THE BEST OF

AMAZING STORIES

The 1940 Anthology

(with the original magazine illustrations)

Edited by
STEVE DAVIDSON
and
JEAN MARIE STINE

Amazing Stories Classics
Produced by Digital Parchment Services

For the best in new science fiction, plus breaking news of the world
of science fiction books, movies, television, games and more, visit
Amazing Stories at **amazingstoriesmag.com**

THE BEST OF
1940 AMAZING STORIES
Contents

PUBLISHER'S NOTE

This special 1940 Retro-Hugo edition of *The Best of Amazing Stories* is not intended to tell World Science Fiction Convention members who or what to vote for (or not to vote for).

At the same time it is not possible for most readers to obtain copies of all the science fiction stories and novels published during 1940 or even those classics that might be ranked among the best. Unfortunately, many of the latter are not in print, and those that are are scattered widely among many different anthologies and not easy to assemble. In fact, the best collection of such stories is undoubtedly Isaac Asimov's and Martin H. Greenberg's *Isaac Asimov's The Great SF Stories 2: 1940* (DAW 1979), a paperback which can be found from used booksellers and which we highly recommend. While there are several other anthologies drawn exclusively from the pages of *Amazing Stories,* they contain few stories from 1940 itself.

Hence, we offer this present book in the hope that it may help contemporary readers become more informed about, at least, some of the better science fiction of the year as it appeared in the pages of *Amazing Stories*. In fact, it is our hope that that this book may inspire our colleagues at *Analog* (formerly the venerable pulp *Astounding Science Fiction*) to publish similar volumes for the retro-Hugos in the future.

RAYMOND A. PALMER

1910-1977

INTRODUCTION

1940 was an important year for *Amazing Stories*—and for its new editor, Raymond A. Palmer. It was also an important year for science fiction in general.

For Palmer it was the culmination of his dream to create a stable of new science fiction writers for *Amazing*, the way John W. Campbell Jr. had done two years earlier with such spectacular success at *Astounding Stories*. Just as Heinlein, Asimov, del Rey, and L. Sprague de Camp had been gathered under Campbell's tutelage, so Palmer gathered Don Wilcox, David Wright O'Brien, Robert Moore Williams, and David Vern Reed under his own. These new authors were very different from Campbell's protégées in style, theme and methodology, yet each group's approach to science fiction was perfect for its publication, given the difference in the two editors' aims.

Hugo Gernsback had been a Vernean, who launched magazine science fiction in 1926 with an *Amazing Stories* footed firmly in the mode of Jules Verne, with awed descriptions of the newly emergent transportation technologies and a travelogue, with just a dash of adventure for spicing, to demonstrate how these wondrous mechanisms functioned. John W. Campbell, Jr. was a Wellsian, who believed science fiction should adhere to the same rules as any other form of literature; should recount an engrossing story, often highly emotionally charged, in which recognizably real people reacted to some believably extrapolated scientific problem or invention, or some postulated future change, resolving them with logic and the scientific method. Raymond A. Palmer, when he assumed the helm at *Amazing Stories* in 1938 (just two years after Campbell became editor of *Astounding*), characteristically charted a different route, all his own.

Palmer admired Campbell's approach but aspired to the kind of large circulation and mainstream readership no other science fiction magazine had ever had, and felt the stories *Astounding* published were too scientifically rigorous and thick with jargon to appeal to a mass audience. Instead, he aimed at publishing a broader, faster moving type of story, designed to be more easily digested and followed, with entertainment stressed over the science. And, just as Campbell preferred his writers to live on the East Coast where he could personally school them to his literary vision, Palmer sought his writers in Chicago, where *Amazing* was published and edited, so he could instruct them personally in writing precisely the type of story he wanted.

Since the Windy City had long been famed as a literary, musical and artistic hotbed, Palmer was not long in building his stable of writers, which included such stalwarts as the highly underrated Rog Phillips, David Wright O'Brien, David Vern Reed (of Batman fame), Don Wilcox, Chester. S. Geier, the Livingston brothers (Herbert and Berkeley), Leroy Yerxa, Frances Deegan, Richard S. Shaver, and others quite popular then but of lesser fame today. He also opened his pages to anything such important authors as Ray Bradbury, Nelson S. Bond, Eando Binder, and Robert Bloch cared to write, enabling them to earn a full-time living from their writings—notably Bond's Lancelot Biggs stories and Popul Vuh trilogy, Bloch's Lefty Feep series and *The Dead Don't Die* (a novel he would later adapt as a movie for television), Binder's Adam Link series, which kicked off with the much filmed novelette "I, Robot" (not to be confused with the Isaac Asimov book which came much later), and Bradbury's breakthrough "I, Rocket," which, in accordance with its title, is narrated by the spaceship itself.

Yes, 1940 was the year it all came together for Ray Palmer. From then on *Amazing Stories'* readership and circulation would continue to grow, even through and after the war, in a triumphal arc that would end when Palmer was brought down by a combination of two men who, though Palmer had done everything to promote their careers, had apparently become covetous of his position. Alongside these two were the more snobbish of Campbell's writers, convinced that the Shaver Mystery stories, published in the late 1940s, were giving science fiction a bad name (if not smell). Under its new editors, rather than achieving illustrious heights, as his betrayers promised *Amazing's* publishers it would, the magazine's readership plunged to an all-time low, as did its story content. That is, until it was rescued a decade later by a woman of impeccable taste and discernment, Cele Goldsmith, who raised the publication's standards while discovering the likes of Thomas M. Disch, Ursula K. Le Guin, Keith Laumer, and Roger Zelazny, to name only a few.

As the stories in this volume make clear, Palmer adopted a number of specific strategies for reaching a wider audience not overly familiar with science fiction tropes. In many stories, rather than setting the stories against a complex futuristic background or filling them with a multitude of scientific details, he would set them in the present and focus his authors on exploring the permutations of a single idea. Another method of making *Amazing*'s stories palatable to those not yet initiated into sf's special language and assumptions was to embed the speculative elements in familiar plots or situations, such as the highly popular screwball-comedy treatment (a movie-audience favorite of the time, e.g. *Bringing up Baby, His Girl Friday*). Finally, to bolster a yarn's readability factor, when scientific explanation threatened to become too extensive and/or dense, Palmer would pull overly technical material out of the body of the story and bury it at the bottom of a page as a footnote, where readers could easily choose their level of engagement with it.

You will see all these elements on display in the stories reprinted here, which we believe are among the most outstanding Palmer published in *Amazing* during 1940. Guiding our selections are what we feel are three key signifiers of quality: 1) reader reaction as reflected in the magazine's letter columns, 2) a story having been deemed worthy of reprint by the field's most able anthologists (Groff Conklin, Philip Strong, Isaac Asimov, Damon Knight, Martin Greenberg, *et al)*, and 3) our own personal reading of all twelve issues published that year.

In this Introduction, we are not going to analyze each story or try to point out why it is worthy of consideration as one of the year's best. We believe our readers are sufficiently perceptive to do that for themselves. We also recognize that one person's "best" is another's "worst." Instead, we are going to present them as they appeared in the magazine, with the original blurbs and all the illustrations. However, there are three stories we do feel deserve a bit of comment.

The gem of the year, a novelette which still enjoys classic status today, was undoubtedly "The Voyage that Lasted 600 Years," the first story ever set on board a ship making a generations-long voyage to a distant star. Once again *Amazing* was in the lead with a cornerstone sf idea that remains a vital part of the field to this day (beating out Robert A. Heinlein's "Universe," which is often misremembered as the first use of a generation starship, by a full year). Written by Palmer stalwart Don Wilcox, it features social commentary, cultural extrapolation, romance, and a slam-bang-action ending, all at novelette length without ever seeming hurried, due to the ingenious narrative strategy Wilcox adopts.

As far as we can ascertain, Nelson S. Bond's novella, "Sons of the Deluge" (just two thousand words too short to qualify as a novel), is the first story about characters who travel back through time and unwittingly become famed figures of legend. If it is not the first, it is certainly one of the first and far and away the best up to the time of its writing— and certainly beats out anything published by Gernsback, with its full-bodied characters, polished dialogue, and globe- and time-trotting plot (beating out Manly Wade Wellman's novel on a similar theme, *Twice in Time*, by several months). Bond is undeservedly forgotten today, perhaps because stylistically speaking, his work was so superior to that of even the best pulp science fiction writers that the majority appeared off screen, so to speak, in the slick and higher paying magazines.

Finally, we must mention Donald Bern's "The Three Wise Men of Space," which, while it is an exemplar of all that is connoted by the world "schmaltz," feels as apt at this time in word's history as it must have seemed when it literally closed out the year as the last story in the December 1940 issue of *Amazing*. This fact relends it some of the gravitas it must have held in a U.S. for which the European war was inevitably marching and would find itself unwillingly thrust into a World War in just a short twelve months. Hitler was already pursuing all of Europe, grinding it under his heel, and was dropping battalions of bombs on the U.K. (particularly London) every night. In the U.S., the vision of a global conflagration was a source of unease on everyone's mind—and rightly so, since bombs would be falling on Pearl Harbor in the same month just one short year later. Here, Donald Bern, who had a background in advertising, turns a mordant eye on humanity in 1940, in a story that ends like the snap of a rubber band.

As we noted earlier, 1940 wasn't just a great year for *Amazing Stories*, it was a great one for science fiction in general, and we would be remiss in not acknowledging that fact. Campbell had hit his stride the year before with the first stories by Heinlein ("Life-Line," "Misfit"), A. E. van Vogt ("Black Destroyer," "Discord in Scarlet") and Asimov ("Trends"), and the first top-of-their-form blockbusters by recent arrivals Lester del Rey ("The Day is Done," "Luck of Ignatz") and L. Sprague de

Camp ("Divide and Rule," "The Gnarly Man"—bought for *Astounding* but published in *Unknown Worlds* to help fill that fledgling publication's pages). In 1940 Campbell continued to pump out all-time classic stories and novelettes like "Martian Quest," Leigh Brackett's first published story; Heinlein's "The Roads Must Roll" and "Coventry"; del Rey's "The Stars Look Down" and "Dark Mission"; Van Vogt's "Vault of the Beast"; Rocklynne's "Quietus"; Asimov's "Homo Sol"; Malcom Jameson's "Admiral's Inspection" (first of the award winning Bullard saga); Harry Bates' "Fairwell to the Master" (filmed as *The Day the Earth Stood Still*); P. Schuyler Miller's "Old Man Mulligan"; de Camp's "The Warrior Race," and Jack Williamson's "Hindsight", to name only too few.

It was a great year for novels too, as any year must have been that produced Robert A. Heinlein's *If This Goes On...*—a novel far more audacious and human than any that had appeared in a science fiction magazine before. And L. Ron Hubbard, later of Scientology fame but then a fresh-cheeked young writer, was not far behind Heinlein in daring and innovative subject matter, slamming out three psychological masterpieces, novels that have stood the test of time: *Final Blackout, Death's Deputy*, and *Fear*. Nor did the novel-length goodies the magazines produced end there. 1940 also saw the publication of *Slan*, the novelistic debut of A. E. van Vogt's, an up-and-coming writer who would change the face of science fiction and give his name to the recomplicated, wheels-within-wheels story, a tale so powerful Stephen King would copy its opening narrative structure at the beginning of the first chapter of his own sci-fi classic, *Firestarter*. They were all high standards to meet and yet two more novels managed the trick: Norvell Page's nightmarishly logical meditation on what the coming of a true supermutant would be like, *But Without Horns*; and Manly Wade Wellman's story of a modern man cast into the past, whose attempts to find a place for himself in Renaissance Florence turn him into one of history's most celebrated figures, *Twice in Time*.

Amazing and *Astounding* may have been the magazines to beat, but the other science fiction magazines also produced stories so memorable they are still anthologized today. *Super Science Stories* gave us Asimov's "Strange Playfellow" (aka "Robbie") the foundational story in his classic "Robot" series, plus the first collaboration between Pohl and Kornbluth—"Before the Universe"—and Heinlein's "Let There be Light." *Astonishing Stories* produced Ross Rocklynne's "Into the Darkness," the first story in his landmark cosmic drama, "Darkness," told from the point of view of living suns, and the initial story in Asimov's pioneering "Half-Breeds" trilogy. *Planet Stories* presented "The Forbidden Dream," the first of Rocklynne's "Hallmeyer, Destroyer of Worlds" stories, dark interplanetary secret-agent thrillers which prefigure the work of John le Carré by a quarter-century in questioning Western foreign policy and its search for economic hegemony—and also the first story from a newcomer soon to hit the heights and become an sf household name, "The Stellar Legion" by Leigh Brackett, whose evocative style and highly-charged story telling quickly made her the readership's number one favorite, leaving the magazine's male authors to straggle along in her wake, doing their best to emulate her work. *Thrilling Wonder Stories* gave sf fans Clark Ashton Smith's "The Great God Awo," Sam Merwin's "Exiled from Earth," and the much-reprinted "The Impossible Highway" by Oscar J. Friend. Over at *Amazing*'s then-sister magazine, *Fantastic Adventures*, Palmer offered "The Prince of Mars Returns," Philip Francis Nowlan's first work since 1929's "Airlords of Han" (the second "Buck" Rogers story), and mainstream novelist James Norman's hilarious "Oscar, Detective of Mars," which began a notable series.

Across the pond, the UK's first science fiction magazine, *Tales of Wonder,* was in its fourth year under the able editorship of British journalist and long-time fan Walter Gillings, whose discernment would lead him later to publish early work by Arthur C. Clarke and the first story by the immortal trickster Eric Frank Russell. Gillings brewed up a nice cuppa science fiction for his readers, featuring reprints from the best of the Gernsback publications mixed with stellar stories by a new generation of fledgling future fiction authors. In 1940, Gillings dished out the exciting "Experiment in Genius" by William F. Temple (of *Four-sided Triangle* fame) and Erik Frank Russell's ingenious "I, Spy."

1940: An amazing year for *Amazing Stories,* for science fiction—and for science fiction readers everywhere.

DISCLAIMER

These works of pulp fiction have been adjudged a classic of both historical and literary value and, as such, are presented for the entertainment and education of contemporary audiences. The text and illustrations are reproduced as originally published. They contain some material which, given our comparative cultural advances since 1940, may now be considered offensive to readers. While they can be read for entertainment, these stories can also be read as cultural text and as a window into the worldview of a previous era—along with that era's implicit presuppositions, for better and worse. The views and beliefs represented in these stories do not represent those of the current editors or publishers.

The Voyage That

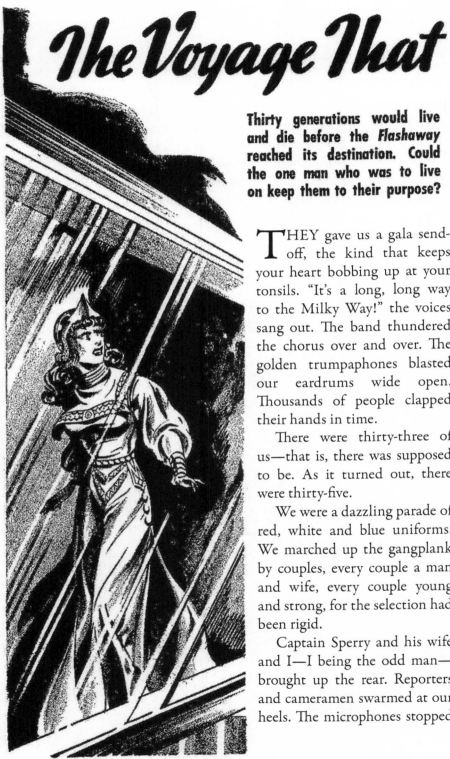

Thirty generations would live and die before the *Flashaway* reached its destination. Could the one man who was to live on keep them to their purpose?

THEY gave us a gala send-off, the kind that keeps your heart bobbing up at your tonsils. "It's a long, long way to the Milky Way!" the voices sang out. The band thundered the chorus over and over. The golden trumpaphones blasted our eardrums wide open. Thousands of people clapped their hands in time.

There were thirty-three of us—that is, there was supposed to be. As it turned out, there were thirty-five.

We were a dazzling parade of red, white and blue uniforms. We marched up the gangplank by couples, every couple a man and wife, every couple young and strong, for the selection had been rigid.

Captain Sperry and his wife and I—I being the odd man—brought up the rear. Reporters and cameramen swarmed at our heels. The microphones stopped

Lasted 600 Years

by DON WILCOX

Grimstone gripped his automatic tightly as he stepped from the animation machine.

KRUPA

us. The band and the crowd hushed.

"This is Captain Sperry telling you good-by," the amplified voice boomed. "In behalf of the thirty-three, I thank you for your grand farewell. We'll remember this hour as our last contact with our beloved Earth."

The crowd held its breath. The mighty import of our mission struck through every heart.

"We go forth into space to live—and to die," the captain said gravely. "But *our children's children,* born in space and reared in the light of our vision, will carry on our great purpose. And in centuries to come, *your children's children* may set forth for the Robinello planets, knowing that you will find an American colony already planted there."

The captain gestured goodbye and the multitude responded with a thunderous cheer. Nothing so daring as a six-century nonstop flight had ever been undertaken before.

An announcer nabbed me by the sleeve and barked into the microphone, "And now one final word from Professor Gregory Grimstone, the one man who is supposed to live down through the six centuries of this historic flight and see the journey through to the end."

"Ladies and gentlemen," I choked, and the echo of my swallow blobbed back at me from distant walls, "as Keeper of the Traditions, I give you my word that the S. S. *Flashaway* shall carry your civilization through to the end, unsoiled and unblemished!"

A cheer stimulated me and I drew a deep breath for a burst of oratory. But Captain Sperry pulled at my other sleeve.

"That's all. We're set to slide out in two minutes."

The reporters scurried down the gangplank and made a center rush through the crowd. The band struck up. Motors roared sullenly.

One lone reporter who had missed out on the interviews blitzkrieged up and caught me by the coattail.

"Hold it, Butch. Just a coupla words so I can whip up a column of froth for the *Star*— Well, I'll be damned! If it ain't 'Crackdown' Grimstone! "

I scowled. The reporter before me was none other than Bill Broscoe, one of my former pupils at college and a star athlete. At heart I knew that Bill was a right guy, but I'd be the last to tell him so.

"Broscoe!" I snarled. "Tardy as usual. You finally flunked my history course, didn't you?"

"Now, Crackdown," he whined, "don't go hopping on me. I won that Thanksgiving game for you, remember?"

HE gazed at my red, white and blue uniform.
"So you're off for Robinello," he grinned.

"Son, this is my last minute on Earth, and *you* have to haunt me, of all people—"

"So you're the one that's taking the refrigerated sleeper, to wake up every hundred years—"

"And stir the fires of civilization among the crew—yes. Six hundred years from now when your bones have rotted, I'll still be carrying on."

"Still teaching 'em history? God forbid!" Broscoe grinned.

"I hope I have better luck than I did with you."

"Let 'em off easy on dates, Crackdown. Give them 1066 for William the Conqueror and 2066 for the *Flashaway* take-off. That's enough. Taking your wife, I suppose?"

At this impertinent question I gave Broscoe the cold eye.

"Pardon me," he said, suppressing a sly grin—proof enough that he had heard the devastating story about how I missed my wedding and got the air. "Faulty alarm clock, wasn't it? Too bad. Crackdown. And you always ragged *me* about being tardy!"

With this jibe Broscoe exploded into laughter. Some people have the damnedest notions about what constitutes humor. I backed into the entrance of the space ship uncomfortably. Broscoe followed.

Zzzzipp!

The automatic door cut past me. I jerked Broscoe through barely in time to keep him from being bisected.

"Tardy as usual, my friend," I hooted. "You've missed your gangplank! That makes you the first castaway in space."

We took off like a shooting star, and the last I saw of Bill Broscoe, he stood at a rear window cursing as he watched the earth and the moon fall away into the velvety black heavens. And the more I laughed at him, the madder he got. No sense of humor.

Was that the last time I ever saw him? Well, no, to be strictly honest I had one more unhappy glimpse of him. It happened just before I packed myself away for my first one hundred years' sleep.

I had checked over the "Who's Who Aboard the Flashaway"—the official register—to make sure that I was thoroughly acquainted with everyone on board; for these sixteen couples were to be the great-grandparents of the next generation I would meet. Then I had promptly taken my leave of Captain Sperry and his wife, and gone directly to my refrigeration plant, where I was to suspend my life by instantaneous freezing.

I clicked the switches, and one of the two huge horizontal wheels—one in reserve, in the event of a breakdown—opened up for me like a door opening in the side of a gigantic doughnut, or better, a tubular merry go round. There was my nook waiting for me to crawl in.

Before I did so I took a backward glance toward the ballroom. The one-way glass partition, through which I could see but not be seen, gave me a clear view of the scene of merriment. The couples were dancing. The journey was off to a good start.

"A grand gang," I said to myself. No one doubted that the ship was equal to the six-hundred-year journey. The success would depend upon the people. Living and dying in this closely circumscribed world would put them to a severe test. All credit, I reflected, was due the planning committee for choosing such a congenial group.

"They're equal to it," I said optimistically. If their children would only prove as sturdy and adaptable as their parents, my job as Keeper of the Traditions would be simple.

BUT how, I asked myself, as I stepped into my life-suspension merry-go-round, would Bill Broscoe fit into this picture? Not a half bad guy. Still—

My final glance through the one-way glass partition slew me. Out of the throng I saw Bill Broscoe dancing past with a beautiful girl in his arms. The girl was Louise—my Louise—the girl I had been engaged to marry!

In a flash it came to me—but not about Bill. I forgot him on the spot. About Louise.

Bless her heart, she'd come to find me. She must have heard that I had signed up for the *Flashaway*, and she bad come aboard, a stowaway, to forgive me for missing the wedding—to marry me! Now—

A warning click sounded, a lid closed over me, my refrigerator—merry go round whirled— Blackness!

CHAPTER II
Babies, Just Babies

IN a moment—or so it seemed—I was again gazing into the light of the refrigerating room. The lid stood open.

A stimulating warmth circulated through my limbs. Perhaps the machine, I half consciously concluded, had made no more than a preliminary revolution.

I bounded out with a single thought. I must find Louise. We could still be married. For the present I would postpone my entrance into the ice. And since the machine had been equipped with *two* merry-go-round freezers as an emergency safeguard — oh happy thought—perhaps Louise would be willing to undergo life suspension with me!

I stopped at the one-way glass partition, astonished to see no signs of dancing in the ballroom. I could scarcely see the ballroom, for it had been darkened.

Upon unlocking the door (the refrigerator room was my own private retreat) I was bewildered. An unaccountable change had come over everything. What it was, I couldn't determine at the moment. But the very air of the ballroom was different.

A few dim green light bulbs burned along the walls—enough to show me that the dancers had vanished. Had time enough elapsed for night to come on? My thoughts spun dizzily. Night, I reflected, would consist simply of turning off the lights and going to bed. It had been agreed in our plan that our twenty-four hour Earth day would be maintained for the sake of regularity.

But there was something more intangible that struck me. The furniture had been changed about, and the very walls seemed *older*. Something more than minutes had passed since I left this room.

Strangest of all, the windows were darkened.

In a groggy state of mind I approached one of the windows in hopes of catching a glimpse of the solar system. I was still puzzling over how much time might have elapsed. Here, at least, was a sign of very recent activity.

"Wet Paint" read the sign pinned to the window. The paint was still sticky. What the devil—

The ship, of course, was fully equipped for blind flying. But aside from the problems of navigation, the crew had anticipated enjoying a wonderland of stellar beauty through the portholes. Now, for some strange reason, every window had been painted opaque.

I listened. Slow measured steps were pacing in an adjacent hallway. Nearing the entrance, I stopped, halted by a shrill sound from somewhere overhead. It came from one of the residential quarters that gave on the ballroom balcony.

It was the unmistakable wail of a baby.

Then another baby's cry struck up; and a third, from somewhere across the balcony, joined the chorus. Time, indeed, must have passed since I left this roomful of dancers.

Now some irate voices of disturbed sleepers added rumbling basses to the symphony of wailings. Grumbles of "Shut that little devil up!" and poundings of fists on walls thundered through the empty ballroom. In a burst of inspiration I ran to the records room, where the ship's "Who's Who" was kept.

THE door to the records room was locked, but the footsteps of some sleepless person I had heard now pounded down the dimly lighted hallway. I looked upon the aged man. I had never seen him before. He stopped at the sight of me; then snapping on a brighter light, came on confidently.

"Mr. Grimstone?" he said, extending his hand. "We've been expecting you. My name is William Broscoe—"

"Broscoe!"

"William Broscoe, the second. You knew my father, I believe."

I groaned and choked.

"And my mother," the old man continued, "always spoke very highly of you. I'm proud to be the first to greet you."

He politely overlooked the flush of purple that leaped into my face. For a moment nothing that I could say was intelligible.

He turned a key and we entered the records room. There I faced the inescapable fact. My full century had passed. The original crew of the *Flashaway* were long gone. A completely new generation was on the register.

Or, more accurately, three new generations: the children, the grandchildren, and the great-grandchildren of the generation I had known.

One hundred years had passed—and I had lain so completely suspended, owing to the freezing, that only a moment of my own life had been absorbed.

Eventually I was to get used to this; but on this first occasion I found it utterly shocking—even embarrassing. Only a few minutes ago, as my experience went, I was madly in love with Louise and had hopes of yet marrying her.

But now well, the leather-bound "Who's Who" told all. Louise had been dead twenty years. Nearly thirty children now alive aboard the S. S. *Flashaway* could claim her as their great-grandmother. These carefully recorded pedigrees proved it.

And the patriarch of that fruitful tribe had been none other than Bill Broscoe, the fresh young athlete who had always been tardy for my history class. I gulped as if I were swallowing a baseball.

Broscoe—tardy! And I had missed my second chance to marry Louise—by a full century!

My fingers turned the pages of the register numbly. William Broscoe II misinterpreted my silence.

"I see you are quick to detect our trouble," he said, and the same deep conscientious concern showed in his expression that I had remembered in the face of his mother, upon our grim meeting after my alarm clock had failed and I had missed my own wedding.

Trouble? Trouble aboard the S. S. *Flashaway,* after all the careful advance planning we had done, and after all our array of budgeting and scheduling and vowing to stamp our systematic ways upon the oncoming generations? This, we had agreed, would be the world's most unique colonizing expedition; for every last trouble that might crop up on the six-hundred-year voyage had already been met and conquered by advance planning.

"They've tried to put off doing anything about it until your arrival," Broscoe said, observing respectfully that the charter invested in me the authority of passing upon all important policies. "But this very week three new babies arrived, which brings the trouble to a crisis. So the captain ordered a blackout of the heavens as an emergency measure."

"HEAVENS?" I grunted. "What have the heavens got to do with babies?"

"There's a difference of opinion on that. Maybe it depends upon how susceptible you are."

"Susceptible—to what?"

"The romantic malady."

I looked at the old man, much puzzled. He took me by the arm and led me toward the pilots' control room. Here were unpainted windows that revealed celestial glories beyond anything I had ever dreamed. Brilliant planets of varied hues gleamed through the blackness, while close at hand—almost close enough to touch—were numerous large moons, floating slowly past as we shot along our course.

"Some little show," the pilot grinned, "and it keeps getting better."

He proceeded to tell me just where we were and how few adjustments in the original time schedules he had had to make, and why this non-stop flight to Robinello would stand unequalled for centuries to come.

And I heard virtually nothing of what he said. I simply stood there, gazing at the unbelievable beauty of the skies. I was hypnotized, enthralled, shaken to the very roots. One emotion, one thought dominated me. I longed for Louise.

"The romantic malady, as I was saying," William Broscoe resumed, "may or may not be a factor in producing our large population. Personally, I think it's pure buncombe."

"Pure buncombe," I echoed, still thinking of Louise. If she and I had had moons like these—

"But nobody can tell Captain Dickinson anything..."

There was considerable clamor and wrangling that morning as the inhabitants awakened to find their heavens blacked out. Captain Dickinson was none too popular anyway. Fortunately for him, many of the people took their grouches out on the babies who had caused the disturbance in the night.

Families with babies were supposed to occupy the rear staterooms—but there weren't enough rear staterooms. Or rather, there were too many babies.

Soon the word went the rounds that the Keeper of the Traditions had returned to life. I was duly banqueted and toasted and treated to lengthy accounts of the events of the past hundred years. And during the next few days many of the older men and women would take me aside for private conferences and spill their worries into my ears.

CHAPTER III
Boredom

"**W**HAT'S the world coming to?" these granddaddies and grandmothers would ask. And before I could scratch my head for an answer, they would assure me that this expedition was headed straight for the rocks.

"It's all up with us. We've lost our grip on our original purposes. The Six-Hundred-Year Plan is nothing but a dead scrap of paper."

I'll admit things looked plenty black. And the more parlor conversations I was invited in on, the blacker things looked. I couldn't sleep nights.

"If our population keeps on increasing, we'll run out of food before we're halfway there," William Broscoe II repeatedly declared. "We've got to have a compulsory program of birth control. That's the only thing that will save us."

A delicate subject for parlor conversations, you think? This older generation didn't think so. I was astonished, and I'll admit I was a bit proud as well, to discover how deeply imbued these old graybeards were with *Flashaway* determination and patriotism. They had missed life in America by only one generation, and they were unquestionably the staunchest of flag wavers on board.

The younger generations were less outspoken, and for the first week I began to deplore their comparative lack of vision. They, the possessors of families, seemed to avoid these discussions about the oversupply of children.

"So you've come to check up on our American traditions, Professor Grimstone," they would say casually. "We've heard all about this great purpose of our forefathers, and I guess it's up to us to put it across. But gee whiz, Grimstone, we wish we could have seen the Earth! What's it like, anyhow?"

"Tell us some more about the Earth..."

"All we know is what we get second hand..."

I told them about the earth. Yes, they had books galore, and movies and phonograph records, pictures and maps; but these things only excited their curiosity. They asked me questions by the thousands. Only after I had poured out several encyclopedia-loads of Earth memories did I begin to break through their masks.

Back of this constant questioning, I discovered, they were watching me. Perhaps they were wondering whether they were not being subjected to more rigid discipline here on shipboard than their cousins back on Earth. I tried to impress upon them that they were a chosen group, but this had little effect. It stuck in their minds that *they* had had no choice in the matter.

Moreover, they were watching to see what I was going to do about the population problem, for they were no less aware of it than their elders.

Two weeks after my "return" we got down to business.

Captain Dickinson preferred to engineer the matter himself. He called an assembly in the movie auditorium. Almost everyone was present.

The program began with the picture of the Six-Hundred-Year Plan. Everyone knew the reels by heart. They had seen and heard them dozens of times, and were ready to snicker at the proper moments— such as when the stern old committee chairman, charging the unborn generations with their solemn obligations, was interrupted by a friendly fly on his nose.

W HEN the films were run through, Captain Dickinson took the rostrum, and with considerable bluster he called upon the Clerk of the Council to review the situation. The clerk read a report which went about as follows:

To maintain a stable population, it was agreed in the original Plan that families should average two children each. Hence, the original 16 families would bring forth approximately 32 children; and assuming that they were fairly evenly divided as to sex, they would eventually form 16 new families. These 16 families would, in turn, have an average of two children each—another generation of approximately 32.

By maintaining these averages, we were to have a total population, at any given time, of 32 children, 32 parents and 32 grandparents. The great-grandparents may be left out of account, for owing to the natural span of life they ordinarily die off before they accumulate in any great numbers.

The three living generations, then, of 32 each would give the Flashaway a constant active population of 96, or roughly, 100 persons.

The Six-Hundred-Year Plan has allowed for some flexibility in these figures. It has established the safe maximum at 150 and the safe minimum at 75.

If our population shrinks below 75, it is dangerously small. If it shrinks to 50, a crisis is at hand.

But if it grows above 150, it is dangerously large; and if it reaches the 200 mark, as we all know, a crisis may be said to exist.

The clerk stopped for an impressive pause, marred only by the crying of a baby from some distant room.

"Now, coming down to the present-day facts, we are well aware that the population has been dangerously large for the past seven years—"

"Since we entered this section of the heavens," Captain Dickinson interspersed with a scowl.

"From the first year in space, the population plan has encountered some irregularities," the clerk continued. "To begin with, there were not sixteen couples, but seventeen. The seventeenth couple-.—" here the clerk shot a glance at William Broscoe—"did not belong to the original compact, and after their marriage they were not bound by the sacred traditions—"

"I object!" I shouted, challenging the eyes of the clerk and the captain squarely. Dickinson had written that report with a touch of malice. The clerk skipped over a sentence or two.

"But however the Broscoe family may have prospered and multiplied, our records show that nearly all the families of the present generation have exceeded the per-family quota."

At this point there was a slight disturbance in the rear of the auditorium. An anxious-looking young man entered and signalled to the doctor. The two went out together.

"*All* the families," the clerk amended. "Our population this week passed the two hundred mark. This concludes the report."

The captain opened the meeting for discussion, and the forum lasted far into the night. The demand for me to assist the Council with some legislation was general. There was also hearty sentiment against the captain's blacked-out heavens from young and old alike.

THIS, I considered, was a good sign.

The children craved the fun of watching the stars and planets; their elders desired to keep up their serious astronomical studies.

"Nothing is so important to the welfare of this expedition," I said to the Council on the following day, as we settled down to the job of thrashing out some legislation, "as to maintain our interests in the outside world. Population or no population, we must not become ingrown!"

I talked of new responsibilities, new challenges in the form of contests and campaigns, new leisure-time activities. The discussion went on for days.

"Back in my times—" I said for the hundredth time; but the captain laughed me down. My times and these times were as unlike as black and white, he declared.

"But the principle is the same!" I shouted. "We had population troubles, too."

They smiled as I referred to twenty-first century relief families who were overrun with children. I cited the fact that some industrialists who paid heavy taxes had considered giving every relief family an automobile as a measure to save themselves money in the long run; for they had discovered that relief families with cars had fewer children than those without.

"That's no help," Dickinson muttered. "You can't have cars on a space ship."

"You can play bridge," I retorted. "Bridge is an enemy of the birthrate too. Bridge, cars, movies, checkers—they all add up to the same thing. They lift you out of your animal natures—"

The Councilmen threw up their hands. They had bridged and checkered themselves to death.

"Then try other things," I persisted. "You could produce your own movies and plays—organize a little theater—create some new drama—"

"What have we got to dramatize?" the captain replied sourly. "All the dramatic things happen on the earth."

This shocked me. Somehow it took all the starch out of this colossal adventure to hear the captain give up so easily.

"All our drama is second-hand," he grumbled. "Our ship's course is cut and dried. Our world is bounded by walls. The only dramatic things that happen here are births and deaths."

A doctor broke in on our conference and seized the captain by the hand.

"Congratulations, Captain Dickinson, on the prize crop of the season! Your wife has just presented you with a fine set of triplets— three boys!"

That broke up the meeting. Captain Dickinson was so busy for the rest of the week that he forgot all about his official obligations. The problem of population limitation faded from his mind.

I wrote out my recommendations and gave them all the weight of my dictatorial authority. I stressed the need for more birth control forums, and recommended that the heavens be made visible for further studies in astronomy and mathematics.

I was tempted to warn Captain Dickinson that the *Flashaway* might incur some serious dramas of its own—poverty, disease and the like—unless he got back on the track of the Six-Hundred-Year Plan in a hurry. But Dickinson was preoccupied with some family washings when I took my leave of him, and he seemed to have as much drama on his hands as he cared for.

I paid a final visit to each of the twenty-eight great-grandchildren of Louise, and returned to my ice.

CHAPTER IV
Revolt!

MY chief complaint against my merry-go-round freezer was that it didn't give me any rest. One whirl into blackness, and the next thing I knew I popped out of the open lid again with not so much as a minute's time to reorganize my thoughts.

Well, here it was, 2266—two hundred years since the take-off.

A glance through the one-way glass told me it was daytime in the ballroom.

As I turned the key in the lock I felt like a prize fighter on a vaudeville tour who, having just trounced the tough local strong man, steps back in the ring to take on his cousin.

A touch of a headache caught me as I reflected that there should be four more returns after this one—if all went according to plan. *Plan!* That word was destined to be trampled underfoot!

Oh, well (I took a deep optimistic breath) the *Flashaway* troubles would all be cleared up by now. Three generations would have passed. The population should be back to normal.

I swung the door open, stepped through, locked it after me.

For an instant I thought I had stepped in on a big movie "take"—a scene of a stricken multitude. The big ballroom was literally strewn with people—if creatures in such a deplorable state could be called people.

There was no movie camera. This was the real thing.

"Grimstone's come!" a hoarse voice cried out.

"Grimstone! Grimstone!" Others caught up the cry. Then — "Food! Give us food! We're starving! For God's sake—"

The weird chorus gathered volume. I stood dazed, and for an instant I couldn't realize that I was looking upon the population of the *Flashaway*.

Men, women and children of all ages and all states of desperation joined in the clamor. Some of them stumbled to their feet and came toward me, waving their arms weakly. But most of them hadn't the strength to rise.

In that stunning moment an icy sweat came over me.

"Food! Food! We've been waiting for you, Grimstone. We've been holding on—"

The responsibility that was strapped to my shoulders suddenly weighed down like a locomotive. You see, I had originally taken my job more or less as a lark. That Six-Hundred-Year Plan had looked so air-tight. I, the Keeper of the Traditions, would have a snap.

I had anticipated many a pleasant hour acquainting the oncoming generations with noble sentiments about George Washington; I had pictured myself filling the souls of my listeners by reciting the Gettysburg address and lecturing upon the mysteries of science.

But now those pretty bubbles burst on the spot, nor did they ever re-form in the centuries to follow.

And as they burst, my vision cleared. My job had nothing to do with theories or textbooks or speeches. My job was simply to get to

Robinello—to get there with enough living, able-bodied, sane human beings to start a colony.

Dull blue starlight sifted through the windows to highlight the big roomful of starved figures. The mass of pale blue faces stared at me. There were hundreds of them. Instinctively I shrank as the throng clustered around me, calling and pleading.

"One at a time!" I cried. "First I've got to find out what this is all about. Who's your spokesman?"

THEY designated a handsomely built, if undernourished, young man. I inquired his name and learned that he was Bob Sperry, a descendant of the original Captain Sperry.

"There are eight hundred of us now," Sperry said.

"Don't tell me the food has run out!" "No, not that—but six hundred of us are not entitled to regular meals." "Why not?"

Before the young spokesman could answer, the others burst out with an unintelligible clamor. Angry cries of "That damned Dickinson!" and "Guns!" and "They'll shoot us!" were all I could distinguish.

I quieted them and made Bob Sperry go on with his story. He calmly asserted that there was a very good reason that they shouldn't be fed, all sentiment aside; namely, because they had been born outside the quota.

Here I began to catch a gleam of light.

"By Captain Dickinson's interpretation of the Plan," Sperry explained, "there shouldn't be more than two hundred of us altogether."

This Captain Dickinson, I learned, was a grandson of the one I had known.

Sperry continued, "Since there are eight hundred, he and his brother—his brother being Food Superintendent—launched an emergency measure a few months ago to save food. They divided the population into the two hundred, who had a right to be born, and the six hundred who had not."

So the six hundred starving persons before me were theoretically the excess population. The vigorous ancestry of the sixteen — no, seventeen — original couples, together with the excellent medical care that had reduced infant mortality and disease to the minimum, had wrecked the original population plan completely.

"What do you do for food? You must have *some* food!"

"We live on charity."

The throng again broke in with hostile words. Young Sperry's version was too gentle to do justice to their outraged stomachs. In fairness to the two hundred, however, Sperry explained that they shared whatever food they could spare with these, their less fortunate brothers, sisters and offspring.

Uncertain what should or could be done, I gave the impatient crowd my promise to investigate at once. Bob Sperry and nine other men accompanied me.

The minute we were out of hearing of the ballroom, I gasped, "Good heavens, men, how is it that you and your six hundred haven't mobbed the storerooms long before this?"

"Dickinson and his brother have got the drop on us."

"Drop? What kind of drop?" "Guns!"

I couldn't understand this. I had believed these new generations of the *Flashaway* to be relatively innocent of any knowledge of firearms.

"What kind of guns?"

"The same kind they use in our Earth-made movies—that make a loud noise and kill people by the hundreds."

"But there aren't any guns aboard! That is—"

I knew perfectly well that the only firearms the ship carried had been stored in my own refrigerator room, which no one could enter but myself. Before the voyage, one of the planning committee had jestingly suggested that if any serious trouble ever arose, I should be master of the situation by virtue of one hundred revolvers.

"They made their own guns," Sperry explained, "just like the ones in our movies and books."

INQUIRING whether any persons had been shot, I learned that three of their number, attempting a raid on the storerooms, had been killed.

"We heard three loud bangs, and found our men dead with bloody skulls."

Reaching the upper end of the central corridor, we arrived at the captain's headquarters.

The name of Captain Dickinson carried a bad flavor for me. A

century before I had developed a distaste for a certain other Captain
Dickinson, his grandfather. I resolved to swallow my prejudice. Then
the door opened, and my resolve stuck in my throat. The former Captain
Dickinson had merely annoyed me; but this one I hated on sight.

"Well?" the captain roared at the eleven of us.

Well-uniformed and neatly groomed, he filled the doorway with
an impressive bulk. In his right hand he gripped a revolver. The gleam
of that weapon had a magical effect upon the men. They shrank back
respectfully. Then the captain's cold eye lighted on me.

'Who are *you*?"

"Gregory Grimstone, Keeper of the Traditions."

The captain sent a quick glance toward his gun and repeated his
"Well?"

For a moment I was fascinated by that intricately shaped piece of
metal in his grip.

"Well!" I echoed. "If 'well' is the only reception you have to offer,
proceed with my official business. Call your Food Superintendent."

"Why?"

"Order him out! Have him feed the entire population without
further delay!"

"We can't afford the food," the captain growled.

"We'll talk that over later, but we won't talk on empty stomachs.
Order out your Food Superintendent!"

"Crawl back in your hole!" Dickinson snarled.

At that instant another bulky man stepped into view. He was almost
the identical counterpart of the captain, but his uniform was that of the
Food Superintendent. Showing his teeth with a sinister snarl, he took
his place beside his brother. He too jerked his right hand up to flash a
gleaming revolver.

I caught one glimpse—and laughed in his face! I couldn't help it.

"You fellows are good!" I roared. "You're damned good actors! If
you've held off the starving six hundred with nothing but those two
dumb imitations of revolvers, you deserve an Academy award!"

The two Dickinson brothers went white.

Back of me came low mutterings from ten starving men.

"Imitations—dumb imitations—what the hell?"

Sperry and his nine comrades plunged with one accord. For the next ten minutes the captain's headquarters was simply a whirlpool of flying fists and hurtling bodies.

I have mentioned that these ten men were weak from lack of food. That fact was all that saved the Dickinson brothers; for ten minutes of lively exercise was all the ten men could endure, in spite of the circumstances.

BUT ten minutes left an impression. The Dickinsons were the worst beaten-up men I have ever seen, and I have seen some bad ones in my time. When the news echoed through the ship, no one questioned the ethics of ten starved men attacking two overfed ones.

Needless to say, before two hours passed, every hungry man, woman and child ate to his gizzard's content. And before another hour passed, some new officers were installed. The S. S. *Flashaway's* trouble was far from solved; but for the present the whole eight hundred were one big family picnic. Hope was restored, and the rejoicing lasted through many thousand miles of space.

There was considerable mystery about the guns. Surprisingly, the people had developed an awe of the movie guns as if they were instruments of magic.

Upon investigating, I was convinced that the captain and his brother had simply capitalized on this superstition. They had a sound enough motive for wanting to save food. But once their gun bluff had been established, they had become uncompromising oppressors. And when the occasion arose that their guns were challenged, they had simply crushed the skulls of their three attackers and faked the noises of explosions.

But now the firearms were dead. And so was the Dickinson regime.

But the menacing problem of too many mouths to feed still clung to the S. S. *Flashaway* like a hungry ghost determined to ride the ship to death.

Six full months passed before the needed reform was forged.

During that time everyone was allowed full rations. The famine had already taken its toll in weakened bodies, and seventeen persons—most of them young children—died. The doctors, released from the Dickinson regime, worked like Trojans to bring the rest back to health.

The reform measure that went into effect six months after my arrival consisted of outright sterilization.

The compulsory rule was sterilization for everyone except those born "within the quota"—and that quota, let me add, was narrowed down one half from Captain Dickinson's two hundred to the most eligible one hundred. The disqualified one hundred now joined the ranks of the six hundred.

And that was not all. By their own agreement, every within-the-quota family, responsible for bearing the *Flashaway's* future children, would undergo sterilization operations after the second child was born.

The seven hundred out-of-quota citizens, let it be said, were only too glad to submit to the simple sterilization measures in exchange for a right to live their normal lives. Yes, they were to have three squares a day. With an assured population decline in prospect for the coming century, this generous measure of food would not give out. Our surveys of the existing food supplies showed that these seven hundred could safely live their four-score years and die with full stomachs.

Looking back on that six months' work, I was fairly well satisfied that the doctors and the Council and I had done the fair, if drastic, thing. If I had planted seeds for further trouble with the Dickinson tribe, I was little concerned about it at the time.

My conscience was, in fact, clear—except for one small matter. I was guilty of one slight act of partiality.

I incurred this guilt shortly before I returned to the ice. The doctors and I, looking down from the balcony into the ballroom, chanced to notice a young couple who were obviously very much in love.

THE young man was Bob Sperry, the handsome, clear-eyed descendant of the *Flashaway's* first and finest captain, the lad who had been the spokesman when I first came upon the starving mob.

The girl's name—and how it had clung in my mind!—was Louise Broscoe. Refreshingly beautiful, she reminded me for all the world of my own Louise (mine and Bill Broscoe's).

"It's a shame," one of the doctors commented, "that fine young blood like that has to fall outside the quota. But rules are rules."

With a shrug of the shoulders he had already dismissed the matter from his mind—until I handed him something I had scribbled on a piece of paper.

"We'll make this one exception," I said perfunctorily. "If any question ever arises, this statement relieves you doctors of all responsibility. This is my own special request."

CHAPTER V
Wedding Bells

ONE hundred years later my rash act came back to haunt me—and how! Bob Sperry had married Louise Broscoe, and the births of their two children had raised the unholy cry of "Favoritism!"

By the year 2366, Bob Sperry and Louise Broscoe were gone and almost forgotten. But the enmity against me, the Keeper of the Traditions who played favorites, had grown up into a monster of bitter hatred waiting to devour me.

It didn't take me long to discover this. My first contact after I emerged from the ice set the pace.

"Go tell your parents," I said to the gang of brats that were playing ball in the spacious ballroom, "that Grimstone has arrived."

Their evil little faces stared at me a moment, then they snorted.

"Faw! Faw! Faw!" and away they ran.

I stood in the big bleak room wondering what to make of their insults. On the balcony some of the parents craned over the railings at me.

"Greetings!" I cried. "I'm Grimstone, Keeper of the Traditions. I've just come—"

"Faw!" the men and women shouted at me. "Faw! Faw!"

No one could have made anything friendly out of those snarls. "Faw," to them, was simply a vocal manner of spitting poison.

Uncertain what this surly reception might lead to, I returned to my refrigerator room to procure one of the guns. Then I returned to the volley of catcalls and insults, determined to carry out my duties, come what might.

When I reached the forequarter of the ship, however, I found some less hostile citizens who gave me a civil welcome. Here I established myself for the extent of my 2366-67 sojourn, an honored guest of the Sperry family.

This, I told myself, was my reward for my favor to Bob Sperry and

Louise Broscoe a century ago. For here was their grandson, a fine upstanding gray-haired man of fifty, a splendid pilot and the father of a beautiful twenty-one-year-old daughter.

"Your name wouldn't be Louise by any chance?" I asked the girl as she showed me into the Sperry living room.

"Lora-Louise," the girl smiled. It was remarkable how she brought back memories of one of her ancestors of three centuries previous.

Her dark eyes flashed over me curiously.

"So you are the man that we Sperrys have to thank for being here!"

"You've heard about the quotas?" I asked.

"Of course. You're almost a god to our family."

"I must be a devil to some of the others," I said, recalling my reception of catcalls.

"Rogues!" the girl's father snorted, and he thereupon launched into a breezy account of the past century.

The sterilization program, he assured me, had worked—if anything, too well.

The population was the lowest in *Flashaway* history. It stood at the dangerously low mark of *fifty!*

Besides the sterilization program, a disease epidemic had taken its toll. In addition three ugly murders, prompted by jealousies, had spotted the record. And there had been one suicide.

As to the character of the population, Pilot Sperry declared gravely that there had been a turn for the worse.

"They fight each other like damned anarchists," he snorted.

THE Dickinsons had made trouble for several generations. Now it was the Dickinsons against the Smiths; and these two factions included four-fifths of all the people. They were about evenly divided—twenty on each side—and when they weren't actually fighting each other, they were "fawing" at each other.

These bellicose factions had one sentiment in common: they both despised the Sperry faction. And—here my guilt cropped up again—their hatred stemmed from my special favor of a century ago, without which there would be no Sperrys now. In view of the fact that the Sperry faction lived in the forequarter of the ship and held all the important offices, it was no wonder that the remaining forty citizens were jealous.

All of which gave me enough to worry about. On top of that, Lora-Louise's mother gave me one other angle of the set-up.

"The trouble between the Dickinsons and the Smiths has grown worse since Lora-Louise has become a young lady," Mrs. Sperry confided to me.

We were sitting in a breakfast nook. Amber starlight shone softly through the porthole, lighting the mother's steady imperturbable gray eyes.

"Most girls have married at eighteen or nineteen," her mother went on. "So far, Lora-Louise has refused to marry."

The worry in Mrs. Sperry's face was almost imperceptible, but I understood.

I had checked over the "Who's Who" and I knew the seriousness of this population crisis. I also knew that there were four young unmarried men with no other prospects of wives except Lora-Louise.

"Have you any choice for her?" I asked.

"Since she must marry—and I know she *must*—I have urged her to make her own choice."

I could see that the ordeal of choosing had been postponed until my coming, in hopes that I might modify the rules. But I had no intention of doing so. The *Flashaway* needed Lora-Louise. It needed the sort of children she would bear.

That week I saw the two husky Dickinson boys. Both were in their twenties. They stayed close together and bore an air of treachery and scheming. Rumor had it that they carried weapons made from table knives.

Everyone knew that my coming would bring the conflict to a head. Many thought I would try to force the girl to marry the older Smith—"Batch", as he was called in view of his bachelorhood. He was past thirty-five, the oldest of the four unmarried men.

But some argued otherwise. For Batch, though a splendid specimen physically, was slow of wit and speech. It was common knowledge that he was weak-minded.

For that reason, I might choose his younger cousin, "Smithy," a roly-poly overgrown boy of nineteen who spent his time bullying the younger children.

But if the Smiths and the Dickinsons could have their way about it, the Keeper of the Traditions should have no voice in the matter. Let me insist that Lora-Louise marry, said they; but whom she should marry was none of my business.

They preferred a fight as a means of settlement. A free-for-all between the two factions would be fine. A showdown of fists among the four contenders would be even better.

BEST of all would be a battle of knives that would eliminate all but one of the suitors. Not that either the Dickinsons or the Smiths needed to admit that was what they preferred; but their barbaric tastes were plain to see.

Barbarians! That's what they had become. They had sprung too far from their native civilization. Only the Sperry faction, isolated in their monasteries of control boards, physicians' laboratories and record rooms, kept alive the spark of civilization.

The Sperrys and their associates were human beings out of the twenty-first century. The Smiths and the Dickinsons had slipped. They might have come out of the Dark Ages.

What burned me up more than anything else was that obviously both the Smiths and the Dickinsons looked forward with sinister glee toward dragging Lora-Louise down from her height to their own barbaric levels.

One night I was awakened by the sharp ringing of the pilot's telephone. I' heard the snap of a switch. An *emergency* signal flashed on throughout the ship.

Footsteps were pounding toward the ballroom. I slipped into a robe, seized my gun, made for the door.

"The Dickinsons are murdering up on them!" Pilot Sperry shouted to me from the door of the control room.

"I'll see about it," I snapped.

I bounded down the corridor. Sperry didn't follow. Whatever violence might occur from year to year within the hull of the *Flashaway*, the pilot's code demanded that he lock himself up at the controls and tend to his own business.

It was a free-for-all! Under the bright lights they were going to it, tooth and toenail.

Children screamed and clawed, women hurled dishes, old tottering granddaddies edged into the fracas to crack at each other with canes.

The appalling reason for it all showed in the center of the room— the roly-poly form of young "Smithy" Smith. Hacked and stabbed, his nightclothes ripped, he was a veritable mess of carnage.

I shouted for order. No one heard me, for in that instant a chase thundered on the balcony. Everything else stopped. All eyes turned on the three racing figures.

Batch Smith, fleeing in his white nightclothes, had less than five yards' lead on the two Dickinsons. Batch was just smart enough to run when he was chased, not smart enough to know he couldn't possibly outrun the younger Dickinsons.

As they shot past blazing lights the Dickinsons' knives flashed. I could see that their hands were red with Smithy's blood.

"Stop!" I cried. "Stop or I'll *shoot!"*

If they heard, the words must have been meaningless. The younger Dickinson gained ground. His brother darted back in the opposite direction, crouched, waited for his prey to come around the circular balcony.

"Dickinson! Stop or I'll shoot you dead!" I bellowed.

Batch Smith came on, his eyes white with terror. Crouched and waiting, the older Dickinson lifted his knife for the killing stroke.

I shot.

The crouched Dickinson fell in a heap. Over him tripped the racing form of Batch Smith, to sprawl headlong. The other Dickinson leaped over his brother and pounced down upon the fallen prey, knife upraised.

Another shot went home.

Young Dickinson writhed and came toppling down over the balcony rail. He lay where he fell, his bloody knife sticking up through the side of his neck.

IT was ugly business trying to restore order. However, the magic power of firearms, which had become only a dusty legend, now put teeth into every word I uttered.

The doctors were surprisingly efficient. After many hours of work behind closed doors, they released their verdicts to the waiting groups.

The elder Dickinson, shot through the shoulder, would live. The younger Dickinson was dead. So was Smithy. But his cousin, Batch Smith, although too scared to walk back to his stateroom, was unhurt.

The rest of the day the doctors devoted to patching up the minor damages done in the free fight. Four-fifths of the *Flashaway* population were burdened with bandages, it seemed. For some time to come both the warring parties were considerably sobered over their losses. But most of all they were disgruntled because the fight had settled nothing.

The prize was still unclaimed. The two remaining contenders, backed by their respective factions, were at a bitter deadlock.

Nor had Lora-Louise's hatred for either the surviving Dickinson or Smith lessened in the slightest.

Never had a duty been more oppressive to me. I postponed my talk with Lora-Louise for several days, but I was determined that there should be no more fighting. She must choose.

We sat in an alcove next to the pilot's control room, looking out into the vast sky. Our ship, bounding at a terrific speed though it was, seemed to be hanging motionless in the tranquil star-dotted heavens.

"I must speak frankly," I said to the girl. "I hope you will do the same."

She looked at me steadily. Her dark eyes were perfectly frank, her full lips smiled with child-like simplicity.

"How old are you?" she asked.

"Twenty-eight," I answered. I'd been the youngest professor on the college faculty. "Or you might say three hundred and twenty-eight. Why?"

"How soon must you go back to your sleep?"

"Just as soon as you are happily married. That's why I must insist that you—"

Something very penetrating about her gaze made my words go weak. To think of forcing this lovely girl—so much like the Louise of my own century—to marry either the brutal Dickinson or the moronic Smith—

"Do you really want me to be *happily* married?" she asked.

I don't remember that any more words passed between us at the time. A few days later she and I were married—and most happily!

The ceremony was brief. The entire Sperry faction and one

representative from each of the two hostile factions were present. The aged captain of the ship, who had been too ineffectual in recent years to apply any discipline to the fighting factions, was still able with vigorous voice to pronounce us man and wife.

A year and a half later I took my leave.

I bid fond good-by to the "future captain of the *Flashaway,*" who lay on a pillow kicking and squirming. He gurgled back at me. If the boasts and promises of the Sperry grandparents and their associates were to be taken at full value, this young prodigy of mine would in time become an accomplished pilot and a skilled doctor as well as a stern but wise captain.

Judging from his talents at the age of six months, I was convinced he showed promise of becoming Food Superintendent as well.

I left reluctantly but happily.

CHAPTER VI
The Final Crisis

THE year 2466 was one of the darkest in my life. I shall pass over it briefly.

The situation I found was all but hopeless.

The captain met me personally and conveyed me to his quarters without allowing the people to see me.

"Safer for everyone concerned," he muttered. I caught glimpses as we passed through the shadows. I seemed to be looking upon ruins.

Not until the captain had disclosed the events of the century did I understand how things could have come to such a deplorable state. And before he finished his story, I saw that I was helpless to right the wrongs.

"They've destroyed 'most everything," the hard-bitten old captain rasped. "And they haven't overlooked *you.* They've destroyed you completely. *You are an ogre.*"

I wasn't clear on his meaning. Dimly in the back of my mind the hilarious farewell of four centuries ago still echoed.

"The *Flashaway* will go through!" I insisted.

"They destroyed all the books, phonograph records, movie films. They broke up clocks and bells and furniture—"

And I was supposed to carry this interspatial outpost of American civilization through *unblemished!* That was what I had promised so gaily four centuries ago.

"They even tried to break out the windows," the captain went on. "'Oxygen be damned!' they'd shout. They were mad. You couldn't tell them anything. If they could have got into this end of the ship, they'd have murdered us and smashed the control boards to hell."

I listened with bowed head.

"Your son tried like the devil to turn the tide. But God, what chance did he have? The dam had busted loose. They wanted to kill each other. They wanted to destroy each other's property and starve each other out. No captain in the world could have stopped either faction. They had to get it out of their systems..."

He shrugged helplessly. "Your son went down fighting..." For a time I could hear no more. It seemed but minutes ago that I had taken leave of the little tot.

The war—if a mania of destruction and murder between two feuding factions could be called a war—had done one good thing, according to the captain. It had wiped the name of Dickinson from the records.

Later I turned through the musty pages to make sure. There were Smiths and Sperrys and a few other names still in the running, but no Dickinsons. Nor were there any Grimstones. My son had left no living descendants.

To return to the captain's story, the war (he said) had degraded the bulk of the population almost to the level of savages. Perhaps the comparison is an insult to the savage. The instruments of knowledge and learning having been destroyed, beliefs gave way to superstitions, memories of past events degenerated into fanciful legends.

The rebound from the war brought a terrific superstitious terror concerning death. The survivors crawled into their shells, almost literally; the brutalities and treacheries of the past hung like storm clouds over their imaginations.

As year after year dropped away, the people told and retold the stories of destruction to their children. Gradually the legend twisted into a strange form in which all the guilt for the carnage *was placed upon me!*

I WAS the one who had started all the killing! *I, the ogre,* who slept in a cave somewhere in the rear of the ship, came out once upon a time and started all the trouble!

I, the Traditions Man, dealt death with a magic weapon; I cast the spell of killing upon the Smiths and the Dickinsons that kept them fighting until there was nothing left to fight for!

"But that was years ago," I protested to the captain. "Am I still an ogre?" I shuddered at the very thought.

"More than ever. Stories like that don't die out in a century. They grow bigger. You've become the symbol of evil. I've tried to talk the silly notion down, but it has been impossible. My own family is afraid of you."

I listened with sickening amazement. I was the Traditions Man; or rather, the "Traddy Man"—the bane of every child's life.

Parents, I was told, would warn them, "If you don't be good, the Traddy Man will come out of his cave and get you!"

And the Traddy Man, as every grown-up knew, could storm out of his cave without warning. He would come with a strange gleam in his eye. That was his evil will. When the bravest, strongest men would cross his path, he would hurl instant death at them. Then he would seize the most beautiful woman and marry her.

"Enough!" I said. "Call your people together. I'll dispel their false ideas—"

The captain shook his head wisely. He glanced at my gun.

"Don't force me to disobey your orders," he said. "I can believe you're not an ogre—but they won't. I know this generation. You don't. Frankly, I refuse to disturb the peace of this ship by telling the people you have come. Nor am I willing to terrorize my family by letting them see you."

For a long while I stared silently into space.

The captain dismissed a pilot from the control room and had me come in.

"You can see for yourself that we are straight on our course. You have already seen that all the supplies are holding up. You have seen that the population problem is well cared for. What more do you want?"

What more did I want! With the whole population of the *Flashaway* steeped in ignorance—immorality—superstition—savagery! *

Again the captain shook his head. "You want us to be like your friends of the twenty-first century. *We can't be.*"

He reached in his pocket and pulled out some bits of crumpled papers.

"Look. I save every scrap of reading matter. I learned to read from the primers and charts that your son's grandparents made. Before the destruction, I tried to read about the Earth-life. I still piece together these torn bits and study them. But I can't piece together the Earth-life that they tell about. All I really know is what I've seen and felt and breathed right here in my native *Flashaway* world.

"That's how it's bound to be with all of us. We can't get back to your notions about things. Your notions haven't any real truth for us. You don't belong to our world," the captain said with honest frankness.

"So I'm an outcast on my own ship!"

"That's putting it mildly. You're a menace and a troublemaker—an *ogre!* It's in their minds as tight as the bones in their skulls."

The most I could do was secure some promises from him before I went back to the ice. He promised to keep the ship on its course. He promised to do his utmost to fasten the necessary obligations upon those who would take over the helm.

"Straight relentless navigation!" We drank a toast to it. He didn't pretend to appreciate the purpose or the mission of the *Flashaway,* but he took my word for it that it would come to some good.

---

*Professor Grimstone is obviously astounded that his charges, with all the necessities of life on board their space ship, should have degenerated so completely. It must be remembered, however, that no other outside influence ever entered the *Flashaway* in all its long voyage through space. In the space of centuries, the colonists progressed not one whit.

On a very much reduced scale, the *Flashaway* colonists are a more or less accurate mirror of a nation in transition. Sad but true it is that nations, like human beings, are born, wax into bright maturity, grow into comfortable middle age and oft times linger on until old age has impaired their usefulness.

In the relatively short time that man has been a thinking, building animal, many great empires—many great nations—have sprung from humble beginnings to grow powerful and then wane into oblivion, sometimes slowly, sometimes with tragic suddenness.

Grimstone, however, has failed to take the lessons of history into account through the mistaken conception that because the colonists' physical wants were taken care of, that was all they required to keep them healthy and contented. —Ed.

"To Robinello in 2666!" Another toast. Then he conducted me back, in utmost secrecy, to my refrigerator room.

I AWOKE to the year of 2566, keenly aware that I, was not Gregory Grimstone, the respected Keeper of the Traditions. If I was anyone at all, I was the Traddy Man—the ogre.

But perhaps by this time—and I took hope with the thought—I had been completely forgotten.

I tried to get through the length of the ship without being seen. I had watched through the one-way glass for several hours for a favorable opportunity, but the ship seemed to be in a continual state of daylight, and shabby-looking people roamed about as aimlessly as sheep in a meadow.

The few persons who saw me as I darted toward the captain's quarters shrieked as if they had been knifed. In their world there was no such thing as a strange person. I was the impossible, the unbelievable. My name, obviously, had been forgotten.

I found three men in the control room. After minutes of tension, during which they adjusted themselves to the shock of my coming, I succeeded, in establishing speaking terms. Two of the men were Sperrys.

But at the very moment I should have been concerned with solidifying my friendship, I broke the calm with an excited outburst. My eye caught the position of the instruments and I leaped from my seat.

"How long have you been going *that way?*"

"Eight years!"

"Eight—" I glanced at the huge automatic chart overhead. It showed the long straight line of our centuries of flight with a tiny shepherd's crook at the end. Eight years ago we had turned back sharply.

"That's sixteen years lost, gentlemen!"

I tried to regain my poise. The three men before me were perfectly calm, to my astonishment. The two Sperry brothers glanced at each other. The third man, who had introduced himself as Smith, glared at me darkly.

"It's all right," I said. "We won't lose another minute. I know how to operate—"

"No, you don't!" Smith's voice was harsh and cold. I had started to reach for the controls. I hesitated. Three pairs of eyes were fixed on me.

"We know where we're going," one of the Sperrys said stubbornly. "We've got our own destination."

"This ship is bound for Robinello!" I snapped. "We've got to colonize. The Robinello planets are ours—America's. It's our job to clinch the claim and establish the initial settlement—"

"Who said so?"

"America!"

"When?" Smith's cold eyes tightened.

"Five hundred years ago."

"That doesn't mean a thing. Those people are all dead."

"I'm one of those people!" I growled. "And I'm not dead by a damned sight!"

"Then you're out on a limb."

"Limb or no limb, the plan goes through!" I clutched my gun. "We haven't come five hundred years in a straight line for nothing!"

"The plan is dead," one of the Sperrys snarled. "We've killed it."

HIS brother chimed in, "This is our ship and we're running it. We've studied the heavens and we're out on our own. We're through with this straight-line stuff. We're going to see the universe."

"You can't! You're bound for Robinello!"

Smith stepped toward me, and his big teeth showed savagely.

"We had no part in that agreement. We're taking orders from no one. I've heard about you. You're the Traddy Man. Go back in your hole—and stay there!"

I brought my gun up slowly. "You've heard of me? Have you heard of my gun? Do you know that this weapon shoots men dead?"

Three pairs of eyes caught on the gleaming weapon. But three men stood their ground staunchly.

"I've heard about guns," Smith hissed. "Enough to know that you don't dare shoot in the control room—"

"I don't dare miss!"

I didn't want to kill the men. But I saw no other way out. Was there any other way? Three lives weren't going to stand between the *Flashaway* and her destination.

Seconds passed, with the four of us breathing hard. Eternity was about to descend on someone. Any of the three might have been splendid pioneers if they had been confronted with the job of building a colony. But in this moment, their lack of vision was as deadly as any deliberate sabotage. I focused my attack on the most troublesome man of the three.

"Smith, I'm giving you an order. Turn back before I count to ten or I'll kill you. One...two...three..."

Not the slightest move from anyone. "Seven...eight...nine..." Smith leaped at me—and fell dead at my feet.

The two Sperrys looked at the faint wisp of smoke from the weapon barked another sharp command, and one of the Sperrys marched to the controls and turned the ship back toward Robinello.

CHAPTER VII
Time Marches On

FOR a year I was with the Sperry brothers constantly, doing my utmost to bring them around to my way of thinking. At first I watched them like hawks. But they were not treacherous. Neither did they show any inclination to avenge Smith's death. Probably this was due to a suppressed hatred they had held toward him.

The Sperrys were the sort of men, being true children of space, who bided their time. That's what they were doing now. That was why I couldn't leave them and go back to my ice.

As sure as the *Flashaway* could cut through the heavens, those two men were counting the hours until I returned to my nest. The minute I was gone, they would turn back toward their own goal.

And so I continued to stay with them for a full year. If they contemplated killing me, they gave no indication. I presume I would have killed them with little hesitation, had I bad no pilots whatsoever that I could entrust with the job of carrying on.

There were no other pilots, nor were there any youngsters old enough to break into service.

Night after night I fought the matter over in my mind. There was a full century to go. Perhaps one hundred and fifteen or twenty years. And no one except the two Sperrys and I had any serious conception of a destination!

These two pilots and I—*and one other*, whom I had never for a minute forgotten. If the *Flashaway* was to go through, it was up to me and *that one other—*

I marched back to the refrigerator room, people fleeing my path in terror. Inside the retreat I touched the switches that operated the auxiliary merry-go-round freezer. After a space of time the operation was complete.

Someone very beautiful stood smiling before me, looking not a minute older than when I had packed her away for safe-keeping two centuries before.

"Gregory," she breathed ecstatically. "Are my three centuries up already?"

"Only two of them, Lora-Louise." took her in my arms. She looked up at me sharply and must have read the trouble in my eyes.

"They've all played out on us," I said quietly. "It's up to us now."

I discussed my plan with her and she approved.

One at a time we forced the Sperry brothers into the icy retreat, with repeated promises that they would emerge within a century. By that time Lora-Louise and I would be gone—but it was our expectation that our children and grandchildren would carry on.

And so the two of us, plus firearms, plus Lora-Louise's sense of humor, took over the running of the *Flashaway* for its final century.

As the years passed the native population grew to be less afraid of us. Little by little a foggy glimmer of our vision filtered into their numbed minds.

THE year is now 2600. Thirty-three years have passed since Lora-Louise and I took over. I am now sixty-two, she is fifty-six. Or if you prefer, I am 562, she is 256. Our four children have grown up and married.

We have realized down through these long years that we would not live to see the journey completed. The Robinello planets have been visible for some time; but at our speed they are still sixty or eighty years away.

But something strange happened nine or ten months ago. It has changed the outlook for all of us—even me, the crusty old Keeper of the Traditions.

A message reached us through our radio receiver!

It was a human voice speaking in our own language. It had a fresh vibrant hum to it and a clear-cut enunciation. It shocked me to realize how sluggish our own brand of the King's English had become in the past five-and-a-half centuries.

"Calling the *S.S. Flashaway!*" it said.

"Calling the *S.S. Flashaway!* We are trying to locate you, *S.S. Flashaway.* Our instruments indicate that you are approaching. If you can hear us, will you give us your exact location?"

I snapped on the transmitter. "This is the *Flashaway.* Can you hear us?" "Dimly. Where are you?"

"On our course. Who's calling?"

"This is the American colony on Robinello," came the answer. "American colony, Robinello, established in 2550—fifty years ago. We're waiting for you, *Flashaway.*"

"How the devil did you get there?" I may have sounded a bit crusty but I was too excited to know what I was saying.

"Modern space ships," came the answer. "We've cut the time from the earth to Robinello down to six years. Give us your location. We'll send a fast ship out to pick you up."

I gave them our location. That, as I said, was several months ago. Today we are receiving a radio call every five minutes as their ship approaches.

One of my sons, supervising the preparations, has just reported that all persons aboard are ready to transfer—including the Sperry brothers, who have emerged successfully from the ice. The eighty-five *Flashaway* natives are scared half to death and at the same time as eager as children going to a circus.

Lora-Louise has finished packing our boxes, bless her heart. That teasing smile she just gave me was because she noticed the "Who's Who Aboard the *Flashaway*" tucked snugly under my arm.

The Monster OUT OF SPACE

by MALCOLM JAMESON

This was no planetoid wandering in the void. It was a living monster, threatening to eat whole worlds. Could Berol's science stop it?

"GRAB something, folks, and hang on. I'm putting this little packet down on her tail!"

Bob Tallen shoved home the warning-howler switch, pushed the intership phone transmitter away from him, and jabbed the ignition control for the reversing tube.

Before the blasts fired, he threw two turns of his sling around him and thrust himself easily against the braces. Sudden decelerations were all in the day's work for him. He lay there grinning at the dismayed cries wafted to him from the laboratory compartment just behind. He heard the crash of glass even above the vibration of the belching tube.

The trim little *Sprite* shuddered, then bucked. Slowly and tremblingly, she began her turn. It was not often the exquisite little yacht of Fava Dithrell experienced the rough and ready hand of a Space Guardsman at her throttle. Usually the ship took a more demure pace.

"Bob! What happened?"

Fava herself had laboriously clawed her way to the control room, pulling along by the grab-irons in the fore-and-aft passage. Walter Berol, panting and dripping rusty-colored slime, clung uncertainly behind her. Both looked startled, but Berol also looked sheepish.

"Breakers ahead," announced Tallen calmly. "Some bonehead of a lighthouse tender forgot to recharge the beacon, or it's been robbed, or a meteor hit it. Anyhow, I thought I'd heave to and have a look-see."

"B-but...why so suddenly?" complained Berol, looking ruefully at his reeking smock... That is, we..."

In an instant the surface of the world-monster was a livid hell of action and death..

"Sudden is my nature," answered Bob Tallen serenely, jutting his jaw a trifle. "The situation called for a stop. So I stopped. It's as simple as that."

"Oh," said Berol.

"Walter was showing me how to use the laboratory he rigged up for me," explained Fava with a little flush, "and we were looking at a culture of those *vermes horridons* those nasty pests that overrun Dad's plantations on Titania. You spilled 'em all over him when you reared back like that!"

"Tough," commented Tallen, looking casually up at the pulsating red light on the control board. It indicated a considerable celestial body not far ahead.

"I thought he could take care of himself. He's as big and husky as I am."

"Oh, I get it," Berol spoke up with a good-natured laugh. "The big bad caveman was up here all alone, and he thought it was time he got in an inning."

"Boys! Boys!" protested Fava. "Don't spoil our vacation. You sound like a pair of infants."

Walter Berol grinned.

Bob Tallen laughed too. "What the hell! Nothing like a little emergency to pep up a party. Trot out the space suits, Fav, and we'll all take a stroll as soon as I can put this can alongside that rock, whatever it is."

Fava tapped her foot in annoyance, but there was a twinkle in her smoldering black eyes. She got a big kick out of the friendly rivalry of her two suitors. She liked them both immensely, even if they were as different as the poles.

Bob Tallen—Commander Tallen of the Space Guard—was bold, impetuous and able. He already had every decoration the Systemic Council could bestow. He would tackle a herd of Martian *felisaurs* barehanded if Fava were threatened, and never think twice while he was doing it. She liked him for his swift decisions and his daring.

WALTER Berol—*Doctor* Berol to the world, director of the Biological Institute—was easily more clever, but cursed with an incurable shyness that had all but wrecked his career. Yet, given time, he could solve any problem. Moreover, he was considerate and possessed of a droll sense of humor that made him good company anywhere. He was solid gold, even if not spectacular.

Fava felt the ship lurch as Tallen cut out two more tubes. The visiplate was glowing now, and a strange object was coming into focus.

"I'm damned," muttered Tallen, looking from his "Asteroid List" to the visiplate and back again. "Listen to this." He read:

The planetoid is known as Kellog's 218, and is a coffin-shaped iron body with some quartz inclusions. A Class R-41 buzzing beacon is installed, its period—

"Pear-shaped, I'd call it," said Fava. "It's a funny-looking thing, isn't it?"

"Looks like a rotten canteloupe impaled on an iron bar," remarked Berol.

"And at that end—where that pink, mushy-looking stuff is," exclaimed Fava, with growing excitement, "it seems to be covered with high grass!"

"Yes," said Berol, watching narrowly, "and it's undulating—as if in a breeze!"

"Nonsense," growled Bob Tallen, staring at the visiscreen. "How could there be wind on a boulder like that—and where did you ever see grass beyond Mars?"

It was a queer sight they saw in the visiplate—a writhing, doughy mass seemingly plastered on one end of Kellog's planetoid. And there was no beacon.

"Watch yourself!" called Tallen. "I'm landing."

WHEN Walter Berol and Fava were well up onto the first of the doughy terraces, they were astonished at how differently it appeared than as they had seen it from the ship. What they thought was mushy substance turned out to be a firm but yielding covering, much like dressed leather.

The waving grasses on closer examination appeared to be clusters of bare stalks of the same dirty pink material standing like wild bamboo. Yet their eyes had not deceived them. The grasses *did* move, gently undulating as do the fronds of huge marine growths in terrestrial oceans.

"What do you suppose *those* things are?" Fava suddenly asked, looking down after the two had advanced a bit between two avenues of the strange clumps. At the girl's feet, scattered in the pathway, were little crimson knobs, like half-buried tomatoes.

"They look squishy," Fava said, and kicked one with her toe.

Her shrill scream followed so instantly that Berol was dazed. The nearest of the clusters came to life with startling speed. A snaky antenna dived downward like the curving neck of a swan and threw its coils around Fava. Paralyzed by the swiftness and unexpectedness of the attack, Berol stared dumbly as the groping tip took two more turns and was creeping onward to enwrap the girl's leg.

Berol fumbled at his belt for his hand-ax, and yelled hoarsely into his helmet microphone for Bob Tallen. Tallen could not be far away.

Before Berol could free his ax, he heard Fava's strangling gasp. The crushing pressure of the tentacle had choked off her breath. Horrified, he saw her being lifted upward; glimpsed a yawning, purple slit opening up a few feet beyond.

Berol's blood ran cold, but he attacked the clutching tentacle with all the fury he could muster. The first blow rebounded with such violence as to almost hurl the hatchet from his hand, but he struck and struck again. He saw little nicks appear, and a dark, viscous fluid ooze out, splattering. Half blinded by tears of helpless rage and sweat, he kept on hacking.

Then he knew he could not raise his arm, and he felt the lash of some heavy thing across his shoulders. His faceplate was fogged and he could not see, but he felt the hideous nuzzling beneath his armpit and then the cold, rib-cracking constriction as another of the frightful antennae seized him. He had only time to cry out once more:

"Help, Bob—Fava—Bob..."

Then he fainted.

"HE'S coming round."

It was Bob Tallen, speaking as through a bloody mist. Berol knew, from the sweet abundance of the air, that he must be out of his suit. He must be on the ship, then. He stirred and opened his eyes, saw Fava hanging over him, looking at him anxiously. Then he remembered—those entwining, crushing, cruel tentacles; and the vile, sticky blood of the beast—gaping, waiting, slimy and nauseating. Berol shuddered. But Fava was safe!

"It's okay, old man," he heard Tallen's reassuring voice. "You've been pretty sick, but it's all over now. We're hitting the gravel at Lunar Base in an hour, and there's an ambulance waiting. In a couple of weeks you'll be good as new."

"That...thing...was...organic," Berol managed. "Did...you..."

"Forget it," said Tallen. "The sky is full of weird monsters. I burned that one down with my flame gun, and that's that. I daresay that rock was swarming with 'em, but never mind. It's two hundred million miles away now."

Berol tried to forget it, but he could not. He could not forget that he had been at Fava's side when she was imperiled, and that he had failed. It was Tallen who blasted the monster down—whether it was animal or vegetable or some hideous hybrid.

So he was thinking as he tossed and fretted in his room in the great hospital in Lunar Base, knowing that Bob Tallen was making hay while the sun shone. Tallen was still at the base, fitting out the new cruiser *Sirius* which he was to command. He had all his evenings free, however, and these he spent in company with Fava...

"You are a dear, sweet boy and I'm fond of you," Fava told Walter Berol, as she walked out with him the day he was discharged. They were on the way to the launching racks to see Bob Tallen take off for his shakedown voyage. "But the man I marry must be resourceful, masterful. I'm sorry... I don't want to hurt you...but..."

"It's to be Bob, then?"

She nodded, and suddenly the universe seemed very empty. Then a feeling of unworthiness almost overwhelmed him. Yes, she was right. He lacked the red-blooded qualities she admired in Bob Tallen. He was not fit mate for her.

But as suddenly another emotion surged through him. It was the old primeval urge—old as the race itself—of a man balked of his woman. He meant to have her, Tallen or no Tallen.

"You will not marry Bob," said Walter Berol quietly.

CHAPTER II
The Heavenly Monster

FAVA'S voice had been urgent, frightened.

"Come over to Headquarters at once! I am so afraid—for Bob."

Walter Berol stood only for a moment on the landing deck atop his great laboratory before stepping into the gyrocopter, but in that moment he cast an uneasy glance at the serene star-spangled canopy overhead. Disquieting thoughts were running through his mind.

In the three weeks since Bob Tallen and the *Sirius* had departed, many disturbing reports had come in from the asteroid belt. Eleven sizable planetoids were missing from their orbits—vanished! A dozen assorted cargo ships were overdue and unreported. A lighthouse tender had sent a frantic S.O.S. through a fog of ear-splitting static, and had been choked off in the middle of it with the words, "We are being engulfed..."

The gunboat *Jaguar,* sent to aid the tender, had not been heard of since. It was all very inexplicable. It was ominous.

Berol strode past the grim-faced sentries outside the General Staff Suite. As Director of the Biological Institute, he could enter those carefully guarded precincts. Inside, the room was jammed with officers, listening intently and gazing at the huge visiscreen. Fava sat beside an Admiral Madigan, fists white as snow as she clutched the arm of the chair. Berol stopped where he stood. A deep bass voice was coming in through the Mark IX televox.

"That's Bill Evans, in the *Capella,*" whispered someone.

"...we've finally caught up with the thing, whatever it is, and are close aboard now. We have circumnavigated it twice, but there is not the slightest trace of the *Jaguar* or any other ship."

Walter Berol was staring at an incredible landscape slipping beneath the *Capella's* scanner. It was a dirty pink, and studded with many curious knobs of writhing tubular matter. It looked soft and mushy, very much like a rotten pumpkin. It strangely resembled the bulbous end of Kellog's 218. Berol shuddered at the memory. Evans went on, "...the waving clumps mentioned by the *Jaguar* just before her radio went dead are not visible. All I can see is mounds of what looks like Gargantuan macaroni lying in heaps. The skipper is about to land. In a minute or so I'll give you a close-up. Stand by!"

There was a raucous blare of unusually heavy static, and when the voice did begin again, it was hard to make out the words. The static distorted the visuals, too, so that the screen was a blur of crawling pink light and no more. Presently the operators managed to eliminate the worst of the noise, and the voice came through once more, bellowing out against the deafening barrage of sound.

"...surface very deceptive...quite hard and tough. A landing party has gone out through the lock and is cutting samples of the surface with drills and axes. One man is chopping at a huge crimson growth as big as a barrel. Hold on—one of those hillocks of collapsed tubing is moving! The things are whipping around like snakes! Some of them have shot straight up into the air, and others are curling all around us!"

Berol edged his way through the crowd. Fava was breathing hard. Admiral Madigan's jaw was granite and his eyes never wavered from the screen.

"...they are tentacles! One has wrapped itself around our bow, and another group has caught us amidships. That is why we roll and pitch this way. The captain is clearing away the Q-guns. In a minute we will blast out—you'd better cut down on your power until that is over. There he goes..."

A dull roar filled the room and the walls trembled. Then the volume dropped. Brilliant scarlet light slashed and stabbed across the visiplate, and then it went almost black as if obscured by thick, oily smoke.

"...all stern tubes in full discharge. The surface of the planetoid—if this damn thing *is* a planetoid—is smoking furiously. Several clusters of the antennae astern of us have been burned away. We're still hung here, though. Looks like the impulse of the tubes is not enough to tear us loose from that grip forward..."

A wail of unearthly static drowned out the laboring voice. Then, "...trying the bow-tubes now. Wait. No, they can't get out that way...the spacelock is submerged and we're twisting over fast! A huge crevasse has opened up under us. We're sinking into it! The whole port is covered. We *a-a-awrk!*"

The voice ceased, choked off, and the light on the screen went out abruptly. In the dark room no one spoke for an instant. Berol felt, rather than saw, the tension among the hardened Space Guard officers. Fava's hand crept into his and clung to it.

The *Capella* had just gone to the doom they had so nearly missed, for there was no mistaking the similarity between this monster of unguessable nature and the menace on Kellog's 218.

"RAISE *Sirius!*" broke in Admiral Madigan's voice, crisp and angry. "What the hell is Tallen doing all this time?"

But the *Sirius* was there, hovering over the spot where the *Capella* had been, her shattering Q-rays lashing down, searing acres of the ravenous false asteroid. She turned on her televox so that those at Headquarters could see the quivering, sizzling terrain below. Clumps of the three hundred foot antennae were being roasted to a sooty ash, and swelling and popping with evil gases as they did. Bob Tallen's voice came through, strong and clear, barking out strident orders.

Nothing the *Sirius* could do, however, could save her floundering sister. The upper turret of the *Capella* sank out of sight, and the scorched, leathery integument closed over it. In a few minutes there was only a livid, ashen scar, and even that mark faded.

Commander Bob Tallen's face came onto the screen, huge in its close-up.

"Heat does it," he said tersely. "Send me all you've got, and hydrogen feroxite by the ton. I'll blast the damn thing to shreds, and then burn the shreds."

As the face faded, Admiral Madigan sprang into action.

"Out of here, all of you! Squadrons Three, Six and Ten take off at once. Report to Tallen when you get there. All reserve flotillas will install heavy-duty flame projectors and take on fuel to capacity. Report to me the instant you are ready."

He jerked out other curt orders and the officers hastened from the room. Fava had withdrawn to one side, looking on with eyes wide with horror. How well she knew the grip of those merciless tentacles! For there could be no mistaking that the monstrosity she had just been watching was the same as that on Kellog's 218, grown larger. And she sickened at the memory of the slimy fissures the vile beast seemed to open at will. It filled her with dread, for Bob Tallen was going to attack the thing, and he was rash, so reckless in his daring.

"Oh, Walter!" she cried, clutching Berol by the arm. "Do you think..."

Walter Berol shook his head gloomily.

"It is too late for brute force. The thing is too big. We should have found out something about its nature and destroyed it when it was little. But it must be four miles in diameter now, and growing as it feeds. All our fleet can have no more effect than a swarm of gnats nibbling at a rhinoceros. If it is to be attacked at all, it must be through its biological processes. Bob is attempting the impossible."

Admiral Madigan wheeled, a smile of cold scorn curling on his lip.

"So! The dreamer leans from his ivory tower to look us over and tell us we're wrong. Well! And what is the solution the great brain has to offer? Quickly! This is an emergency—men have died before our eyes!"

"I—don't—know," said Dr. Berol slowly. "It will take time, research. I will begin at once..."

"Bah!" snorted Madigan. "Research! It is lucky that there are men of action at hand. Like our Tallen."

He turned away abruptly, leaving Walter Berol standing where he was, his face aflame. Dull anger rose in his breast, but there was pity mingled with it—pity for the blind arrogance of these self-styled men of action, who thought they could control this colossal menace with their puny weapons.

For of all the men in that room, only Berol realized to the full the immensity of the threat that hung over the Solar System. If the monster had drifted in as a spore from the beyond, consumed cosmic gravel until it was big enough to digest a body like Kellog's iron planetoid, where would it stop? After the asteroids, what would it devour? The planetary moons, perhaps. And after those?

In that instant Walter Berol resolved to stop this Mooneater—and knew that he would face ridicule and obstruction. But the pink menace was more than a threat to the race—it had become a personal symbol. The creature, whatever its nature, had attacked the woman he loved, then crushed and humiliated him in her presence. Now it had brought the taunt of this space admiral.

"Fava," he said abruptly, "I want the use of the *Sprite.*"

"And if I refuse it?"

"Then I shall commandeer it in the name of the Institute."

THE air of quiet finality in his tone startled her. He had used it once before—the day he said she would not marry Bob Tallen. She looked at him wonderingly, then shrugged prettily. Let him try; he meant well. But she was sure he would fail. Out in the cold, gravityless vacuum of space he would fail as he always had outside his laboratories. That did not matter. What did matter to her just then, was that she saw a pretext to be near her sweetheart.

"Very well, Walter," Fava agreed, smiling. "But remember, I am rated as a laboratory helper—and the *Sprite* is my yacht. I intend going, too."

"But the danger..."

"Bob is in danger too," she said simply.

"**D**EAD," murmured Walter Berol. On the table in the *Sprite's* flying laboratory lay a clumsy Venusian rockchewer—the *Lithovere Veneris* — a queer, quartz-eating variety of armadillo. Seen through the fluoroscope, all its internal organs were still.

"A twentieth of a grain of *toxicin** has no effect—a tenth kills it."

"So you think—" Fava was looking on.

"No. It is merely worth trying. The Mooneater's internal chemistry may be the same; it may not. We have twelve drums of the stuff on board. I want to plant it on the monster's next victim. Then we will watch for the effect."

The next victim was the small planetoidal body Athor. Men had learned something of the predatory habits of the pink invader. This tremendous monstrosity swerved from orbit to orbit by the manipulation of magnetic fields, which it set up with a howling of static. Inexorably it pursued the cosmic body until it overtook it. Then, without any crash of collision, the marauder would split open along its leading face and take the planetoid bodily into itself. The maw would snap shut and the Mooneater would move on, bigger and more ravenous, to its next prey.

Fava set the *Sprite* down in the dismal Athor canyon known as South Valley. There was barely time for what they had to do, as the Mooneater was already a huge and growing disk in the black sky. They could even make out the lightning playing over its surface where Tallen's cruisers hung in a cloud, ever blasting, burning and harassing. Time after time they had scarified its surface, until there were only black stumps where the antennae clumps had been, but as often the monster grew fresh ones.

Walter Berol put on a space suit and with four of his crew sought a cave in which to cache their deadly drug toxicin. But hardly had they emerged from the lock when, with a fiery swoop, a huge warship settled

---

* *Toxicin,* a powerful chemical substance which is capable of breaking down and dissolving the proteins of certain living creatures, such as the rock-chewer of Venus, described here as an armadillo-like creature.—Ed.

to the ground nearby. A dozen helmeted figures sprang from its airlock and bounded toward the grounded yacht.

"What are you fools doing here? This asteroid was ordered evacuated thirty hours ago!"

The voice was Bob Tallen's, harsh and angry.

Then in astonishment Tallen recognized the familiar lines of the *Sprite,* and knew the man before him was Berol.

"My God!" shouted Tallen hoarsely. "Fava here? Get out—at once—while you can!"

He pointed to the oncoming Moon-eater, which now filled a quarter of the sky.

"I see it," replied Walter Berol. "We will leave as soon as we dump some drums of chemicals. I am planting a dose of poison..."

"Arrest this man!" Bob Tallen whirled on the bluejackets who had followed him.

The sailors from the *Sirius* pounced on Berol and bore him protesting and struggling into the *Sprite,* Tallen following close behind. Inside the yacht Tallen snapped orders to the other ship. The airlocks of both vessels rang shut, and on the instant they plunged upward with streaking wakes of flame.

"Look," said Bob Tallen dramatically, pointing back at the asteroid.

The Mooneater was no more than four diameters away. It had opened its maw, revealing a slimy, purplish cavern. Five minutes later the ghastly pseudo-lips were closing in on the periphery of little Athor. Then there was but a livid line to mark where the asteroid had gone. The pink monster rolled on, heedless of the massed cruisers stabbing at it with their Q-rays and heat guns.

EVERYONE gasped a little. "If it had not been for me," Tallen went on, his face a thundercloud, "you—and Fava—would be inside there. I have placed you under restraint to save you from your own idiocy. This is a man's game. It is no time to play around with theories. Action is what is required now."

"You've been in action for two months," retorted Walter Berol with pointed irony. "The Mooneater, I believe, has approximately trebled its volume in that time. If that is how effective action is, I think it is high time somebody did a little *thinking.*"

"That's my worry," snapped Tallen. "The Autarch, head of the Systemic Council, has given me this job. When I want help, I'll ask for it. Until then, you are to keep out of my way."

CHAPTER III
Pursuit

FROM Mars the destruction of Deimos was plainly seen. Every eye, every telescope, every pair of binoculars was trained on the oncoming scourge. Batteries of cameras drank in every detail through telephoto lenses. Photographic plates were made from ultra-violet and infra-red rays. At every vantage point the Omnivox announcers set up their mikes and described the battle to the thoroughly aroused citizenry of the Solar System.

Bob Tallen, now a Space Guard commodore, had set up his controls in the south tower of the administration building in Ares City. He was ready for the final test of strength between his forces and the hitherto irresistible pink menace. Under his direction Deimos was honeycombed with galleries and tunnels—miles of mines packed with tens of thousands of tons of feroxite. Around Mars' equator, heavy siege guns had been placed to assist the ships in their bombardment. In one tremendous concentration of flame and violent detonation Tallen proposed to blast the marauder to bits.

The *Sprite* was safely tucked away in Martian Skyyard, and to permit. Fava and Walter Berol to witness his triumph, Tallen had made room by his side for both of them.

Fourteen cruisers of the first class, and many dozen lesser ones, had trailed the Mooneater from the asteroid zone, hammering incessantly at it as they followed. Day after day they had pumped high explosives into it and played fierce flames upon its ever-sprouting tentacles. Hundreds of cargo ships shuttled between the fleet and the bases, bringing fresh supplies of fuel and ammunition. As a demonstration of the sustained application of brute force in massive doses, Tallen's campaign had no precedent. Now he was ready for the kill.

"It won't work, Bob," said Berol mildly, as he watched the huge pink orb advancing on Mars' tiny moon. "The thing is organic, I tell you."

"So what?" barked Tallen. "If it lives, it can be killed, can't it?"

"*If* you can apply enough force at one time. That is what you cannot do. You are trying to kill an elephant by jabbing it with a penknife. Being organic, the creature is capable of self-repair. That is where you're licked. You've got to upset its organic functioning..."

"*I'll* upset its functioning," said Bob Tallen grimly, his eye on the monster. It was within one diameter of Deimos. He jabbed the button before him—three times. The attack was on.

A cloud of cruisers darted between the yawning mouth of the Mooneater, letting their salvos go into its open chasm. Others smothered its rear areas with raging flame. And as the Mooneater advanced relentlessly in spite of all, until its hideous pseudo-lips closed on the little satellite, Bob Tallen pressed the key that set off the radio-controlled mines.

"OOOOh! Look!" screamed Fava, gripping Berol's arm. "Bob has won! He has torn it to shreds!"

For a few minutes it appeared he had. An immense blister rose as one side of the Mooneater swelled to accommodate the terrific blast of the expanding feroxite gases within. Then the monstrosity burst shatteringly in scores of places, as in a chain of terrestrial volcanoes, tearing great strips of the beast's entrails. Gaping streamers and shreds of purplish flesh were flung out into the void, rent by the explosion. Other strings of viscid stuff drooled from the jagged slot that had been a mouth, only to flash into flame as the ray-guns lashed at them.

Then the throaty roar of thousands of heavy guns from Mars drowned out all other sound. The moment the ships were clear, the artillery opened up, slamming salvo after salvo into the harried monster. Huge hunks of the featherlike hide were torn out, leaving ragged craters. Tentacles were blown to flying fragments and ripped away by their roots. With an outpouring of static that exceeded any before, the monster turned away from Mars and headed back toward the asteroids.

B OB Tallen glared incredulously after the retreating raider. He had hurt it—yes. But it was still *intact!* It had not disgorged the satellite it had just devoured. It was on its way back to complete the clean-up of the asteroids. Cruiser after cruiser fell away from it and headed back to Mars. They were out of ammunition. The great stroke had been made—and had failed!

"With your permission, Commodore Tallen," remarked Walter Berol dryly, "I will take up my researches where I left off. I notice that your high explosive shells have a penetration of something like three hundred feet. When you consider that the Mooneater is upwards of ten miles in diameter, it ought to be clear that you are doing little more than irritating its hide. It must be attacked from within, not externally."

"Research and be damned to you!" Bob Tallen flung at him, reckless in his anger and disappointment. "You keep yelping about what science can do—well, show us! Only keep out of my way."

"I will do that," replied Berol coldly. He rose and left the room, and he did not glance at Fava as he left. He realized the challenge had been given and accepted. His first job was the conquest of the Mooneater. His personal affairs could wait. After all, if the Mooneater was to be permitted to glut itself without Mint on the planet bodies of the Solar System, the time was not far off when personal affairs would cease to exist. From that moment Walter Berol dedicated himself to the destruction of the pink monster.

BEROL did not go near the *Sprite*. Instead he took the space tender *Jennie* from the Martian branch of the Biological Institute and went up and into the orbit of defunct Deimos. Floating there in tumultuous disorder were the gouts of viscous matter ejected from the wounded Mooneater, intermingled with long streamers of jagged and torn tissue. Berol gathered tons of the stinking, filthy stuff and carried it down to the branch laboratory on Mars.

For many weeks he immersed himself in the examination of his specimens. He and his aides sectioned, cultured and analyzed. He was amazed at what he found. The monstrosity was built of proteins! * By some freak of internal chemistry, the creature could actually transmute the heavier elements to lighter ones: convert iron to flesh, and quartz to organic fluids.

Yet despite his discovery of the macrocosmic nature of the monster's structure—it had individual cells as big as apples—he could learn little

---

*Protein; an albuminous compound derived from a proteid, one of a class of important compounds found in nearly all animal and vegetable organisms, and containing carbon, hydrogen, oxygen, nitrogen, and sulphur. —Ed.

of its constitution as a whole, and nothing of its vital organisms. What he had wag bits of the epidermis, or the droolings from its surface fluids. His task was as hopeless as that of reconstructing a whale from a few square inches of torn blubber.

Berol was still doggedly working at his quest when an "All-System" broadcast broke the stillness of his study. When the Autarch spoke, everyone listened.

"The peoples of the Solar System are advised that the Supreme Council has decreed that the wasteful war on the invader popularly known as the Moon-eater shall cease. In spite of the gallant efforts of the Space Guard, it has destroyed all our asteroids, including Ceres and the moons of Mars. It is now close to a thousand miles in diameter and quite beyond our power to control..."

Dr. Berol gasped. He had lost touch with the outside world and did not know that things had come to such a pass.

"It is ordered, therefore, that all the satellites of the System of less than the destroyed planet bodies be evacuated immediately, and that scientists of every category abandon whatever research they may be engaged in at present, and concentrate on the problem of rendering Jupiter habitable. Our mathematicians have extended the curve of the Mooneater's consumption, knowing the size of the planetoidal bodies remaining, and have computed with great accuracy the date of extinction of each of our planets, Only Jupiter is so huge that the Mooneater can never grow large enough to swallow it, "The Autarch has spoken!"

WALTER Berol sat staring at the dead amplifier long after that final click. So Bob Tallen was beaten. The Autarch was beaten. The human race was beaten. It meant extinction, for it was unlikely that great king of planets could ever be made habitable for man. And if it should, there was not enough transportation in the System to convey the populations there...

Berol, too, was beaten. He realized that. All the feverish work of recent weeks was wasted. He had reached no conclusions, he had not found the fatal toxin that would kill the monster. Nor had he any clear notion of how to introduce it if he had it. It is true a cobra can kill a bull by the prick of a fang. But Berol had no proven poison, nor the means of injection. And now came the order to drop all work. His failure was complete, for the Autarch's dictum was final.

Wearily he pressed a button on his desk.

"Close our files on the Mooneater," he told his laboratory chief. "Let me have the index on the 'Flora and Fauna of Jupiter'."

FAVA Dithrell burst excitedly into Walter Berol's study.

"Walter," she cried, "the Mooneater is here! It is passing Europa now!"

"There is nothing we can do about it," said Berol. "We have orders to disregard it. Anyhow, Callisto is safe for the present."

When Berol had moved his headquarters to be close to Jupiter, he was not greatly surprised to find that Fava was already there as a helper. The order of the Autarch had been for engineers of every degree and all scientists to work on the Jupiter project, and Fava was known as an amateur biologist. Berol had long suspected that she applied for a position in the Callistan laboratories because Bob Tallen was based on nearby Io. Since he had been pulled off the Mooneater hunt, Tallen had been put in charge of the evacuation of Jupiter's minor satellites.

"The Mooneater," Fava was repeating. "It's behaving queerly, Walter. It passed the small outer satellites without touching one of them."

"Hm-m," he mused. "That *is* odd. It may be significant." He drummed the desk with his fingers. "Perhaps it has reached its full growth; it may consume less hereafter."

The behavior of the Mooneater was odd, indeed. It skirted Jupiter's moons on a lazy, incurving spiral, and then departed from the Jovian* System without molesting even its smallest satellite! Speculation was rife. Had the monster attained its optimum—its maximum size? That could be it: each race of creatures has a limiting size. Only time could answer.

But as the panic subsided among the Jovian colonists, screaming accounts of the exodus from the Saturnian System began filling the news. The pink monstrosity was heading that way, and all of Saturn's moons, with one exception, were of edible size.

* Jove and Jupiter are interchangeable mythological terms. Jovian is the adjective. —Ed.

On rolled the Mooneater. It slid past Phoebe, past Hyperion and Rhea and all the other little moons. It touched none of them, but went on in close to the great semi-liquid planet. There, astoundingly enough, it swam into the midst of the Ring and stayed, floating for weeks about Saturn as a self-elected satellite! Then, as unaccountably as it had come, it left, and spiraled outward to intercept Uranus.

Walter Berol learned of it only because Fava told him. Her father's ranches were located on Titania, and she feared the properties were doomed. Berol shook his head gloomily. There was nothing he could do. The Autarch had repeatedly refused to permit him to resume his efforts. The head of the Council had gone so far as to threaten stern disciplinary measures if the matter was brought up again.

But Fava's account of the Moon-eater's actions in the vicinity of Saturn had a galvanic effect on Walter Berol. He jumped up excitedly.

"Yes, yes—of course! I might have anticipated it. The answer lies there, surely. She would have gone into the Rings for no other purpose—"

"*She!*" snapped Fava, her fears scurrying before her sense of outrage. "Why confer *my* sex on that unspeakable monster?" She stamped her tiny foot angrily.

"Yes—she!" Berol fairly shouted. "Don't you understand? We have to deal now with more of the accursed things—thousands, millions of them, perhaps. We must go there at once and stamp out her hellish progeny!"

FAVA was staring at him dumfounded. Such a display of excitement was very rare with Walter Berol. He talked on, vehemently.

"This monster was small once—how small we never knew. In the beginning it probably consumed cosmic sand and gravel, then boulders, then moons. Now it is mature, and like all other living things, it is under the compulsion to reproduce. She has laid her eggs in the Ring gravel!"

Fava's tension broke with a merry tinkling laugh. "Walter, have you gone crazy? Eggs! How fantastic!"

"Not at all. There can be no other conclusion. We see the cycle of the monster's life beginning all over again —with sand and gravel, and small diameter bodies near at hand. Like the bee, the ant and the beetle, she deposits her eggs where food suitable for the newborn is the most abundant. Why else would she abstain from eating those satellites herself? We know her appetite. Hers is the mother instinct!"

Fava gasped. It was a bold idea, but plausible. The Mooneater was a living creature, no one doubted that.

"But will the Autarch—" she began.

"To hell with the Autarch and his one-track mind!" Berol yelled, snatching up his head covering. "Your yacht, Fava—it is completely equipped. We'll defy them all. The existence of the race depends on us. In those baby Mooneaters is the clue to their structure, their chemistry. Come!"

CHAPTER IV
The Fatal Depths

"WE ARE practically at Ring speed now," said Anglin, Fava's sailing master.

All about them hung the glittering quartz and crystalline iron nuggets that swing forever about Saturn in broad bands.

"Good," said Walter Berol. "Turn on the ultraviolet beam."

He slipped on a space suit and went out onto the hull. For a long time he sat, holding a long rod that had a butterfly net at its end, studying the reflected rays sent back by the Ring particles. All about them seemed to be a sort of fog, so filled was the space with suspended dust and sand. Few of the little stones that compose the Ring are larger than marbles. It was a perfect feeding ground for embryo Mooneaters.

It was more than an hour before Berol caught the first embryo, but once he learned the peculiar lemon-yellow light with which they fluoresced, he began hauling them in by the dozens. They were not unlike basketballs—leathery, pinkish orange spheres covered with downlike fuzz. Those tiny hairs were what in time would come to be the horrid tentacles that held smaller prey—until one of the myriads of slitlike mouths could open beneath.

Walter Berol turned the job of catching the creatures over to a pair of deck-hands, and then hurried below with his first specimens. Triumphantly he slammed them down onto the dissecting table before Fava.

Swiftly, and under her watchful gaze, he slit one of the creatures open, cutting it from pole to pole with a green scalpel. He laid bare the hooplike formation of ribs ranged after the fashion of earthly meridians. His knife revealed the heavy circumpolar muscles that pulled the ribs to one side when in the act of eating huge masses. And under the viscid, purplish jelly that filled the body cavity, Berol found the palpitating green organ that must be the brain.

As rapidly as his fingers could fly, Berol traced the outflung intricacies of the branching green nerve-trunks, even to where they terminated at the skin in the tiny red specks that picked up the motor impulses[1]. Berol found the arterial tubes that conveyed the purple life-juices from the central reservoir, and he located the many subsidiary stomachs that lay under the fissured openings. Within an hour he had a clear understanding of the monster's anatomy.

"Bring me a needle of *toxicin*," he ordered.

Fava injected the poison in one of the living specimens, but it had no effect. Then she tried heteraine, and totronol[2]. The totronol was also harmless, but the heteraine had a definite narcotic effect. It caused a temporary paralysis of the parts where it was injected.

"That's something," muttered Berol, after they had exhausted the list of drugs and poisons. "Now for disease germs."

Ranged about the compartment were phials and phials of bacilli. There were samples of the bacteria that caused every disease of man, beast, plant or known monster of the airless, dark planets. There were *skuldrums*—sluglike lumps of fatty stuff that was the fatal enemy of the Plutonian lizard-cats. There were the thready spirochetes that plagued the Venusian rock-chewers, driving them to madness. There were others—globular, tubular, disk-shaped, some winged, some ciliated, some with fins. Each was sure death to some other living thing.

"Here," Berol said to Fava, handing her a tray full of ripped-out nerve ganglia and greenish brain fibre. "Find out whether any of these bacteria thrive in this stuff. I'll tackle the blood angle. Hurry!"

Fava blinked in mock dismay. Walter Berol had never spoken to her

---

1. It was Fava's kicking at one of those red nerve-ends that had caused the tentacle to grasp her. —Ed.

2 *Fleteraine is* a narcotic drug, extremely poisonous to humans in anything but infinitesimal doses, although it is a distillate of the paralysis-spray of the Venusian giant boa. *Totranol is* an Earth drug which totally destroys the motor nerves of the spinal column, inducing a permanent and quickly fatal paralysis.—Ed.

in such a brusque and authoritative manner. But she did not dislike it. She took the tray and went.

In ten hours they found the parasite they sought. It was a thin, pale worm—the *illi ulli,* parasite worm of the Venus fish life! Once it was introduced into the green nerve stuff, it multiplied at a terrific rate and quickly consumed it all.

"Now for the grand test," said Berol, as he leaned over a baby Mooneater with a hypodermic filled with a liquid that was crawling with the *illi ulli.* A quick jab, and the thing was done. Within an hour the leathery ball was a flabby corpse, its nervous system gutted by the ravenous worms. As it died, its multitude of slitlike mouths gaped open, gasping like the gills of an air-strangled water fish.

"Eureka!" whooped Dr. Berol, leaping into the air.

THE *Sprite* lurched forward, her jets screaming under forced discharge. Berol slewed the periscope about and took a look astern. Thousands of the leathery balls that might have grown into Mooneaters were springing into fiery incandescence, then exploding with silent *plops!* as the full energy of the backlashing rocket stream struck them. Berol knew there must be many thousands more of them, but someone else would have to sweep them up. He had bigger and more urgent game ahead. But first he must go into Iapetus for some needed supplies.

"Fava, while I am getting my rigging on board, your job is to make the *illi ulli* grow. I want 'em big—as big as possible—as big as anacondas, if you can do it. Force mutations on them with the X-ray, and feed them the synthetic diet I prescribed. Cull out the larger ones and let 'em propagate, and so on."

He snatched up a set of headphones and got through to the Governor of Iapetus. He lied glibly in a manner that simply amazed Fava. For Walter Berol issued a multitude of crisp orders —and said they were in the name of the Autarch and the Systemic Council! And he was probably already down on the punishment list for having vacated his post on Callisto without permission!

"I want," Berol snapped, "two large-capacity cargo ships loaded and ready to hop off tomorrow night. Here is the list of what is to be on board them."

It was an odd list: a two hundred foot derrick, a Myritz-Jorkin drill rig, complete with drill-bits and spare cutting heads; a hundred thousand feet of steel cable on spools; a three-inch detonon gun, with a thousand rounds of H.E. ammunition, but the shells to be unloaded except for delicate fuses; and twenty drums of 80% heteraine solution. With that equipment he wanted a drill crew of huskies and roughnecks from the gas fields of Io.

"That is all," barked Berol, as the acknowledgment came back. He yanked the jack from its socket and turned, to find Fava still by him.

"Well?" he said tartly. "Why aren't you nursing those worms along? Time flies!"

"I wanted to tell you, Walter, that I think you are wonderful." For the first time in many months Fava dropped the bantering tone she usually used toward him. "I had no idea you could be so—masterful! I didn't know...well, that you could *do* things... I—I..."

His impatient frown melted. Then he laughed uproariously for the first time since his encounter with the Mooneater on Kellog's 218.

"Oh, I see. Even you fell for the popular superstition that scientists have to be drier—than—dust, impractical boobs."

"B-but," she stammered, "you were always so clumsy...so timid... outside the laboratory..."

"You saw me trying to do things I didn't know how to do. That is all. But I am back in the laboratory—the whole Solar System is my laboratory now. I'm doing the work I know best. The difference is in the scale of it. I am on my way to inject an animal with disease germs. Since its hide is five or six *miles* thick, it calls for a gigantic needle." He laughed a little grimly.

"SURE!" said old Harvey Linholm, the gigantic six-foot-ten master rigger who had been supplied with the drilling gear. "We see the whole damn idea. Me and my men will go to hell and back with you, Doc, if it comes to that. We've lost plenty to that moon-gobbling, howling menace, and we're fed up with it. Besides, I'd as soon die right now takin' a crack at the thing as wait and go to Jupiter. I can't see livin' on giant Jupiter—think of what I would weigh there!"

Berol grinned. He turned to the captains of the two supply ships.

"All right, then. Take off at once and proceed to the spot I gave you the geodetics of. I'll overtake you. After that, follow me down."

He hurried away and mounted the ramp up the side of the *Sprite's* launching cradle. An obviously agitated Fava overtook him as he was about to enter the ship.

"We've lost," she moaned. "The *gendarmes* are on the way to seize you. The Autarch has learned of your assumption of authority here and has ordered you brought to the Earth in irons for trial."

"They'll have to hurry," said Walter Berol grimly, swinging the door open. "I'm taking off in ten seconds, Autarch or no Autarch."

"That's not all," Fava said in a low voice. "Bob Tallen has found out where I am and is on his way here to get me. I had a message from him forbidding me to have anything more to do with you."

"Ah," said Berol. "Perhaps Bob could tell us how the Autarch happens to know so much about our expedition."

"Yes," she nodded, and it was almost a whisper.

Berol's face hardened. "I am shoving off—now! You may come or not. Please yourself."

"Let's hurry then," Fava said, closing the lock door behind her. "The police and Bob won't be far behind."

T HE Mooneater was as huge as Luna. Led by the *Sprite,* the little flotilla circled in, warily, surveying the forest of clutching tentacle tips, now reaching thousands of feet into the sky. Lower and lower they flew, until at times they were diving between rows of the clumps.

"Shoot at the red spots," directed Berol, pointing out the nerve-ends. "Or at those greenish veins."

The detonon gun crew slammed in a shell—a shell loaded with the numbing drug heteraine instead of its usual high explosive. They aimed and fired, and as the missile tore its way into the monster's nerve fibre, the nearest group of tentacles lashed and writhed in fury. Eight, nine, ten—shot after shot ripped into the antennae's controlling ganglia. Then the clutching, whipping arms went limp and collapsed their full two miles in length onto the pink plain beneath.

The ships circled and came back to shoot down another set of antennae. By the time they slid to a stop on the horny hide of the Mooneater itself, the doped tentacles lay in mountainous piles for several miles around them.

"Quick!" commanded Berol, the moment they were at rest. "All hands outside! Squirt more heteraine into every nerve-end you see. We must anesthetize this entire area."

Men scampered about the grounded ships with big cans of heteraine strapped to their backs, jabbing sharpened pipes into the quivering nerve-ends. In a little while that part of the Mooneater was as inert as the floor of a crater on Luna herself. Beyond the narcotized section, the rest of the tentacles could be seen in agitated motion, twisting and clutching. Walter Berol anxiously scanned the black void from which he had come, but he saw no sign of the jet flames of his pursuers. He might accomplish his purpose yet.

After the anesthetic squads came the riggers. They unloaded the ships where they lay on the Mooneater, and by the time the first rest period had come, the derrick was up. Ten hours later, the hole was spudded in. Then the drill-bits began to grind, gnawing their way down through the horny hide of the monster like 'steel augers through an ancient cheese.

From time to time Fava and her steward made the rounds of the nerve-ends and shot fresh injections of the deadening drug into them. It was of utmost importance that they keep the monster numb and quiet where they worked, as its slightest shudder would have all the effect of a devastating earthquake. They might lose not only their drill-bits, but the derrick. And somewhere near about must be one of those auxiliary mouths that could engulf them all in a moment.

IT was at a depth of just seven miles that grizzled Harvey Linholm announced his drilling was through. Sticky, viscous purple blood was welling up and spreading lazily about the lip of the hole. That meant they were through the tough outer skin and down into the tenderer tissues beneath.

"Pump it out and set your casing," Berol said, and went to see about his snakes.

Under Fava's forced feeding they were monstrous serpents now, ten feet or more in length, and more fecund and voracious than ever. Selection and high-speed evolution had done miracles. They were unbeautiful worms—slender, eely creatures with forked tails and transparent skins, but they had insatiable appetites and bred at an astonishing rate. Walter Berol felt certain they would do the work he expected of them.

Berol stepped under the derrick presently and gazed down the shiny barrel of the well. To one side stood fourteen crates of selected *illi ulli,* a portable flame-cutter, and a shoulder-size container of heteraine, along with hypodermic injection pipes. The worms were hungry, as always, and squirming and hissing venomously to show their irritation at being cooped up in the long cylindrical baskets. Berol put on the heteraine container and grasped the flame-thrower, then reached for the sling that was to lower him into the depths.

A spasm of revulsion and cold fear suddenly swept over him, and for a moment he shut his eyes out of sheer horror. Thirty-seven thousand feet down into the tissues of this monster—and through a slender forty-inch hole! All the confident self-assurance that had sustained him until then oozed from the biologist. His former timidity threatened to take control again, and his resolution faltered. He was badly rattled.

For in that instant Walter Berol ceased to think of the Mooneater as a mere laboratory specimen, even though a colossal one, but rather as a living adversary. He was about to do what countless generations of men had done before him—enter into mortal hand-to-hand combat with a ruthless enemy!

Vaguely he sensed that Linholm was watching him, awaiting the signal to lower away. And back of the silent group of drillers was a small helmeted figure—Fava. She, too, was watching. And then, as in a vision, Berol was aware of the millions of helpless humans everywhere whose existence hung on his own hardihood. And Bob Tallen was on the way to stop him.

"Lower away," Walter Berol managed, and hoped dumbly that his voice did not reveal the quaver he felt in his soul.

The gleaming neochrome casing quickly turned to a dead black, as he shot past its thousands of fathoms. Down, down he plunged. Then, after what seemed centuries, his pace began to slacken and he knew he must be nearing the bottom. He ceased to feel the slick metal walls, realized he was hanging in a subterranean cavern. His next sensation was that of being plunged knee-deep in slimy mud, only the mud was warm and clinging, like a live thing.

Berol snapped on his crest lamp and looked about him. He was in a huge purple cavern, lined with slime-dripping tissue, and interlacing purple tubes told him he was looking at Gargantuan capillaries. Over in a corner was a bulbous lump of green mush—the creature's nerve stuff—a minor ganglion, no doubt, for the functioning of the antenna clump immediately overhead.

Berol stood dear and sent the sling back up. Now they would send down the baskets of *illi ulli*. Until they came, he sloshed about in the stinking mire, slashing at the nerve-leads with his machete and injecting each one with a few ounces of heteraine. By the time his serpents came, he had openings ready for their entry into the monster's nervous system.

He unhooked the first of the baskets with trembling hands, but steadied himself with the thought that he was now at the culminating moment of his great experiment. A few more steps, and he would know whether he had succeeded. He had gone too far to weaken, and he tried to shut out of his imagination the seven miles of solid organism that separated him from his kind.

T HE pale serpents wriggled vigorously through the muck the moment Berol released them. Their instinct seemed to direct them unerringly, for they made straightway for the nearest nerve fibres. Berol saw their evil-looking heads nuzzle into the incisions he had made, and their forked tails give a final flip as they wriggled out of sight. Then he could hear the horrid gurgling as the half-starved reptiles gnawed into the green substance.

The tenth basket was down and unloaded before Berol felt the cavern shake ominously. That meant the first batches of snakes had penetrated the nerve-trunks beyond the anesthetized area, and that the Mooneater was feeling pain. Berol knew he must expect more of these mountainous shudders, and only hoped his cavern would not collapse until he had at least got all his snakes started. At their rate of propagation Berol was confident he had enough for his purpose.

Laboriously he made his way back to the spot beneath the trunk. Basket number eleven was due. But it was not a basket that came. It was a space-suited figure—a diminutive figure that fell with a rush, and floundered for a moment in the slime on the animal floor.

"You—Fava!" Berol exclaimed.

"Hurry—oh, hurry!" the girl cried. "Come up while there is time! Bob Tallen has come—is landing near us...

The floor beneath them heaved mightily, flung them far apart. Berol's light jarred out, and it was several seconds before he could get it on again. When he did, he saw the place they were in had been squeezed to a third its former volume, and its shape completely changed.

He glanced upward at where the hole had been, but it had been smashed flat. Two lengths of the neochrome casing stuck out, twisted and bent almost beyond recognition. The Mooneater had had a violent convulsion, and the two humans inside it were trapped!

Walter Berol fought his way to Fava, ducking under writhing capillaries and proceeding on his hands and knees at times. Fava gasped, "He—Bob—is blasting his way in! Q-rays and flame guns...He burned down those antennae to the north of us..."

"The blundering fool!" exclaimed Walter Berol. "The one thing he should not have done. If this brute is excited at this stage, we are all lost!"

It looked as if they were indeed, for one terrific upheaval followed another in quick succession. Twice Berol was completely buried in vile semi-liquid tissue, and only his space suit saved him from suffocation. And twice he found Fava again and clung to her. At last the shudderings and quakings diminished; then ceased altogether.

It seemed a forlorn hope, but Berol thought of trying it. He jabbed viciously at his phone button, and monotonously began calling Linholm on the surface. There was a faint chance the thing's writhings might penetrate the heavy roof of monster hide over them.

Then Berol thought he heard a voice, and a little later he got Linholm.

"Things are pretty bad, Doc," Lin-holm was saying. "I can't help you—not for a day or so. The derrick is down... The 'earthquake' did that... Can you stick it out until I get the derrick set up again and a new hole drilled?"

Walter Berol groaned. Bob Tallen had played hell for fair.

"What about Tallen's cruiser?" Berol demanded anxiously.

"It's gone," came the answer, so faint it could hardly be heard.

"Gone away?"

"No. Gone down. It landed, blazing away, about a thousand yards to the west of us. A bunch of them tentacle things wrapped themselves around it, and the next thing I knew...it wasn't there. It sank plumb into the monster."

BEROL snapped off the phone and stared at Fava. Now he had the explanation of the violent upheavals. It was Bob Tallen's attack and the monster's reaction to it. Tallen's blasting at the edge of the narcotized area had awakened the beast, and it had fought back in its customary manner. The end had been the usual one—Tallen's ship had been engulfed.

The biologist sat stunned for a moment, hardly conscious that Fava was lying alongside him, clinging. His thoughts were a strange mingling of satisfaction and despair. He had inoculated the Mooneater—it would die, in time. He felt sure of that. But he and Fava were trapped, and in the tremendous convulsions that were sure to attend the monster's death agony, they would die, too. He did not mind so much for himself. But Fava...

Then he thought of Bob Tallen and his entombed *Sirius*. That was another bit of dramatic irony. The would-be rescuer who had brought death instead of life—and was doomed to die himself. Now he lay a thousand yards away in the corroding acids of one of the monster's minor stomachs—

Walter Berol jumped as if prodded with a bayonet. Inside the *Sirius* there might be safety! It was a race with time. Could the Mooneater digest the warship in advance of its own death struggle? Berol clambered to his feet and dragged Fava up with him.

"Come," he said, and led the girl to the west wall of their deformed cavern.

He handed her the heteraine outfit while he hung on to the flame-cutter. In a few jerky words he told her what he was trying to do, and his explanation seemed to put new life into her, though both of them knew their chances of finding the cruiser were slim. Compasses were useless inside a creature that emanated erratic magnetic waves, and everywhere there was a hopeless jumble of intertwined blood capillaries and nerve-trunks. The two victims could easily be lost in the first hundred feet.

But they plodded on. It was five hundred feet before they came to a nerve-trunk that had any green substance left in it. The *illi ulli* had done their work well, for in the next few hundred yards they saw many mother serpents accompanied by their huge broods of infant snakes. It was not until after that, that Fava had to use heteraine shots to paralyze the tissues ahead of them.

Berol doggedly burned away or cut the barriers that they encountered. Twice he backtracked to check his orientation. It was *well* he did, for he discovered on both occasions he and Fava had a tendency to veer off to the north. Aside from hacking out their path, he tried not to think at all. To do that would lead to madness, for there was really no basis for hope.

CHAPTER V
Brain vs. Brawn

AT last they came to the tough stomach wall, and the breaching of it took the last erg of energy in the flame-gun. Berol tossed it into the muck, and jerked back the folds of tissue to allow some of the fuming acids within to flow past. He helped Fava through the hole, and they plunged on, thankful for their acid-resistant suits.

"Too late," said Berol grimly, as he looked up at the hulk that had been the crack cruiser *Sirius*. Her outer hull was gone, leaving only a few gaunt frames, pitted and eaten to knife-thin plates which crumbled at the touch.

Corroded decks hung limply, like damp cardboard, dripping slime. All that was left of the ship was the armored central compartment that housed the gyros and the control room.

Yet so good did this man-made thing look, dilapidated and dissolving though it was in this cavern of horrors, that both Berol and Fava instinctively drew closer to it. The biologist helped the girl climb the collapsing decks, and cleared away the slimy mud that clung there. He noticed that no more of it came, and attributed that to the paralysis of this region worked by his worms.

The armored compartment seemed to be tight, so Berol carefully scraped about one of its doors until he had laid the metal bare. Then he tapped with the handle of his knife.

There was an answering tap, after a little. In a moment the door was cautiously opened, and a helmeted officer peered out. It must have been a shock to him to see all the ship outside his compartment gone, and in its place a vague blackness lit only by the crest lamp on one of the suited figures before him. He let them in, and carefully closed the door behind.

Bob Tallen stood in the center of the control room, an expression of deep concern on his face. But as be recognized Fava, he broke into a smile, though obviously a forced one.

"Thank God we found you!" he exclaimed, striding forward as if to embrace her.

"*You* found *us?*" Fava laughed merrily. "Why, you big, clumsy, heroic lummox of a meddler! If you only knew what we've gone through to find *you,* just to tell you to keep your shirt on and you'll be all right!"

Bob Tallen's jaw dropped in sheer amazement. Then he caught on.

"Poor Favikins—I understand. But you're safe now..."

"Don't Favikins' me," the girl retorted. "I'm more right in my head than I ever was. I know ability when I see *it—now!* We were doing fine— Walter and I—until you came blundering in and upset everything with your stupid interference.We have inoculated this monster with some home-grown spirochetes of our own invention, and it's dying. In about an hour it'll heave up and throw us back onto the surface—where we would be right now, if *you* hadn't butted in!"

Bob Tallen could only stare at her, not knowing how to take her sudden fury.

"And let me tell you one more thing, Robert M. Tallen! I demand you return to Callisto at once, and failing that I am coming after you. Demand, indeed! And who told you that you were anybody's intended husband?"

Just then a violent temblor shook the remainder of the ship until every fixture in it rattled deafeningly. There was a succession of quick heaves, and men had to hang on to stanchions to keep their places.

"Friend Mooneater's sick," remarked Walter Berol blandly. "Stand by for a quick rise!"

THE next fifteen seconds was a tumultuous kaleidoscope. The core of the acid-eaten ship must have turned completely over five or six times before it came to rest. It was an experience such as none of the occupants ever wanted to go through again.

Then Walter Berol boldly opened the door, and they looked out onto as fantastic a landscape as ever a *troolum* *addict imagined. Everywhere huge chasms had opened and thick purplish stuff was puffing up in sickly bubbles. Antennae drooped and collapsed. The Mooneater's surface billowed like a typhoon-swept ocean. The monster was dying. A quarter of a mile away lay the *Sprite* and her two tenders, on their sides, but otherwise unhurt.

"Come, Walter," said Fava. "Now that Bob's all right, we can finish what we started."

"Right-ho!" Berol grinned, and he picked the girl up in his arms and strode away across the heaving plain.

"Look at him," muttered Bob Tallen in disgust. "Showing off his strength! Some people are just too conceited to live!"

---

* A *troolum* addict indulges in the chewing of the troolum weed, a Martian plant with the power to effect the brain in a delusory manner. Paradoxically, though the Martian name troolum sounds as though the drug induces "true" appearing visions, the exact opposite is the fact. Troolum visions are wild, impossible, incredibly fantastic, and yet, the victim believes implicitly in all he sees. —Ed.

TRUTH isa

By DAVID WRIGHT O'BRIEN

•

Suddenly the citizens of Weston found themselves in a plague of truth, and there was the devil to pay that a few lies might easily have prevented

•

ALMOST everyone in Weston saw the planes that morning. Crowds pouring from the subways and elevateds on their way to work stopped in the middle of the business district to crane their necks heavenward in gaping astonishment. Traffic became horribly snarled, and the policemen let it stay that way while they, too, watched the writing in the sky.

Ordinary commercial smokewriting would not have merited more than a passing glance from the citizenry of

Lance Randall and Professor Merlo fought to get through the panic stricken crowd.

Weston. But this was certainly different. To begin with there were ten planes printing the sky message. Secondly, they were flying so low that it appeared as if they would inevitably crash into the office buildings of the district. And last but not least, there was the message itself.

"HONESTY," it read, "IS THE BEST POLICY!"

The skywriting continued for another half hour, during which time the message must have been spelled out fifty times in all. Then the smoke planes departed, and Weston was shrouded by the cloak of blue vapor left in their wake.

ON the twenty-first floor of the Radio LJ Building, located in the heart of Weston, Jack Train, staff announcer for Station W-E-S-T, left the window where he had been watching the skywriting. It was two minutes to nine, and he was due in Studio F at nine o'clock.

"Whew!" snorted Train, "those ships were flying so low you could even smell the smoke." He sniffed deeply as if to prove it to himself.

"Funny smoke at that," he said as he entered Studio F. "It's sort of sweet and fresh smelling."

He cleared his throat and looked at the glass partition behind which the engineer was sitting. The engineer signaled the "on-the-air."

"Goooood morning, ladies and gentlemen. This is Jack Train, your Pobo Toothpaste announcer, greeting you. Have you brushed your teeth today? Don't forget, Pobo is the Toothpaste Supreme. It gives your molars that brilliant lustre so necessary to movie stars. It removes dirty, dingy stains."

As if in a dream, Train heard his voice continuing gaily on past the point where the commercial ended.

"Yes indeed. It removes stains. It removes enamel. Give it a little time and it removes your teeth, too!"

THE business man was coughing slightly. Smoke always made his throat harsh, and those blankety-blank skywriters spread enough smoke around the city to gag a man. He turned into his office building and was standing in front of the elevator when someone slapped him on the back. It was Jones, another business associate whom he hadn't seen in several weeks.

"Good old J. T.," boomed Jones. "Glad to see you, old boy. How have you been? Where've you been keeping yourself? Really great to see you, great!"

A mechanical smile came to the businessman's face as he opened his mouth to reply. Something, at that moment, seized control of his tongue.

"You're a damned liar," he heard himself saying. "We hate one another's guts and you know it."

LINDA Meade, salesgirl in Weston's most exclusive millinery shop, brought forth another hat for Mrs. Blythe. It was the fourteenth hat that Linda had tried on the society matron in the last half hour. Mrs. Blythe coughed disapprovingly as Linda adjusted the hat. "Terribly smoky in here, m'dear."

"It's from those skywriters, madam," Linda explained patiently. "They flew so low that the entire city seems to be filled with it."

Mrs. Blythe, hat on head, began peering this way and that into the mirror before her. She turned to Linda, smiling sweetly. "What do you think of this one, m'dear?"

"It makes you look," said Linda, horrified at what she knew was coming, "like a rather pretty mountain goat!"

LANCE Randell placed the telephone back in its cradle and turned to face Professor Merlo. "It's a call from the airport," he stated. "The planes are all in. They've covered the city with our smokewriting."

Professor Merlo, a sparse, bird-like little man, ran a nervous hand through his white hair. "Fine," he said, "splendid. In another hour we should be getting reports on the effect of our experiment."

Randell grinned. "You mean *your* experiment, Professor. *Your* experiment, not mine."

"Without your financial backing," the Professor reminded him, "it would still be a dream. It is yours as much as mine." He beamed fondly on the rugged young man.

"It's still hard to believe," said Randell reflectively. "A gas made from Truth Serum. If it has effect, Professor, are you still sure it will make everyone tell the truth?"

"Yes, my boy. Dishonesty will be an impossibility, providing the gas works." "Utopia?"

"Maybe. We must first see what effect it has on one city. If it works on Weston we can change the world. At the end of this hour, every citizen in Weston should be affected by it."

Lance Randell lit a cigarette as the Professor fell silent. For the first time in his life, Randell told himself, he was putting his wealth to a good use. A world of Truth! Little shivers of excitement ran through him at the thought of how near they were to changing the course of destiny. He drummed his fingers impatiently on the arm of his chair. This waiting was nerve-racking.

Restlessly he went to the window and gazed for a moment at the serenity of the countryside. "Nice out here," he observed. "So quiet. But right this minute, this peace is killing me."

He turned back from the window. "If you don't mind, I'm going into the city."

Professor Merle smiled. "Go ahead. I'm a little old to be impatient. I'll stay here to get the reports, and then you might drive back to give me a first-hand account."

Randell grabbed his hat. "Swell. Soon as I take a look at our Utopia, call you."

A few minutes later, behind the wheel of his roadster, Randell said to himself, "Somehow this is like—like playing God!"

It sent a shudder through him.

IT was only a fifteen minute drive from Professor Merlo's suburban laboratories to the city limits of Weston, but Randall tried to make it in ten. Halfway there, two sirens began to scream behind him.

"Pull over," snarled the motorcycle copper on his right. Randell brought his car to an abrupt stop. His pursuers walked over to his car. They looked grim and determined and were pulling little black books from their hip pockets.

"Thought you'd shake us at the city limits, eh?"

"I suppose you're gonna tell us you didn't know how fast you was going?" said the second, a tall, morose fellow, the sarcasm dripping from him. "A lousy seventy-five per."

Randell would have sworn that it wasn't his own voice replying with such cheerful unconcern. "Yes," he heard himself saying, "I had been hoping to shake you fellows at the city limits. You wouldn't have been able to pinch me in Weston, y'know. I was not, however, doing seventy-five. Last time I looked, I was inching up close to ninety."

During the ominous silence that followed this announcement, Randell collected the pieces. He sniffed the air suspiciously. Yes, there it was, that faint, sweet freshness! No wonder: the Truth Gas extended all the way to the city limits!

Suddenly the realization hit him. The officers, themselves, must be affected by the gas, too!

Randell kept his face straight during his next question. "Haven't you policemen ever broken the speeding laws?"

The policemen started to speak and stopped. They looked at each other queerly. "Of course," they declared in stupefied unison. "Lots of times!"

"Fun, ain't it?"

"Great sport," said the flabbergasted motorcycle cops.

"Now," said Randell severely, "after admitting that you break the speed laws yourselves, adding that it's great fun, do you still think you ought to give me a ticket?"

"No," said the morose cop, with an oddly bright glance. "It wouldn't be fair!"

"Well," said Randell, putting his car into gear, "so long, then!"

In his rear vision mirror Lance Randell could see the bewildered motor cops standing at the city limits, scratching their heads. He couldn't hold back any longer. He broke into peals of laughter. But he wasn't laughing by the time he arrived in Weston's business district.

CHAPTER II
The Unexpected Truth

DORIS MARTIN sat at her neat little desk in the ornate offices of Lance Randell Enterprises, Inc., sorting the batch of morning mail. The clock on her desk told her that it was almost ten o'clock. She sighed. The Boss could be expected about noon, if he came in at all that day.

At the thought of Lance Randell, Doris permitted herself another sigh, and still sighing she stared for a moment into the mirror. An oval face, framed by auburn hair and presenting a pert, freckled nose, level gray eyes and mischievous mouth, stared back at her.

The mouth smiled, revealing an even row of dazzlingly white teeth. "You," declared the mouth, "might as well be an office fixture." Doris snapped the compact shut. She coughed slightly. The office seemed terribly smoky this morning. Probably due to those planes that had been skywriting over the city.

She got up to close the window next to her desk when she saw the familiar blue roadster roll up in front of the building. She watched the rugged figure of her boss get quickly out of the car and walk swiftly to the entrance.

She walked back to her desk and sat down, making a conscious effort to assemble the mail. It wasn't any use. There were little thoughts spinning around in her mind...

Doris heard the doorknob turning, and her heart did a more than its usual routine flip-flop. Randell came into the room.

"How's the staff?"

He always said that to her. It was his standard form of greeting, rain or shine, day in and day out. And he seldom waited for an answer. He just kept walking into his office.

Doris followed him.

"Here's your mail, Mr. Randell," she said, keeping her voice carefully impersonal.

She watched him while he sorted swiftly through the letters, noticing the way he hunched his wide shoulders in preoccupation. Then fearing that he might glance up, she turned back to some trivial matter.

"Ahhh." She knew from the sound of his sigh that he'd come to the letter he *was* looking for. The perfumed message from the bubble dancer.

"Darling," Randell read to himself, "even a day away from you seems like simply years." As he read on, all thoughts of the past twenty-four hours vanished. From time to time he repeated his sigh. Finally there was the signature, "Your darling Edie."

He looked up from the letter, entranced. "She's wonderful," he said rhetorically to his secretary, "isn't she?"

"Do you mean Miss Dalmar?" Doris heard herself reply.

Randell seemed startled back to reality. He wasn't expecting an answer to his statement. "Why, yes," he said "who else would I mean?"

Doris was flustered. Something had happened. She never meant to say that. It just popped out, and to her astonishment a torrent of words were following her first unintended sentence. She heard her voice continue.

"If you mean she's wonderful," Doris was saying, "I don't think she is. As a matter of fact I think she's nothing but a cheap, gold-digging little vixen. If you'd remove her warpaint, keep her away from the beauty parlor, and eliminate the dubious glamour of her profession, you'd see nothing but a washed-out, frizzled haired little know-nothing!"

RANDELL's jaw was hanging foolishly agape at the outburst.
"You are just sap enough," Doris went on, "to think that she loves you. She hasn't room enough in that shallow heart of hers for love of anything but money and herself. You have plenty of money, and that's what she's after. Everyone in town knows it but you." Her voice was shaking now, and she knew that she would be crying in another minute.

Automatically Doris was picking up her things, moving toward the door. "It probably never entered your skull that there might be someone in the world who'd care for you even if you didn't have a —"

She was at the door, now, her hand on the knob, speaking again. "It probably never occurred to you that someone could love you so much that nothing else mattered except to see you do something with your utterly pleasant and equally worthless life besides waste it on a bubble dancer!"

For five full minutes Lance sat on the edge of his desk, staring at the door.

"Well, be damned," he kept repeating to himself. "Well, be damned!"

His brain was going through the futile thought mechanisms that confront any man when trying to arrive at a logical reason for the actions of a woman. Suddenly the explanation flashed before him. He had forgotten all about the experiment, all about the gas! Doris was affected by the Truth Gas, that explained it all!

But if she—no, it couldn't be. Lance tried to eliminate the logical conclusion to his deductions. With a sinking feeling he was realizing that if the Truth Gas was the cause of her outburst, what she said must have been true, even about Edie!

Lance dashed for the door. There was only one answer to the agony of doubt that filled his mind. Edie was the only person who could supply that answer!

CHAPTER III
The Plague Grows

THE ash tray next to the radio in Professor Merlo's study was heaped with cigarette stubs. Slumped in an armchair before the radio ever since Randell's departure, Professor Merlo had been listening to news flashes from the scene of his Truth Gas experiment. To be precise about it, the bulletin was read at 9:45.

"The Weston Board of Health," said the announcer, "is investigating the rumor that an odd epidemic of insanity has broken forth in the heart of the city's business district. Victims of this strange malady are reported to be possessed with the desire to make preposterous and often insulting statements. As yet, however, these rumors have not been authenticated." Professor Merlo smiled. The announcer concluded with, "This bulletin has come to you through the courtesy of the Weston Daily Herald, the World's Worst Newspaper!"

Professor Merlo had guffawed. Now several hours after that, however, his laughter was changed to shocked amazement.

"It can't be so," the white haired little man was telling himself. "All this is but the first spasm. When it has spent itself, everything will settle into our expected pattern. Out of it will grow perfect order and Utopia. It is only natural that confusion should be the first result of such an experiment. By noon everything should be well again!"

But even as he spoke, the Professor had a feeling of uneasiness. He'd been saying the same thing for the last hour and a half. The Professor gulped, his Adam's apple bobbing along his scrawny neck like an egg in a hose. He wished fervently that Randell would return.

The radio news announcer was jabbering excitedly once more. Dully, like a man expecting an unavoidable blow, Merlo turned his head to listen.

"As the strange epidemic of mass insanity grows in Weston, today, it has been learned that three more suicides have occurred in the business district. These happened when the owners of Weston's three largest department stores leaped to their deaths rather than meet the financial ruin facing their establishments."

The Professor shuddered. He was expecting something like that ever since the bulletin of an hour ago which stated that the clerk's in the downtown department stores were selling all goods at less than cost price. Fifteen minutes after that particular bulletin it was announced that delighted shoppers were buying up every bit of stock in the stores— at a net loss of several million dollars to the owners of the stores.

The announcer was babbling on, "This brings today's death rate to the staggering total of one hundred persons. Many of these, as you probably learned in previous flashes, were victims of murder."

PROFESSOR Merlo cringed, remembering the thirty-or-so husbands whose wives dispatched them to their Maker over blood-stained breakfast tables, the fifty-odd revenge slayings perpetrated by persons who learned of long-concealed treacheries by friends or partners, the suicides whose doctors were forced to admit that they were victims of incurable diseases.

"God," Professor Merlo muttered, covering his face with his hands, "God!"

"Police have stated," continued the announcer, "that they are as yet unable to control the army of a thousand men and women who have formed a marching brigade through the streets of- the city. These marchers, victims of the strange malady, were all thrown out of work early this morning when they told insulted employers what they thought of them. At present they are fairly orderly, but it is feared that, once they realize their power, looting and bloodshed will result."

Professor Merlo winced, thinking of the hundreds more who would join the marchers the moment the department stores were shut down.

The telephone was jangling insistently, and Merlo crossed the room slowly to where it stood. He knew what the call would probably be. He'd had nine of them already. He picked the receiver off the hook. "Yes?"

"Hello, Professor Merlo?" a voice on the other end inquired. In an almost toneless whisper the Professor admitted it was.

"This is J. Weems Sharp," said the voice. The Professor was sure of the call now. "Yes," said Merlo, "I think I understand what you're calling for. You want to tell me that you're withdrawing your endowment from my Civic Scientific Foundation."

The voice was amazed. "Yes, that's right. How did you know?"

Merlo ignored the question. "You want to withdraw your endowment from the Foundation because you are quite willing to admit that you don't give a damn for the betterment of your fellows."

"That's right," agreed the voice. "I never cared what happened to the masses. No sense in my wasting money on other people when I can keep it all for myself. I was a chump to let you talk me into it for the past ten years. Now it can go to the devil, I—" Professor Merle put his thumb down on the hook, breaking the connection.

"That makes the tenth one," he told himself bitterly, beginning to pace the floor. "They can all tell the truth, now. They'll admit that they're miserly monsters, and refuse to give any more to scientific charity. It's just about the end of my Foundation. Oh Lord," he thought, "for ten years I've been able to play on the hypocrisy of those money-bags, making them shell out money for the good of their fellowman, pleasing their egos by giving their charity a lot of publicity. But now," he shuddered, "they admit that they don't give a damn for charity!"

THE Civic Scientific Foundation had been the pride and joy of Merlo's existence, and seeing it crumble was one of the hardest blows of the day. Ten years of progress was being wiped out in the space of several hours.

It was clear to the Professor, now, what he and Lance failed to take into consideration before the experiment. People affected by the Truth Gas would not only tell what they *knew* to be true, but would also admit to things which had been lying under the hypocritical cloak of their subconscious thoughts for years. In other words, the gas was exposing ideas which people never even previously suspected they cherished!

"Something," muttered the tightlipped scientist, "has to be done, and done fast." He paused before the window. And as he looked out across the country-side, it seemed as though nature itself had fallen under the mood of gloomy foreboding. The sun was hidden behind ominous formations of black rain-laden clouds.

CHAPTER IV
Lance Makes a Test

If Lance Randell hadn't been so preoccupied with the doubts that clouded his romance he might have noticed the growing confusion in Weston. As it was, however, he looked neither left nor right as he put his high-powered roadster into gear and shot out for the Weston Tower Hotel where the blonde Edie had an apartment.

The crowds that were beginning to surge through the streets escaped his notice, the clang of speeding ambulances and police wagons failed to enter his brain, so one-tracked was his determination.

In a little less than three minutes after he'd left the office Randall drew up in front of the elaborate canopy marking the entrance to the skyscraping Weston Tower Hotel. Edie's apartment was on the fortieth floor, and Randell didn't bother to telephone from the lobby. He crossed the room swiftly and stepped into an elevator.

Edie Dalmar, when she opened the door, was astonished to see a breathless and strangely intense Lance Randell standing there with his hat in his hand. For a moment her oval, doll-like features registered amazement, then Weston's Loveliest Bubble Dancer regained her composure. She arched delicately penciled eyebrows in a smile.

"Daahhling, what a surprise! What are you doing heah at this hour?"

Lance entered the room and put his hat on the mantel. He turned and spoke.

"Edie, there are some things I have to ask you. It's very important, and I don't want you to be angry with me."

Edie moved sinuously across the room, smoothing her dark hair with scarlet nailed fingers. She sat down on the couch and turned violet eyes on Lance. "Why, deah, ah don't know jes' what it's all about, but go right ahead and ask me anything you want to."

Lance removed an enormous, floppy Cupid doll from the cushion next to her and sat down. For a moment he was silent. This wasn't going to be easy. He knew that any question he'd ask would bring a starkly truthful answer. But he had to know. He forced himself to speak.

"Edie, do you really love me?"

The bubble dancer opened her slightly petulant lips to protest, but

Lance went on. "I mean, do you love me for myself? Is it, is it me that you love, or is it my money?"

There, Lance told himself, it was done. He felt his heart hammering wildly as Edie started to speak. He felt as though the answer would mean the difference between life and death.

"Why, daahhling, of course I love you! Honey, whatevah made you fancy that I cared a speck about your money? I'd marry you even if you were a pauper!"

Randell was ecstatic in his relief. They were all wrong! Doris had been a spiteful, jealous wench. Edie was true! He knew it all along, Edie was true! She didn't give a damn for his money. She loved him for himself alone.

By now, however, Edie was pouting. Two enormous tears began to trickle down her cheeks. She was sobbing silently, dabbing at her eyes with a scrap of lace.

"HONEYY," said Randell, sensing that he had wounded her feelings, "I never meant to doubt you, honestly. I'm sorry I ever asked you, but I was desperately unsure. I had to know. Please forgive me."

Edie, however, was not so easily consoled. She increased her snuffling. "You thought I, I, I, I was cheap!" she wailed.

Lance Randell had a sudden inspiration. "Edie!"

No reply, merely more snuffling. "Edie," he repeated. This time she looked up.

"What?" she asked between sobs. "You know that coat you admired so much the other day?"

Edie's snuffling lessened perceptibly. "Yes?"

"I'd like you to have it as a present, dear."

Gone were the tears, silenced was the sobbing. Edie's doll face was wreathed ha smiles. She was in his arms. "Daahhling," breathed Edie.

"My dear," said Randell.

The floppy Cupid doll looked up from the floor where it had been dropped, its button eyes shining cynically.

WITH singing heart Lance left Edie's apartment. The world was once more righted, and now he had time to think of the second most important thing in his life, the experiment. Then, too, he'd almost forgotten that Merlo was waiting for a call from him back in the laboratories.

He glanced at his watch. 10:30. Plenty should be happening by now. The gas had had more than an hour and a half to take effect on the populace. There should be some interesting developments. There were.

As he stepped from the elevator into the lobby, Randell was immediately aware that things were popping in the Weston Tower Hotel. There had been a scant twenty people sitting about in the spacious room when Randell had first arrived there. Now, not more than a half hour later, the place was literally jammed with people. Everyone seemed to be talking at once, and in the voices there was a growing undercurrent of hysteria.

The fever spot seemed to be located around the Room Desk, and Randell began elbowing through the mob, moving in that direction.

"Stand back, buddy!"

Lance Randell was in the front of the circle around the Desk, when a blue-clad arm shot out to stop his progress. He noticed, then, that a cordon of eight policemen had blocked off a space around the Desk, and were holding the crowd back.

In the middle of the space, face downward, lay a gray haired man dressed in morning coat and striped trousers. His head was pillowed in a pool of his own blood, and his right hand held a death-like clutch on an automatic pistol.

"Horrified, Randell addressed the policeman who barred his way.

"What happened, Officer?"

"Suicide," was the terse reply. "Shot himself while we were on the way to get him."

A pop-eyed little man on his right supplied Lance with the rest of the information. "It's Gordon Carver," the little man blurted. "He's killed himself, rather than go to jail."

Gordon Carver! Randell was stunned. Gordon Carver was Weston's greatest philanthropist, most charitable millionaire, a leading citizen! He looked at the millionaire's body, so queerly sprawled out across the cold marble floor. The pop-eyed champ was still talking.

"Yeah," said Pop-Eyes, "he called the Police about a half an hour ago, confessed that he had committed some crime years ago, and was an escaped convict. He told them to come to the Weston Tower Hotel, that he'd be waiting in the lobby to surrender to 'em." Pop-Eyes paused to shudder. "I guess he couldn't stand the thought of going back to prison, so he plugged hisself just as the cops walked in the lobby."

SUDDENLY Lance Randell knew that he had to get away from that circle. He fought his way back through the crowd, feeling that he might succumb to nausea at any moment. The voices all around him were still floating to his consciousness. "What's happened to this town?" "It's the end of the world." "Terrible, out in the streets, rioting." "I saw a little child...killed..."

Randell found a telephone booth, managed to push inside. With a hand that trembled slightly, he fished through his pockets until he found a nickel. Then he was dialing Professor Merlo's number. After what seemed like an eternity he heard the old scientist's voice.

"Professor, it's me—Lance. I—" he was cut off by the sharp voice on the other end of the wire.

"Yes," he heard Merlo saying, "I know all about it. Got it all through news flashes. We haven't any time to lose. Have to act quickly. Where are you?"

"At the Weston Towers, but—" Kendall began.

"Stay there," Merlo continued, "I'll meet you as quickly as possible. Every moment that this gas stays over the city means more lives. I think I've hit on a solution."

"How? What?" Randell began. Then he cursed. Merlo had hung up.

What did the old man mean? What possible solution could there be? They had no anti-toxin to the gas. They knew that it would wear off in twenty-four hours, of course, but in twenty-four hours—. He shuddered at the thought of what was in store for Weston if the gas held that long!

A feeling of utter hopelessness, complete futility came over Randell as he stepped back into the lobby of the Weston Towers. Another twenty-four hours before the gas would drift from the city. Twenty-four hours in which hell would rage unchecked! The thought was staggering. Foolishly, it occurred to him that he was suffering the same emotions that Dr. Frankenstein had known upon creating his monster.

Then and there his heart went into a sickening tailspin. He had forgotten about Edie I If this bedlam was going to continue throughout Weston, no one would be safe. He had to get her out of the city, had to get her to safety while there was still time. Desperately, Randell began to push back through the crowded lobby toward the elevators.

CHAPTER V
Lance Gets a Shock

PROFESSOR Merlo waited a moment after hanging up on Lance Randell. Then he picked up the telephone again and dialed a number. As the receiver buzzed in his ear he drummed his fingers impatiently on the table, staring out the window at the darkening skies.

"It should work," the old man muttered to himself. "It has to work." Then he heard a voice on the other end of the wire.

"Weston Contractors," said the voice.

Merlo began speaking excitedly, emphatically, allowing his listener no time for interruptions. After several minutes he concluded, "Is everything straight? It's a question of time. I want them there as quickly as possible."

"Certainly, Professor," was the reply. "I understand. We'll get them there as fast as is humanly possible. But such an enormous load of sand, I can't imagine what you intend—"

"Damn you," shouted Merlo, his face purpling, "you don't have to imagine. All you have to do is get them there, and get them there in a hurry!"

"Yes, Professor," the voice was startled, "never fear. They'll be there on time."

Merlo slammed the instrument back on its cradle and stood up. He seized his hat from the top of a bookcase and stamped out of the room. A few moments later he was turning his black sedan out of his garage and onto the highway leading to Weston. Then he pushed the accelerator down to the floorboards...

Less than a mile from the Weston Tower Hotel, a pretty, red-headed young girl was being swept along by the semi-frantic crowds thronging the business district. For the first time since she dashed tearfully from the offices of Lance Randell Enterprises, over an hour ago, Doris Martin was becoming aware of the frenzied hysteria gripping the city.

Despair at what she said to the man she loved had driven her into the streets, made her wander about aimlessly, until finally, Doris Martin knew what she had to do. And she was going to do it. No one on earth could stop her.

People were passing her, crowds elbowed by, the ordinary hum of the city increased to a tone approaching an angry howl, but Doris walked on, scarcely conscious of anything but the pavement beneath her feet. Where she was going, how long she'd been walking, nothing made any difference.

"Watch where ye're goin', sister!"

Doris had a confused vision of a fat red face peering angrily at her. A sweaty, shirt-sleeved fellow in a sailor straw had wrapped his pudgy hand around her arm and jerked her backward. Her first instinct was one of anger, and she started to speak.

"Ya wanna get kilt?" The fat man was pointing to the cars rushing by in the street, and then Doris realized that they were standing on the curbing, that the fat fellow had pulled her out of the path of the automobiles hurtling past them.

Her ears were torn by the screech of hastily applied automobile brakes. Out of the corner of her eye she saw a black sedan jolting to an abrupt stop. Terrified, she stood rooted in the center of the street.

"Good God, girl," someone shouted. "I might have killed you!" Doris saw that it was the driver of the sedan, and that he was climbing out of his car. The driver was walking over to her now, his face white, jaws shut.

"Doris!" The driver stopped short in shocked amazement.

IT was then that she recognized Professor Merlo. He had her by the arm, was propelling her to his car and talking rapidly. "What are you doing here? Life isn't safe anywhere in Weston. You must be mad to be roaming the streets while this turmoil is raging. Don't you know, haven't you seen it?"

They were in Merlo's sedan now, once more moving along in the stream of traffic. Doris found her voice at last. "Where are you going, Professor? What, what has happened to the city?"

"Plenty," Merlo snapped. "We're going to the Weston Towers. Lance is there, waiting for me. There's a lot to be done. Can't explain it all now."

At the mention of Lance, Doris paled. "Good!" she said firmly. "I was on my way there. I've a little business of my own there."

"Not with Lance, I suspect?" said Merlo, looking at her with less surprise than he might have.

"No," Doris' voice was amazingly different. "I'll tend to that—"

Suddenly the little black sedan shot across an intersection at the same moment that a lumber truck came hurtling through from the side street. It was too late for Merlo to swing the sedan out of its path. The sickening, futile squealing of brakes preceded the rending crash of a side-on collision. In the blackness that was closing around him, Merlo heard a woman scream...

IT had only been his dogged determination that enabled Lance Randell to get Edie Dalmar to leave her apartment. At first she was coyly amused at his insistence that she dress and leave with him immediately. Then, as she began to notice the unsmiling set to his mouth, the feverish gleam in his eyes, she became a little frightened and decided to humor him.

They stepped out of the elevator into the lobby and Randell looked swiftly through the crowd in an effort to see if Merlo had arrived yet. Edie tugged at his sleeve.

"Jus' what is this heah all about, daahling?" she demanded.

Randell tore his eyes from the crowd. Wordlessly he took her arm, piloting her across the room to a quiet corner. They found a lounge.

"What's this all about?" repeated Edie, her voice oddly different in accent. She jerked her arm out of his grasp.

"Look, Honey," he began in a rush of words. "As I said before. Something terrible has happened to the city. I can't tell you any more than that for the present. You'll have to trust me. It isn't safe in Weston any more, and I'm going to get you out of here as soon as Merlo comes!"

Edie's starry eyes narrowed perceptibly. "Have you gone daffy?"

Lance Randell groaned. Then, remembering Edie had seen nothing of the effects of the gas, hadn't even heard of it yet, he made another effort to explain.

"Listen, Darling. Weston is a city suddenly gone mad. Something has happened. It's no longer safe to go out into the streets. Business is being ruined. Financial houses are collapsing. Lives are being taken recklessly.

You must understand me, you have to believe me. If this keeps up, dear, everything will be ruined. It begins to look like you'll have to keep your promise about marrying me even if I were a pauper." Lance stopped abruptly. Edie was staring at him strangely.

"What's that you just said?" she demanded frigidly.

"I said that all business is being ruined. It means that all my investments will be wiped out if this continues, that I'll be a pauper," said Lance in confusion.

"Are you sure of that?" Her tone was like an Arctic breeze.

"I'm afraid so." Randell had pushed his hat back on his forehead and was staring in amazement at the expression that crossed Edie's face.

"Then," said Edie deliberately, "you might as well get out of my sight, you boob. Do you think for a minute that I have any time for a pauper. Why, you sap, all I ever wanted was your dough. This little gal looks out for herself. If you haven't got the bankroll I can get a guy that has." She was standing up now, looking scornfully at him. "Excuse me, chump. I'm leaving. Don't bother to come again!"

Feeling as if he had just been thoroughly gone over by a steam roller, Randell sat gazing in aching astonishment at Edie's retreating back.

CHAPTER VI
Sand—And Rain

FOR a time Lance Randell was unable to do anything more than stare dumbly into space. Edie Dalmar's sudden change had affected him just as forcibly as a left hook to the jaw, leaving him dazed, uncomprehending, paralyzed. His first reactions were those of hurt and bewilderment, bitterness and heartbreak. Then reason began to return, and with it the demand for an explanation of her actions.

She undoubtedly was acting under the effects of the gas, he was certain of that much. But why hadn't she spoken the truth when he talked to her in her apartment? Why didn't the gas influence her until they were down in the lobby?

Suddenly Randell looked at his watch. He remembered at that moment that Merlo should be somewhere in the lobby. The Professor had had more than enough time to get there. His personal troubles vanished as he realized once more that as every moment passed Weston was coming closer and closer to the brink of utter madness. And then, as he glanced in the direction of the revolving doors at the hotel entrance, he gasped.

A grotesque caricature of a man was entering. On his head was a battered fedora, mashed down over wild white hair and a blood-caked brow. His suit was literally ripped to shreds, the left pants leg torn off at the knee, and the coat sticky with oil and blood. He looked wildly about for an instant-

Randell gasped again, "Professor Merlo I..."

In several swift strides Randell was at the old man's side. He threw an arm around his waist and half-carried him over to a couch. "Wasn't sure I'd make it," Merlo said faintly. "There was an accident. Truck. Hit me from the side. Doris, Doris Martin was in the car with me. I must have been out cold for five minutes. When I came around, she was gone. Couldn't look for her. Came the rest of the way by cab. Had to tell you. We must work fast!"

"Where is Doris—" But Randell stopped, fighting to drive all other thoughts from his mind. One thing alone was more important than any others. "Remember you said you'd found a solution?"

"Yes," Merlo said quietly. "It's in the weather."

Lance Randell felt suddenly sick inside. The old man was out of his head, delirious from the accident. His mouth felt dry, and all at once he knew it was all over.

They were beaten. There would be no solution. The one chance of saving the city was in the Professor's plan. And that plan had evidently been jarred from the old man's mind in the collision. Automatically he listened, while the Professor went on:

"Did you notice the weather?"

"No," Randell said, trying to keep the bitterness from his voice.

"Rainclouds," said Merlo, "huge formations of them above Weston. I called the weather bureau. But the rain isn't expected until evening. Then it will be too late. We can't wait for evening, Lance. We must have rain, now. Evening will be too late." The Professor stopped, and looked at Lance strangely. "My God, Lance, don't you see what I'm getting at? Do you think I'm out of my head? Rain! Rain! It'll save us, man. Remember your elementary chemistry! The rain will destroy our Truth Gas, will disintegrate its molecular formation! Water can do that to gas, don't you see?"

There was life once more in Randell's expression, hope in his eyes as he spoke. Gone was his conviction that Merlo was babbling. "Good Lord, I see what you mean, Professor! But you said that rain isn't expected until evening."

"That's what I said," agreed Merlo, "but we're going to *make rain,* Lance. Now!"

Randell was visibly perplexed, but he waited while Merlo continued.

"I've ordered sand," said the Professor, "twelve trucks of it. They should be at the Weston Airport this minute. I've hired airplanes. They're the type used in spraying vegetation and smoking orchards. Those planes are going to fly above the raincloud formations. They're going to bomb the clouds, with sand."*

"But..."

"With sand!" repeated Merlo. "The sand will shatter the cloud formations, release the rain on the city immediately!"

LANCE Randell was on his feet. "You say the planes and the sand are waiting at the Airport?"

Merlo nodded. "I'd planned that we both go to the field. It will make it easier if there are two of us to direct the operations."

The youth helped the old scientist to his feet. "Think you'll be okay, Professor?"

"I think so," said Merlo. But his face was a sickening white.

Randell looked quickly at the Professor, indecision crossing his face. At that instant confusion broke forth in the lobby of Weston Towers, signaled by a hoarse shout of horror the direction of the elevators. Then a woman screamed and every voice in the place became raised in bedlam.

---

*Nothing is so tantalizing to drought sufferers as rainclouds which, because of some peculiar quirk in atmospheric conditions, refuse to precipitate rain. In the southwestern section of the country, considerable success in the past was achieved by airplanes which sprayed or "bombed" with sand stubborn rainclouds above drought-stricken crops or sun-baked city streets. Action of the sand on the clouds released the rain. —Ed.

The Professor and Randell wheeled in the direction of this fresh outburst. People were rushing back and forth in front of a corner elevator like so many frightened chickens. They seemed desperately eager to get away from that particular spot.

Then they saw the cause of the terror, a mousey little man who was standing alone in the elevator, shouting hysterically. The fellow had one hand on the controls and the other was clutching a small, vial-like object.

"Going up, going up, going up," his voice carried to where Randell and Professor Merlo were standing.

"Good Lord," someone cried, "stop him before it's too late."

"Get the Manager," a woman was screaming. "He wants to kill himself."

Lance cursed in anguish. Another one. He struggled through the retreating crowds until he stood behind a cordon of the more courageous spectators, some twenty feet from the elevator row. Merlo had followed directly behind him.

"Get back," the bespectacled little fellow in the elevator was shouting. "Get away from here, all of you, unless you want to come with me!"

The man peered owlishly at the crowd through the thick lenses of his glasses, raising the object in his hand aloft. "This is nitroglycerine! It can blow us all to eternity! *Stand back!*"

Instinctively, the row in front of Lance and Merlo surged back. Lance turned to Merlo. "It's another suicide attempt!"

The little man was shouting at the crowd again. "I'm going up through this roof. Up in a blaze of glory. Glory, for the first time in my miserable life! I've been kidding myself too long. My worthless hide doesn't mean a thing in the scheme of things, and all the time I've been a miserable failure, a fraud. But this morning I stopped lying to myself. Now I'm going out—out and up—with this nitro in my hand! Who wants to come along, eh? Who wants to come along?"

The Professor put a hand to his head, wiping away beads of perspiration. He looked at Randell. "There's nothing we can do about it."

"Good God," Randell cried, "we can't let him kill himself. It's our fault if he dies!" His voice had become anguished, impassioned, and Merlo placed a quieting hand on his arm.

"Steady, Lance. We couldn't foresee all this. There's nothing we can do about it. Every minute we stand here means at least ten such similar deaths throughout the city. Our duty is at the Airport. Let's get out of here, immediately."

Suddenly Lance Randell trembled. Then he quieted.

"You're right. Sorry. Let's get going!" He turned, pushing back through the crowd, when he noticed that Merlo was not moving. The Professor stood frozen motionless, staring in astonishment at the elevator.

"*GOING up! Going up!*" Randell heard the demonical little man chanting. He also heard a gasp from the crowd, heard Merlo mutter a familiar name incredulously. Randell spun around to face the elevator.

"Doris!" the name tumbled from his lips in horror, for from a side entrance to the lobby Doris Martin was walking in a direct line toward the madman's elevator!

In the brief agonized glimpse Lance Randell had of the girl he could see instantly that something was wrong. She walked with the measured step of a sleepwalker, her face blank, eyes unseeing. And in the shocked hush that fell over the lobby he heard her muttering almost inaudibly.

"Lance Randell, you're a fool. A fool." She seemed to be sobbing. "I love you, Lance. She'll never take you..."

"*GOING up! Going up!*" The wild cry of the maniac rang out through the sudden silence like an unclean cackle. He swung the grilled doors of the elevator open momentarily, and in that instant Doris Martin, unseeingly, stepped inside the cage. "Ha—ha! Going up, sister! Glad you're coming along!"

As the elevator door clanged shut Lance Randell's mind became a crimson blot. With an animal snarl he lashed out at the bodies that had blocked his way to the elevator, beating a path before him, hurling himself through the opening. He didn't notice Merlo barging along behind him. He didn't notice anything but the cage with the little suicide and the dazed young girl.

A wild laugh came from the tiny cage, and Randell shouted as he saw it start upward. The light above the door flickered white. Merlo was beside Randall by this time, grabbing him by the arm. He wheeled as he felt the old man's fingers digging into his sleeve.

"What in the hell are we standing here for?" Randell yelled. "Doris is in that elevator, and by God I'm going after her!"

"Get a grip on yourself, Lance," Merlo's fingers dug deeper into his arm and his voice was low, fierce. "Remember what I told you, man. In every moment that we're delayed from the Airport, something like this happens somewhere else in Weston. We've wasted too much time already!"

The Professor's voice brought calm back to Randell, calm and agony at the full import of the situation. "Professor," he muttered shakily, "Doris will be blown to eternity. I have to follow!"

"You'll be sacrificing a hundred lives for one."

Randell looked at the small puddle of blood forming beneath Merlo's leg. "Can you make it alone, Professor?"

"You love the girl?" The Professor's voice was soft.

"Yes... I never realized..." said Randell, and he realized with bitter irony that the Truth Gas was at work once more.

Merlo held out his hand. "I'll make it, Lance, somehow. God give you luck, lad, and speed!" Then the Professor was gone, moving unsteadily off through the crowds. The open door of an adjoining elevator caught Randell's eye and he stepped toward it without hesitation.

"Don't be a fool," snapped a voice directly behind him.

Lance Randell wheeled to see a tall, broad shouldered fellow standing behind him. "Keep out of that elevator. Get back into the crowd. There's a lunatic loose in an elevator with a vial of nitroglycerine. We're clearing the lobby."

"Thanks," Randell grated, "for the information!" As he spoke his fist swung simultaneously. The efficient-looking young gentleman went down heavily. The elevator doors closed with a wild clang.

Lance Randell grabbed the controls of the car, throwing them forward instantly. In his heart was the horrible fear that he'd wasted too much time, that he would be too late. The car lurched forward from the quick start, then shot upward. From the moment when he first spied the insane operator in the elevator, something had been hammering at the back of his consciousness. It seemed to hinge, somehow with Edie Dalmar. And now, with every second holding the answer between life and death, he racked his brain in an effort to hit upon a plan.

H E knew that his only hope of stopping the suicide,, saving Doris, lay in that elusive subconscious discovery. He glanced swiftly about the narrow confines of the cage, mentally thanking God that it was not one of the modern, room-type elevators enclosed on all sides. Instead, the upper-half of the walls were merely spaced iron grillwork, making it possible to see across the shaft from one elevator- to another.

He peered out through the grill. With a silent prayer of thanks he saw that the cables in the adjoining shaft were moving slowly.

"He's taking his time," he muttered. "If I can catch the car before he drives it through the roof I—" Suddenly the elusive plan that had been hiding in his subconscious was crystallized for Randell. He had it.

Of course! The Truth Gas didn't carry to the upper floors of the hotel. It was a heavier than air substance. That accounted for Edie being unaffected by it when she was in her apartment!

His plan was clear in his mind, now. He knew that his one chance of saving Doris lay in forcing the lunatic to the upper floors of the Hotel without discharging the nitro. Once above the gas, the little man would return to normality, would listen to reason.

The little car shot past the twenty-fifth floor. Five floors more and Randell caught a glimpse of the understructure of his quarry's elevator.

Face taut, Randell began to slow his own cage. Three seconds, and he was adjoining the death car. He threw his controls back to stop.

"*Ha!*" He could see the crazed little man turn from where he stood at the controls of the car. He peered through the grillwork at Randell.

Suddenly the suicide's voice cackled, "So you want to come along, too?"

His eyes sweeping desperately across the tar in an effort to see Doris, Randell called, "Where's the girl?"

The little man glanced downward in devilish amusement. "She's lying on the floor. Passed out a moment after we started up."

Randell was talking rapidly, "You can't take that girl to her death. For the love of heaven, man, she has nothing to do with you or your life. Let her out!"

Another hysterical burst of laughter from the demented little fellow was the only answer. Randell opened his mouth to speak, when the other car began to ascend once more. Cursing, he threw the controls forward again.

"32" flashed by.

"33" dropped past.

"36" faded by, and cold sweat trickled off Randell's forehead, smarting into his eyes. He forced himself to look upward, catching a glimpse of the car above. Suddenly he cursed. Something was wrong.

The other car had come to a stop, and was bobbing between floors. "He's going to drop the nitro," Randell thought desperately. He slowed his tiny cage down until he was beside the other.

Looking across the shaft, he was startled. Neither Doris nor the nitro-man was visible!

Instinctively he called out, "Doris!" The silent elevator shafts echoed and re-echoed his cry.

He set his controls, rushing to the grillwork wall, trying to get a better view of the cage in the opposite shaft. Then he saw them. In one corner of the elevator Doris was lying face downward. In the front, next to the controls, the madman was stretched out flat on his back. Next to his open hand was the vial of nitroglycerine—rolling gently back and forth on the floor of the car!

With a numbing sensation of horror, Randell saw that the controls of the car were not set correctly, that they might slip any moment!

Steeling himself, he swept his eyes across the cage in the opposite shaft, looking frantically for some solution to the dilemma. The car was stuck between floors, making it impossible to get to it from a hall door.

Randell realized as much instantly. There was only one other solution, and breathing a silent supplication for time, he set to work on the wall grillwork of his cage.

Precious moments rushed by as he began the laborious effort required to unscrew the thick screen fastenings. It would have been a difficult enough job with tools, but Randell had only his hands, and inside of two minutes they were torn and bleeding.

SOBBING under his breath, knowing that the controls might loosen in the opposite car at any instant, Lance Randell paused only to wipe away the sweat that clouded his eyes. Then at last one side of the screen was loosened.

It was enough. Calling on every last ounce of strength, he pulled backward on the grilling, bending it enough to push his head and shoulders through the scant opening. Hoisting himself up to the ledge where the screening began, he stood teetering, looking down thirty-seven floors of elevator shaft.

He closed his eyes for a moment, grating his teeth against the pain he knew was coming, then seized one of the black, greasy cables with his lacerated hands. It was an almost superhuman act of will that let him swing his feet from the comparatively safe ledge of his own car out into space.

For an agonized second, Randell was sure that his grip on the cable was loosening, that he was going to pitch headlong down the shaft. He wrapped his legs around the huge black coil, hoping to God that the grease wouldn't make such a grip impossible. It was now or never.

One hand lost the cable. The motion made him slide several sickening feet. His hand caught the grilling on the death car, held him there.

With his free hand Randell went to work on the screen fastenings of the cage in which Doris was lying. Time was a blur now, and every frantic second spent in tearing at the bolt fastenings seemed like a section of eternity. He knew he wasn't going to make it, felt his legs growing weak in their grip around the cable, felt the flesh tearing open wider and wider on the hand clutching the coil. But he continued feverishly.

The grilled siding was almost opened, one more bolt, it was loose...

Through the daze of sweat, exhaustion and pain Randell knew that he had to throw all his weight over the half-side of the death car, and as he realized the fact, he caught a split-second vision of the vial of nitroglycerine on the floor, of the control lever that might slip with the slightest jarring of the cage.

He grabbed, releasing all but his legs from the cable, got his elbows over the side of the car. Now his legs were free, and he was clambering into the tiny elevator, making for the controls..

DORIS stood close against Lance Randell, and his arms were around her. They stood in the street outside the Weston Towers. The angry howl of the city had subsided to a tranquil hum, above which could be heard the drone of many airplanes, growing softer, fainter.

Tiny grains of sand were falling in many places over the city, but they were unfelt, locked in droplets of rain. And the rain kept falling gently, steadily, washing away the madness and sorrow and death that a plague of truth had given freedom to.

Lance Randell looked down at the girl.

"Why, darling," he said softly, "you're crying!"

She turned her face upward. "No," she murmured, "it's just the rain on my cheeks."

He drew her tighter. "Liar," he whispered...

PAUL REVERE *and the* TIME MACHINE

By A. W. BERNAL

Before our staring eyes the oaken floor seemed to melt and the top of the Time Swing rose up through it!

Backward into the past went the Time Swing, and when it returned it had a strange passenger—a man who had to get back to 1775 or America was doomed.

"LORD!" gulped Walter. I found myself unable to reply—I was gaping at *it* on the floor and making noises like water in the drain. I wasn't scared; I wasn't even surprised. I was simply paralyzed. After a while I glanced up at Walter's sagging features. His eyes were big as light bulbs.

"Well," I managed, finally, "it works." I gestured at the floor.

"Yeah," exhaled Walter mournfully, like the last drink in the bottle. "Yeah..."

I stared down at *it* again, at its funny three-corner hat, at the lacy ruffles around its throat, at the tight white pants with grease spots on them. It was just like a masquerade—only Walter and I both knew it wasn't any masquerade. That was why Walter's hair stood out from his head like wires. That was why my heart was going like a punching bag.

It, or rather, *he* lay motionless on the floor, in all the dirt and scrap metal, his face the color of an uncooked biscuit. But he'd groaned, and so we knew he was alive—a little, anyhow. He had a nice sort of face, leathery from outdoor exposure, and he wore a silly white wig that was slipping of the back of his head along with his triangle hat. I could just glimpse sparse chestnut-colored hair beneath. And he had a little brown wart on the left of his nose, with two long black hairs pluming from it. The nose itself was three shades redder than a firecracker, with an alcoholic lace of tiny blue veins arabesquing through it to form a dainty design. All in all, he was a work of art.

And all this while the machine ticked on behind us, like a huge clock warming up to strike the hour. Walter suddenly seemed to grow aware of the dolorous tick-tick-ticking beside him, and reached out mechanically to shut the thing off. It stopped with a wheeze as he flipped a switch, and began to settle a few inches toward the floor.

I wouldn't have cared if it had settled right through the floor into the cellar—in fact, I more than half-expected it to. But it didn't. It just relaxed and stood there.

The man on the floor sighed heavily. Then he wrinkled his carrot nose till the little wart would have crawled right into his eye if it had only been open. But his eye remained clamped shut.

"Well, Walter, he's yours... What are you going to do with him?" I asked at length.

Somewhere in the dim, vast labyrinth of Walter's brain, my question set off an alarm and he began to wake—slowly, though. "Yeah," he muttered, and the words clung to his lips like autumn leaves to an ash heap, "what *are* we going to do with him?"

"We?" I smiled. *"You!* Include me out—with bells on!"

"Hank—you can't!" Walter was getting panicky. "You're in this with me. You've got to help me now—he's coming to!"

"I know—that's why I'm going." But Walter was onto my arm like a drowning man, and after one look at him, I thawed. "Okay, okay, I'll stick... Why don't we pick him up?"

"The whiskey, Hank—quick!" cried Walter.

"Who for—us?" I asked, reaching where I knew Walter kept the bottle. I nipped at it myself in transit. "This'll pick him up," I husked, passing it to Walter's trembling hand. "It'll burn out his vocal cords, but it'll pick him up.

He's had a bad shock—he needs a bracer," Walter explained tersely, rooting the bottle in the man's mouth. Scotch vanished in giant gurgles, then the man's eyes flicked like little electric sparks. He looked fleetingly at Walter's worried face, said, "More!" then wrapped his lips around the bottle-neck again.

When the quart flask had been halved, he sighed and relaxed again, flat on the floor.

"He's all right, now," sighed Walter, almost happily. "I think he's just drunk."

And that was how we brought Paul Revere into the 20th Century...

OF course, at first we didn't know it was Paul Revere; that is, we didn't recognize him by his looks. We hadn't hoped for such a distinguished catch. Walter had explained everything to me. He explained and explained every time I went over to his shop with a new part —the only trouble was, he never quite made sense.

You see, I'm a mechanic. Oh, I putter around with electricity some, and I can fix an electric toaster or even a doorbell; but I'm not what you'd strictly call a scientist. Walter is, though, and that's how come we had the fuss.

Back about two years ago, Walter read a book, and well, he couldn't see why, if there was a Fourth Dimension, you couldn't monkey around with it. So he called me over one day and told me he had a machine he wanted me to help him make.

He just told me what he wanted and I fixed it up for him, or if there was no such thing I invented it. Sometimes it wasn't as simple as it sounds, thinking up ways to bend everyday iron and copper into fool whichigigs that would fit in the way Walter said they ought to. But he paid for all of it, and I did it.

Walter said things about no single instant of Time ever being lost. Time was really "an eternally conceived Present along which one focussing instant travels endlessly at uniform speed in one direction." Like a big road ready for use in all sections at once. One end of the road is the Past. One is the Future. The instant *Now* is like an automobile on this big road of Time. It started at one end, the Past, and is heading for the other—the Future—and wherever it happens to be, why, that's the Present.

Get it? Neither do I, but that's what Walter always kept saying to me.

But to get on with things, the only reason Time never got balled up was because some mysterious force kept the car of Now headed always in the same direction — Futureward — and once it passed a point it never came back again, never re-focused on it.

Well, Walter figured that if he could only build a machine which would reach into the Fourth Dimension, he could then reach *Pastward* along this roadway of Time. And if he could do that, then there was no reason why he couldn't send things into other times or bring things into our time.

This machine which Walter designed and I helped build took quite a while, and when we had it done, it would hardly stay together.

Well, the machine looked something like a cross between an oil well, a porch swing, and a Grandfather's clock, if you get what I mean. When Walter started the motor, the wheels and the seat would start swinging back and forth, and when it began to go fast enough, it would sort of blur and disappear.

At this point it was, according to Walter, "shifting gears" and revolving its direction into the Fourth Dimension. After a moment of this shifting, it would suddenly whirl into sight again and start slowing down, bringing to us whatever it had caught from the Time Walter had sent it to.

For some reason, it always went into reverse; the Future was somehow untouchable—and that's something that never bothered me a bit, even though it drove Walter nearly wild.

We kept trying it out, until one night the machine took my straw hat and brought back a bird instead; but I couldn't wear a sparrow, and I told Walter so. But he just kept gawking at the bird, watching it fly around, till it finally flew out of the window. "It's *alive*," he kept yelling. "Alive!"

That same night Walter warned me not to say a word to a soul, but to come back again the next night and we'd try for a real catch. Real catch! *Wow!*

SO here he was on the floor of Walter's house, on the outskirts of Boston, snoring away as though he were home in his own century. As I started to say once before, we didn't know he was Paul Revere then: to us he was just somebody with a pigtailed wig that didn't fit him and a pair of dirty breeches a size-and-a-half too tight.

We scuttled him up onto the table, where his big boots smashed a packet of vacuum tubes I'd set there just to make sure they would be safe. After a while then this thing we'd gotten sat up blinking stupidly from Walter to me and back again. The liquor Walter had funneled into him was beginning to take full effect with the subtlety of a sledgehammer.

He grunted, fumbling in a pocket for a watch bigger than my alarm clock. "'Sblood! What is the hour, good gennelmen? I've work to do this night.-

"How—how do you feel after your—trip?" asked Walter.

The fellow was squinting past the raven-tressed wart on his nose to study the face of his Big Ben. He was muttering to himself.

"Barkeep! Barkeep! A mug of ale and I must be off. Haste, prithee!" He fought himself into a sitting position, and belched manfully.

Walter tried to break it gently, like a salesman with his foot in the door. "Ah, Mr.—ah—what is the name, sir?' he limped, stalling.

"Name?" the aroma of good old English ale he sent my way was thick enough to bear a foam. "*My* name? 'S Paul—Paul Revere, by my powdered, pasted periwinkle! Name, thrice-blessed name of a gennelman and a—a gennelman, sirs." He smacked his lips. "And now, my ale, barkeep! Thunderation, but I must go!" He cocked one eye at us and belched again. "A thousand pardons," he mumbled, "a thousand pardons. Barkeep—saddle my good mount Brondelbuss, for I must be off and away! I tell thee there's riding to be done this night!"

"I beg your pardon, Mr.—Mr. Revere," Walter had begun—and then it hit him like a truck. "Ride? Revere? *Paul* Revere? YOU?" He nearly stabbed him dead with that long bony finger of his. "Lord, Hank, it's—PAUL REVERE!"

"S-s-sh! " Paul Revere clapped a big hand over his loose lips, wildly waving the other at Walter. "S-s-sh—don't shout m' name. I'm on serious business for the colonies—secret business!"

"For Pete's sake," I yelped, "he's a G-Man of yesterday!"

But he ignored me and Walter jabbed me angrily in the ribs.

"Prithee," rambled on the man out of the Past, "writhe, keep m' name quiet, or you'll give me away to these common tipplers here." Then, picking up my tool-kit from the table and trying to peer in it, he roared: "By my saddle-girth! Is my tankard empty yet?"

I saw my chance. "S'cuse me, Mr. Revere," I put in, handing him his wig and hat, which had fallen off his head when we'd rolled him onto the table, "but here's your wig, sir. And maybe you can tell me something of a brand new straw hat, size—"

Hank!" Walter flagged me down, as Revere put his wig on backward so that its pigtail draggled into his mouth. "It's Paul Revere himself, don't you understand? Just think, Hank—the 18th Century—one hundred and fifty years —and he's here with us, alive and breathing! Paul Revere out of history —right here with you and me!"

" 'S'LIE!" thundered Revere, banging my tool kit on the table with a smash. "I don't come from—from where you said, at all. I live right here in village, an' my credit should be good for one ill smidgeon of ale. By my powder horn and candle-snuffer, though —I'll never come here again unless I get some service! I've riding to do this night, I tell thee!"

He rolled off the table onto his feet, immediately sagging as if someone were pulling him at the pockets. Walter gave him a shove and flattened him on the table again.

Walter was almost hysterical, his eyes dancing as he looked at the calendar on the wall behind us.

"Hank—look! It's the eighteenth of April!"

" 'Struth, 'tis!" boomed Revere. He grabbed his wig and swung it exultantly by its pigtail. "April the eighteenth, '75, and Paul Revere'll make history tonight. History, I say—one if by land, two if by sea... Another ale and I'll have eyes like a hawk! Barkeep! 'Swounds, where *is* the poltroom?"

"One if by land—" I croaked in surprise. "Hey, that's in the poem!"

"Twah!" Revere howled, wriggling his head back into his wig, now turned completely wrongside out. "Glory be, good gennelmen, and I swear a merry oath—'tis no poem. 'Tis a song! One if by land—two if by sea—I've a tankard of ale that's due to me! A pox on us all—where's my ale?"

"It's getting close to midnight," said Walter suddenly, his eyes wide.

"Midnight! Too late for ale—history's in the making. One if by land, two if by sea—and Revere'll send the alarm ringing through every Middlesex village from Charleston to Lexington and back again!"

Paul Revere notched his belt. He shot his feet at the floor with a sudden flurry of determination. "Must go," he boomed.

"Well, if you gotta go—" I began, but Walter butted in.

For the past couple of minutes, Walter had stood with his mouth open and his face a complete blissful blank. But now he suddenly quivered all over, grabbed Paul Revere by his coat sleeve, and moaned: "Hank! Hank! We can't let him go out of here—what'll we do?"

"What's this?" Revere hooted, regarding us with his bloodshot eyes. "Brigands in the tavern? Rascals, let me free!"

He jerked his arm loose with a twist that buckled his legs under him and he finally compromised by sinking to one knee. "Whew," he muttered, eyes closed desperately, "I'm not so steady as I might be, with what I've to do this night. Help me to horse—strap m' feet to the stirrups. Blast my boiled buttons, I've drunk too much for duty!" He sighed, and sank a little further toward the floor.

Walter was still just staring at him. "Hank," he pleaded, turning my way, "don't you get it? We've got to get him back in the machine right away! Don't you see? We've botched up history, Hank. This is the eighteenth of April —the night of his famous ride. The British man-of-war Somerset is on her way into the Charles' River this very instant!"

"HUH?"
"Oh, you dope!" Walter exploded. "Can't you see that if Paul Revere doesn't get back to his own Time to warn the colonists, the American Revolution may never come off?"

"HUH?"

That was when it hit me. "But, Walter, that's old stuff—it's been done and forgotten a hundred and fifty years ago!"

"Don't be a mucklehead! Can't you grasp the fact that the Past is just as real as the Present? Use your head, Hank. Look—Paul Revere, in '75, on the eighteenth of April, was all set to make history as planned, wasn't he?"

"Yeah, but—"

"Shut up. Now, all at once a couple of blamed fools like us reach into the Past where we have no business, and snag Revere out of his own

Time and yank him into our own year-1940!"

"Yeah, but—"

"Shut up. Now, here's Paul on the floor of our room in 1940, half-crocked on ale and the Scotch we loaded him with a while back. How d'you suppose he's going to be in two different centuries at once?"

"Well, he's here now—"

"So he can't be back in '75 where he should be! And if he isn't back in history where he belongs, he can't warn the minute-men that the British are coming. And if he can't do that, General Gage on the Somerset will land his troops and probably wipe out the American military supplies at Concord and cripple our forces like they intend to do. *And* they'll capture John Hancock and Samuel Adams, too—they're part of what Gage is after! And if that happens, then the Revolution'll be over before it gets going, and the Redcoats'll win and retain America as a British colony, and then— Oh, Hank, we've gone and bungled things so the whole history of our nation will be remade in a single night, and a hundred and fifty years of American freedom will be blotted out—be non-existent."

"Walter," I tried to calm him, "now, Walter, it can't happen that way. What's done is done—history is history, and— And, look, Walter! Maybe it'll come out all right anyway!"

"Maybe," cried Walter, a wild gleam in his eye, "but we don't dare take that chance! Hank, we've not a second to lose. We've got to get Paul Revere back to his own time before the British ruin everything!"

So there we were.

It was half past ten. In a little over an hour back there in that other world where Paul Revere should have been, the Redcoats would be sighted by Paul's buddy in the belfry and the signal would be flashed to Revere himself, on the other side of the river.

And it was up to us to meet a crisis which occurred a hundred and fifty years before we were born!

How we went about it I don't know.

While I worked on the machine with every tool I had, Walter was in no less of a dither pouring black coffee down the throat of a very much bewildered Paul Revere. By dint of much shouting and repetition, and the aid of a bucket of cold water in the groaning hero's face, Walter was finally able to bring him to the realization that something was definitely haywire. We raced like madmen against the ominous ticking of the wall clock, fighting against each second that drove us that much closer to the moment when the Old North Church belfry should gleam with a lantern light back there in '75.

FINALLY I wheeled, "Ready!"
I wrapped my wrench around the last loose nut. Sweat cascaded down my face in a regular Niagara, but I was done, and it was just past eleven o'clock. "Throw him in the cage!" I panted.

Walter was busy all this time going over the situation endlessly with Paul Revere. "Don't you understand?" he moaned hoarsely. "It's our fault... It's the Fourth Dimension."

"Fourth Dimension? 'Sblood and pantaloons! Could you repeat it all just once more, citizen?"

"It's no use," Walter wept. "It just isn't any use!"

"Looky!" I shrieked now, getting almost as mad as I was scared. "This is 1940. You're from 1775 and you must get back. See?" Then I gave him a good hard shove toward the cage of the Time Swing, and, "Now you get the drift, buddy," I finished, "we got no time to lose. Hop in!"

"But, good gentlemen—" He was getting a little of our own anxiety, now. Who wouldn't, with two bleary-eyed and chalky faces gaping at him. Paul Revere was cold sober now—cold sober and plenty panicky.

"You—you don't mean the Redcoats have already come?"

"You see, *Einstein—*" Walter began.

"Skip Einstein—" I shoved Walter away. I jerked Paul Revere to his feet by the lapels of his funny coat. "Now, squat!"

He squatted. Huddled there in that big metal cage, surrounded on all sides by wheels and pistons, his eyes were popping with an uncomprehending fright.

"How'll he find out what the British are going to do?" Walter turned to me.

"For Pete's sake — tell him!" I yelped, busy wrapping Revere's numb fingers around some arm-supports on the sides of the cage. "Now hang on tight so you won't spill out somewhere in the Gay Nineties." Then to Walter again: "Tell him—you know how it all came out! Tell him—and for God's sake, *throw that switch!*"

Walter's eyes lit up. "We know what happened, don't we? By sea!

Two lamps, Revere—that's the signal! *Two,* man, d' you understand?"

Paul Revere was nodding so hard his wig slid off into his lap. "By sea—" he was echoing, like a school kid, "two lamps in the Old North tower. By sea! I knew it!" His face dropped again. "But Brondelbuss — what have you done with my horse?"

"Sit still! Walter—that *switch!*"

Walter leapt at the control-panel, his hands buried in switches up to his wrists. "Close your eyes and count twenty," he sputtered, "then grab the first horse you can find—and light out for Lexington!"

"But—" Revere began...

Then Walter slammed everything home.

THERE came a wheeze, a jerk, a whirring thump, and the Time Swing trembled into life.

Then Walter howled. "Grab 'er, Hank—she's tipping!"

Faster and faster, and the old machine was beginning to groan and strain forward like it always did. I made a jump for her supports and hung on, the nuts and bolts I had so laboriously tightened a minute ago hopping about me like popcorn.

Then the gear-shifting began. Our anachronistic friend was now nothing more than a bluish blur with a frightened look running across it, slowly creeping off at right angles to everything else in the universe— climbing into that infernal Fourth Dimension.

Walter gulped. "I—I think it's working."

The next second I thought he'd drop dead. Two of the wildly stomping beams of the rocking oil-well support of the Time Swing tore unexpectedly loose from their moorings, and the whole kaboodle of machinery waltzed in a crazy circle right across the room, leaving me holding about twenty pounds of loose ends in my hands. I stabbed Walter with a look and whirled back.

The seat in the cage was empty.

"It's busted," said Walter, dully.

I couldn't believe it myself.

There came a long pause.

"We'll soon know," Walter said quietly.

I didn't feel any too good all of a sudden, either. After all, even if my forefathers didn't come over on the Mayflower, I am an American, and proud of this Depression-bitten promontory of ours. And right at this moment I loved America, and I hated to think that Walter and me had tossed her right smack in the laps of the Redcoats back there on that fateful night a century and a half before either of us was born.

"Hank." If there had been a deep pit under the floor of Walter's shack, that is where his voice would have come from. "He didn't make it. The Swing didn't hold long enough. He couldn't have made it. We threw him out in some unknown year—threw him away forever..."

I looked at the clock and shook my head. "He'd have had time to make it, too. Ain't quite eleven yet. Had till midnight, didn't he?"

"Yeah," mourned Walter gently. "'T'was twelve by the village clock.' he quoted sadly, " 'when he galloped into Medford town.' Yes—if only the machine had held, he'd have made it in good time." Walter sighed.

"Yeah. And then we'd still be American citizens, huh?"

"YES, Hank." He was slowly shoving parts of the machine back together again. Absently, I chipped in with my wrench on a few bolts.

"We lost the Revolution, huh?"

"We will—at dawn, I guess, Hank. Throw me that bundle of wire, will you?"

I tossed it to him. I tightened something more with my wrench. "I wonder if he didn't make it, though," I said.

"No, Hank. I'm afraid not."

"What'll he do, Walter, wherever he is, huh?"

"Go on being an engraver, I suppose. That's his trade, you know—engraving. He—hey, listen! What—what's *that?*"

"What?"

"That!"

I heard it all right, only I didn't want to.

"Listen, Hank."

I listened again. I heard it again. I moaned.

"Hank." It was a whisper, deep-hidden in some frozen crater of the moon. "Hank... We're mad. D'you know that, Hank? Mad as loons...!"

From faraway outside it had come—that thudding and hoarse shouting. From faraway down the road. Then nearer, nearer it came, until we could make out words—words being cried out in a wild voice.

Walter and I were staring at each other, petrified. Then Walter broke.
-That voice—" he choked, "can it be—?"

It was a barroom baritone, and it was bawling: "The Redcoats are coming...up, up, and to arms!"

But I couldn't believe we were insane. "Walter," I babbled, "is it— can it—?"

"No—Good Lord, no!"

But all the time the hoofbeats grew louder, and so did that hoarse voice. Together they came thundering down the road toward Walter's place while we held our breaths. The hooves were thudding away just outside now—a moment more and they'd be past. But no —they stopped!

-Whoa!" crackled a human klaxon, just outside our door—"Whoa, I said, confound it!" That voice was unmistakable—I could almost smell the ale come floating through the door when it spoke. "Whoa, plague take thee!"

Then out of that night and into our shack thundered our Paul Revere. The door slammed open with a crash and a burly figure in lace shirt and white pants stood limned against the darkness, waving its triangle hat like a drunken college boy. "To arms, good people! The British regulars—" But they never came in that particular sentence. It rattled away as though someone had stuffed Revere's big mouth with pebbles. I could have tightened up those bulging eyeballs with my wrench, the way they popped out of their sockets.

"Odd's blood, gentlemen, is it *thee* again?" He was appalled.

"How the devil did you get back here?" Walter shouted.

Revere made no reply, he simply wheeled and dashed for the steps.

But Walter and I were right after him. "Get him, Hank," screamed Walter, spilling down the steps, landing a-sprawl in the dirt. I leapt over his rolling body and dashed after Revere. Before he even got near his horse, I had him around the waist.

"Pox take thee, let me be! What devil's potion have I drunk this night to have such visions? Let me go, quietly, I beg of you, sir Devils."

But Walter had now picked himself up. "It's only us, Mr. Revere— there's been some kind of an error." Judging from his agonized expression, this was scarcely good news to our captive, and he trembled like a leaf.

"Prithee, good demons," he was pleading like a child, "only let me go."

Then Walter let out a yelp. He dangled a wrist before my face. "Let's step on it, Hank—we've still half an hour to midnight! There's still a chance!"

Between us we managed to drag the big hulk inside, though we had to do it by his bootstraps to keep him from bolting. As it was, he writhed in a frenzy of despair and fear, clinging for a full minute to the doorknob, swinging there as if it were the handle of the Pearly Gate itself, before we could pry him loose and shut the door.

"No, no, good gentlemen, I beg you!" he blubbered. "I prithee, pretty devils, let me be!"

"Can it, boy," I barked. "It's just a bad dream, see? But if you don't sit still, I'll wrap this monkey wrench around your ears. Get me?"

Walter flew around the room. I thought he had a dozen hands, the way he was working over that control board and jamming do-businesses into the stomach of our battered machine.

"BE ready in a minute," he was rattling. "Put him back in the cage...I hope we get him back in time, I hope! We still got ten minutes... Keep him still, Hank! Mullivaney's nag, he must've had, eh, Hank? Hand me that insulator. Wasn't in the Past at all, just thrown horizontally half a mile along the Fourth, through solids and all... I hope we got her set right—but we got to take the chance 'cause we're lost anyway, if we don't... Ah, now, Hank! Hold him steady —we're ready to shoot!"

"Revere," I breathed, "fly away home! You get the first nag you see—"

"What, good sirs—" I swear I could almost see tears in his rolling eyes—"*again?*"

"Yes—you want the colonies to get the jump on the Redcoats, don't you?" "I do, by God!"

I'll be darned if he wasn't a real American, too!

"Great, then!" crackled Walter. "In exactly two seconds you'll be back in the Revolution—"

He stopped, like a phonograph running down. I felt my own heart clanking into my boots.

For, with one wild cry, his face turning ocean green, Paul Revere had melted out of my grasp and slipped prone on his face in the cage of the Time Swing. The rocket-trip through the Fourth Dimension and our mauling had been too much for his cargo of mixed ale and Scotch. The Man of History was out!

And once more the hungry hands on the clock began eating up our precious minutes!

We had been through all this once before tonight, but this time we were up against a stupor which would have done credit to Bacchus! It seemed like centuries, the time it took to get one of those eyes open again—and yet it seemed that those clock-hands were over toward midnight like race h:rses on the stretch.

Finally, with less than six minutes to go before Zero Hour, Paul Revere groaned and tried to sit.

"I—I'm not—not well." he whispered, in a masterpiece of understatement, the ocean green of his face ebbing and flowing like a tide.

"Oh, Lord—try to get up:" wept Walter. "Try, Revere—you must try!"

"Five minutes!" I screamed at both. *"Five!"*

But screaming and moaning and even trying were all no good. It had been a feat of sheer superhuman will for Revere to open that one eye—he had shot his bolt. He was through.

"Hank," 'Walter's restless syllables kept running on and on, "Hank, we got to get him up. Hank, if we only had a few minutes more, Hank, we *got to—*"

"Four minutes to twelve," I heard myself groan. Then I shut up. Walter had got a solution. I saw it in his glazed eyes.

Two seconds he spent in unhooking the control panel from its moorings. One second more he took to plug in a long cord in its place, with a complicated gadget from his desk dangling from its end. Another second and he had shoved me clean off my feet into the swaying, rickety cage, smack on top of our prone hero. And then, with a chortle that must have been heard round the world, he plunged home a button-series on the gadget he held in his hand and leapt on the bodies of me and Revere.

The cage began to quiver.

"Hey—" it was my voice, but I didn't know I was yelling. "Hey—the machine is moving!"

Walter had a funny grin on his face. "I know," he said, rolling off me and sitting up. "You and me are taking Paul Revere *home!*"

I nearly fainted dead away. Because we were!

I HAD trouble in focusing my eyes: they persisted in trying to look about three ways at once. Then they drew blank for what may have been a minute or one hundred and fifty years. And then we stopped with a thud.

I smelled dirt. I rolled off of Walter and struggled to sit up. The landscape whirled about me like a merry-go-round. Before I could see clearly, I scrabbled around with my fingers and felt *grass* below me. Anyway, I kept telling myself silently, we're not in the house.

All at once, with a jolt, it all settled down. On a patch of greensward, before a lighted old barn of a place, sat Walter and me. Beside us lay a very quiet Paul Revere. One look at that house before us told me we had made the trip all right; nothing like that shack was ever built in Oakville!

"Well." breathed Walter, awe in his voce, "how does it feel to be in good old '75. Hank?"

I didn't answer. I didn't feel like it. "Come on—bring the hero."

Walter had climbed to his feet and was staggering off toward the lighted house, which bordered a road of sorts. I squinted through the darkness of a moonless night and saw that Walter was reeling in a long piece of cord. I remembered that he had thrown the coil of it into his pocket back—back there, before we started. He was winding it in, and I figured he must be looking for the crack in Time we had slipped through—for on the other end of that precious cord was the Time Swing and 1940!

I helped Revere to his feet, and we plodded unsteadily after Walter. He was heading straight toward the house ahead of us, reeling in wire as he went.

"Be with you in a minute," he called over his shoulder to me; "but if we lose this cord, we don't get back home!"

"Take all the time you want, pal," I urged. Saving America might be pretty vital, but so was getting home again.

As we neared the building across the road, I made out a sign swaying above its door: INNE of Ye FOWLE & SPITTE. I could tell by the sudden pulse of life in the hulk I was dragging behind me that Paul

Revere had caught that sign, too.

"Your local tavern?" I asked, and he nodded weakly. I began to worry about the Redcoats again. "Your horse must be hereabouts, then, eh?" I went on.

"Here is where I stood," he managed thinly, "when your incantations found me. Yonder stands Brondelbuss..."

"Some horse," I said, spotting the plug as he spoke; and then I turned to call out to Walter. "It's just about twelve by my clock. What do we do now?"

At my words, a sad-hearted hound bayed mournfully at the lumpy moon above us. In the still night air, the braying must have carried for miles.

Walter was holding up a hand. "Listen to that, Hank!" he breathed. I saw he was pretty awed by it all. "That dog brayed that way in the middle of the night a hundred and fifty years before we were born! Think of it, Hank! We've rolled back the years to Boston, 1775! Boston—a little village in a brand new continent—with its few hundreds of souls all asleep around us...men and women who have been dead for more than a century! But tonight, Hank, thanks to us, we know they are alive again!"

I decided it was time we did something. I felt creepy. "Snap out of it, dreamy," I said, shaking him. "If you got that cord safe, let's spread the word about the British before it's too late."

"Lord, yes!" gasped Walter. "I'd almost forgotten our mission, in the miracle of just being here. Old *Boston,* Hank! 1775!"

He was in a most wonderful mood suddenly, fears and doubts gone like nothing. "Maybe this inn has a road map," he cracked, pushing open the oaken door.

I followed and Revere wobbled along behind me. A thick smell assailed us that was no different than that in any gin mill in 1940. Walter forged on ahead, like a man in a dream.

"HO!" rang a basso voice from behind the stout, reeking old bar. "Revere, I thought ye'd slipped anchor to perform a duty this night!"

Revere did not reply. He left me to roll over to a nearby table, where he plunked himself down limply, his head held between his hands.

"Revere," the giant behind the bar was booming again, a note of anxiety and suspicion in his voice, "Methought ye'd be in Lexington by this. Who are these—men?"

Walter had followed a line of electric cord straight across the smoky, candle-lighted room, saying not a word to anyone. Then, while the bartender stared, and I stared, and Revere didn't even look up, something very peculiar occurred.

Right smack at Walter's feet there came a hissing and a whirring—and before our staring eyes the thick oaken planks of the floor seemed to melt, and the top of the cage of the Time Swing rose up through it!

It was uncanny, to say the least. And not a soothing sight to the monster who owned the joint! The bartender reached up for a huge blunderbuss high above the bar, and even Revere got to his feet.

"By my tops'le and spanker," croaked the barkeep, slamming the gun on his bar, "what in Satan's own name is going on over there?"

Walter, sneezing from the dust which was still settling in a cloud about that end of the big room. But it was me to whom he spoke. "Look at that, Hank, there's a funny one for you! After *we* stopped, the cage moved on—through the Fourth Dimension—a few additional space-seconds. The last couple of yards of this cord just materialized through Time-Space. Wonderful!"

If this was gibberish to me, it was worse than that to the barkeep. He looked sternly at Revere and bawled angrily: "Revere, you sot! Who are these friends of yours who come wrecking my inn? I thought—"

But Revere interrupted him with a wail: "They are not my friends! They're not men at all—they're wicked demons conjured up by some British magician!"

In a moment of stunned silence that followed, I began to sweat cold drops as big as grapes. You could scarcely blame Revere for thinking we were evil spirits summoned to fight against him by witchcraft, after all the hard luck he'd had with us and our manufactured miracle. But it did put us in a bad spot. One peep at the size of barkeep convinced me he could rub me and Walter together until we were powder. And by the look on his face, I knew he wanted to.

What with machinery which would not yet be invented for a hundred years, popping up from his cellar—I could readily believe he thought we were exactly what Revere had called us—good old-fashioned, New England-hatched demons!

"Walter, never mind the Redcoats," I whispered, "pull that cord and let's get home!" Home! What a wonderful word!

WALTER, unheeding, said, "I—I know this looks a bit unusual, but there is a national crisis tonight, and we —we came over to help."

"Stow it!" Barkeep was in an ugly mood. He strode across the tavern floor in three steps. The stout oak planks creaked beneath his weight. He picked up a small tree-trunk and slammed it into place across the door, barring us inside with his wrath.

"Revere," he grated like the roar of a bull, "tell me this. Be ye drunk or drugged?"

"Drugged," Revere managed to grunt, without lifting his head from the table. "Demons—and they drugged me. I swear it."

Barkeep put his heavy hands on his hips and glared at Walter and me. He spat into a cuspidor with venom and force. He hoisted his pants, and I noticed that, as his arms flexed, his muscles bulged tightly beneath his shirt.

I forgot all about the colonies. "Walter, let's you and me go home!"

"Stow it!" Barkeep drowned me out. "Hark, ye slithering things in the guise of men." Slowly he began rolling up his sleeves. "Now, be ye men or be ye demons, I know by the work ye've done tonight that the pair of ye are British-sent scum. Ye've kept matey here from his ridin', and now ye'll answer to Jim Toddy for it."

And then he lowered his thick head and ran for us.

I leapt for the cage, which stuck out of the floor like a cellar-door, yelling: "Walter—he thinks we're trying to help the Redcoats! Come on!"

But Walter never budged. Something came over his thin body. He tensed, stiff as a ramrod. Then Toddy lunged past the spot where a second ago Walter had been standing. I had never seen Walter move so fast. He had waited solidly as a rock until the man's rush closed the distance between them. Then he had whipped aside like a toreador, and stuck out his foot. And the barkeep flashing by, roared like a bull and went down with a crash that shook the ground.

I looked at Toddy's face as he picked it off the floor, and ducked my head. But I had to raise it again to see how Walter was going to die.

Walter stood firm: white and pale, but firm. Toddy roared in at him, seized poor Walter in a bear's grip and his baboonish thumbs went round Walter's throat. But Walter, though blue with pain, was not licked yet. He whipped a hand behind him, seized a bottle by the neck.

Crash! Spangles of glass shot out like sparks. Toddy shuddered, shook his thick head, and went sprawling onto the floor with a sound like thunder.

Walter struggled up, color coming back into his face with every pump of his pounding heart. He clutched the bottle neck, now all that was left whole of his make-shift weapon, and stared at the huge man at his feet. There was no need for further action, though. Toddy was prone among sawdust and glass fragments; the blow had removed him from combat.

"How—how did you think of doing, that, Walter?" I managed to ask, climbing out of the cage again.

He shook his head, wiping his brow with a shaky hand. "I don't know. I only thought of how mad I was that this big lump should try to stop us from our duty..."

"Come on, man," I said. "If it's duty you're after, let's get some horses."

Walter was hiding the precious coil of wire which held the switch of the Time Swing in its end, when suddenly there came a thumping at the door. I froze where I stood.

REVERE had been dazedly trying to pull himself together. Whether he saw the fight, I don't know. But now he was staggering over to the door, fumbling to open it.

"Don't open that!" I cried out.

He ignored me. "Just a moment, dear," he was saying, "I saw you looking through the window." He struggled to hoist the bar from its slots, and then lifted up the latch, just as the pounding began again. Revere fell back, as the door swung open, and began feverishly to straighten his messy clothes.

It was a woman.

"Oh, ye did see your wife through the window, did ye now, ye old reprobate?" she cried, bustling up to Paul Revere, oblivious to the rest of us. "Ye told me ye were out on civic business, out on patriotic duty, didn't ye, Paul Revere? And where I find your horse tonight I've found the beast a dozen times—hitched before Jim Toddy's saloon!"

"Listen, dear," Revere explained, frantically dusting off his wig and wriggling into it, "I was delayed by these—"

Mrs. Revere turned and saw us. Her eyes narrowed. "So! You're the minute-men, I've heard tell about! Look at ye, now! Where did ye find those oddments ye are wearing? Drunkards, draggin' my husband off, making him—"

"Get out of here!" I yelled, all at once. "Scram! Don't any of you old-fashioned idiots realize what's happening? Do you think we have any time for family quarrels?" I came up alongside Revere's wife, my eyes probably popping, if they gave the slightest indication of how I felt. "Hit the road!" I yelled.

The poor woman took a step back, then another, and with a sudden cry ran out of the place.

"Get a horse!" I turned on Revere viciously. "Go out and get on some kind of a horse. You can't pin the failure of the Revolution on me! Get out and ride, you dang-blasted son-of-a-hero, before I—'

And just then, Revere broke down. He laid his head on a table and cried. "Gentlemen, or demons—whatever ye may be—I cannot. My wife will never forgive me for this. *You* do what you can to help the colonies. God protect them! But *I'm* going home to explain matters to my wife!"

It was precisely at that instant that I heard Walter's voice beside me, like the sound of a ghost.

"The dawn!" His lips were barely moving as he pointed through the shuttered windows to a grey streak across the horizon. "It's almost morning!" Without another word, he went through the door, staggering, and sank limply down on the stoop.

I stood in the tavern for some minutes, listening to the stentorian breathing of the still unconscious barkeep, and the sobs from the drunken Paul Revere. They were the only sounds in a vast quiet.

I went out and sat down beside Walter. I couldn't understand what had happened, but some things I knew. We had wasted one of the most historic nights in Time, trying to manage a drunken hero, fighting a belligerent barkeep, and arguing with a shrewish housewife...and in that time, the magnificent ride that Paul Revere should have made— had been forgotten!

"We must have become mixed up in our calculations somewhere," Walter was saying, softly. "We probably didn't even get here until it was too late."

"There isn't anything we can do?"

"No."

A moment later, Walter suddenly leaped high into the air. *"Hank!"* he *"Hank! I've got it!* We'll take Revere into the machine again. We'll go back a few more hours, and, begin again, and this time we'll make sure."

I didn't wait another second. Together, we dashed back into the tavern...

THERE was no one there. Paul Revere and the barkeep had both vanished. Only a little back-door, swinging in the morning breeze, indicated two men had disappeared...fleeing from demons from another age...

"Now what, Walter?"

"I'll tell you what! We're going out to find him and put him on the Swing." He started to go out that little backdoor, going to Heaven alone knows where, when I seized his arm.

"Listen!" It was the second time that night.

There were horses in the distance, and shooting. The short bursts of rifle fire blasted the quiet morning air.

"They're coming for us!" I gasped. ""Revere and the barkeep have gotten help. We've got to get out of here."

We can't!" Walter said, with a strange firmness. "We've got to make them understand. We're sacrificing the heritage—"

"Heritage! We'll sacrifice ourselves! You know by now we're through. All I want now is to die in my own time."

Walter was about to say no when I let him have it. He had fallen halfway to the ground when I caught him and lugged him to the rickety Time Swing. I strapped the both of us in.

The horses were sounding louder now, the shots closer.

A million strange switches stared me in the face. I monkeyed with them the way I had seen Walter do, turned a lever which said, "Reverse," and held on for life. Horses were galloping past the tavern.

Just then the door opened and a grimy man in a three-cornered hat strode in. He carried a gun in one hand, which he suddenly threw up and aimed at us. And then the whole world seemed to blur, like faces in an unsteady stream, and the machine quivered. My stomach twisted, and I heard the sound of a musket going off somewhere, and something soft brushed by me...

Walter's workroom was swimming by at an angle, spinning on a mad pivot. There was a sudden rain of machinery, a swift jerk, and the leather straps that held me gave and spilled me out on the floor, with Walter following.

The most magnificent traitors in history had returned, after doing a job that no one on Earth could undo, selling out a nation that had paid in blood for a victory that had been wiped out.

Walter was sitting up, a foolish smile on his face. "Hell," he said, "I *feel* like an American."

I got up and peered through the drawn curtains of the room. The dawn was coming up. Soon the sun would be shining over this land, the same sun that never set on British soil. And yet it all looked the same to me. History might have changed, but maybe Boston had been left out of it. It was impossible to believe that our world had been so changed.

The room was the same, the furniture the same. The street outside, even the street-name, *Adams Street* was the same; I could read it from where I stood. "Walter," I said, suddenly, "do you suppose the British would have let us keep the same names on our streets —names of Revolutionary heroes?"

"Maybe," he said, glumly. The idiot's smile had left him, and he was returning to full consciousness. "Just history, that's all. We've changed every book ever written about it—like that." He tried to snap his fingers, but it didn't work.

"Exactly." I almost whispered it. "That's where we can find out exactly what we've done." I lurched at the bookcase, and dragged out one of the musty volumes of the—I cursed the thought—*Encyclopaedia Brittanica*. Swiftly I ran through the pages on the American Revolution...

IT was all the same...all the same...
"Walter! Look at this!"

But Walter had thought of something else. He had been reading another book. "It's all right!" he shouted, *"Hank, it's all right."* He threw the book down on the floor, yelling, "Yankee Doodle," jumped after it, opened it again, and lying there, he read to me.

"On the night of April 18th, when the British were planning to seize the Concord military supplies and arrest John Hancock and Samuel Adams, and thus quash the Revolution before it started, a prominent patriot named Paul Revere was to catch a signal flashed from the Old North Church belfry and ride at midnight, spreading the alarm. But, in some peculiar circumstance, never clarified, Revere was captured on the outskirts of Boston, in the company of his wife, by a British scouting patrol. Fortunately for the colonists, however, Revere's friend, William Dawes, was on hand when the signal showed from the historic old church..."

I couldn't listen any more. I screamed and swooped down on Walter. "What's this all about?" I yelled. "Who is—was—this William Dawes—God bless him?" Then I remembered the man who had shot at us, the grimy man in the three-cornered hat, coming into the Tavern, his ride long over, just as the Swing had begun.

"Hank," said Walter, closing the book solemnly, "this is a lesson to you. You don't know your American history; you're a dope. Bill Dawes was left out of the poem because Longfellow couldn't find a rhyme for his name. When Revere didn't show up—due, as we now know, to his being somewhere in the Fourth Dimension with us—Dawes just naturally up and went. The Paul Revere ride is a story, but the truth is in the books, and anyone can check on it. Matter is, with fools like you, not even bothering to—"

"Why, you—"

"Out of my way," said Walter.

"Where you going now?"

Walter didn't answer. I could hear him stomping around downstairs, then coming back up. And in his hand he held two axes. "Here," he said, handing me one.

I wish you could have heard the noise we made, laughing and yelling at six in the morning, as we swung those stocky little axes at the Time Swing.

A horrid scream came from Torri's lips.

The LIVING MIST

By RALPH MILNE FARLEY

Warden Lawson had a strange power over the convicts of his prison, but Spike Torri was a different proposition. Then came the Mist—a mist that was living! And the life in it was that of Spike Torri!

WARDEN Lawson sent for "Spike" Torri around three that afternoon. This was another break for me, because the Boston *Times* had sent me down for a Sunday feature and I had run smack into a pair of fair-sized riots. I plastered my eye against the peek-hole in the adjoining room and got ready.

Torri came in a moment later. Slim, dapper even in prison grays, he walked over to stand in front of the warden's big walnut desk.

"What the hell is this?" Lawson barked. "You're not going to make a monkey out of me! Ten years you get for a bank job. So you put on an act when you get here, promise to reform, and like a horse's neck I make you a trusty a year ago. So today we have two riots—count 'em, two!—one in the dining hall, the other in the yard, and you refuse to spill the beans. Louse!"

Torri had been white-faced when he came in. Now the color came back to his cheeks, although his poise had been perfect all through. He rubbed his chin reflectively, grinned—the guy had charm, I'll admit that—and then spread out his hands.

"Warden," he said, "I thought it was about something serious. Like maybe you thought I was the skunk in the woodpile. Now, Warden, you wouldn't want me to be a stool pigeon, would you?"

"Yes," Lawson snapped, "I would! I'm running a prison, not a finishing school. If we don't get to the bottom of this, there'll be more trouble and some guys will get shot. You wouldn't want that to happen, would you?" Lawson pleaded.

Torri shrugged disarmingly. "Just between you and me, Warden," he said, "would that be much of a loss to the world?"

Touché! Lawson sprang up, fists clenched. Torri stood his ground, sure of himself, amused, knowing he was in the clear.

"Get out of my office!" the warden snarled. "Play games with me, huh?"

He advanced threateningly. Torri, half the size of the huge prison official, backed tactfully to the door and felt for the knob.

"By the way, Warden," Torri said as he got the door open, "I'm getting paroled in a month, you know. Going to work in my Dad's wholesale meat business. And," he added softly, "your daughter promised to marry me when I drove her to town yesterday."

"What!" Lawson got apoplectic. "How dare you say such a thing! Why, you're only a jailbird! A cheap common punk that I took pity on! So that's the way you repay me—ingrate!" Lawson balled his big fists. "Get back to your hole!" he thundered. "Yes, you — Number Six-eight-seven-three-five! And your privileges are revoked!"

If Torri had been a man, he would have planted his feet on the floor and talked back. Maybe that was what Lawson had hoped for. This, after all, was the crucial test. But Torri couldn't measure up to it. His cool agate eyes fell to the floor. His cheek muscles twitched spasmodically. He—cringed.

"Yes, sir," said Spike Torri meekly, and backed out the door.

I came in the room a moment later. Lawson was mopping his brow.

"Boy, that was a close one!" he breathed. "If that fellow had taken a poke at me he could have had Margery and my best wishes. But I knew the guy had a yellow streak in him—I was just hoping to make a man of him in other ways. Well, live and learn."

"You're," I said, "telling me!"

Lawson relaxed. "You're okay, son. Come on, I'll take you on a tour through the place myself. Then we'll have supper together. Help to round out your article—I'm just a family man at heart, and all that stuff. There'll be just Margery, Dr. Avery, and you and me."

I was glad the invitation came from him. If Warden Lamont Lawson, head of the State Penitentiary, had a daughter who gallivanted around with a prison trusty—hell, I wanted to meet the girl and see what made her tick. I had already met Avery—a frank, broad-shouldered young fellow just out of his internship.

The trip through the prison was interesting enough. Lawson had installed an efficient organization and it worked like a clock. The print shop, mill and foundry ran much like their counterparts on the outside, and the prisoners seemed to have an unusual amount of freedom. The riots, Lawson explained to me, were the result of overcrowding and an insufficient appropriation for food.

"We do the best with the funds at our disposal," he said. "If the people stand for slums and unemployment, we're going to have crime. I'm the fellow that's got to take it in the neck, when that happens. Society's chickens all come home to roost—right here!"

Supper that evening was a restrained affair. Lawson and I couldn't help thinking of the two riots—and Spike Torri. Young Dr. Avery was naturally diffident, evidently more so than usual tonight. He stared steadily at Margery Lawson with a sort of hurt, appealing look in his eyes.

Well, I couldn't blame him any—not for looking. Margery, in the popular parlance, was an eyeful. Clear-cut, almost cameolike features, burnished copper hair, and dark blue eyes which seemed troubled, though she said little. When she did speak, she ignored Avery completely. Trying to size her up, I could not for the life of me understand how this girl had fallen for a shallow punk like Torri. Sure, he'd fooled the warden. But you can't fool a woman, brother—they've got intuition!

After the dessert, Margery got up, saying she had a headache, and withdrew to her room with almost tactless haste. Lawson, Avery and I lit our cigars, and Lawson turned on the radio to a dance program.

After a bit: "Margery's a strange child," the warden began awkwardly.

Young Avery's sensitive face twitched. "She is just a child," he mumbled. "Maybe that's the reason."

I, of course, kept my mouth shut. My ears, too—officially. My article in the Boston *Times* would be concerned strictly with my prison tour. A good newspaperman, after all, prints news—not gossip. What the public doesn't know will never hurt it. Besides—

The dance band abruptly blacked out. We all sat up, tensing. Maybe Hitler had just taken over Greece—

"Flash! Your local newscaster, Benny Bartlett, has just learned that Spike Torri, notorious bank robber, escaped from the State Penitentiary tonight! The eight p. m. checkup revealed Torri missing from his cell. The cell-block is closed by double-doors, and both sets of locks are intact. So is the lock on Torri's own cell!

"Folks, I've got it exclusively that Torri's cellmate claims to have been asleep and to have heard nothing! According to Deputy Warden

Herman Wagner—"

Lawson jerked to his feet and switched off the radio.

"That damned local station!" he growled. He grabbed up the French phone from its stand and barked:

"Central 7997! Emergency! Yeah, this is Warden Lawson... Wagner? What the hell is going on? Why did you give out that story? How do you know Torri isn't hiding in the place somewhere?... *What?* You *didn't* give it out? You... Huh? You called here and my phone didn't answer? Why man, you're crazy—I've been here all evening!"

Avery and I stared at each other.

"Now get this," Lawson barked. "Phone that fool radio station, tell them you found Torri hiding in the prison laundry... Yeah, that's right. Then send a squad out with the bloodhounds. I'll meet you at the 'hollow'—that's where he'll be heading."

Lawson slammed the receiver down and slumped into a chair. His face seemed to have gone pale, and his eyes had a staring look about them.

"Something's screwy around here," he muttered. "Sherman, I've been holding out on you. Funny things have been going on around here lately, but I just couldn't place my finger on what's wrong."

That's me, Roy Sherman. "You mean," I said, "something uncanny—"

Lawson got up heavily and put a hand on my shoulder.

"Son," he said, "you came down here for a story. Well, I'm afraid that's just what you're going to get."

CHAPTER II
The Monster Rises

THE three of us emerged into the sweet-scented summer moonlight. A cooling breeze swept in from Cape Cod, a mile away. A manhunt on such a night seemed incongruous. One of the prison guards, running up, met us on the sidewalk.

"The dogs are headed for Richard's Woods, sir," he panted.

Lawson motioned to Avery and me to get into his car, which was parked at the curb, and soon we were speeding over the two-lane highway.

We flushed another guard at the outskirts of the woods, halted.

"The hounds are in there, sir," he reported. "Near the—the—"

He glanced inquiringly in my direction. Lawson nodded his shaggy head.

The man continued. "They're near the 'hollow', Warden." His voice was tinged with awe.

The night seemed suddenly not quite so warm and balmy as we drove on.

"I don't hear any baying," I remarked, with an attempt at calmness.

"Avery cut their vocal cords. Baying would give the chase away. Silent hounds are more terrifying to the pursued," Lawson said.

A cloud passed across the face of the moon, and I shuddered. Black night, heavy thickets shrouding the gaping mist-filled maw of the "hollow," which was a swamp-like depression in the woods, and a pack of silent bloodhounds relentless on the trail of a fugitive from justice—I shuddered again.

Lawson stopped the car moments later. About half a dozen guards had gathered, with their electric torches, carbines and sawed-off shotguns. One guard held two straining hounds in leash.

Deputy Warden Wagner lumbered up to report. "The dogs have traced him into that thicket, just as you expected. We then circled it, but there is no trail out. He must be still in there."

"Good!" Lawson snapped. "But keep dogs and men out until daylight. Might fall into the 'hollow' in the dark. Surround the place until morning."

Dr. Avery stayed on, but Warden Lawson and I drove back to town. Before turning in at my hotel, I wired my paper about Torri's escape and told them I was on the track of further news, which was about to break. The writing of the prison feature could wait—it was a Sunday article, anyway.

Shortly before daybreak, the warden called for me and drove me out to Richard's Woods again. As soon as it was fully light, we plunged into the thicket from all sides, alert and armed. The bloodhounds led the way straight to the rim of the hollow, where they recoiled with evident terror. I didn't feel much better myself at what I saw.

There was a saffron mist at the bottom of this pit within the hollow. It seemed to be seething with strange activity. Even as we peered down, *the saffron mist gathered itself into* a *stringy ball and floated upward!*

As the tenuous mass reached the level of the ground, from its evil midst a tentacle suddenly lanced out at Dr. Avery. He threw up his hands before his face, staggered backward from the hollow, tripped and fell. One of the hounds sprang forward protectively, only to receive the tentacle like a whiplash square across its muzzle.

The next moment the poor animal was writhing on the ground and pawing at the wound—or burn, rather, like that of a branding iron. Avery picked himself up, deftly tied a handkerchief across the dog's muzzle, pinioned its legs with its leash, and—assisted by one of the guards—carried it out gently to the car. There could be no doubt that the dog had been seriously burned.

Meanwhile the nauseous orange-yellow cloud had drifted up, over the tops of the trees, and away out of our sight. The bottom of the hollow now lay exposed to view for the first time, Lawson told me in an aside.

"For the—first time?" I asked him. "What is this, a sulphur deposit? Funny that no one seems to have heard anything about it, until now."

"Not at all," Lawson contradicted. "The town here, you know, is quite a summer resort. The prison is far enough on the outskirts not to cause an unpleasant atmosphere. But this hollow here—well, the local people keep quiet about it, so that it won't get into the newspapers. Be bad for the tourist trade, you know. Especially since the prison is located here, too."

WE crowded to the edge of the pit then and peered over its steep sides. The depression was much deeper than we had thought, and in its bottom were tightly packed the yellowed bones of thousands of small birds and animals. And—lying atop this pile was the skeleton of a man, contorted as though its owner had died in agony; a skeleton literally picked clean of flesh.

"Spike Torri!" Lawson remarked grimly with a sweep of his hand. "He tried his luck just once too often."

Several of the guards, religious fellows, nervously crossed themselves.

No one cared to risk crawling down into the hole to fetch this grisly relic, so ropes and grappling hooks were brought, and the bones were hoisted out.

From Bertillon measurements and the records of the prison dentist, it was unquestionably identified as the last physical remains of Spike Torri.

Later, Warden Lawson gave out a statement to the press that Spike Torri had been drowned in a pond in the woods, and that the reason for the earlier official false announcement of Torri's capture was to allay popular fear of a criminal at large. My own account, wired exclusively to the Boston *Times,* was more complete, but it did not mention the hollow and its legend.

Of course, the part about the hollow did eventually leak out in and around the town, and scores of inquisitive persons visited the spot. But by that time the abortive escape of Spike Torri had ceased to be news, and if anything much about the hollow got into the papers I didn't notice it.

Margery Lawson shut herself up in her room, and refused to see anyone, even Dr. Avery. And the young prison physician respected her grief, though he could not respect the cause of it. For it was only too obvious that the girl had fallen for this sleek ex-gangster.

Some subconscious hunch held me in town. I wrote up my Sunday feature article and mailed it in to the *Times.* Yet still I lingered. And, to kill time, I read all the local news.

And all at once I began to notice scattered items about the loss of cows and horses and other stock at various points throughout the county. Always the skeleton would be found, picked clean of flesh. The losses usually occurred at night.

Finally these items came to the attention of others than myself. Wolves were suspected, although none had been seen in this vicinity for a generation. I hired a car and toured the countryside, interviewed farmers (some of whom claimed to have actually seen the wolves), and wrote up a crackerjack of a yarn about it all for my paper.

But Warden Lawson, Dr. Paul Avery, and I had our own theory.

One evening when I was visiting at the warden's house, the phone rang. Lawson answered it. I paid no particular attention, until I noticed that he was frantically juggling the center of the phone-rest with one forefinger.

"Operator! Operator!" he barked. "I've been disconnected. Who was calling? All right, ring them back, please. They don't answer? That's strange. Well, keep trying them, and call me."

He replaced the phone in its cradle, then turned toward Avery and me, a strained expression on his face.

"That was Deputy Wagner's voice. He said 'Hello.' Then there was a choking gurgle, and the line went dead. I'm going over across to the prison. Something's wrong."

THE three of us hurried with him across the street. We rang and rang the doorbell at the main entrance, but no one came. We walked around under the wall and shouted up at several of the sentry boxes, but received no response. There were lights in the main office on the second floor, where Deputy Wagner should have been. We threw stones up against the lighted windows, but without rousing anyone.

Lawson charged back into his own house like a man gone berserk, dialed the headquarters of the local police and the captain of the local National Guard company.

"Jail break!" he snapped. "Rush all available men to the State Penitentiary, and surround the place!"

We had scarcely returned to the street again, when the screaming of motorcycle sirens signaled the arrival of the first detachment of police. These took up positions at strategic points around the gray stone buildings. A half hour later a sleepy company of national guardsmen trotted up. Machine guns were set up opposite the principal exits. Yet still not a sound came from within the prison, to indicate what the mutinous inmates were up to.

Equipped with a powerful long-focus electric flash, Warden Lawson began a tour around the walls.

"You two better keep under cover," he cautioned Avery and me. "The cons are probably armed."

"How about yourself?" I replied.

He laughed harshly. "Wouldn't dare pot *me*." It was the only time I ever heard him boast of his strange power over his charges.

Anyway Avery and I went with him. He trained his beam on the top of the wall and swept it along. It came to a stop on something white. We craned our necks and peered up through the darkness.

The white object was a human skeleton lying atop the wall, with one bony arm trailing down over the edge.

"We might have known," Avery breathed.

Sledgehammers were brought, and two husky policemen battered down the main door. Then, preceded by a squad of soldiers with automatic rifles and pistols alert, we entered the prison. Not a single living soul greeted or opposed us.

In the main office sat another human skeleton, slumped over the desk, with one bony hand resting on the cradle-phone. Every shred of flesh and clothing was gone, except on the head. The head was intact. Dr. Avery lifted it up, and the agonized fat face of Deputy Herman Wagner stared at us, pop-eyed, its jaw fallen open and frozen in that position.

A gasp of horror rose in unison. Then we all raced through the building, searching for what we knew instinctively we would find.

On the bare wires of the bunks in the guards' squad-room lay the skeletons of the day shift—with heads intact.

"Whoever did this was kind enough to leave identification easy," the captain of the soldiers commented grimly.

"Don't!" groaned the warden. "Each of these men was an old friend of mine."

At the entrance to the cell-block we found two seated skeletons. Heads intact, of course. But when we came to the cells, there was a difference; for, in the case of all the prisoners, the skulls too had been picked clean.

Sickened to our souls, we turned away. Warden Lawson, walking like a man in a dream, his eyes distant and vacant, extinguished all the lights, locked all the inside doors, and requisitioned a squad of soldiers to guard the battered entrance until morning.

Paul Avery edged up to me, his normally luminous brown eyes now slits, and whispered, "The mist has fed well this night."

His words snapped me out of my horrified daze. Bidding the distracted warden a "good evening" which he scarcely noticed, I raced back to my hotel and phoned my city editor the scoop of the year.

I HAD just hung up, when the operator rang me back.
"Paul Avery speaking. Come over as quickly as you can. Mr. Lawson, is taking this situation too hard, and Margery and I can't handle him."

I hopped a taxi and sped to the warden's home. Margery and Dr. Avery, with solemn faces and fingers entwined, met me at the door and ushered me into the den.

There sat Margery's father, his big body slumped in a chair, his bushy mane of hair rumpled, his leonine head in his strong hands.

"It's all my fault," he kept moaning in a monotone. "All my fault."

And nothing that the three of us said could snap him out of his stupor of remorse.

CHAPTER III
Abortive Attack

THE next few days were hectic ones for me. The inquest at the prison was front-page stuff. Staff writers from all the leading dailies in the country flew in, but I still maintained the inside news track.

The town was jammed with curiosity seekers, who even dared to invade the depths of the hollow and cart away its grisly contents, bone by bone. Hawkers appeared on the streets, selling miniature skeletons and little bottles filled with orange-yellow gas. It was the Lindbergh kidnap trial all over again, and worse.

Through it all Warden Lawson moved like a sleepwalker, but whether stunned into mental numbness or lost in unfathomable thoughts, we three who watched over him were unable to determine.

Together so constantly, Margery and Paul Avery became very close friends. They became so close, in fact, that one afternoon they slipped down to the church rectory and were married quietly by the minister.

Quiet, too, was the mist. The orange-yellow menace had not been sighted since its violent and all-embracing attack on the prison.

"It's sleeping off its orgy in some hideout," Avery suggested somberly. "This thing is a horrible monstrosity, and I wish the public would realize it and do something about it."

That was the strange part of it all. First news of the prison outrage had created a sensation. "The mist" had been played up in 96-point headlines. And then editors had begun to get cynical.

"Such a monster is beyond the realm of possibility," they snorted. "What probably happened is that the ventilation system, which runs through the prison's chemical laboratory, became choked with a powerful gas which eats away flesh and then dissipates itself in the air. Probably some convict was experimenting with a highly volatile form of mustard gas, and something went wrong."

I made my own investigation. I checked over every chemical in the place. I examined the records of chemicals bought for the past year by the prison's purchasing officer.

And there were insufficient chemicals, or combinations of them, to have compounded such wholesale death!

Being a newspaperman, I kept my discoveries to myself. Now was not the proper time to go off half-cocked on a wild-eyed tangent. I would have to wait and let things take their course. Of that much I was certain—the mist, whenever it was ready, would strike again.

Meanwhile, a meeting of minds could be of no harm. Margery, Paul Avery and I had numerous discussions on the nature of the mist. Leading scientists throughout the world wrote glib articles explaining the phenomenon as one sort of caustic gas or another; but somehow their explanations didn't sound very convincing.

For one thing, they all ducked what seemed to me to be the most significant fact of all, namely, that the heads of all the prisoners had been left fleshless, while the guards had kept their skulls intact. I felt that this was somehow the key to the whole morbid puzzle. Obviously the mist did things by calculation; obviously there was diabolical method in its madness...

Gradually the furor died down. Warden Lawson ceased to be a personality of news interest. Indeed, he ceased to have any individuality at all. He simply sat through the days with head bowed in his hands, as in a constant daze.

The newspapers had forgotten all about the affair at the State Penitentiary when the mist struck again. One morning a badly frightened farmer living on the outskirts of town phoned in to report that the whole of the adjoining farm was blotted out by yellow fog.

I WAS now representing a chain of papers, in addition to the Boston *Times*. I hastened to the scene by taxi, snapped shot after shot of the huge gaseous amoeba, and sent the films off by twin carrier pigeons. Our cameras take all pictures in duplicate, and it was well this time that they did. For as my two birds circled up after being released from their cage, a yellow tentacle lanced out, flicked one of them and dragged it back fluttering into the writhing mist. The other pigeon, with a terrified upsurge, escaped.

Shortly thereafter, crowds of morbid sightseers began to arrive. But now the holiday spirit, which had been evident during the inquest, was markedly absent. The present onlookers were intent and grim.

A stiff wind was blowing toward the mist from one side, but that did not seem to affect it other than to ruffle its pulsating surface. Someone suggested fighting it with fire, and instantly the crowd went determinedly to work piling up hay and fence rails along the boundary. Soon hot tongues of fire were lapping out at the tendrils of yellow mist.

The mist cringed back at the contact, and the throng let out a yell of triumph. The mist gave way, retreated, then surged aloft in a compact saffron ball, clear of the flames, to reveal for the first time the condition of the farm which it had invaded.

With the exception of one small shed, surmounted by a radio aerial—*radio* had been Farmer Johnson's hobby—not a building remained standing. There was not a tree, shrub, plant or even a blade of grass left on the entire farm. Alongside what had once been the barn, there lay now the bleached skeletons of two cows.

I got some excellent pictures, and released two more pigeons.

When the borderline fires died down, the ball of yellow fog descended again. Once more it spread out over the entire farm, licking out misty tentacles at the crowd until the people stampeded back to a safe distance. Then the mist relapsed into quiescence.

Later in the day, so I learned, the village fire department, called to extinguish a grass fire which had spread with a change in the wind, tried squirting both water and chemicals at the mist, but without any evident result.

That evening at the Lawsons', during a lull in the conversation, I was idly twiddling the dials of the radio set when the following message suddenly blared forth. I can give it verbatim, inasmuch as it was later reprinted in all the newspapers.

"We, the Mist, address the people of this State. We wish to live at peace with you. Do not attack us again with fire. Not that fire can hurt us, for you have seen that it cannot. But attacks on us irritate our patience. Do not try it again.

"As we said, we wish to live at peace with the world. Feed us two fat steers per day, and we will remain within the confines of the Johnson farm. Refuse us this very reasonable request, and we shall go on a rampage.

"No telling then where we shall strike. No citizen will be safe. You have already seen an example of our power in our raid on the State Penitentiary. We await an official reply on our own wave-length: fifteen-point-three."

SILENCE then. A creepy feeling ran down my spine.
"What the hell is this?" I muttered. "I don't get it. I don't get it at all."

Margery said, "I don't see how it could use the radio."

That's what got me sweating. "I've heard of screwy things, but never of a mist making up to a microphone."

Avery pursed his lips and said, "I think I've heard that voice before."

An expression of reminiscence and of pain flashed across Margery's face. Her jaw set and her blue eyes narrowed. "That was Spike Torri's voice," she said. "I could never forget it."

"But Torri is dead!" I exclaimed. "The Mist got him." (I didn't realize it then, but the Thing had assumed the proportions of a monster from that point on in my mind. It was a living Thing now—the Mist.

Paul Avery looked at me. "I wonder," he said. "I wonder if he is dead." That brought Warden Lawson out of his daze. The whole of his face lighted up, and his bushy black brows twitched He tensed his lips, snapped his fingers several times, nodded his head contentedly—and then lapsed back into quiescence.

All that evening we hung by the radio, waiting for an official reply from the State capital. But Governor Maverick, a shrewd politician, merely called in the press and issued a statement that he had begun an immediate investigation. He would, he said, have some definite news within twenty-four hours.

That gave me an idea. I phoned the State House and got the Governor's assistant secretary on the wire. He and I had been roommates at college.

"Joe," I said, "what's the payoff?"

His voice got very low. "For cripes' sake, don't let it get out that this came from me. Phone Professor Mordecai Miller at Harvard—you know, the world's leading authority on chemical poison. Tell him that you figure he's been called into the case—because who else would know what to do? So naturally he'll say 'yes,' that the Governor just got in touch with him."

"Thanks, pal," I said. "Call this number"—I gave him the listing—"if anything else breaks, huh? I won't be here, but leave word for me to call back."

So I phoned Professor Miller and got him just as he was about to leave on a chartered plane.

"Naturally I have been summoned by the Governor," he snapped. "Who else would be called in?"

Didn't like himself much, did he? I got my paper three minutes later.

We broke the news of Miller's imminent arrival hours ahead of any other sheet in the country.

Next morning I went out to the Johnson farm. Miller had been there for a couple of hours and had been working since before dawn, supervising the assembling of several trunkloads of laboratory apparatus. Although it was seven o'clock, a huge crowd had already gathered. Paul Avery had come with me, but he had insisted that Margery remain at home.

The local militia company was there, too, with a lot of peculiar-looking gadgets like fire extinguishers. And a dozen or more oil trucks.

Avery and I introduced ourselves to Professor Miller, a tall, lean, scholarly gentleman with a brown Vandyke beard and an expression of intense intolerance.

Avery started to tell him that the Mist was a living creature, possessed of a high degree of intelligence, and to be fought as such. But the Professor brushed him impatiently aside with a contemptuous, "What degrees do you hold, Dr. Avery?" and continued about his business.

OIL from the trucks was sprayed into the Mist from all sides. The Mist merely parted to let the streams through, then closed again like a trap when the streams petered out. Professor Miller's white teeth grinned with satisfaction through his brown beard.

The troops, with their engines of war at equal intervals, now surrounded the Johnson farm. Three shots from a revolver by their captain was the signal for them to get into action. Scores of flames belched in unison from their flame-throwers.

With a mighty hiss, the Mist recoiled inwardly from all sides. And the fuel oil, previously sprayed in and now uncovered, blazed up with a roar. The Mist had been trapped, taken by surprise. It contracted into a compact orange-colored ball in the very center of the farm, as the fire surged toward it.

Then with an upcurving wave along its entire periphery, the Mist sprang outward in all directions. A saffron tidal wave, it came. It blanketed the flames. Angry tentacles, like flames themselves, lanced out at the surrounding crowd, which scattered stumblingly with shrieks of terror.

When it was all over, and the Mist had withdrawn again to the proper confines of the Johnson farm, the flames had been blotted out, and the place was ringed with a row of human skeletons, all but one of which had its head still intact. That one exception was the skeleton of the late Professor Mordecai Miller of Harvard; *his* skull was eaten clean.

CHAPTER IV
Appeasement

O N our silent return to town, Margery Avery met us at the door with a long face and tears in her blue eyes. "Father's gone," she announced. "Gone? What do you mean, gone?" I demanded.

"I mean exactly that. Gone, skipped, fled! The Governor phoned demanding father's resignation as warden. Instead of replying, he just merely kissed me goodbye, and left."

She flashed a glance at her husband, and he added, "For some time I have thought his mind affected."

I stared first into Avery's clear-eyed virile face, then into Margery's smoothly chiseled features. Something was wrong here. Their reaction wasn't what one would expect under the circumstances. I sensed this, although I couldn't quite put my finger on it. But then, when do human beings ever react exactly as we expect them to?

I dashed into the house and made for the telephone, then hesitated. "Go ahead and call the *Times*," said Margery. "We don't mind."

I stared at her for a moment, then shrugged my shoulders, and put in a call for Boston, collect.

While I was talking to the City Desk, Margery and Avery tuned in on shortwave station 15.3, the Mist's "official" wave-length. As I hung up, they got the following:

We, the Mist, speaking. Now that we have added the mind of Professor Miller to our already composite mentality, we now know more about our own gaseous composition than the rest of the world will ever know. We are invulnerable. Why try to make war upon us, when all we wish is to live at peace with our neighbors?

If you refuse to make peace, then it is you who have become the aggressors, and we shall be reluctantly compelled to retaliate with whatever weapons are at our command. We can match frightfulness with frightfulness, if that be what the world wishes.

But, if our extremely reasonable terms are met, we shall take over no more territory. We, the Mist, have spoken.

Paul Avery squared his broad shoulders. "Well," he announced, "this confirms what I have suspected for some time. For years the Mist led a low state of almost vegetative existence in the bottom of the Richard's Woods hollow, feeding on plant life and on the bodies and minds of small animals and birds and insects. Then, by accident, Spike Torri stumbled into its maw.

"Now, at last, the Mist possessed a human mind, the most brilliant though depraved brain in American gangsterdom. Led by this distorted mentality, this Thing swept out of its hollow, attacked the State Penitentiary and absorbed the minds of all the other criminals there.

"But it was careful not to absorb the minds of any of those who were on the side of law and order; hence the untouched heads of Deputy Wagner and the prison guards. Professor Miller is just screwy enough that the Mist is willing to take a chance on adding him, too."

"Well," said Margery, with a touch of sarcasm in her voice, "now that we know all about it, what are we going to do?"

SHE amazed me! So calm and unaffected by this revelation that her former lover had become an amoeboid vampire, a menace to mankind! But, then, I never could quite understand this girl.

Avery answered, "We *don't* know everything. We know merely the composition of its mind. Before a successful attack can be made upon it, we must learn the nature of its body."

Thereafter the press was filled with scientific speculation as to what the Mist was, how it was able to "broadcast," whether it had a voice and knew how to speak over a microphone, or whether by its very nature it could set radio waves in motion.

A few days later Paul Avery moved his own laboratory apparatus from the now vacant penitentiary to a room in the Lawson house, and set to work to devise some sort of gadget for taking a sample of the Mist.

"For," as he declared, "we obviously cannot learn its real nature unless and until we analyze it."

"And even then," I said, "I wonder. What would a chemical analysis of the human body teach us of human powers and capabilities?"

Avery merely shrugged his broad shoulders. "We can but try."

To assist him with his work, he hired a gross repulsive person, introduced to me merely as "Old Tom." Scalp close-clipped. Face clean-shaven. No eyebrows or eyelashes. Lips pendulous and drooling.

I took an instant dislike to the fellow. He gave me the creeps. There was something elusively familiar about him, which just escaped me. Avery said that Old Tom was an ex-convict who had formerly assisted him in the prison laboratory, and that I had probably met Old Tom in my tour of the place. He had been released, his term completed, just in time to escape being devoured by the Mist.

But this explanation did not satisfy me. A newspaper reporter learns to sense when facts are being withheld from him. And furthermore, I had the uncanny feeling that Old Tom's gimlet eyes were fixed upon me whenever I turned my back.

I told Avery that I objected to his having a jailbird in his employ.

"Who knows but what he's in cahoots with Spike Torri?" I added.

Avery replied, "I need Old Tom in more ways than one. Not only can he help me in my laboratory work, but he can also keep us in touch with the underworld. *You* will appreciate that—later." Nor would he tell me what he meant by that last crack.

Margery sided with her husband, and so Old Tom stayed on. He must have known of my objections, and that they had been overruled, for now his fat face seemed always to bear a leer of triumph.

Curiously enough, New York's underworld chose that very week to line up behind a new leader. Crime reporters described him glowingly as a veritable mastermind; a big, heavyset man with a dominating personality.

One evening I found Paul Avery reading the papers. He looked up at me calmly, his finger pointing to the front-page account of New York's latest big shot.

"I told you his mind was affected," he said.

"What do you mean?" I demanded.

"Get on to yourself, Roy. That's Margery's father, and he's turned criminal in a big way."

I looked at him as though he were insane.

"You're nuts! I never heard of anything so screwy in my life."

Avery regarded me quizzically. "Wait and see," he said. "Wait and see."

THE State made one more attempt to destroy the Mist. One of the largest bombing planes available was borrowed from Mitchel Field on Long Island, to try to blast out the yellow fog that squatted low on the Johnson farm. The press, but not the populace, had been tipped off in advance, and so I was there on the sidelines at the impromptu press gallery.

The mist was unusually quiet that day, as the plane flew low above it on a reconnaissance flight. But it seemed to me that there was a tenseness and alertness to its quietude. From constant observation, I believed that I had learned to sense its moods.

After circling the farm once, the bomber flew straight across and loosed one two-thousand-pound bomb in the very center of the farm. A geyser of yellow gas, streaked with black dirt, spouted upward from the impact of the projectile; then bent suddenly in the direction of the departing ship. It lanced out with one rope-like tentacle, seized the luckless plane and yanked it down like a lassoed steer. Eager yellow fingers reached up from the surface of the Mist to meet the ship as it fell.

A moment later the Mist divided, leaving a narrow swath extending straight from the sidelines to the wreck of the plane. As we stared fascinated, yellow tentacles sprouted from each side-wall of the fog, reached into the cockpit and hauled out the struggling pilot. Holding the man suspended just off the ground, by one tentacle wrapped tightly around his neck, the Mist extended other tentacles and stripped the flesh from his writhing bones.

Horrified, unable to help, I shuddered and turned my face away from the grisly scene. A gasping sigh in unison escaped the crowd of newshawks. I opened my eyes and turned back. The Mist had closed in again, and was quiescent.

But as we gaped at its blank wall of yellow, it parted once more, disclosing a crater of dirt where the radio shed had stood. Rising from the ground, the Mist formed itself into letters of smoke, like those of a sky-writer:

"REBUILD!"

"Why should we rebuild?" someone shouted from the crowd.

The sky-writing oozed together again, and then reformed as:

"OR ELSE!"

We all broke, raced our cars to the nearest phones, and relayed this latest warning to our respective papers.

The reaction by the State authorities was immediate. Complete short-wave sending and receiving apparatus was rushed to the Johnson farm, and a courageous young radio engineer (under promise of ten thousand dollars anyway, and a substantial pension for his family if he should never return) entered a rift in the Mist, and rebuilt the station. The Mist permitted him to go and come without interference, as he brought in load after load of necessary materials. He was on the job for nearly a week.

From his reports, the public learned at last how the Mist, although possessing no voice as such, had been able to broadcast. For the Mist resumed communication with the world before the young engineer had rebuilt the radio shed's microphone. Thus it demonstrated only too graphically that in some manner, it had the power to set up an electrical disturbance in the tubes, capacities or inductances of the Johnson short-wave set.*

FINALLY the young radioman shouted, "One more trip, and it will be finished." He emerged from the cleft which stretched from the newly built shed to the edge of the farm. Then he shouted back:

"I fooled you, Mist. The radio set is complete and in working order; and I have escaped you!"

The cleft closed together with a snap, and from the already tuned loud-speakers set up in the press gallery, there intoned the voice of Spike Toni:

"That act of bravado was unnecessary. If he had trusted us, what is about to happen would not take place."

The voice sounded quite annoyed, it seemed to me. And that night the young electrician, his wife and their baby daughter died horribly in their beds, stripped of all their flesh—except the heads.

This latest outrage convinced the State authorities that no one was safe. So Governor Maverick promptly entered into an agreement with the Mist, whereby the Mist was to keep within the confines of its present territory, and was to be fed cattle at State expense, as long as it did so.

---

*In order for the mist to produce any sort of reaction in the Johnson short-wave set, it must have been capable of generating electrical impulses, perhaps similar to static. We might assume that the mist had the same power to produce positive electricity as clouds do, and thus cause lightning by attracting ground charges to it. Possibly the intelligence of the cloud was able to formulate static noises into recognizable words. —Ed.

CHAPTER V
The Antidote

THE events of the next few weeks can be summarized in brief. There was a sameness in their ominous monotony. Time after time the Mist oozed out of its agreed boundaries and occupied additional adjoining farms. Each time a new arrangement was solemnly agreed to, promising the Mist a larger, daily supply of steers, in return for its solemn agreement now at last to stay put.

A special railroad branch was built up to the edge of the Mist, to accommodate the daily cattle train. The town boomed as never before from the thousands upon thousands of tourists who converged from all over the continent to see this freak of nature. A large semicircular grandstand was built along one boundary of Mistland.

Yet, with each disregard of former commitments by the Mist, with each further extension of fog-enshrouded territory, there were popular rumblings. There was increased insistence by a growing faction of public opinion, that someday this policy of appeasement would have to come to an end, that someday America would have to fight the Mist to a showdown, or become completely its slave.

Meanwhile the State Penitentiary had been reopened, and Paul and Margery Avery had been ousted from their State-owned home to make room for the new warden. My two young friends moved to a cottage, on a small island in the bay close to the mainland, and I moved in to live with them. Old Tom was there too, of course, helping Avery in his laboratory and doing odd jobs around the place, though he frequently was absent for several days at a time, on "business of his own." The nature of this business was not confided to me.

I saw very little of Avery and Margery, so busy was I on my reportorial work. I could sense that the two of them walked in the shadow of a great fear, and so were not very communicative. Avery did not go near the Mist, but built device after device in his laboratory, only to discard them all.

"I want to be sure in advance that it will work," he explained to me. "For I feel certain that our enemy will give me only one chance, and I can't afford to fail."

Meanwhile, New York's new Public Enemy Number 1 was doing

all right by himself. He held up an armored car down on Wall Street, a feat heretofore considered well-nigh impossible, in view of the way the financial sector is policed. He organized a new restaurant racket, and the District Attorney's office nearly went crazy trying to get frightened restaurant owners to sign complaints.

So fantastic became his exploits, in fact, that he literally crowded the Mist off the front page. My paper was about to recall me to Boston, because the quiescent activities of the Mist no longer rated a staff correspondent.

But now I found, dropped right into my lap, a new source of copy. Old Tom, by virtue of his previous gangland connections, was able to give me tips about the activities of this new Public Enemy Number 1 well in advance of the stories breaking in the press. And so I stayed on.

But the Mist, jealous at being elbowed out of the limelight, demanded that my stories be suppressed. The Governor ordered me to stop. I claimed my constitutional right of "freedom of the press," and certain elements promptly threatened to run me out of the State.

"Pipe down!" Avery advised me, "I'm ready to give you some *real* news."

He led me into his laboratory, and showed me what he had devised.

IT was a strong steel bottle lined with shatterproof glass. Its mouth was capped by a hermetic shutter, which could be opened or closed at will by an electric impulse sent along a pair of long wires, which also served as a tow-rope for the bottle.

With a vacuum pump Avery exhausted the air from the bottle, and then sealed it. All was in readiness.

I drove him out to the Mist in the car I'd bought. At his command, I turned the car around facing toward town again, and sat at the wheel with the motor running. Avery approached the wall of yellow smoke.

Swinging the bottle round and round his head by its wire rope, he let go and launched it far into the midst of the Mist. Click! Click! He pressed two electric buttons in quick succession. Then he hauled in on the cable, hand over hand for dear life.

That portion of the Mist nearby seethed in angry confusion; then reared up over us, with pawlike knobs projecting from its upper edge, like a panther preparing to pounce.

Clutching his precious bottle close to his chest, Avery raced to the car and plunged in beside me. We were off and away. And after us, like a swirling tornado, roared the Mist.

It had taken the Mist several seconds to gather itself together after that first abortive pounce, and so we got several hundred yards head start. But now, although we were tearing along over the concrete at not less than eighty-five, the yellow smoke-cloud slowly and steadily gained upon us.

"We aren't going to make it!" Avery groaned, glancing back as I drove the car across the Simpson's Creek Bridge and entered town.

I glanced back too, just in time to see the Mist halt abruptly at the edge of the creek, and rear up into the air like a cowboy's horse reined suddenly back onto its haunches. Then it veered to the westward, upstream.

I slowed down just in time to avoid running into an interstate bus.

We reached the cottage without further pursuit. Neither Margery nor Old Tom were anywhere about, but at the moment we had forgotten them.

Avery and I went at once to his laboratory. He was pale and shaking like a leaf, not so much because of the yellow death from which we had just escaped, as from the fear that his quest would prove fruitless.

With trembling hands, he sucked the contents of the steel bottle into a vacuumized glass container. Then he sank into a chair from sheer relief. For the vacuum container was now filled with seething yellow gas! The daring attempt had not failed.

Margery came in carrying a pail; and in response to her husband's frantic query as to where she had been, she explained that she had gone down to the rocks to get some sea water for her aquarium, Margery's greatest hobby.

Avery proudly showed her his capture. "Now to analyze it," he announced.

The sample of mist was now boiling more violently. As we clustered about it, it burst its prison asunder with a clatter of broken glass, hung above our heads for a moment, then fled and cowered in one corner of the room.

"Don't let it escape!" Avery cried in frantic tones.

I SLAMMED the door, and he pulled down and latched the only window. Ripping off her blouse, Margery stuffed it under the door and into the keyhole.

"We've got you, Mr. Mist!" Paul Avery exclaimed in triumph.

But his joy was short-lived. The ball of gas swelled to twice its size. Tentacles trickled out in all directions from its base. And then this synthetic octopus began to crawl slowly forward.

Margery's blue eyes went wide, she clenched her two hands in front of her face and shrieked. The creature sprang upon her and stifled her screams, with one rope-like arm wrapped round and round her smooth young throat.

Avery glanced frantically about for some weapon, saw the pail of sea water, snatched it up and hurled its contents squarely at Margery and the beast.

And there was no longer any beast there! Not a trace of mist remained!

Margery sank dripping to the floor, and began to sob convulsively. But even as he sprang to comfort her in his strong arms, Paul Avery's brown eyes glowed with triumph.

"Margery, dear," he soothed. "Believe me, we've got it licked! We know the antidote. Salt water will destroy the Mist! The Mist doesn't even dare to pass over an arm of the sea. It tried to follow me home, but recoiled when we crossed Simpson's Creek. We are safe from it here on this island."

Margery stopped her sobbing, and smiled up at her husband with shining eyes.

A darkness suddenly enshrouded the room. I flashed a glance at the window. A thick yellow fog had engulfed the house. Wisps of yellow haze were beginning to seep in around the window.

Avery and Margery immediately sensed the situation.

"Salt!" Avery cried.

But I wondered. The Mist had got up sufficient courage to cross the channel between our island and the shore. Was it no longer allergic to salt?

"In the kitchen!" Margery answered. "There's a bag of salt in the cabinet."

She tore open the door, then recoiled in the face of the dense yellow fog gathered in the hallway.

Avery remembered a cup of salt on one of the laboratory shelves. As tenuous tentacles reached in through the doorway to seize his wife, he hurled a handful of salt past her. The Mist retreated precipitately. Avery followed it with cup in hand, drove it from the house with pinches of salt, as Margery rushed for the kitchen and snatched up the precious bag of white ammunition from the kitchen cabinet.

Then before the Mist could return, we closed all the doors and windows. Next we mixed up a salt solution in tubs and pails and bowls, emptied out all the fire extinguishers and filled them with salt water, and packed all the door and window cracks with salt-soaked cloths. We were now prepared to withstand a siege.

"That's all very well," I objected, as we paused panting from our labors, "but unfortunately the Mist can eat wood. You saw how it destroyed the buildings on the Johnson farm. Undoubtedly it is gnawing through your roof right now."

To my surprise, Avery chuckled. "I'm going to phone the fireboat, give the Mist a real load of antidote."

BUT he couldn't raise "central."
Gradually the realization dawned on us that, somehow, the Mist had cut the telephone wires. We afterward discovered that this had been very simply accomplished by eating away the insulation, thus permitting a short-circuit between the two twisted cords.

"Well," Avery declared, "I'll have to go for help."

We begged him not to, but he insisted. I offered to go instead; but, when I realized that the only way to keep clear of the Mist would be to *swim* clear to town, and when I took a good look at Avery's broad shoulders, I piped down.

So Avery stripped himself and smeared his body with salt. Then, fire extinguisher in hand, he flung open the front door. The circumambient Mist recoiled, as Avery raised his weapon menacingly. Then he dashed out, and the yellow fog closed over him. We heard a splash.

Craning our ears, we fancied that we could hear a rhythmic ripple, as of a swimmer, growing gradually fainter, but we couldn't be sure—it might have been merely the waves on the rocks. At last silence. The Mist surged in at us again, and we slammed the door in its face. Once more we packed the cracks, and waited. Waited.

But we did not sit and wait. Extinguishers in hand, we patrolled the house. Holes began to appear in the inside walls; but we drove back, with squirts of saline solution, the yellow fog which filtered in.

Faster and faster we had to work, as more and more holes appeared. Finally we retreated to the laboratory, barricaded the door and waited.

Holes appeared in the door and walls. Frantically we fought. Our lungs became raw with exertion. At last we had to quit. Not only were we too tired to struggle any further, but our last supply of salt water was exhausted. Margery crept into my arms and whimpered, as we awaited the inevitable end.

But the intruding jets of yellow vapor ceased their infiltration. Withdrew, even. It became lighter out.

"Look, Margery!" I cried, dragging her to the window.

All around us the Mist was rising. It was drifting away. I could make out the lines of the shore; the bulk of a boat.

It was the town fireboat, all its streams of salt water playing upon our little island. We were saved!

Margery and I rushed out of the house to greet Avery, as the fireboat docked and he sprang ashore. Soon the young couple were in each other's arms.

Far overhead hung an angry churning ball of yellow smoke, which finally shot off to the northwestward in the direction of the Johnson farm. The Averys' cottage looked as though it had been through the mill, but its burns were not too many to be patched up.

I went immediately ashore to phone the story to my paper, and soon the State was buzzing with plans for a concerted attack on the Mist with fire engines and salt water.

CHAPTER VI
The Trick

THE Mist promptly put a stop to these plans. That night the Thing went on a violent rampage. When morning dawned, the death toll of men, women and children, far and wide, mounted to over a thousand! The Mist must have divided itself into hundreds of separate units, in order to accomplish such a carnage.

Then came its broadcast ultimatum to the Governor:

We, the Mist, insist that you give a definite promise that there shall be no more attacks upon us. And no more encirclement. We are to be free to expand as and where we see fit. Cattle are to be furnished to us, adequate to our needs.

That part of our mind which was the mind of Professor Miller has devised a defense against salt water, so Dr. Avery's discovery has been in vain.

But as indemnity for his attack upon us, we demand that his wife Margery be delivered up to us with the next load of cattle. That part of us which was Spike Torri desires to blend his soul with hers.

Refuse our demands, and there will be another shambles. We, the Mist, have spoken.

Governor Maverick immediately acceded to all of these demands, except one. To the honor of his memory, be it said that he refused to deliver up Margery Avery, declaring that he would not send one innocent human victim to death, regardless of what reprisals might follow such refusal.

That night the Governor died in his bed, a skeleton stripped except as to the head.

We rushed Margery to a cell in the penitentiary and organized a squad of guards equipped with fire extinguishers loaded with salt water. Margery was let alone.

"All of which proves," I announced the next day through my paper, "that the Mist's claim that its absorbed Professor Miller has discovered an antidote for salt water, its mortal enemy, is sheer nonsense."

Throughout the country, the citizenry began to arm themselves with salt-water defenses. And as if this were not turmoil enough, gangland, undoubtedly led by ex-Warden Lamont Lawson, struck simultaneously and effected an epochal haul of banks and jewelry stores.

The reaction of the Mist to the arming of America was surprisingly conciliatory. Over the air, it announced that for the present, it would refrain from further reprisals, if the U. S. Government would capture and deliver up to it Public Enemy No. 1—the man whose identity only Avery and I knew about. Incredible or not, I had to admit that the second-hand description of New York's new criminal mastermind could only point to one man.

The Mist concluded:

For we need this criminal's brain to add to our already

superhuman mind. The State can kill two birds with one stone by delivering him up: rid yourselves of a notorious gangster, and comply with our demands. I might add that this criminal genius was once known in this region as Lamont Lawson, warden of the State Penitentiary.

TO say I was startled would be to put it mildly. The secret which Avery and I had so closely guarded was now common public property. How would poor Margery take it?

Margery took it altogether too well. When I tried to soothe her, she became distant, almost impolite. I was so shocked that words failed me altogether.

At any rate, the Mist's suggestion captivated the public imagination, and soon the President, the Governors of most of the States, the Mayors of many cities, and even public-spirited private citizens were offering a rapidly snowballing reward for the capture of Lamont Lawson, dead or alive.

I came unexpectedly upon Margery Avery and Old Tom discussing the situation. What I heard was incredible.

"I've a mind to go after that reward. It's stupendous!" Old Tom was saying.

I am an old man, and those millions will mean a lot to those whom I love. Also think of the service to my country!"

"Oh, you dear, dear man," Margery cried, flinging her arms around the repulsive creature and kissing him full on the mouth.

They hadn't noticed me. I turned and staggered from the scene, my arm across my eyes. Margery Avery, conspiring to betray her father into a living death! I would have thrashed any man who breathed that such a thing was possible.

And now, how to warn Paul Avery without smearing Margery? This problem was still unsolved when a few days later, on my return from a jaunt to town, Avery, his large brown eyes shining, his broad young shoulders resolutely squared, beckoned me into his laboratory and pointed dramatically to an object on the floor. *It was Lamont Lawson, bound and gagged!*

"Now for the reward, and to save the world," he declaimed.

I recoiled in horror. "You too?" I cried.

"Certainly. We planned it that way." *"You planned it that way!"* I was absolutely thunderstruck.

"Yep—Mr. Lawson, Margery and I. We had you fooled all the while. Please forgive us. But there was too much at stake to trust even you."

Margery joined us. Avery stepped over to the bound figure and snatched off its black wig and glued-on eyebrows.

Before me now lay—Old Tom!

"Oh, so it isn't Mr. Lawson! It's only Old Tom!" I exclaimed in relief. "Serves the fellow right for his treachery.

Avery removed the gag and helped the bound figure to sit up. From it came the familiar booming voice of ex-Warden Lamont Lawson.

"Treachery, my hat! Never went away, except for excursions into gangland. Merely shaved my head. Posed as Old Tom. Never was any Old Tom except me."

"But why give yourself up to the Mist?" I remonstrated. "Surely this young couple would rather have you than all the rewards in the world."

"You know we would, Dad," Margery breathed. There were tears in her blue eyes.

"Yes, I know, child," he replied, looking up at her. "But I've made up my mind. There's no turning aside now."

There came a knock at the front door. As Margery went to answer it, Paul Avery hastily replaced the wig, eyebrows and gag on Mr. Lawson. Then the police entered and carted him away. We never saw him again.

I COULD not speak for a full minute. Finally I got a grip on myself. "Paul," I exclaimed, "for God's sake, let me in on this before I go nuts. It—it just doesn't make sense!"

He came over and put a soothing hand on my shoulder.

"Take it easy, old man. There really isn't such a great mystery to it. You see, the warden felt that Torri's death at the hands of the Mist was his own responsibility. He brooded over it for days. Then, that night when it made its first broadcast, Lawson knew that Spike Torri, whose voice the Mist was using, had been absorbed by the monster.

"That woke him up from his despondency. He realized, then, that the only way that he could come into contact with the Mist, was to so build himself up as a gang leader that the Mist would want to absorb him for his criminal mentality."

Margery broke in, "That's it exactly. You see, through his position as warden, Dad knew just which criminals to contact in New York. So he bought some padded-out clothes, shaved his head and eyebrows, and got some false hair and a pair of brows. You see, he didn't want to look too much like himself.

"When he was in New York, he used the fake makeup, which made him resemble his real self. When he showed up here as Old Tom, his nostrils and cheeks were distorted with putty, his face was smeared with dirt, he wore dirty old clothes and he removed his false makeup."

I was so stunned by the whole trick, as well as by the sickening certainty of the final outcome, that I couldn't say another word. I went up to my room, locked the door and for long hours sat at the open window, gazing out over the rocks and the sea.

CHAPTER VII
The Devil Disappears

GANGLAND, of course, raised hell. Deprived of the best brain ever to come their way, they were like a flock of sheep without a leader. They actually became so brazen as to send unsigned telegrams to the new Governor, demanding Lamont Lawson's release. They threatened to charter a plane and bomb the State capital to smithereens.

Caught between two fires, the authorities were nevertheless more afraid of the Mist than of the combined forces of gangdom. A double guard was placed around the State Penitentiary, and no rescue was effected or even attempted.

Knowing the Mist as we did, we fully expected it would decide to stand for no delay, but would invade the prison in search of its victim. Yet we miscalculated the Mist's colossal ego.

Everything, the Mist stated, must come off according to Hoyle. Lamont Lawson would have to be turned over to the Thing after an appropriate official ceremony on the Johnson farm!

That was too much for me. I got the City Desk on the phone.

"Dan, this is Sherman. Listen—send me out a relief on this Mist business, will you? Honest, I can't take it any more. I can't stand to see Lawson being swallowed up like that..."

There was an awkward silence. Then I heard, "You can have a month's vacation, Roy. After that crazy ceremony. But you knew Lawson, you admired him, and you're the man who's got to cover his last bow. Write anything you like—we'll print it."

SO it finally came off, two days later. Paul and Margery Avery went out alone to sit on the rocks, their hands clasped tightly together. The reaction had set in now. They realized they had been party to a magnificent sacrifice—and a ghastly tragedy. They sat there now, silent, tears streaming down their cheeks.

I took the little launch to the mainland. Then I got my car out of the garage and drove to the Johnson farm.

There was a tremendous crowd gathered on the sidelines. Yet not a soul might have been there, so silent was every throat.

Promptly at ten o'clock an official limousine drew up. Out of it stepped Governor Maverick's successor and Lamont Lawson, in the custody of two prison guards. The little party proceeded amid packed silence to a little bandstand built for the occasion. The Governor took a last look at Lawson, standing there perfectly calm, an unfathomable smile on his face, and shuddered. Then he approached a microphone.

From my place in the press gallery I craned my neck forward, fascinated, sickened, incredulous.

The Governor raised his voice. "Mist, we are ready!"

The saffron, nebulous monster divided itself in a narrow cleft, whose opening was directly in front of the Governor's stand. While everyone strained forward, horrified, Lamont Lawson was led from the stand to the seething entrance.

The Thing spoke then:

We, the Mist, gratefully accept this gift from the people. With this new super-mind which you have added to ours, we are now invincible. There can be no stopping our expansion. Lamont Lawson—step forward into my midst.

Down the narrow corridor Lawson strode, right into the very depths of the monster. He never faltered, he never once looked back. His heavy shoulders swung jauntily, and I could not be sure but I thought his fists were clenched.

The Mist resumed:

We, the Mist, shall no longer temporize or pretend. From now on, our bargains with mankind will be merely truces. You shall purchase dearly each pause in our inexorable advance.

Our next demand is that we be fed Margery Avery, to be our wife; and Dr. Paul Avery, to feast on, all but the head. For no brain that is on the side of law and order shall ever pollute our composite mentality.

By then Lamont Lawson had disappeared into the bowels of the Thing. Like the closing of a trap the gelatinous corridor snapped shut. Suddenly the air was split with the Mist's angry voice—the voice of Spike Tonni. The words were no longer impersonal, but strident, angry.

"Now look here, Warden! I'm running this show! Don't try to bulldoze me!"

THE booming laugh of Lamont Lawson came back, confident, triumphant.

"Why, you two-bit punk! And the rest of you mugs that are in on this—get back in your holes, where you belong! We may all be disembodied spirits here, but that doesn't change a damned thing, get it? To me, you're still a bunch of rats and I'm the boss. Want to make anything of it?"

With a great convulsion, as of two wrestlers suddenly covered with a blanket, the Mist writhed inward on itself. Seething, churning, it wrapped itself finally in a compact ball. Then it rose slowly into the air, heading southeast.

I heard later that the yellow cloud-ball passed over our cottage, and halted just above and beyond the beach. Then, spreading apart, its tentacles formed into the letters P-A-U-L. Reforming, it spelled out M-A-R-G-E-R-Y.

There was a violent churning as the thing rolled inward again into its compact ball. There was a brief struggle before the last tentacle was sucked into the orange-yellow mass.

Then the Mist rose into the sky, heading nebulously out to sea.

Warden Lawson was herding his vicious charges into oblivion.

The Day TIME

Dave Miller pulled the trigger—and time stopped! Was he the only man left alive?

*A*LL *Dave Miller wanted to do was commit suicide in peace. He tried, but the things that happened after he'd pulled the trigger were all wrong. Like everyone standing around like statues. No St. Peter, no pearly gate, no pitchforks or halos. He might just as well have saved the bullet!*

D AVE MILLER would never have done it, had he been in his right mind. The Millers were not a melancholy stock, hardly the sort of people you expect to read about in the morning paper who have taken their lives the night before. But Dave Miller was drunk—abominably, roaringly so—and the barrel of the big revolver, as he stood against the sink, made a ring of coldness against his right temple.

STOPPED MOVING

by BRADNER BUCKNER

Dave Miller pushed with all his strength,
but the girl was as immovable
as Gibraltar.

Dawn was beginning to stain the frosty kitchen windows. In the faint light, the letter lay a gray square against the drain-board tiles. With the melodramatic gesture of the very drunk, Miller had scrawled across the envelope:

"This is why I did it!"

He had found Helen's letter in the envelope when he staggered into their bedroom fifteen minutes ago—at a quarter after five. As had frequently happened during the past year, he'd come home from the store a little late...about twelve hours late, in fact. And this time Helen had done what she had long threatened to do. She had left him.

The letter was brief, containing a world of heartbreak and broken hopes.

"I don't mind having to scrimp, Dave. No woman minds that if she feels she is really helping her husband over a rough spot. When business went bad a year ago, I told you I was ready to help in any way I could. But you haven't let me. You quit fighting when things got difficult, and put in all your money and energy on liquor and horses and cards. I could stand being married to a drunkard, Dave, but not to a coward..."

So she was trying to show him. But Miller told himself he'd show her instead. Coward, eh? Maybe this would teach her a lesson! Hell of a lot of help she'd been! Nag at him every time he took a drink. Holler bloody murder when he put twenty-five bucks on a horse, with a chance to make five hundred. What man wouldn't do those things?

His drugstore was on the skids. Could he be blamed for drinking a little too much, if alcohol dissolved the morbid vapors of his mind?

Miller stiffened angrily, and tightened his finger on the trigger. But he had one moment of frank insight just before the hammer dropped and brought the world tumbling about his ears. It brought with it a realization that the whole thing was his fault. Helen was right—he was a coward. There was a poignant ache in his heart. She'd been as loyal as they came, he knew that.

He could have spent his nights thinking up new business tricks, instead of swilling whiskey. Could have gone out of his way to be pleasant to customers, not snap at them when he had a terrific hangover. And even Miller knew nobody ever made any money on the horses—at least, not when he needed it. But horses and whiskey and business had become tragically confused in his mind; so here he was, full of liquor and madness, with a gun to his head.

Then again anger swept his mind clean of reason, and he threw his chin up and gripped the gun tight.

"Run out on me, will she!" he muttered thickly. "Well—this'll show her!"

In the next moment the hammer fell...and Dave Miller had "shown her."

MILLER opened his eyes with a start. As plain as black on white, he'd heard a bell ring—the most familiar sound in the world, too. It was the unmistakable tinkle of his cash register.

"Now, how in hell—" The thought began in his mind; and then he saw where he was.

The cash register was right in front of him! It was open, and on the marble slab lay a customer's five-spot. Miller's glance strayed up and around him.

He was behind the drug counter, all right. There were a man and a girl sipping cokes at the fountain, to his right; the magazine racks by the open door; the tobacco counter across from the fountain. And right before him was a customer.

Good Lord! he thought. Was all this a—a dream?

Sweat oozed out on his clammy forehead. That stuff of Herman's that he had drunk during the game—it had had a rank taste, but he wouldn't have thought anything short of marihuana could produce such hallucinations as he had just had. Wild conjectures came boiling up from the bottom of Miller's being.

How did he get behind the counter? Who was the woman he was waiting on? What—

The woman's curious stare was what jarred him completely into the present. Get rid of her! was his one thought. Then sit down behind the scenes and try to figure it all out.

His hand poised over the cash drawer. Then he remembered he didn't know how much he was to take out of the five. Avoiding the woman's glance, he muttered:

"Let's see, now, that was—uh—how much did I say?"

The woman made no answer. Miller cleared his throat, said uncertainly:

"I beg your pardon, ma'am—did I say—seventy-five cents?"

It was just a feeler, but the woman didn't even answer to that. And it was right then that Dave Miller noticed the deep silence that brooded in the store.

Slowly his head came up and he looked straight into the woman's eyes. She returned him a cool, half-smiling glance. But her eyes neither blinked nor moved. Her features were frozen. Lips parted, teeth showing a little, the tip of her tongue was between her even white teeth as though she had started to say "this" and stopped with the syllable unspoken.

Muscles began to rise behind Miller's ears. He could feel his hair stiffen like filings drawn to a magnet. His glance struggled to the soda fountain. What he saw there shook him to the core of his being.

The girl who was drinking a coke had the glass to her lips, but apparently she wasn't sipping the liquid. Her boyfriend's glass was on the counter. He had drawn on a cigarette and exhaled the gray smoke. That smoke hung in the air like a large, elongated balloon with the small end disappearing between his lips. While Miller stared, the smoke did not stir in the slightest.

There was something unholy, something supernatural, about this scene!

With apprehension rippling down his spine, Dave Miller reached across the cash register and touched the woman on the cheek. The flesh was warm, but as hard as flint. Tentatively, the young druggist pushed harder; finally, shoved with all his might. For all the result, the woman might have been a two-ton bronze statue. She neither budged nor changed expression.

Panic seized Miller. His voice hit a high hysterical tenor as he called to his soda-jerker.

"Pete! *Pete!*" he shouted. "What in God's name is wrong here!"

The blond youngster, with a towel wadded in a glass, did not stir. Miller rushed from the back of the store, seized the boy by the shoulders, tried to shake him. But Pete was rooted to the spot.

Miller knew, now, that what was wrong was something greater than a hallucination or a hangover. He was in some kind of trap. His first thought was to rush home and see if Helen was there. There was a great sense of relief when he thought of her. Helen, with her grave blue eyes and understanding manner, would listen to him and know what was the matter.

HE left the haunted drug store at a run, darted around the corner and up the street to his car. But, though he had not locked the car, the door resisted his twisting grasp. Shaking, pounding, swearing, Miller wrestled with each of the doors.

Abruptly he stiffened, as a horrible thought leaped into his being. His gaze left the car and wandered up the street. Past the intersection, past the one beyond that, on up the thoroughfare until the gray haze of the city dimmed everything. And as far as Dave Miller could see, there was no trace of motion.

Cars were poised in the street, some passing other machines, some turning corners. A street car stood at a safety zone; a man who had leaped from the bottom step hung in space a foot above the pavement. Pedestrians paused with one foot up. A bird hovered above a telephone pole, its wings glued to the blue vault of the sky.

With a choked sound, Miller began to run. He did not slacken his pace for fifteen minutes, until around him were the familiar, reassuring trees and shrub-bordered houses of his own street. But yet how strange to him!

The season was autumn, and the air filled with brown and golden leaves that tossed on a frozen wind. Miller ran by two boys lying on a lawn, petrified into a modern counterpart of the sculptor's "The Wrestlers." The sweetish tang of burning leaves brought a thrill of terror to him; for, looking down an alley from whence the smoke drifted, he saw a man tending a fire whose leaping flames were red tongues that did not move.

Sobbing with relief, the young druggist darted up his own walk. He tried the front door, found it locked, and jammed a thumb against the doorbell. But of course the little metal button was as immovable as a mountain. So in the end, after convincing himself that the key could not be inserted into the lock, he sprang toward the back.

The screen door was not latched, but it might as well have been the steel door of a bank vault. Miller began to pound on it, shouting:

"Helen! Helen, are you in there? My God, dear, there's something wrong! You've got to—"

The silence that flowed in again when his voice choked off was the dead stillness of the tomb. He could hear his voice rustling through the empty rooms, and at last it came back to him like a taunt: "*Helen! Helen!*"

CHAPTER II
Time Stands Still

FOR Dave Miller, the world was now a planet of death on which he alone lived and moved and spoke. Staggered, utterly beaten, he made no attempt to break into his home. But he did stumble around to the kitchen window and try to peer in, anxious to see if there was a body on the floor. The room was in semi-darkness, however, and his straining eyes made out nothing.

He returned to the front of the house, shambling like a somnambulist. Seated on the porch steps, head in hands, he slipped into a hell of regrets. He knew now that his suicide had been no hallucination. He was dead, all right; and this must be hell or purgatory.

Bitterly he cursed his drinking, that had led him to such a mad thing as suicide. Suicide! He—Dave Miller—a coward who had taken his own life! Miller's whole being crawled with revulsion. If he just had the last year to live over again, he thought fervently.

And yet, through it all, some inner strain kept trying to tell him he was not dead. This was his own world, all right, and essentially unchanged. What had happened to it was beyond the pale of mere guesswork. But this one thing began to be clear: This was a world in which change or motion of any kind was a foreigner.

Fire would not burn and smoke did not rise. Doors would not open, liquids were solid. Miller's stubbing toe could not move a pebble, and a blade of grass easily supported his weight without bending. In other words, Miller began to understand, change had been stopped as surely as if a master hand had put a finger on the world's balance wheel.

Miller's ramblings were terminated by the consciousness that he had an acute headache. His mouth tasted, as Herman used to say after a big night, as if an army had camped in it. Coffee and a bromo were what he needed.

But it was a great awakening to him when he found a restaurant and learned that he could neither drink the coffee nor get the lid off the bromo bottle. Fragrant coffee-steam hung over the glass percolator, but even this steam was as a brick wall to his probing touch. Miller started gloomily to thread his way through the waiters in back of the counter again.

Moments later he stood in the street and there were tears swimming in his eyes.

"Helen!" His voice was a pleading whisper. "Helen, honey, where are you?"

There was no answer but the pitiful palpitation of utter silence. And then, there was movement at Dave Miller's right!

Something shot from between the parked cars and crashed against him; something brown and hairy and soft. It knocked him down. Before he could get his breath, a red, wet tongue was licking his face and hands, and he was looking up into the face of a police dog!

Frantic with joy at seeing another in this city of death, the dog would scarcely let Miller rise. It stood up to plant big paws on his shoulders and try to lick his face. Miller laughed out loud, a laugh with a throaty catch in it.

"Where'd you come from, boy?" he asked. "Won't they talk to you, either? What's your name, boy?"

There was a heavy, brass-studded collar about the animal's neck, and Dave Miller read on its little nameplate: "Major."

"Well, Major, at least we've got company now," was Miller's sigh of relief.

For a long time he was too busy with the dog to bother about the sobbing noises. Apparently the dog failed to hear them, for he gave no sign. Miller scratched him behind the ear.

"What shall we do now, Major? Walk? Maybe your nose can smell out another friend for us."

They had gone hardly two blocks when it came to him that there was a more useful way of spending their time. The library! Half convinced that the whole trouble stemmed from his suicide shot in the head—which was conspicuously absent now—he decided that a perusal of the surgery books in the public library might yield something he could use.

THAT way they bent their steps, and were soon mounting the broad cement stairs of the building. As they went beneath the brass turnstile, the librarian caught Miller's attention with a smiling glance. He smiled back.

"I'm trying to find something on brain surgery," he explained. "I—"

With a shock, then, he realized he had been talking to himself.

In the next instant, Dave Miller whirled. A voice from the bookcases chuckled:

"If you find anything, I wish you'd let me know. I'm stumped myself!"

FROM a corner of the room came an elderly, half-bald man with tangled gray brows and a rueful smile. A pencil was balanced over his ear, and a note-book was clutched in his hand.

"You, too!" he said. "I had hoped I was the only one—"

Miller went forward hurriedly to grip his hand.

"I'm afraid I'm not so unselfish," he admitted. "I've been hoping for two hours that I'd run into some other poor soul."

"Quite understandable," the stranger murmured sympathetically. "But in my case it is different. You see—I am responsible for this whole tragic business!"

"You!" Dave Miller gulped the word. "I—I thought—"

The man wagged his head, staring at his note pad, which was littered with jumbled calculations. Miller had a chance to study him. He was tall, heavily built, with wide, sturdy shoulders despite his sixty years. Oddly, he wore a gray-green smock. His eyes, narrowed and intent, looked gimlet-sharp beneath those toothbrush brows of his, as he stared at the pad.

"There's the trouble, right there," he muttered. "I provided only three stages of amplification, whereas four would have been barely enough. No wonder the phase didn't carry through!"

"I guess I don't follow you," Miller faltered. "You mean—something you did—"

"I should think it was something I did!" The baldish stranger scratched his head with the tip of his pencil. "I'm John Erickson—you know, the Wanamaker Institute."

Miller said: "Oh!" in an understanding voice. Erickson was head of Wanamaker Institute, first laboratory of them all when it came to exploding atoms and blazing trails into the wildernesses of science.

ERICKSON's piercing eyes were suddenly boring into the younger man.

"You've been sick, haven't you?" he demanded.

"Well—no—not really sick." The druggist colored. "I'll have to admit to being drunk a few hours ago, though."

"Drunk—" Erickson stuck his tongue in his cheek, shook his head, scowled. "No, that would hardly do it. There must have been something else. The impulsor isn't *that* powerful. I can understand about the dog, poor fellow. He must have been run over, and I caught him just at the instant of passing from life to death."

"Oh!" Dave Miller lifted his head, knowing now what Erickson was driving at. "Well, I may as well be frank. I'm—I committed suicide. That's how drunk I was. There hasn't been a suicide in the Miller family in centuries. It took a skinful of liquor to set the precedent."

Erickson nodded wisely. "Perhaps we will find the precedent hasn't really been set! But no matter—" His lifted hand stopped Miller's eager, wondering exclamation. "The point is, young man, we three are in a tough spot, and it's up to us to get out of it. And not only we, but heaven knows how many others the world over!"

"Would you—maybe you can explain to my lay mind what's happened," Miller suggested.

"Of course. Forgive me. You see, Mr.—"

"Miller. Dave Miller."

"Dave it is. I have a feeling we're going to be pretty well acquainted before this is over. You see, Dave, I'm a nut on so-called 'time theories.' I've seen time compared to everything from an entity to a long, pink worm. But I disagree with them all, because they postulate the idea that time is constantly being manufactured. Such reasoning is fantastic!

"Time exists. Not as an ever-growing chain of links, because such a chain would have to have a tail end, if it has a front end; and who can imagine the period when time did not exist? So I think time is like a circular train-track. Unending. We who live and die merely travel around on it. The future exists simultaneously with the past, for one instant when they meet."

MILLER's brain was humming. Erickson shot the words at him staccato-fashion, as if they were things known from Great Primer days. The young druggist scratched his head.

"You've got me licked," he admitted. "I'm a stranger here, myself."

"Naturally you can't be expected to understand things I've been all my life puzzling about. Simplest way I can explain it is that we are on a train following this immense circular railway.

"When the train reaches the point where it started, it is about to plunge into the past; but this is impossible, because the point where it started is simply the caboose of the train! And that point is always ahead—and behind—the time-train.

"Now, my idea was that with the proper stimulus a man could be thrust across the diameter of this circular railway to a point in his past. Because of the nature of time, he could neither go ahead of the train to meet the future nor could he stand still and let the caboose catch up with him. But—he could detour across the circle and land farther back on the train! And that, my dear Dave, is what you and I and Major have done—almost."

"Almost?" Miller said hoarsely.

Erickson pursed his lips. "We are somewhere partway across the space between present and past. We are living in an instant that can move neither forward nor back. You and I, Dave, and Major—and the Lord knows how many others the world over—have been thrust by my time impulsor onto a timeless beach of eternity. We have been caught in time's backwash. Castaways, you might say."

An objection clamored for attention in Miller's mind.

"But if this is so, where are the rest of them? Where is my wife?"

"They are right here," Erickson explained. "No doubt you could see your wife if you could find her. But we see them as statues, because, for us, time no longer exists. But there was something I did not count on. I did not know that it would be possible to live in one small instant of time, as we are doing. And I did not know that only those who are hovering between life and death can deviate from the normal process of time!"

"You mean—we're dead!" Miller's voice was a bitter monotone.

"Obviously not. We're talking and moving, aren't we? But—we are on the fence. When I gave my impulsor the jolt of high power, it went wrong and I think something must have happened to me. At the same instant, you had shot yourself.

"Perhaps, Dave, you are dying. The only way for us to find out is to try to get the machine working and topple ourselves one way or the other. If we fall back, we will all live. If we fall into the present—we may die."

"Either way, it's better than this!" Miller said fervently.

"I came to the library here, hoping to find out the things I must know. My own books are locked in my study. And these—they might be cemented in their places, for all their use to me. I suppose we might as well go back to the lab."

Miller nodded, murmuring: "Maybe you'll get an idea when you look at the machine again."

"Let's hope so," said Erickson grimly. "God knows I've failed so far!"

CHAPTER III
Splendid Sacrifice

IT WAS a solid hour's walk out to West Wilshire, where the laboratory was. The immense bronze and glass doors of Wanamaker Institute were closed, and so barred to the two men. But Erickson led the way down the side.

"We can get in a service door. Then we climb through transoms and ventilators until we get to my lab."

Major frisked along beside them. He was enjoying the action and the companionship. It was less of an adventure to Miller, who knew death might be ahead for the three of them.

Two workmen were moving a heavy cabinet in the side service door. To get in, they climbed up the back of the rear workman, walked across the cabinet, and scaled down the front of the leading man. They went up the stairs to the fifteenth floor. Here they crawled through a transom into the wing marked:

"Experimental. Enter Only By Appointment."

Major was helped through it, then they were crawling along the dark metal tunnel of an air-conditioning ventilator. It was small, and took some wriggling.

In the next room, they were confronted by a stern receptionist on whose desk was a little brass sign, reading:

"Have you an appointment?"

Miller had had his share of experience with receptionists' ways, in his days as a pharmaceutical salesman. He took the greatest pleasure now in lighting his cigarette from a match struck on the girl's nose. Then he blew the smoke in her face and hastened to crawl through the final transom.

John Erickson's laboratory was well lighted by a glass-brick wall and a huge skylight. The sun's rays glinted on the time impulsor. The scientist explained the impulsor in concise terms*. When he had finished, Dave Miller knew just as little as before, and the outfit still resembled three transformers in a line, of the type seen on power-poles, connected to a great bronze globe hanging from the ceiling.

"There's the monster that put us in this plight," Erickson grunted. "Too strong to be legal, too weak to do the job right. Take a good look!"

WITH his hands jammed in his pockets, he frowned at the complex machinery. Miller stared a few moments; then transferred his interests to other things in the room. He was immediately struck by the resemblance of a transformer in a far corner to the ones linked up with the impulsor.

"What's that?" he asked quickly. "Looks the same as the ones you used over there."

"It is."

"But— Didn't you say all you needed was another stage of power?"

"That's right."

"Maybe I'm crazy!" Miller stared from impulsor to transformer and back again. "Why don't you use it, then?"

---

*Obviously this electric time impulsor is a machine in the nature of an atomic integrator. It "broadcasts" great waves of electrons which align all atomic objects in rigid suspension.

That is to say, atomic structures are literally "frozen." Living bodies are similarly affected. It is a widely held belief on the part of many eminent scientists that all matter, broken down into its elementary atomic composition, is electrical in structure.

That being so, there is no reason to suppose why Professor Erickson may not have discovered a time impulsor which, broadcasting electronic impulses, "froze" everything within its range. —ED.

"Using what for the connection?" Erickson's eyes gently mocked him. "Wire, of course!"

The scientist jerked a thumb at a small bale of heavy copper wire.

"Bring it over and we'll try it."

Miller was halfway to it when he brought up short. Then a sheepish grin spread over his features.

"I get it," he chuckled. "That bale of wire might be the Empire State Building, as far as we're concerned. Forgive my stupidity."

Erickson suddenly became serious.

"I'd like to be optimistic, Dave," he muttered, "but in all fairness to you I must tell you I see no way out of this. The machine is, of course, still working, and with that extra stage of power, the uncertainty would be over. But where, in this world of immovable things, will we find a piece of wire twenty-five feet long?"

THERE was a warm, moist sensation against Miller's hand, and when he looked down Major stared up at him with commiseration. Miller scratched him behind the ear, and the dog closed his eyes, reassured and happy. The young druggist sighed, wishing there were some giant hand to scratch him behind the ear and smooth *his* troubles over.

"And if we don't get out," he said soberly, "we'll starve, I suppose."

"No, I don't think it will be that quick. I haven't felt any hunger. I don't expect to. After all, our bodies are still living in one instant of time, and a man can't work up a healthy appetite in one second. Of course, this elastic-second business precludes the possibility of disease.

"Our bodies must go on unchanged. The only hope I see is—when we are on the verge of madness, suicide. That means jumping off a bridge, I suppose. Poison, guns, knives—all the usual wherewithal—are denied to us."

Black despair closed down on Dave Miller. He thrust it back, forcing a crooked grin.

"Let's make a bargain," he offered. "When we finish fooling around with this apparatus, we split up. We'll only be at each other's throat if we stick together. I'll be blaming you for my plight, and I don't want to. It's my fault as much as yours. How about it?"

John Erickson gripped his hand. "You're all right, Dave. Let me give you some advice. If ever you do get back to the present...keep away from liquor. Liquor and the Irish never did mix. You'll have that store on its feet again in no time."

"Thanks!" Miller said fervently. "And I think I can promise that nothing less than a whiskey antidote for snake bite will ever make me bend an elbow again!"

FOR the next couple of hours, despondency reigned in the laboratory. But it was soon to be deposed again by hope.

Despite all of Erickson's scientific training, it was Dave Miller himself who grasped the down-to-earth idea that started them hoping again. He was walking about the lab, jingling keys in his pocket, when suddenly he stopped short. He jerked the ring of keys into his hand.

"Erickson!" he gasped. "We've been blind. Look at this!"

The scientist looked; but he remained puzzled.

"Well—?" he asked skeptically.

"There's our wire!" Dave Miller exclaimed. "You've got keys; I've got keys. We've got coins, knives, wristwatches. Why can't we lay them all end to end—"

Erickson's features looked as if he had been electrically shocked.

"You've hit it!" he cried. "If we've got enough!"

With one accord, they began emptying their pockets, tearing off wristwatches, searching for pencils. The finds made a little heap in the middle of the floor. Erickson let his long fingers claw through thinning hair.

"God give us enough! We'll only need the one wire. The thing is plugged in already and only the positive pole has to be connected to the globe. Come on!"

Scooping up the assortment of metal articles, they rushed across the room. With his pocket-knife, Dave Miller began breaking up the metal wrist-watch straps, opening the links out so that they could be laid end-to-end for the greatest possible length. They patiently broke the watches to pieces, and of the junk they garnered made a ragged foot and a half of "wire." Their coins stretched the line still further.

They had ten feet covered before the stuff was half used up. Their metal pencils, taken apart, gave them a good two feet. Key chains helped generously. With eighteen feet covered, their progress began to slow down.

Perspiration poured down Miller's face. Desperately, he tore off his lodge ring and cut it in two to pound it flat. From garters and suspenders they won a few inches more. And then—they stopped— feet from their goal.

Miller groaned. He tossed his pocket-knife in his hand.

"We can get a foot out of this," he estimated. "But that still leaves us way short."

Abruptly, Erickson snapped his fingers.

"Shoes!" he gasped. "They're full of nails. Get to work with that knife, Dave. We'll cut out every one of 'em!"

IN ten minutes, the shoes were reduced to ragged piles of tattered leather. Erickson's deft fingers painstakingly placed the nails, one by one, in the line. The distance left to cover was less than six inches!

He lined up the last few nails. Then both men were sinking back on their heels, as they saw there was a gap of three inches to cover!

"Beaten!" Erickson ground out. "By three inches! Three inches from the present...and yet it might as well be a million miles!"

Miller's body felt as though it were in a vise. His muscles ached with strain. So taut were his nerves that he leaped as though stung when Major nuzzled a cool nose into his hand again. Automatically, he began to stroke the dog's neck.

"Well, that licks us," he muttered. "There isn't another piece of movable metal in the world."

Major kept whimpering and pushing against him. Annoyed, the druggist shoved him away.

"Go 'way," he muttered. "I don't feel like—"

Suddenly then his eyes widened, as his touch encountered warm metal. He whirled.

"There it is!" he yelled. "The last link. *The nameplate on Major's collar!*"

In a flash, he had torn the little rectangular brass plate from the dog collar. Erickson took it from his grasp. Sweat stood shiny on his skin. He held the bit of metal over the gap between wire and pole.

"This is it!" he smiled brittlely. "We're on our way, Dave. Where, I don't know. To death, or back to life. But—we're going!"

The metal clinked into place. Live, writhing power leaped through the wire, snarling across partial breaks. The transformers began to hum. The humming grew louder. Singing softly, the bronze globe over their heads glowed green. Dave Miller felt a curious lightness. There was a snap in his brain, and Erickson, Major and the laboratory faded from his senses.

Then came an interval when the only sound was the soft sobbing he had been hearing as if in a dream. That, and blackness that enfolded him like soft velvet. Then Miller was opening his eyes, to see the familiar walls of his own kitchen around him!

Someone cried out.

"Dave! Oh, Dave, dear!"

It was Helen's voice, and it was Helen who cradled his head in her lap and bent her face close to his.

"Oh, thank God that you're alive—!"

"Helen!" Miller murmured. "What—are—you—doing here?"

"I couldn't go through with it. I—I just couldn't leave you. I came back and—and I heard the shot and ran in. The doctor should be here. I called him five minutes ago."

"*Five minutes*... How long has it been since I shot myself?"

"Oh, just six or seven minutes. I called the doctor right away."

Miller took a deep breath. Then it *must* have been a dream. All that—to happen in a few minutes—It wasn't possible!

"How—how could I have botched the job?" he muttered. "I wasn't drunk enough to miss myself completely."

Helen looked at the huge revolver lying in the sink.

"Oh, that old forty-five of Grandfather's! It hasn't been loaded since the Civil War. I guess the powder got damp or something. It just sort of sputtered instead of exploding properly. Dave, promise me something! You won't ever do anything like this again, if I promise not to nag you?"

Dave Miller closed his eyes. "There won't be any need to nag, Helen. Some people take a lot of teaching, but I've had my lesson. I've got ideas about the store which I'd been too lazy to try out. You know, I feel more like fighting right now than I have for years! We'll lick 'em, won't we, honey?"

Helen buried her face in the hollow of his shoulder and cried softly. Her words were too muffled to be intelligible. But Dave Miller understood what she meant.

H E had thought the whole thing a dream—John Erickson, the "time impulsor" and Major. But that night he read an item in the *Evening Courier* that was to keep him thinking for many days.

POLICE INVESTIGATE
DEATH OF SCIENTIST
HERE IN LABORATORY

John M. Erickson, director of the Wanamaker Institute, died at his work last night. Erickson was a beloved and valuable figure in the world of science, famous for his recently publicized "time lapse" theory.

Two strange circumstances surrounded his death. One was the presence of a German shepherd dog in the laboratory, its head crushed as if with a sledgehammer. The other was a chain of small metal objects stretching from one corner of the room to the other, as if intended to take the place of wire in a circuit.

Police, however, discount this idea, as there was a roll of wire only a few feet from the body.

THE MATHEMATICAL KID

by Ross Rocklynne

I WAS walking fast down the quarter-beam tunnel toward my watch on the skipper's bridge, shrugging on my first mate's coat, when, *"Psst!"* he whispered, beckoning me from under the companionway.

I stopped, pivoted my head. It was the twerp. I said, staring, "Well, what the hell do you think you—"

"Sh!" He waved his arms like scissors...

"You're heading for a crack-up!" warned the kid. He said it so often he succeeded in becoming a nuisance. But then...

Behind the cars an avalanche roared down, bent on their destruction.

"Sh! Come here. I've got something important, really important, to tell you!"

So you can see right away he was a twerp—our new cabin boy. It was emergency that made me and Old Scratch—he's the skipper—take him on. Yesterday, just before we hit heaven, he had snuck up the gangway and bearded Old Scratch on the bridge.

Kind of a funny kid, built like an asteroid—hard and rocky, yellow hair sticking out of his head like straw from a scarecrow, eyes glowing like blue neon signs advertising the presence of his turned-up, butt-end-of-a-peanut nose. It was funny, darned funny, that he had showed up just when our regular cabin boy was missing and we were getting ready to shove off.

So we had to hire him. Then Old Scratch and I shooed him off the bridge, and we went on checking and rechecking the orbit figures the Corporation had computed for us.

And now here was the little twerp acting mysterious, as if he had a conspiracy on tap.

"All right," I growled, "spill it!"

"Listen to me!" he hissed, pulling my head down to his with a half-Nelson. "Nobody else will. I tried to tell the captain, but he flew off the handle. Do you know why I took this job?"

I said, sarcastic, "Sure. You was working your way through—"

His neon eyes snapped.

"No, no!" His police siren voice sank to a hoarse whisper. "That isn't it! I took the job because I wanted to save the *Aphrodite* from cracking up! Yes, I did, actually and literally!"

"Hey," I yelped, drawing away, "are you bats? Here we are, only three units out from the mother planet, and you're wobbly already!"

He grabbed my arm excitedly. "You're traveling the EP1x344 orbit, ain't you, Sandy? Well, that's the wrong course. I'm telling you for your own good, and you better switch over to another one quick! The *Aphrodite* is due for a crack-up eight days, seven hours, and forty-three minutes plus or minus from this very second!"

"Stow it, fellow!" I said real sharp. Then I spoke kindly, as I turned away.

"Go to your bunk and climb in, and I'll make your apologies to the skipper. Now get along, and wait until you know something about celestial mechanics before you go letting your one-horsepower brain do a hundred-horsepower job.

"Remember, you're not any Georgie Periwinkle." And I left him with that, though I did feel a little bit guilty, because his face fell a mile. But it was a laugh, him trying to tell *us* we were following a collision course.

THE next day, I left the bridge for a couple minutes and went to the engine room to see what in Hades was causing the sour note in the Wittenberg* howl—the chief engineer told me that there were air bubbles in the lead cable. When I came back up on the bridge, the kid ran out.

He looked at me accusingly, and pointed a stubby forefinger at me and bleated.

"He wouldn't listen to me, and neither would you! You're going to be sorry!"

"Listen, Kid," I said patiently. "I think we've had just about enough of this stuff. I warn you, quit bothering us, or I'll warm the seat of your pants so hot you'll never forget it!"

"What ails that kid?" snarled Old Scratch, his red, puffed-up beacon of a nose winking. He slammed his charts down on the table and glared at me as if I was a source of misery.

"I ought to fire you, damned if I shouldn't, for letting me hire him in the first place!"

"Say," I yelped, "you mean to say I hired him? Why, you old—"

He settled down. "Hold your temper, you old space hound," he snapped. "Maybe we have been up and down around the sun all our lives together, but that don't give you no extra privileges, see?"

"Yes, sir," I simpered.

"Now, Mr. Flabberty!" he growled. "Who's putting crazy ideas in the kid's head? If it's *you*—"

"Aw, be yourself, Cap'n. He's got a touch of the wobblies, that's all."

"See atmospherics then, and have his air regulated. I ain't going to have no wild kid gumming up this run. We got a load of ten-thousand-dollar, airtight automobiles to get to Pluto in the next sixty days, and whadaya think's gonna happen if we don't get them there in time, huh? The Corporation'll give us the bum's rush, that's what!"

---

*Wittenbergs are the motors invented by Silas B. Wittenberg, late in the   century, which supplanted the dangerous rocket drive by direct explosion. In this type motor, the possibilities of control are much extended, and the danger of explosion of the entire fuel supply is eliminated. Lead cables conduct the mixed gases to the outer firing chambers, and prevent static electricity sparks which are quite a problem around metal parts in space. However, a weakness still exists, in the air bubbles which frequently obstruct the cables and cause uneven fuel mixture. This results in a howling noise. —Ed.

"He been bothering you that much?" I demanded, incredulous.

"Damned right he has! Beggin' me with tears in his eyes to change our orbit. Beggin' me if I won't do that, to cut our acceleration down to half a G, for three days at least."

I gasped, "What for?"

He said aggrievedly, "How should I know? He's enough to give anyone the meenies, that's what. I'll begin to believe our course is all wrong myself. Keep him outa here—he worries me."

The skipper shifted on his big feet uncomfortably, cocked an impatient eye at me.

"Recheck our course," he growled. "And then check it again. Go on, you, get going! And when you're finished, put that crazy kid in the brig!"

So I wearily checked and rechecked, and checked again, and I began to think how nice it'd be to step on the kid's face.

I made a mathematical sweep through 10° of the ecliptic plane, and just to make sure went 20° above and below, using the *Ephemeris* and a slide-rule to calculate possible *puncti—and* there wasn't, and would never be, even a rock in our trajectory; not unless it was above 20°, coming in at a 90° angle and at an impossible speed—and we all knew there wasn't anything like that.

So we had clear sailing. The ether was clean. We could plow right through. Hadn't I just calculated it? Sure.

So I knew the kid was wobbly in the bobbly, and it didn't hurt my conscience a bit when I cornered him in the galley and stuck him in solitary. We left him there—two and a half days. Yes, you guessed it— at the end of that time, all hell broke loose!

FIVE days out; and following the EP1x344 trajectory, the Wittenbergs went dead, and the *Aphrodite* coasted. We were on schedule, we were doing a neat hundred-point-oh-three miles per second, and we forgot about the kid.

Then—right in the middle of my snore-watch—I was jolted out of my dreams by Old Scratch's voice screaming from the general audio.

"Attention all!" he roared. "Attention all! Rock ahead! Wittenbergs! *Wittenbergs!* Get them Wittenbergs howling! Lane! Two gravities fore!"

I bounced out of bed, pulled my pants on and went sailing for the bridge. The chief engineer came charging down the corridor in his nightshirt.

"Two gravities fore!" he was gasping. "Jerusalem H. Slim!"

Old Scratch was still blaring into the general audio, when I came in.

"Two gravities fore! Larramie, lay off the pilot blasts—you'll send us through the bulkheads, at this speed! Telescope! Give me the dope on that again, and if you've made a mistake, I'll make a personal autopsy on your gizzard to see what brand you're using!"

"89° to the ecliptic," the telescope man's frightened voice said. "Almost perpendicular. There ain't nothin' like that! 14-16-20-50-100-150160—Great God," he yelled, "the tape reads 163 per. I just don't believe—"

"Shut up!" Old Scratch snarled. "Believe your machines! Two and a half gravities fore!" he roared.

And the Wittenbergs began to whine, and crescendoed upward until a hell of awful sound shook the air. I had to stand at a slant. As I walked toward the console, I felt just like I was walking up a forty-five degree hill, only worse.

"Three gravities fore!" Old Scratch snarled.

"We can't take that!" I panted.

"I'm gonna take it, and soli everybody else. Whip it up—three gravities!"

Chief Engineer Lane began to whip it; and I began to weigh 540 pounds.

"What about the kid?" I whispered.

"To hell with the kid!" he yipped. Three gravities were straining his 200 —600 now—pounds back against his braced chair.

He yelled out, "Four gravities fore!" and that was the end of me. Old Scratch tests out at five gravities, I can take four and a half most of the time. But this was one of my off days. I was forced back against the wall, and saw something big and gray rushing at us in the view-screens.

I couldn't breathe. If that wall hadn't been there, I'd have gone tumbling the whole length of the ship. When Old Scratch added another fraction of a G, I began to give way inside. Everything blurred.

Suddenly the ship swung. It must have, because I fell clear across the room, bounced soggily into another wall. The Wittenberg howl tore at my eardrums. I felt a huge wave of sound and pure vibration surge through the ship. And then *bang!* I was gone—just like throwing a knife switch.

I WOKE up, and felt light as a feather. I opened my eyes. I moved an arm, pivoted my neck, saw a row of beds filled with patients. I groaned. Then I began to get heavier and heavier, as the gravity perspective came back; and soon I knew that something like maybe only one, or one and a half gravities was sitting on me.

"Feeling better?" Dr. Ran Tabor came across the room, grinning all over his drunken face. He was our ship doctor, sort of a renegade from the profession.

Somehow I asked about the kid first.

"Him? Up and around last two hours. Some kid, him. Got bones like rubber bands. But you're brittle from the fuzz on top of your head down to the nail on your big toe. You got two busted ribs."

"Did we—did we crash?"

His brows came up. "Ha-ha! Sure, we crashed. Hard. Ha-ha! Aft section stove in—hospital full—main jets wrecked— Do you blame me for gettin' drunk?" He scowled.

I sank back wearily. "Send me Old Scratch, if he can make it."

Tabor scowled. "Nothin' could hurt that old buzzard."

Old Scratch came charging in after a while, his eyes stormy. He all but shook his fist under my face.

"You!" he snarled. "A big, strong man like you foldin' up under four and a half gravities, and just when I needed you to—"

I yelped indignantly, "Why, you old—"

"Shut up!" Then he softened. "You know what happened? We tried to swerve at the last minute—the pilot blasts. Didn't work. They just twisted us around on our center of gravity, and the ship bounced her stern against the planet, stove in the supply hold, and tore up the main jets into scrap metal.

"So now we're caught here, see? There ain't any way of lifting her. This is a one and a half gravity planet."

He gnawed at his unshaved lip; he glared at me as if he thought I ought to be the angel of deliverance.

"We should be able to lift her some way," I began.

"With the forward jets? Don't be stupid. The firing area ain't enough to lift us from a one-gravity planet, let alone a one and a half. Well, you lay there, and figure something out, and get those ribs healed up, sissy!" Then he went charging out of the hospital.

Couple hours later, the kid came in, his eyes glowing with excitement. He came right up to me. Maybe he thought I was his friend even if I did treat him rough.

"I think I've found something," he said excitedly. "It's wonderful. It really is. But first I have to test it."

"Test what?" I scowled.

"Test the planet," he said in surprise, just as if he was talking about dropping something in a retort and boiling it over a Bunsen burner.

HE got enthusiastic again. "You see, the main thing that's bothering the captain is that this is a one and a half gravity planet, and the ship is so bunged up it can't draw away from anything more than half of that—that's what Old Scratch said.

"So the thing to do," he went on, impressively, "is to decrease the amount of gravity pulling on the ship!"

And he gave me a "see how simple it is!" look.

I groaned, and almost gave up the ghost.

"Who told you about this planet," I said weakly, "and how big is it?"

"Nobody told me about it, and it's three thousand miles in diameter!" Then he stepped back and his neon eyes lost their enthusiasm, and flared with anger.

"You're like Old Scratch and everybody else!" he bleated ragingly. "I told you days ago the ship was going to crack up, and now when it does, you think that somebody else told *me*! I computed it myself! I saw your orbit figures in the Astronomical Section of the *Philadelphia Herald,* and I had just discovered this planet, and I saw right away you were going to crack up.

"I'll fix *you* guys!" he cried. "After this, when I find something, I won't say a word. No, I won't. I'll let you figure it out *yourself— pickle-puss!*"

And then he turned away and marched fuming out of the room. Then for the first time I began to wonder if we weren't misjudging the kid and treating him too harsh. But I forgot all that by what happened next.

TWO days later, the sawbones braced me with a couple yards of adhesive and let me get up. I dressed, feeling wobbly, what with one and a half gravities on me, made my way to my office in the ship, made out a requisition for a pressure suit, and then looked up the maintenance man. He measured me with one eye while he picked a pressure suit off the rack with the other.

The tender let me out the airlock into the middle of a big, smooth, dark plain ringed with low hills about six miles off, I guessed. The stars in the black sky were cold, fixed points of lights, so I knew there wasn't any atmosphere.

At the stove-in stern Of the *Aphrodite,* a half dozen of the boiler boys were at work with oxy-acetylene torches. They were bungling the job, and Old Scratch knew it. But he kept them at it, trying to weld those shapeless masses back into position again.

"Oh, so you're up after takin' it easy two days," he snarled. He glared, but beneath the glare he was a confused, helpless old space hound, wondering how in the devil he was going to get a hundred and ten airtight automobiles to Pluto in the time called for by contract.

"If you've thought of anything, Mr. Flabberty," he growled, sarcastic, "I wish you'd spill it, instead of keeping us in such delightful suspense. How do we get away from this one and a half gravity planet?"

"Easy," I told him, grinning all over my face. "You decrease the gravity to, say, three-fourths of a—"

His face began to screw up, and he took a step toward me.

"That's just what the kid said!" he growled, with murder in his eyes.

I BACKED up. "Hey, wait a minute! Don't blame me if the kid said it," I protested. "And besides, since he did predict the crack-up, he might be right about this, too!"

"My dear Mr. Flabberty! Of course he's right. All we have to do is decrease the gravity. But maybe the planet won't lay down and wave its hind legs in the air like the kid thinks!" he thundered.

"And as for the kid predicting the crack-up, I got my own ideas about *that!* Somehow he found out that the Corporation had deliberately plotted us a bad course. And for why? Why, so they could collect insurance on the old tub, that's why. As soon as we get outa this mess I'm gonna collar that kid and find out just where he got that information, so help me, I am!"

And looking at him, I suddenly began to feel sorry again for the kid. He was just plain poison to Old Scratch.

I looked around. Few miles away, just like we were in the center of a big crater, were a ring of low hills; and beyond that the land stretched away into a clear-cut horizon. I turned around and around, looking for the kid, but I didn't see him.

That was funny. He hadn't been in the ship either. Maybe he'd gone for a walk somewhere. Maybe he'd got lost. "Good riddance!" said Old Scratch disgruntledly. "That'll be one less passenger we have to carry along."

BUT five or six hours later, when we are all eating in the mess hall, the skipper went into a rage, pounding his fists together.

"It ain't enough that we can't lift ourselves," he panted wildly. "It ain't enough that we can't repair the main jets. Now we have to organize a search party, looking for a damned half-pint Jonah!"

But we did do just that, four groups of us starting out under the cold stars in four different directions. We got about two hundred yards away from the ship when Wilkes, our electrician, said in awe.

"Here comes that there moon."

The rest of them had seen that moon, but I hadn't, though I'd heard about it. I gawked. It came thundering over the horizon, like six white horses around the mountain. It was small at first. It got visibly bigger as we traveled along. It came faster, while I almost broke my neck watching the crazy thing. It swooped at us, getting bigger, coming faster.

At the end of an hour it was overhead, five times as big as when we first saw it, and going like Mercury in a planetarium. It couldn't have been more that fifteen, maybe twenty thousand miles away. Then it began to go toward the other horizon, getting smaller, farther away, decelerating.

At the end of two hours, when we reached the foot of the hills, it had completely gone from horizon to horizon, accelerating, growing in diameter, decelerating, shrinking as it set.

"Wow!" somebody breathed. "Crazy moon!"

Old Scratch, still itching to get his hands on the kid, said, "T'hell with it! It's just got a highly eccentric orbit." But, of course, none of us knew why.

WE started up the hill. The ground was rocky with strangely smooth boulders, as if they'd rolled a long ways. There was sand, too, and small pebbles. We topped the hill, the four of us, and stood looking out over the plain.

Suddenly we saw something, a little black dot, rolling along toward us down there on the plain.

Wilkes gasped unbelievingly, "It's an automobile!"

I looked at Old Scratch and saw his face getting redder and redder behind the helmet of his pressure suit. His lips mumbled something. After that we were all silent, waiting while that airtight, torpedo-shaped automobile, made for traveling in rough country over almost any gravity, came nearer and nearer. It started up the hill and stopped about twenty yards from us, with the kid at the wheel.

We stood there in grim silence. The door opened. The kid got out, took one look at our faces, and then scrambled back in. Through his radio headset he panted.

"Don't you come near to me! Don't you touch me. Because if you do, I'll tell my friend the President of the United States. I had to steal the automobile from the hold—I had to test the planet!"

We were looking at the tires of the automobiles. Ripped to shreds. We were looking at the paint job. Dented, scratched, a mess. We started toward the automobile.

But the kid stepped on the starter, swished forward, detoured around us at the last second, and then stopped about forty yards away.

"I promise to ride you back to the ship," he panted excitedly, "if you promise not to get rough with me. Anyway, you *can't* get rough with me!" he pleaded. "I've found a good way to decrease the gravity!"

"We promise not to get rough with you," said Old Scratch, in an 'it gifs candy and ice cream' voice. And so help me, we didn't—then! When we got back to the ship, Old Scratch and I waited around until the kid got his pressure suit off, and had himself exposed. Then we both leaped at him.

"Me first!" said Old Scratch, holding up a hand. And he went at it, and laid it on so thick I didn't have the heart to add any more to what he deserved. We sent him to solitary for two days.

We found later that the car was all out of line. The kid must have put it through some rough punishment, because those cars are built to

withstand a lot. Not that it was going to hurt our contract—we only
had to deliver a hundred cars. We had ten extra, just in case; it was just
the principle of the thing.

Then, with that episode off our hands, we began to drive ourselves
crazy trying to think of ways and means to get off this world. Our
transmitting apparatus wasn't powerful enough to signal somebody to
come and get us.

And if we waited around for somebody like Georgie Periwinkle, the
mathematical genius, to discover this planet and start an exploration,
why we'd all be starved; or, at the least, we wouldn't get our precious
load of automobiles to Pluto.

No matter which way you looked at it, things were an unholy mess.

AND then the kid went and did it again.
We had been bottled up on the planet a week. We had stopped
working on the main jets—they just wouldn't fix. Old Scratch and I
were sitting on the bridge and looking at the walls, hopeless, when the
doors open and in comes the kid.

Old Scratch made an annoyed, tired sound.

The kid's face was flushed. If I didn't know he was just a kid, without
any sense in his head, I might have thought the look in his eyes was
dangerous. So I just looked at him, my mind a billion miles away.

The kid was almost panting with some kind of nervousness.

"Cap'n" he husked, "I know how to get us off this planet!"

Old Scratch muttered to himself, "Yeah? Run off and peddle your
peanuts someplace else. Can't you see we're busy? Besides, you're fired."

The kid's voice trebled. "You better listen to me!" he panted.

Old Scratch looked at him. A gleam came to his eye. The front legs
of his chair hit the floor, and he started to roll up his sleeves.

Quick as sound, the kid leaped back, his eyes just like slits. Suddenly
my breath zipped from my lungs at what I saw.

"Stand back!" he yelped, as I came to my feet and started toward
him.

"Put that paralyzer down!" I snapped. "You want to hurt
somebody?"

"Stand back!" he yipped, fairly dancing on his feet.

But I knew he was just a kid, and that he wouldn't pull the trigger and I started toward him, sore as a boil, when suddenly—well, suddenly. I was out cold. Dead to the world. Something had nudged my brain, had short-circuited certain nerve centers.

And that was absolutely all I knew until I opened my eyes, and there I was in that all-fired ship's hospital again, and Dr. Ran Tabor was breathing his liquory breath into my face.

The quartermaster, the chief engineer, the maintenance chief, and half a dozen others were standing over me. They started yelling all at once. "What happened?"

"Where's the captain?"

"Where's Johnny?"

So I told them, and then they told me.

Old Scratch was gone, not a trace of him or Johnny anywhere! And to tie the whole thing up, the airlock to the freight hold was open, and another automobile was missing!

"He kidnaped him," the quartermaster said. "Well, be a horse's neck. It just don't make sense."

I struggled to my feet, jabbed a finger at Wilkes, Lane and Cummings, the quartermaster.

"Break out another one of them automobiles," I snapped. "We're going to find that kid, and when we get him—"

I DIDN'T know exactly what I would do with him. But it would be something drastic. Something horrible. Something ghastly. Yes, it would! And if I felt that way, how would Old Scratch feel when we finally freed him? I began to get happier with each passing second.

We made the low, sloping hills in fifteen minutes, following the path the kid had taken the time before. We went beyond the hills, winding our way around unbelievably smooth boulders, following the tire tracks through the sand and gravel. We went pretty fast, hitting high as much as we could, and after about an hour we noticed the plain was beginning to slope—all at once. I mean, the whole plain was tilting up.

"Say, that's funny!" said Cummings.

I'll say it was! It got even funnier. The farther we got away, the more the plain sloped. It went past 200, started hitting 30°. After about five hours- we were still following the tire tracks—it went up to 45°!

We must have been four or five hundred miles away from the ship at that time. And the hill stretched endlessly upward, and endlessly to each side, and endlessly downward.

Practically speaking, it was a plateaulike surface, stretching away evenly in all directions, with occasional small hills and swells growing out of it. A lopsided plain!

It was the mightiest, eeriest, most colossal hill I've ever seen or ever will see, because it never seemed to end, though we went up for miles and miles and more miles.

We saw that crazy moon, and did it have an eccentric orbit? It did! It came small over the horizon, and slow. And got smaller, went slower until, even when it set on the horizon that was the apparent top of the hill, it was so distant that we couldn't see it at all!

We pushed on, our mouths open, so absolutely flabbergasted we couldn't say a word. We began to feel lightheaded. We began to make motions that moved us further than we meant them to. We couldn't understand it at all!

And then we saw the automobile, Old Scratch and the kid. Just a tiny black dot way up there, coming toward us at a terrific clip. It detoured swells and small hills, missed boulders and detritus and gullies by hairbreadth turns, coming on as if hell was sitting on its tires!

And then we saw why.

And it sent a chill down our backs as we watched. It was a death race with an avalanche, that was—and *what* an avalanche! It was a mountain of boulders and detritus and talus, and small hills, and it filled the whole horizon.

I stared at it through the windshield, chills racing up and down my spine.

The kid drove like mad, and we could see Old Scratch in the seat beside him, his face florid. They were near now, and Old Scratch was making wild, crazy gestures.

What for? I don't think any of us realized that the avalanche was after us too, until Lane suddenly blasted in my ear.

"Wow! Turn the car!"

"DID I get it then? I did! I wish you could have seen the way I wrenched that wheel over, started the atom-motor to growling! The battered machine squealed, but she yawed over, went into high, made a neat semicircle and started down the hill. Man, did we let her go! There was the colossal hill stretching below us, and the avalanche behind us, and we *went*.

And the kid came after us, just keeping away from the grinding teeth of a moving mountain by the length of a whisker.

We detoured hills, frantically sought routes around gullies, made hairpin turns, yelled with glee when we hit the straightaway. Sand and rock and pebbles skittered under our screaming tires. We plunged down that planetary mountain side as if the fires of hell were singeing the seats of our pants.

Wilkes pounded me on the back until I started coughing.

"It's catching up!" he blasted. "Faster!"

Faster? Ye gods, what did the man want? We were already doing a hundred and twenty. So I threw more mileage in on top of what I already had. And the hill was growing steeper, and I heard Cummings cursing steadily, profanely, unbelievingly.

I knew he was looking down that unending slope, chopped off in a great circle where sat the frightful, star-sprinkled black horizon. But I was the driver, and I was looking at that horizon too, and it made my hair stand right up on end to think I was driving into it!

After a while it became a nightmare. Detour, slam on the brake, scream around impossible curves, start up a hill that ended in a cliff, yaw around, look for a better way out—a straightaway!—and down we'd go.

And I had three mad men in the car with me, so excited they couldn't get scared. Pounding me on the back. Yelling in my ears. Telling me the kid was gaining on us, and that the avalanche was gaining on the kid.

Ye gods, how that avalanche had us at a disadvantage! *It* didn't have to detour! It just took the obstructions along with it.

Everything hazed up. After all, I'd just got out of a sickbed. My hand on the wheel, my feet on the pedals, began just to do the things they had to, without my telling them. So for the last half of the ride, I was just a passenger. And even after the lopsided plain began to level off, I drove like mad.

Lane, Cummings, Wilkes started to cheer like a grandstand of people, all of whom have bet on the right horse, and are right happy about it. They had to take the wheel out of my hands, they had to push in the brake.

When I came out of my daze, the hill was gone—the big one—and the plain was a plain, and not very far away I saw the chain of low hills that circumscribed the plateau on which stood our ship.

Then we got out of the car, and I staggered around like a drunken man, until I saw the kid's automobile come screaming to a stop beside ours. I looked at him, and then I looked in the direction we'd come from.

THE avalanche was gone. As it reached the slow end of the slope, it had begun to lose parts of itself. Finally there had not been any slope to speak of and it had just petered out, dead and gone at the bottom of the five-hundred-mile hillside. Or so I thought. I know what we all felt—Lane, Wilkes, Cummings and I. About the kid, I mean, for exposing us all to the avalanche. We stood around waiting until the kid got out of his car, and I think we all were just waiting for Old Scratch to light into the kid and beat the stuffings out of him.

The kid got out first, his face flushed with excitement. He started toward us, and then stopped when he saw the looks on our faces. He started backing up.

Old Scratch got out of the car. We started to grin all over our faces.

"Now watch the fireworks!" Cummings husked joyfully.

And what started popping was our eyes. And why? Because if this was fireworks, then somebody had lit a whizzer! Old Scratch looked at us and grinned—and then threw an arm around the kid's shoulder!

I couldn't believe it. "But the kid kidnaped you!" I yipped out.

Old Scratch beamed. "Don't I know it? Wow! What a ride! Kidnaping was the only way this here kid could show me what he wanted to show me. It took a hell of a long time for me to get some sense in my head.

"Johnny," he beamed, "suppose you tell these here ignoramuses where that there avalanche come from." He grinned maliciously. And we gaped.

The kid shifted from one foot to another, grinning too.

"It came from the top of the hill," he said, as if that was all he needed to tell us. When we didn't get it, he added what he thought was an explanation.

"That's on the other side of the planet."

"The top of the hill is on the other side of the planet?" I said, trying to be real polite. "Forty-five hundred miles away?"

"Sure," boomed Old Scratch, as if he had known it all along. He began to laugh, his body shaking.

"It's the funniest damn thing I ever run across, so help me, it is! Why, this whole planet is a hill—a mountain—doggoned if it ain't! It's a hill from top to bottom. And the bottom is right where the ship landed—in the center of that ring of hills.

"Them hills is parts of avalanches that rolled all the way from the other side of the planet."

He continued to laugh, until I yelped:

"For Pete's sake, and you in the prime of life! What d'you mean, it's a hill? That we landed at the bottom—"

And then I think I and Lane and Wilkes and Cummings began to get it, and our mouths started to fall open.

THE kid grinned. "Sure," he piped up. "I knew it all along, but you wouldn't listen to me. This world we're on is a big mountain—an off-center planet. The center of gravity isn't in the center of the planet— it's about three hundred miles below the surface. Below our ship, the gravity is greatest." He was anxious for us to understand now.

"Maybe it's neutronium down there," he suggested hopefully.

I was feeling weak, and I sat down on the running board of our car. I looked at him dazedly.

"Go on, Johnny," I said weakly. "Then all we have to do to get off the planet is to decrease the amount of gravity pulling on the ship."

"Sure," the kid said excitedly. "I told you that, and you wouldn't believe me. The farther you go away from the center of gravity, the less it gets—it falls off as the square of the distance from the center."

He was getting enthusiastic now, and we listened to him tell us how to move the ship. That was because we were so dazed we couldn't talk.

"We use a few of the automobiles in the hold," he said, his eyes shining like a thousand watts. "We put two under the forward fins, two under the rear ones, two in the middle."

"But first we jack the ship up," said Old Scratch proudly, and then looked embarrassed as he realized that was pretty obvious.

"We hitch more automobiles up to the nose of the ship with chains," the kid went on. "Then we carry the ship over the plain and to the hills. There we look for a gap in the hills, and clear away some of the big boulders and get the ship over the detritus of the avalanches—maybe by making a roadway out of some rocks—and then we start pulling the ship up the hill!

"And when we get"—he stopped and his eyes got a preoccupied look, and then came back to us—"when we get the ship 733-point-three-nine miles away from where she is now, why, the gravity'll be exactly three-fourths of a G."

"Go on," I said. It was getting more and more like pretty music, the things he was saying.

"Why, then we can make it!" he said excitedly. "We can use the forward jets, and they'll lift us from three-fourths of a G! That'll take about—about two weeks, maybe. That leaves us thirty days to get to Pluto. And we can make it, too!"

His eyes went toward heaven again, and I thought I began to see mathematical symbols parading across his cornea. He said, "Yes, we can! I'll compute you an orbit myself!"

Old Scratch began to laugh. It got so he couldn't stop himself.

"He'll compute us an orbit," he gasped, pointing at the kid. *He'll* compute us an orbit! And it takes an expert what's got a dozen years training behind him to do that.

"Now, you listen, Johnny," he said, speaking very kindly. "You're a smart kid to be able to figure this here planet out, but you ain't *that* smart! You let that there job of computing up to me or Sandy or somebody that knows Planck's Constant* from a board."

The kid's cheeks began to burn.

"You guys are the *dumbest* bunch of pickle-pusses I *ever* ran across! Yes, you are! I tell you you're on a collision course, and you crack up, and *still* you don't' believe me. I figure out a planet for you, and tell you how to get off, and *still* you think I'm just a dumb kid that can't compute an orbit!

"How do you think I knew this was an off-center planet? Why I *knew* that those hills around the ship were just detritus that had rolled

---

*Max Planck was a German physicist, who first asserted that the energy of radiation is emitted and absorbed in integral multiples of certain indivisible "quanta" of energy which depend on the frequency of the oscillation of the electrons. This law of radiation is called Planck's Constant. —Ed.

down the hill? The boulders were so smooth, just like they rolled a long way. And I figured the eccentric anomaly* of that moon, and I knew it came in close and went so fast because it had to, where the gravity was greatest."

"You actually figured the eccentric anomaly of that there moon?" said Old Scratch incredulously. "Now don't pull my leg," he added in warning.

"Sure I did! In my head, too.

I figured exactly where the center of gravity was."

We stared at him harder and harder. Things were beginning to click in my head at last! The kid began to flush. He shifted from one foot to the other, the harder we stared at him. He got a guilty expression on his face. He avoided our eyes, like he thought maybe we had something on him.

"I guess you guys got me pinned down," he blurted out finally, and his lower lip began to tremble. "Now I guess you'll send me back to the Philadelphia Science Institution. But I couldn't stand that dry, stuffy old joint. And when I saw your orbit figures on the paper, I knew you were on a collision course. So I sent a telegram to my friend, the President of the United States, and told him I was running away, and then I waited in an alley until your—"

And by that time I had it. I jumped to my feet, yelping to high heaven: *"Georgie Periwinkle!"*

The kid shifted from one foot to the other, embarrassed and ashamed-looking.

There was a big silence, and then everybody started to explode.

"Wow!" Old Scratch yipped out, and his eyes began to bulge.

Georgie Periwinkle, the mathematical prodigy, with six comets, two new planets—three, now—a new subatomic particle, and a mess of miscellaneous inventions to his credit!

Georgie Periwinkle flushed redder and redder while we stared at him.

"So we'll get to Pluto on time," he said, trying to change the subject.

But we kept looking at him, and finally we started grinning all over

---

*The angular distance of a planet from its perihelion from the sun, which measures apparent irregularities in its movement. —Ed.

our fool faces. Georgie Periwinkle! Did *we* feel wobbly!

The kid said, uncomfortably, "And then I ran away, and I hid in an alley, and waited until your cabin boy came along, and then I hit him over the head with a sandbag, because I had to get his—"

OLD SCRATCH lost his grin. He purpled.

"You hit him over the head so you could get his job?" he yelped. "So *that* was why—"

Suddenly he began to laugh. He got so he couldn't stop himself. He began to laugh tears out of his eyes.

"He hit him over the head!" he yelled. "So help me, if that ain't the funniest—"

About that time I grabbed hold of the skipper and dragged him toward an automobile.

"Come on! We got to get off this off-center planet before you get that way, too!"

I never did like that other cabin boy anyway. No brains. Know what I mean?

"We cant turn back," said Penwig. "This ship is in a dimension where there are no curved lines."

THE STRANGE VOYAGE OF DR. PENWING

BY RICHARD O. LEWIS

Dr. Penwing had a fantastic theory about the Earth, but it wasn't as strange as his voyage through space.

"YOUNG man, do you believe the world is round?"

Bart Finny looked up quickly from the "Men Wanted" column to find a little man with bird-like eyes and wispy gray hair standing before him.

"No," said Bart. He was in no mood to be answering foolish questions. "I believe the world is flat. Flat broke! And in some cases even concavely so!"

To his surprise the little man seemed elated.

"Fine! Fine!" he said. "Remarkable! And now, young man, just one more question: What is the shortest distance between two points?"

"I used to believe that the shortest distance between two points was a straight line," recited Bart. "But lately I have discovered that the shortest distance between the point of college graduation and the point of getting a job is an unending jumble of circles and dizzy loops."

The little man with the bird-like byes seemed more elated than ever. "Marvelous!" he cried. "Such an open mind! You're just the man for the job."

At the word "job," Bart Fines leaped up from his bench, letting the newspaper fall to the ground. "Job!" he gasped. 'Did I hear you say *job*?"

"Yes. I need a mind like yours. One that is entirely open and unprejudiced. Follow me. We have no time to lose."

He wheeled about and started down the walk such a rapid pace

JULIAN
KRUPA
1940

a   t

that Bart, despite his long, athletic legs, had difficulty in keeping up.

The little man, with Bart at his heels, kept up the mad pace for several blocks and then turned abruptly to hurry up the steps of a terrace to a large brownstone house that set some distance back from the street.

Together, they entered the house and went through a living-room, dining-room and kitchen respectively to finally emerge into a long, low-roofed building that had been obviously annexed to the back of the house. From the benches and equipment strewn about, Bart judged this room to be a laboratory or work-shop of some kind.

The little man halted. "I am Dr. Penwing," he said quickly. "I feel that some explanations are in order before we begin our trip?"

"Trip?" Bart's eyes popped open. "Where are we going?"

"To our antipode,* St. Paul Island, just south-west of Australia."

It was Bart's turn to be elated. This was going to be great. He not only had a job, but was going to travel as well. That meant the job would last awhile, too. Several months at least. "I must have time to get a few of my things together," he mentioned.

"That will not be necessary, said Penwing. "We'll be back by noon tomorrow."

"Tomorrow!" Bart's heart sank. Of all the crazy ideas! But it was just his luck. After searching for a job all over this part of the country, he had landed one at last—only to find that his employer was as crazy as a loon.

"I must explain a few things," said Penwing. He glanced at his watch. "And I must hurry," he added. "Otherwise, we run serious chances of running into the moon."

Ye Gods! Bart felt like tearing his hair. How did the moon ever get mixed up in this? "Listen!" he said. "I accepted this job because I thought you had some work for me. But I'm not going on any round trip to Australia and back in twenty-four hours by way of the moon. That's out." He started toward the door. "And I'm leaving!"

Dr. Penwing clutched his coat in desperation. The coat was not a new one and a seam began to give way. Bart stopped. "All right," he said. "Maybe if you get a few more of those silly ideas off your mind you'll feel better."

*An antipode is a point upon the earth's surface diametrically opposed to another given point. —Ed.

THE STRANGE VOYAGE OF DR. PENWING

D R. Penwing's eyes were sparkling. "You see," he said, "I have discovered a *straight line!*" He made the statement with all the pride and emphasis of a man who had just done something as fully remarkable as finding perpetual motion, cold light and a dodo bird all rolled into one.

"I suppose you found it hiding somewhere on a ruler or a yardstick," said Bart.

"Quite the contrary. You see there are no straight lines on either of those devices. In fact, there is no such thing as a straight line."

"I see." said Bart. "And yet you found one."

"What I mean to say is," explained Penwing, "that a straight line is foreign to our world and to our conceptions. We can have a straight line only in relation to something else.* Never a true straight line in relation to all things at once. I mean we could never see such a straight line because the light rays we see travel in curves and not in a straight line dimension."

Penwing turned to a table near at hand. "Here." he said, "is a straight line."

Bart saw nothing on the table except a flat disc with a hole in its center. "It may be there," he said, "but I don't see it."

"Naturally. A straight line is quite invisible. But if you pass your fingers directly above that disc, you'll be able to *feel* the straight line."

Bart reached his hand forward. Much to his surprise his fingers contacted what felt like a badly twisted sliver of steel extending up from the disc-like base. He began running his fingers along the curve of steel and the very next instant he let out a cry of alarm. *His fingers had disappeared from sight.*

Jerking his hand quickly back into reality, he stood staring at it.

"When your fingers disappeared," explained Penwing, "it was

---

*A carpenter's level is straight only in relation to the surface of the earth, which is really a curve. A pilot dropping a bomb from his plane, would see the bomb falling straight beneath him as long as he kept his speed consistent. But to a man on the ground, the falling bomb would fall through a curve caused by the speed of the plane and the pull of gravity. A man on the moon, due to the earth's rotating, would see a vastly different curve, while a man on the sun would see a still more complex gyration. A line that was "straight" in relation to all these men would be quite beyond the concepts of any one of them. —Ed.

obvious that you were moving them along a straight-line dimension."*

Bart looked at the scientist in a new light. Perhaps he wasn't so crazy after all. "But what does all this have to do with the trip and my job?" he wanted to know.

"I'm coming to that," said Penwing. "Here is where I need your open and unbiased mind. I have worked alone with the problem for so long that I am afraid I can no longer approach it with the personal detachment of a true scientist. My own prejudice might bias me in my final decision.

"You see, I have just discovered that the earth is round and..."

"A fellow by the name of Copernicus beat you to that discovery by a few hundred years," mentioned Bart. .

"But he had the wrong idea," argued Penwing. "He believed we were living on the outside curvature of this round earth. But we're not. *We're living on the inside.*"

"Nuts!" said Bart. "If we were living on the inside like Peter Pumpkin-Eater's wife, we couldn't see the moon or the sun or..."

"They're on the inside with us." "But the sun is several hundred thousand times larger than..."

"No!" Penwing glanced at his watch again. "Science has been measuring sizes and distances in curved space with a faulty conception of angles and straight lines. An impossibility. It is like trying to measure the inside curvature of a rain barrel with a carpenter's square.

"Here," he said as he unrolled a large map and spread it out upon the table. "I'll show you how the earth really looks."

The map showed a circular cross-section of the earth. Within the large circle were series of curves. And inside the earth, in the space contained by the crust, were the stars, sun, and moon. The entire concept was of a huge earth, hollowed out, with all of space contained inside it.

"You see," said Penwing, "if I can but prove my theory it will revolutionize the entire concept of science!"

"It certainly would," admitted Bart. "But I still don't see what this

---

*A comparatively recent scientific concept is that all space is curved. Light rays, forces of gravity, sound and heat vibrations, time, everything—all adhere strictly to this *curved* dimension. Therefore, according to Dr. Penwing, anything in the straight-line dimension would be entirely invisible to anyone in this curved dimension of ours. —Ed.

has to do with the trip and my job."

"What I propose to do is to fly in a straight-line dimension from this side of the earth to the other side." Penwing looked at his watch again. "We will leave here at exactly noon and arrive at the other side of the earth at exactly midnight."

"I suppose you will be telling me next that you have a space ship hidden around here somewhere."

To Bart's complete surprise, Dr. Penwing nodded his head. "Come," he said eagerly. "I'll show you."

B ART followed him through the door at the side of the laboratory and out into the sunshine of a back yard that was enclosed by a high, board fence.

There was nothing in the yard except the close-cropped lawn. Bart, slightly bewildered, hurried along at the Doctor's side, his eyes scanning the lawn and seeing nothing.

"Look out!" It was Penwing who shouted.

Bart was in the act of turning his head to ascertain the trouble when he crashed squarely into something that was, as far as he was concerned, an immovable object. It had precisely the same effect upon him as if he had walked into a tree in the dark.

After shaking his head several times to clear it, Bart awakened to the fact that he was sprawled out upon the ground. He sat up and felt gingerly of a battered nose.

"What... What happened?" he asked when he found his voice.

"The space ship," said Penwing. "You bumped into it. I tried to warn you..."

Bart looked slowly about the yard and back again to Penwing. His head was buzzing in confusion. "My eyes must be a bit bad," he said. "I don't see any space ship."

"Of course not," said Penwing. "The ship is built in a straight-line dimension. It would naturally be invisible."

Bart shook his head again and got slowly to his feet. He had a strange feeling that he was getting into a bewildering something that was quite beyond his depth.

He saw Penwing reaching out into the sunshine, saw his fingers clutch something and pull back. There, right in the sun-lit air, appeared an irregular splotch of blackness. The splotch was taller and somewhat wider than a man. Its sides, top and bottom scintillated in a shimmering, obscure light.

"The doorway to the ship," Penwing said. "Go ahead and enter."

Bart stepped cautiously forward into the blackness. For a brief moment, the whole world seemed cloaked in shadow. Then he found himself standing in a round, bullet-like affair some ten feet in diameter. Subdued light glowed from the walls.

He turned about quickly toward the incredible black opening just in time to see a foot and leg appear there. It was Dr. Penwing's foot and leg. Then the rest of Penwing stepped into visibility, turned and closed the door.

Bart slumped down on a leather seat fastened to one wall. He tenderly nursed the large bump that was quickly making itself known on the fore part of his throbbing head. He decided to rest a bit and then get up, quit the whole silly business and go see about getting a sensible job of some kind.

Penwing was over at one side of the ship with his back turned. "I have it all figured out," he said over his shoulder. "A ship like this, built in the straight-line dimension, will be able to fly in a straight line directly to the opposite side of the world with very little resistance. Gravity, flowing along the curved dimension as it does, will be almost negligible. Think what this will mean to space travel in the future."

Bart got to his feet. He felt suddenly giddy and nauseated. The fact that it had been twenty-four hours since he had eaten a last order of doughnuts and coffee did not help his personal comfort in the slightest.

His mind was fully made up. "I've had enough of this," he said, starting for the door. "I'm getting out of here."

Penwing was after him in a flash. "Don't open that door!" he screamed.

"I'd like to know why," said Bart.

"I'm getting fed up with this job." He clutched the handle of the door.

Penwing grabbed his arm. "No! No!" he shouted. "You can't open that door! *You can't open it because we are already several hundred miles away from the earth!*"

BART felt some elemental substance flow out of his whole being. It left him weak and almost speechless. "You...you mean we've actually..."

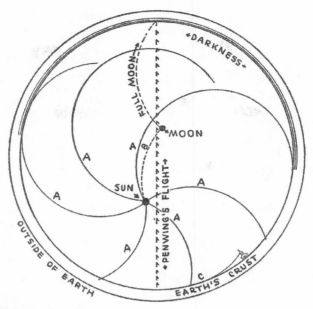

A—*Curved light-rays from the sun.*
B—*Curved light-ray reflecting full moon to dark side of earth.*
C—*Only the spire of the church visible at a distance—giving false impression of earth curving away convexly.*

— EXPLANATION —

Due to Penwing's earth spinning on its axis, all space within the earth spins in a like manner. The space nearest the earth's surface naturally spins at the same speed as the earth, while the space further from the surface spins less and less until, near the vortex, it is not moving at all. (Suspend a bucket of water from a long string and start it to spinning vigorously. You will notice that the water nearest the inside surface of the bucket will soon take up the spinning while the water near the center of the bucket will remain unmoved.)

Light-rays follow this natural curvature of space. Rays from the sun reach that part of the earth nearest it, but the sun's rays curve back upon themselves before reaching the far side of the earth. In this way day and night are accounted for. The moon is seen on the dark side of the earth because the rays of the sun are relayed from the moon by a second curve.

Forces of gravity also follow the curvature of space. (Place a small object in the water near the inner surface of your whirling bucket. You will notice that the object "falls" to the side of the bucket in a decided curve.) Gravity, then, becomes but a simple centrifugal force.

Eclipses of the sun and moon, seasonal changes, the position and action of fixed stars and planets, and all other natural phenomena can be explained readily and simply; but such an explanation would require more space than can be allowed here.

It is easy to understand how our men of science, ignorant of the fact that they were living in a world of curved dimensions, made such gross errors in measuring sizes and distances of the heavenly bodies they saw. —Ed.

A sudden red haze of anger flooded through him. He gripped Penwing by the shoulder. "Listen!" he ground out. "The best thing you can do is to turn this ship around and head back immediately!"

Penwing squirmed away. "But that's impossible," he said. "The ship is built in a straight-line dimension and is flying in a straight-line dimension. Nothing can curve it from its course."

Bart groped his way through his own personal red haze back to the leather seat and sat down again. He was on his way to St. Paul island, just south-west of Australia. Of all the silly things...

"A certain number of rockets started us off," Penwing was explaining. "Our momentum will carry us just slightly past the vortex at the center of the earth. At that point the ship will automatically turn end for end and begin falling toward the other side. A like number of rockets will explode a few minutes before we land, to break our fall."

Bart said nothing. He just sat there holding his head in his hands while disquieting thoughts burned through his brain. What if Penwing's straight line was all foolishness? In that case, the ship, after reaching a spot high above the earth, would turn end for end and plunge earthward with the unwanted help of the second battery of rockets.

And even if Penwing's ideas were correct, there was still the possibility of crashing into the sun or the moon, or of reaching the vortex and sticking there. And, too, St. Paul Island was a very small place in a very large sea. What if the ship missed it a mile or two one way or the other?

Bart glanced about the ship in search of a window; but there were none. They would have been of no practical value anyway, he decided. The straight-line dimension made all other dimensions outside the ship quite foreign to vision.

"You didn't happen to bring along a lunch?" he asked finally.

"Lunch? Lunch?" asked Penwing.

"Yes," said Bart. "It's something you eat."

"Why, no I didn't," stated Penwing. "My daughter usually takes care of things like that; but she was away today. That is why I was in such a hurry this morning. I wanted to do the experiment before she returned."

"And speaking of returning," said Bart, "have you figured out a way of returning from St. Paul Island in case we get there?"

Penwing put his hand to his head and sighed. Then he smiled a bit foolishly. "Do you know," he said, "in my excitement to get started I forgot all about getting back."

Bart groaned audibly. He wondered if there were any jobs to be had on St. Paul Island. Thirteen or fourteen thousand miles by water was a long way to hitchhike.

"I suppose I have really forgotten hundreds of things," Penwing went on. "My mind is like that. I may have even forgotten certain basic factors in my hurried computations."

"It's a poor time to be remembering them now," decided Bart.

"But here is one thing I didn't forget." Penwing reached into his pocket and brought out a small roll of bills. He thrust them toward Bart, "Your pay," he said.

Bart took the bills and counted them. One hundred dollars! That would buy a new suit of clothes and enough coffee, doughnuts and hamburgers to last until he could find a job.

Then he shook his head. "No," he said. "I can't accept that much money for doing nothing."

But Penwing insisted. "I want to pay you now just in case...well, just in case something happens..."

Bart shoved the money into his pocket and sat there grinding his teeth behind tight lips. So! Even Penwing had doubts concerning the success of the trip—wanted to pay off to ease his own conscience. .

BART opened his eyes. He realized that he must have been asleep; but it seemed that only a few minutes had passed since he was just sitting there staring at nothing.

He saw Penwing standing in the middle of the floor, watch in hand. Pen-wing's face seemed troubled and drawn.

"Now what?" asked Bart.

"The rockets," said Penwing. "They should have gone off two minutes ago to check our fall—but they didn't."

Bart was on his feet in an instant. "You mean we're going to crash?"

Penwing looked up at him. "I suppose so," he said. Then a certain look of sadness crept into his small, bird-like eyes. "I guess the experiment is going to be a failure," he added.

"Hang the experiment!" said Bart. "How do we get out of here?"

Penwing said nothing. He just stood there looking at the watch.

Bart had often wondered what the feelings of a man were just a moment or two before certain death. He knew now—just sort of a numb, frozen helplessness during which period everything stood still except the second hand of a watch.

Less than a minute left until midnight. And there would be a full moon...

A faint, buzzing vibration from somewhere beneath his feet broke into his consciousness. "What's that?"

"It's the rocket fuse," said Penwing.

"Then we aren't going to crash!"

"The rockets should be on fully three minutes to check our fall," said Penwing. "It takes the fuse fifteen minutes to reach the rockets. By that time..." It was unnecessary to finish the sentence.

Bart never remembered exactly what happened during those intervening seconds. It seemed to him that he was already dead as far as his sense perceptions were concerned.

Then everything seemed to happen at once. The second hand made its last tick, the floor sprang suddenly upward and a roaring explosion blasted through the ship. Bart knew that the ship was cracking up and felt that he was flying out through one of the sides, flying out into space that was filled with the glowing light of a full moon.

BART was surprised to find that he was still alive. He opened his eyes slowly and found that he was lying on his back on soft grass, lying there looking up at the full moon.

Presently, something else came into his range of vision. At first he thought it was another moon. Then, after getting his eyes to focus properly, he saw that it wasn't.

There just above his head was the face of a young girl. Her golden hair was shimmering in the moonlight and she was smiling down at him. He thought it the most beautiful sight he had ever seen.

"Better take it easy for a while," she said as he tried to rise. Her voice was as soft and as silvery as the moonlight.

Bart closed his eyes again. So this was St. Paul Island! Well, maybe it wasn't going to be so bad after all!

Then a sudden thought struck him. Dr. Penwing!

He sat up quickly. Scattered about him were jagged pieces of the ship that had been jolted out of the straight-line dimension into visibility. Penwing was sitting on the grass with his back against one of the pieces.

"How...how is he?" asked Bart. "Oh, Dad is all right," said the girl. "He was just shaken up a bit."

"Dad?" said Bart. "Your father?"

"Why, yes. I heard an explosion and came hurrying out here to find you and Dad sprawled out in the back yard with a lot of twisted pieces of tin scattered about. I had been wondering where he had gotten to."

"Then...then this is not St. Paul Island?"

"What a silly idea!" She laughed pleasantly. "This is our own back yard."

"I just remembered," put in Penwing. "My watch always gains a couple of minutes every twelve hours. That's why we didn't crash any harder."

"Nuts!" said Bart. Everything had become suddenly clear to him. "We didn't crash and we didn't go anywhere! What really happened is this: The first rockets didn't go off at all; they just left us sitting here in the back yard for twelve hours. Then the second battery of rockets went off all together and exploded the ship—and here we are."

"Marvelous deduction!" applauded Penwing. "Marvelous!" he repeated. "But, of course, it's entirely wrong.

"What really happened, young man, is this: The first rockets sent us on our way as I had planned. We passed the vortex and began falling toward the other side. Then something went wrong with the second battery of rockets. Just as we were about to crash, they exploded the ship and sent us flying out of the straight-line dimension into our own dimension in time to save us from serious injury."

"And, in that case," said Bart, "we would be on St. Paul Island."

"No," argued Penwing. "There is something else I had forgotten. It took us twelve hours to reach the other side, and due to the turning of the earth, it took this back yard exactly the same length of time to get there. Obviously, the ship and the back yard arrived at the other side of the earth at precisely the same instant."

"You can't prove it," said Bart. "You can't disprove it," said Penwing.

"If you two will quit your arguing and come into the house," said the girl, "I'll fix you a hot cup of coffee and something to eat."

THREE WISE MEN OF SPACE

by
DONALD
BERN

Three voyagers from deep in space come to Earth, seeking a place to live in peace—and land amid a hell of Nazi dive bombers!

Ceti drove the ship grimly upward..."One," he counted, "two, three..." and Nazi bombers crashed.

IT was Captain Ceti, peering through the small but powerful telescope of the slim space ship, who first saw the beautiful outlines of the small planet far away in space.

Captain Ceti's single great eye beamed happily, and the useless antenna sprouting from his immense forehead beat the air excitedly. Once, in the faded past, all the intelligent beings on Ceti's planet had conversed or communicated through such an antenna.

But that was long before speech had been invented, long before the planet Floros had become dried by the incessant, fierce heat of its large sun, and long before its decreasing population had been spurred to seek another world to inhabit.

Quickly, Captain Ceti gave orders to his two assistants. This took but a moment, for the Floros men possessed two sets of vocal cords and two tongues and could carry on two conversations at once.

"Eros," he commanded the larger assistant, "fire the repulse tubes and prepare to land within ten million miles!"

Meanwhile his other tongue said:

"Leo, send a message back to Floros that we have at last found a planet which appears habitable!"

His squat, dumpy Floros figure bent as he gazed once more through the telescope.

He reflected dreamily, "And the thousand-year search of our world to find another home can end in success...Leo, this planet is beautiful! I can see vast, green fertile fields, oceans, lakes, rivers! What a change from our dry world!"

Leo was at work sending the message of their happy discovery. The rays that left the transmitting apparatus traveled far faster than light rays* and would reach the home planet in a matter of months, Floros months, whereas radio waves or even electrical impulses would require countless years.

Tears welled from Leo's ball-like eye and ran down over his pudgy, single nostriled nose. Tears of gladness. What a prize this new planet would be!

How thankful the people of his world would be that a planet had been found to which they could migrate, and where they could live and bear their children without the ever-increasing hardship encountered on their own waterless globe!

Then a new thought struck Leo and he turned to the awed Captain Ceti. "Perhaps this sphere is overrun by hostile creatures!" he exclaimed worriedly. "What then?"

Eros broke in, scoffing: "Animals, perhaps, but probably not intelligent, and what is brute force next to our own weapon?"

He nodded his egg-shaped head toward the slender, almost delicate-looking ray-gun tube. Leo frowned.

"You have been too free with the ray gun," he declared. "On planet X236 you killed several intelligent plant life without cause."

"They attacked us!" Eros retorted. "But even so, I wanted to test the ray gun. And we lost nothing, since X236 had too rare an atmosphere to ever become the home of our people."

Leo's continued frown was evidence that this brutal reasoning bore no weight with him. But as they neared the blue, green and brown planet, the frown vanished to be replaced by a happy grin.

Already their apparatus had shown the planet to possess a breathable atmosphere. And the closer the space ship drew to the body, the more certain Leo became that here was a new world for the people of Floros.

"**F**IRE all forward repulse tubes," Captain Ceti ordered Eros after some time had passed.

Eros did as he was bidden and the slim space ship jarred its occupants at each terrific braking blast.

"Circle," said the fleshy captain, and Leo drew back the pilot stick.

The space ship left its straight course to move in a direction paralleling the surface of the sphere. Then they were closing in slowly, steadily, carefully. Captain Ceti put his eye to the telescope once more. Suddenly he gasped.

"Leo, Eros! This planet *is* inhabited! I can make out enormous dwellings and things moving!"

He moved aside to allow Leo to peer through the powerful lens. Leo moved the telescope over the surface of the globe, over its blue waters, its cities, fields.

"There is intelligence here," he said solemnly, gazing at boats on the oceans, at machines that flew through the air, and at vehicles that sped swiftly over the ground.

---

*Einstein's theory postulates that nothing can move faster than the speed of light. Therefore these strange other-world creatures must possess a knowledge of physics far beyond that encompassed by Dr. Einstein in his "Theory of Relativity." —Ed.

Eros elbowed him away from the telescope, put his own great eye to it. A second later he grunted:

"Intelligence, yes, but even that may be dangerous! These beings may become hostile to us."

"Or they may be friendly," Captain Ceti added.

The space ship circled about the planet, gradually braking now and drawing closer to the surface. Closer, closer, finally speeding over a vast expanse of ocean. Then suddenly, a large island was visible below.

"Landing speed!" the pudgy leader commanded, and the forward repulse tubes blasted once more.

Leo pulled a lever at the same instant as Ceti's second tongue rasped, "Wings!" and collapsible wings automatically spread out on either side of the space ship, converting it thereby into an airship, able to move with comparative slowness without falling.

An enormous city came into view. Captain Ceti pointed at a level space near the city.

"A landing field. Bring the ship down there," he ordered. The converted space ship swooped down.

Suddenly, the ship jarred roughly, spilling the Floros men from their seats. A loud impact numbed their ears as the space ship rocked wildly. Leo staggered to the pilot stick, yanked it back. They rose swiftly.

"We're being shot at!" Eros exclaimed. "I saw their guns! They're hostile without knowing who we are or what we want. Let me give them a taste of the ray gun!"

He started toward the fore of the ship where the ray gun was mounted.

"Wait," Leo protested, "help me with the pilot stick. Something is wrong with the control cable—jammed, I think!"

The other two plunged to help him. The space ship was losing altitude, coming once again into the firing range of the hostile creatures below. The very air about it seemed to be exploding.

AFTER a moment the Floros captain shook his egg-shaped cranium and spread wide the three fingers of his hands in a helpless gesture.

"Main cable stuck," he said. "They've got us. See if you can pancake her down gently, Leo."

The landing field was immediately below. Leo brought the ship's flat belly down on the smooth landing field. They came to an easy stop.

Eros was the first to see the tall, beastlike creatures that were approaching the space ship on long, powerful-looking legs. He gasped, paled in fright. Then the other two saw them.

"Six-foot giants!" Ceti exclaimed.

From the average three-foot height of the men from Floros, six feet of height indeed appeared gigantic. These beast-like creatures had hair covering the top of their small heads. They had two small eyes set in each side of their faces; they had two tiny nostrils instead of one large one.

But the most peculiar thing was that instead of being narrow at the top and wide in the middle, as were the bodies of the Floros men, these strange beings were top-heavy and small in the middle. They carried wood and metal sticks, and Leo guessed that these were weapons.

Eros fingered the ray gun nervously.

"Careful with it," Captain Ceti ordered. "We must make them our friends—if possible."

The ugly-looking inhabitants stopped at a distance of seven or eight feet from the space ship. Captain Ceti opened the porthole and bravely wiggled his squat Floros shape out to the open. Then he rose to his full three feet of height and regarded the tall creatures with fearless eyes.

A shocked, ludicrous expression appeared on the others' faces as they looked at the small figure before them.

Ceti cleared his throat.

"People of this beautiful world," he began, "you need have no fear of me or my comrades. We will not harm you. We come on a peaceful but desperate mission."

He halted, realizing his Floros speech was just gibberish to them.

Leo squirmed through the small porthole of the space ship. Then Eros followed, a pencil-size ray gun in his hand.

Suddenly, with a concerted move, the six-footers advanced on the Floros newcomers. Eros brought his ray gun up.

"Wait!" Leo shouted, and tried to knock down his arm. Too late! The trigger was released, a purple ray sprang from the slender tube and enveloped two of the advancing group. They twisted in sudden agony and dropped to the ground heavily.

One of the other creatures exclaimed something that sounded like "blimey!" and at the same instant, the three visitors were pounced upon and thrown to the hard ground. Leo felt his senses fading. For a moment he fought the sensation, then he slumped unconscious.

THERE was a terrific ache in the narrow top of his head. Leo groaned
aloud and opened his great eye. Finally, the spinning world came
to a standstill and he perceived that he was lying on a cot in a cell.

On similar lengthy cots, Captain Ceti and Eros were just stirring to
consciousness. Shortly they were both wide awake, sitting up dazedly.

Captain Ceti passed his three-fingered hand over his forehead with
a pained gesture and gazed helplessly at his two men. His antenna
drooped dismally. He frowned on the sullen Eros.

"You," he grated, "are the fault of this! They weren't going to harm
us, but you killed two of them!"

"They attacked us first, didn't they?" Eros protested shrilly.

THEIR chubby leader swore fluently in the Floros language. Eros
had been disagreeable, sullen and a trouble-maker from the
beginning of the expedition.

Time passed; and then, as the sky was growing dark, bowls of food
were handed the prisoners through the bars of the cell. Then some tall,
bespectacled creature endeavored vainly to converse with them.

"He's a scientist of some sort, I think," Leo said.

The bespectacled being left them finally.

Then a whining, swelling shriek brought them tumbling to the cell's
barred window. For some mysterious reason, large numbers of their
immense captors were scurrying toward what appeared to be some
underground shelters. Some were gazing anxiously at the sky as they
ran. The whine swelled once more and faded away.

It was, had the Floros men known it, an air-raid alarm siren. And then
through the eerie scream came the bass roar of many motors, mounting
quickly to a deafening roar. Airships flew overhead in large numbers.

"There seems to be trouble," Captain Ceti commented.

His casual words were suddenly and almost dramatically verified.
A series of terrific detonations split the air, vibrating the walls and
breaking the cell window. The violent shock threw the prisoners to the
cell floor in a tangle of arms, legs and antennae.

Captain Ceti staggered to his feet, ambled his squat shape to the
window and looked up at the sky. He shook his fist as one of the attacking

ships swooped low and dropped some of its explosive missiles.

"There must be a war going on," he groaned. "Just my luck to get mixed up in something like that!"

A violent, rocking blast burst upon them suddenly. A part of the prison wall dissolved amid the ear-racking detonation. One of the missiles had struck their prison direct!

"Let's get out of here!" Eros bleated.

They scrambled over the debris and crawled through the jagged gap in the wall. As Leo straightened, his large eye caught sight of the spaceship, still standing unmoved on the landing field. The field was a whirl of activity, as airship after airship took to the sky with a revengeful roar to engage the enemy craft above in deadly combat.

But still the explosive shells dropped, gouging craters in the once level ground.

"The space ship will be destroyed!" Leo gasped.

"This is our chance to escape!" Eros exclaimed.

The three tiny Floros men ran toward the space ship. The embattled defenders failed to notice them as they blanketed the darkening sky with an anti-aircraft barrage.

"Release the jammed control cable," Captain Ceti ordered, asserting himself as leader once more.

OBLIVIOUS to the fighting and death raging about him, Leo delved into the mechanisms of the space ship. For a moment Eros gave aid; then as an explosion nearby dug a hole in the ground.

"We'll be blown to bits!" he gasped. "I'm getting out of here!"

He started to run across the open field. An enemy plane swooped low directly above him. Eros ceased to exist.

"That's the end of him," Captain Ceti muttered bitterly, but because of the incessant tumult the busily working Leo did not hear him. Finally Leo's searching fingers found the cause of the jammed control, a fragment of anti-aircraft shell.

"They shot at the space ship, thinking it was an enemy machine," Leo reflected.

They wiggled inside the long tubular space ship just as a new formation of enemy craft zoomed over the field to be met by the alert anti-aircraft batteries. Captain Ceti sprang to the pilot stick, and in a flash the space ship left the ground.

Instantly it was surrounded by a whirling, fighting flight of enemy flying machines. Small pellets from rapidly firing weapons drummed against the space ship. Several whined through the open porthole.

Captain Ceti and Leo exchanged significant glances. Then the captain maneuvered the space ship to an advantageous position as Leo grasped the slender tube of the ray gun and aimed at the peculiarly crossed marking of an enemy craft.

He released the trigger. The airship suddenly wilted, crumpling at the center. It began to spin downward like a wounded bird.

"One!" Captain Ceti counted grimly. He maneuvered to the tail of another enemy ship.

"Two!" he exclaimed a moment later. "Three, four, five, six, seven, eight—"

The attacking aircraft finally turned and fled toward their home base, greatly depleted in number. They had never fought a space ship before!

With a tired sigh, Leo turned from the ray gun. Things on this planet were not as he had hoped they would be. Captain Ceti was also depressed.

"What do we do next?" Leo asked.

Ceti increased the speed of the space ship and headed toward the coldness of outer space. After a short while, Leo pulled the collapsible wing lever and they idled through vast emptiness at seven miles a second. For a moment longer the captain was silent, his large forehead wrinkled in thought. Then he said:

"I'll dictate a message home."

Leo sat down at the transmitting apparatus.

People of Floros,

I am sorry to report that the planet mentioned in my last message is not, after all, an ideal world—not just now, at least.

It is inhabited by hostile beings who shower explosive death on each other.

They are much the way we were in the distant past, and I have no doubt that their wars will end as have ours.

Perhaps then, people of Floros, it will not be too late to migrate there.

Captain Ceti.

The slim space ship gathered speed and left the planet that called itself Earth far behind.

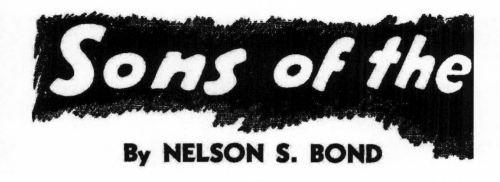

Sons of the

By NELSON S. BOND

12,000 years into the past Duke Callion and Joey Cox sped, in a desperate attempt to save the civilization of Aztlan from the Deluge.

Intrigue and treachery sweep the Atlantean city as the day of the Deluge draws near, and Duke Callion battles to avert an ancient tragedy. Inexorably the Deluge roars down, forcing Duke Callion and Joey Cox to fulfill an ancient legend.

AUTHOR'S NOTE

This story is not pure fantasy. All references to places, persons and happenings have a basis in fact or legend. No one can say that this story did happen. But for that matter, no one can say that it did NOT happen. All I say is that—it MIGHT have happened!

—Nelson S. Bond.

CHAPTER I
The Man in the Cantina

He was a tall man; tall and distinctly fair, though long exposure to the blazing suns of Mexico had tanned him a deep, coppery bronze. But his hair was wheat-yellow and the tiny hairs on the backs of his hands a sun-bleached silver.

His eyes were pale, sea-faded blue, sunk in cavernous pits beneath high ridged cheekbones; shaded by twisting brows. His nose was a thin-bridged arch that jutted from a forehead tall and sloping as that of any antique marble. He looked like some old Egyptian deity, wakened and newly come from the Valley of the Kings. Aquiline. Proud.

Behind me I heard an agonized scream as one of my less fortunate followers tumbled into a hole that had no bottom.

All in all, he was not the sort of person you would expect to find brooding; sipping cheap, thin ale in the back room of an odorous native *cantina*. "Duke" Callion, noticing him, nudged his companion. The gesture was unnecessary, for Joey Cox was already staring at the man. Now he murmured his perplexity.

B-b-beats me, Duke. American?"

"I don't know," said Duke. "Maybe. We'll see."

Fat Pedro, proprietor of the establishment, stared at the two wayfarers. He said curiously:

"You have come far, *senores*?"

Duke replied, shortly, "Far enough." He motioned the barkeep to draw two glasses of beer, nodded toward the mysterious stranger. "*Americano*?"

Fat Pedro's small eyes rolled. He knife-edged the foam off two sweating steins; placed them before Duke and Joey. He leaned far over the counter to whisper hoarsely:

"El es loco, senores. Muy loco!"

Duke grinned. A lean, reckless, lopsided grin.

"That makes three of us," he said. "Come on—let's go meet him, Joey."

He started toward the man's table. With a speed astonishing in his gourd-like frame, Fat Pedro reached out to clutch his arm. The barkeep's face was frightened.

"*Por favor, senor!*" he pleaded. "Go not near him. It will but cause *molestia*. Trouble!"

Duke shook his arm free. "Trouble in Chunhubub, eh?" he laughed. "Well, why not?" And he continued moving toward the stranger, Joey at his heels. A little bit more trouble, Duke reasoned, could hardly make any difference. They were already in it up to their necks.

Soldiers of fortune, he and Joey had just quitted the service of rebel Generalissimo Hernandez Lopez for the very best of reasons. Because neither Generalissimo Lopez nor his troops existed any longer. A surprise attack by the Federals at Tehuantepec had decimated the rag-tag war machine of Lopez. Lopez himself had been courteously but firmly shot before the whitewashed courtyard wall of the District jail.

There signal honor had been paid him when no less a dignitary than the Governor of the District himself had rolled and placed between his lips a cigarette. Unhappily, Generalissimo Lopez had not enjoyed the favor. A volley of polite, but adequate, gunfire had expelled life from his body even as his lips expelled their first blue streamer of smoke.

Following which, Duke and Joey had found themselves friendless in the heart of a country which has little love for stray—and defeated—rebels. By foot, horseback and mule, they had beaten a path cross-country to Yucatan. It was, they knew, useless to attempt an escape from a large port, such as Vera Cruz. But with a little luck, and with the aid of the few remaining *pesos* in their money belts, it was possible they might find a way of leaving the country through one of the smaller Peninsula ports.

No native, they knew, could resist the lure of the posters offering "Ps. 2000" for the apprehension of either, dead or alive. But if they could manage to find a friendly American or Englishman— And here, in this sleepy little *cantina,* was a man who might be persuaded to their cause.

So ran Duke Callion's thoughts as he moved across the room toward the stranger's table, conscious of the odd hush that had fallen over the room; conscious, too, of the scarcely veiled hatred in the native's eyes fastened on his back, and of the fact that behind him, Fat Pedro had taken time from his interminable bar-wiping to cross himself in a gesture at once indignant and fearful...

SURPRISINGLY, the white stranger did not seem to resent the approach of the two Americans. His shaggy eyebrows lifted as they drew near; then he rose to greet them with utterly unexpected courtesy. His voice was deep and smooth as cat's fur. And he spoke—in English!

"Welcome, my friends. You do me a great honor."

"The honor is ours, sir," Duke corrected gravely. "Forgive our intrusion, but I judged we three were fellow strangers in a foreign land, and—"

There was no way of anticipating the man's swift reaction. The hawk-like lines of his face hardened instantaneously. His pale eyes seemed to flicker in their jetty depths. His voice was suddenly harsh; imperious.

"Foreign land, sir? There are no such. *All* lands are those of the sons of Aztlan!"

Then, as Duke and Joey stared at him in shocked bewilderment, he relaxed. The corded muscles on the backs of his hands softened. The strange light died in his eyes. He said, slowly:

"Your pardon, please. Sometimes I forget. And—and all things are not as they once were..."

It was an apology; yet it was not an apology. One of Caesar's proud *centuriones,* addressing a subject barbarian, might have used that same haughty tone. Duke glanced at Joey. Joey's hand gestured significantly, and his lips framed the word, "Nuts!"

Duke stifled a grin, and sat down. Crazy or not, the man might be able to help them. He said cordially:

"My name is Callion, sir. Dave Callion. Or more often—Duke. And this is my friend, Joey Cox."

The stranger nodded quietly.

"I am Quelchal," he said gravely. "Quelchal, of the—" He paused in midsentence; his eyes resting on his empty stein. He looked up sharply, his voice rasping to the barkeep, "Empty! By Bel, dog of an innkeeper, must I give you the lash to get service here! More beer! And quickly!"

Duke stirred restlessly. Angry faces were looking up from all about the room. Evidently this was not the first time Quelchal had created a commotion. And evidently the man was far from popular with the glowering natives.

Fat Pedro waddled from behind the bar. Beads of perspiration streaked his greasy forehead. His mouth was sulky. He leaned over the table.

"*Senores,*" he muttered, "I ask you to leave—now! This disturbance I do not like. *Por favor!*"

The tall stranger rose. He said scornfully:

"You ask us to go, eh? That is well. We cannot talk in this sty, anyway. Come, my friends, let us go before this seller of cheap swill expires of fright and our bellies retch with the stench of this putrid stuff!" He put a hand into his pocket. Metal danced on the table. "For the beer, *olla gordo!*"

Resentful or not the "fat pot" was a tradesman. He glared at the coin; mouthed complainingly:

"For the hundredth time, *senor,* not that money. I have no use for it. *Mexicano,* yes! *Americano,* yes! But *that*—"

Pig! Eater of pigs!" Quelchal retrieved the bit of metal; thrust it back into his pocket. "If you will not have this, take nothing! I go! Come, my friends!"

He stalked toward the door. Fat Pedro's face darkened. He spat something in his native tongue; so swift that even the two soldiers of fortune could not catch it. There was a sudden movement in the *cantina*. A figure brushed by Duke; slipped toward the disappearing Quelchal. Something caught the glint of sunlight, shimmering evilly.

It was instinct—sheer instinct—on Duke's part. He left his feet in a swooping dive. His arms locked about the knees of Quelchal's attacker; welded a band of steel there. Metal clattered on the floorboards. The man whom Duke had tackled grunted once, heavily, and lay still.

Suddenly the place was in an uproar. As Duke rose to his feet, something whisked by his head to dig into the wall beyond and cling there, vibrating a melody of death. Joey's excited voice shrilled, "D-d-duke! B-beat it!"

Quelchal had turned in the doorway. He hesitated now; moved as though to come back. Before he could do so, Duke and Joey hurtled toward him; slammed him backward into the street.

Angry figures spilled after them like bees buzzing from a broken hive. Duke's hand streaked to his hip. His gun coughed bluntly. A leaden messenger splatted on the lintel above the heads of their pursuers. Its challenge froze the natives in their tracks. For an instant. Then they were scrambling for the security of the *cantina*.

Voices screamed vile epithets. That of Fat Pedro was loudest of all as the barkeep clamored for his *argento*. Duke dug a few coppers from his pocket; tossed them toward the now vacant doorway. He shouted warningly, "Get that, fat one, *after* we've gone!"

Behind him, Joey said mournfully:

"Trouble. Nothing but trouble. I wish I was home in Cincinnati!"

Quelchal stood quiet and aloof; as calm and unmoved as though nothing had happened. His mood was meditative.

"Eaters of entrails! I shall have them burned in tallow. Better yet, they shall be buried in scorpions—"

Duke, his automatic still covering the doorway, rapped impatiently:

"Yeah! But meanwhile, they'll be getting up nerve to come out after us. What do we do now?"

Quelchal was silent for a moment. Then:

230 OF AMAZING STORIES - 1940

"We will go to my place," he said quietly. "It will be safe there."

CHAPTER II
He From Aztlan

THERE was nothing queer about Quelchal's "place"—from the outside. It was a typical Mexican adobe hut, entering from the main street of the little Yucatan town by means of a narrow, shaded *arceo* which widened at its far end into a court.

A solitary frayed, despondent palm made an oasis of shade in the center of the court. The hut itself had but one doorway, and only two tiny, paneless windows; mere niches in the baked clay. But its walls were thick, and inside there was welcome relief from the interminable down-pouring of the tropic sunlight. As they entered, Duke heaved a deep sigh of relief. He did not need Quelchal's urging to toss himself on a cool mat of reeds.

Joey Cox was nervous. Like Duke, he had divested himself of his heavy gunbelt, but unlike his friend, he did not relax in the grateful coolness. He padded about the dim room restlessly, peering into shadows as though suspicious of lurking dangers.

"D-d-duke—I don't like it!"

Duke Callion grinned. It was his temperament to take things as they came. Fight, fun or frolic—they were all much the same to the reckless young Irish-American. He grinned at his stuttering companion lazily.

"Don't like what? Those greasers at the *cantina?*"

"N-n-not them. I don't mind them so much. B-b-but this Quelchal, or whatever his name is. I think we ought to pull out of here. The guy's nuts!"

Duke nodded amiably. "All right. So he's nuts—then what?"

"Then let's blow."

Duke stretched luxuriously.

"And leave this coolness? Not on your life. I'm going to stay right here—until tonight, anyway. Anyhow," he straightened and looked at his companion significantly, "Quelchal's a white man. He may be able to help us get to the coast. Get a boat out of the country."

Joey said stubbornly, "W-w-we've made out all right by ourselves before. We don't n-n-need help from—"

"Duck it!" Duke clipped succinctly. Quelchal was entering the room. He bore on a wickerwork tray a carafe, three glasses, and a small vial of liquid. He approached the two friends and nodded with more than customary geniality.

"I see you are relaxing, my friends. That is well. Soon you will be completely rested."

He poured water into each of the three glasses; then, with precise fingers, added to each glass a few drops from the tiny bottle. Joey glanced at Duke; then back at Quelchal suspiciously.

"What's that stuff?" he demanded.

Quelchal smiled. "Drink, my friend, and learn."

Joey squinted at his glass dubiously. "I'm not drinking anything," he said, "until I know what it is. For all I know—"

Duke drawled, "Don't be a sap, Joey!" and took his glass. He lifted it toward Quelchal briefly. "Good luck!" he said—and swallowed.

Swallowed—then stared. Whatever Quelchal had put into the water from his little vial, *did* something! There was no change in the taste of the water. But the effect—

It was as refreshing as a cold plunge on a hot day. As stimulating as the keen bite of alcohol to tired muscles. Of a sudden, Duke's weariness and exhaustion were gone, and his body seemed to have found new life, new vigor, from some unsuspected well of strength. He felt awake. Alive.

"Sa-a-ay!" He looked at Quelchal in amazement.

The tall stranger smiled again; that slow, grave smile that Duke could not help but like.

"We call it," he said, *"ambrosia."*

Duke repeated enthusiastically, "Ambrosia! That's a good name for it. It's like the stuff the gods used to drink in Olympia. That stuff—"

A STRANGE sadness swept the smile from Quelchal's face. He said, in a far-away tone:

"Olympia—no! Or, maybe yes. There were some of the barbarians who called it that."

Joey Cox had followed Duke's example. Now shining eyes and a subtle lifting of his shoulders indicated that he, too, had felt the magic of the potion. He said:

"O-o-olympia? B-b-barbarians? Hey, what's it all about? W-w-what are you guys saying?"

Quelchal's eyes met Duke's searchingly. His voice was strangely pleading. He said:

"Callion...Duke Callion...I think you are beginning to understand. Aren't you?"

There was a curious sensation of lightness, eeriness too bewildering for comprehension, tugging at the fringes of Duke's intelligence. Memories half-forgotten through years of adventurous living were corning back to him slowly; tantalizing him with a thought too absurd to be true. Quelchal's words reached beyond the frontals of his mind; stirred some latent spark of imagination. He said, hesitantly:

"Quelchal—there *is* a thought in my mind. But it is so wild...so fantastic..."

"Not wild. Not fantastic." Quelchal beckoned the two Americans to his side; stepped with swift, sure strides to a far, dim corner of the room. Even in that half-light, his eyes seemed to glow feverishly. His hand made an impatient gesture toward a wall rack on which stood a number of small objects. "Look!" he said. "These—have you ever beheld anything of their kind?"

That the things were *old*—incredibly old—Duke knew instantly. And that they were not born of any civilization known and understood by modern man, he knew, too. A ring was there; a ring of strangely greenish metal which in the faint light shimmered weirdly. There were coins...coins of no nation recorded in history. Coins surmounted with odd hieroglyphics; embossed with the effigy of a monstrous snake entwined about a stark and leafless tree. There was a smooth metallic cylinder there, graven with indecipherable figures.

Quelchal's long, bronzed fingers swept a metal tablet from the shelf. He placed it into Duke's hands. Once again, as in the *cantina,* his voice was oddly harsh and commanding.

"This symbol, Duke Callion—you have seen it somewhere before? It means anything to you?"

Duke stared—and memory flooded back suddenly. He was a boy again, delving into a strange fantastic book from his father's library. A book which reported to tell of an ancient civilization built around a—a crooked mountain. Of an ancient race, fabulously potent, fabulously wise.

His lips groped for half remembered words. He said:

"Cosmos, the Mad Monk! The crooked mountain. The mountain of Cal...of Calhua..."

Quelchal almost ripped the tablet from Duke's hands. He raised it high over his head, eyes gleaming and thunder rolled in the chanting of his voice.

"Calhuacan!" he cried. "At last one who *knows!* Aye, Duke Callion, it *is* the Mount of Atlantis. And *I—*"

Despite himself, Duke felt dread expectation rolling over and through him in great, omnipotent waves. Suddenly he knew what Quelchal's next words must be. But he framed the question. "And you—?" he asked.

There was the clarion call of trumpets in the voice of the golden stranger. Pride, too. Hauteur...and victory. And glory.

"And I, my friend," he said, *"I—am an Atlantean!"*

CHAPTER III
The Years Between

IT was Joey Cox who broke the silence. Stammering Joey Cox, whose awed tone proved that even *his* complacent pragmatism had been shaken by Quelchal's proud pronouncement. He said, in a hushed but querulous tone.

"A-a-atlantean? What does he mean, Duke? W-what's an Atlantean?"

There was a dreamlike quality to Duke Callion's answer. The words seemed to spring from some deep well of his consciousness; some forgotten corner of his memory.

"It was centuries ago," he said slowly, as though he repeated an almost lost knowledge. "Plato said it was nine thousand years before *his* time. That would make it twelve thousand years from today.

"There was a land—an island—opposite the mouth of the Mediterranean Sea. A large island which was the remnant of an Atlantic continent. It was known to the ancient world as—Atlantis.

"It was here that man first rose from barbarism to civilization. These were the Elysian Fields, Olympus, the Gardens of the Hesperides, Asgard, Valhalla. The gods and goddesses of later civilizations were actually but memories—race memories—of the ancient kings and queens of this island. The acts attributed to the gods in our mythology are but a confused recollection of real historical events."

Joey said confusedly, "B-b-but how is it I n-never heard of this place before? There's n-n-no island at the m-m-mouth of the Mediterranean Sea, Duke."

"No. Not now. Because it sank. Sank beneath the sea, in a gigantic catastrophe, with more than sixty million inhabitants. The sea opened and swallowed Atlantis—or so the legend tells in a terrible convulsion of nature. In a single day and night."

Duke stopped suddenly. He had been repeating his fragments of knowledge concerning Atlantis more to reawaken his own memories than for Joey's benefit. Now his own words roused him to the incredibility of Quelchal's claim.

"But, Quelchal, I don't understand. You said that you were an Atlantean. The descendant of Atlanteans—that is what you meant?"

"Not a descendant, Duke Callion." Quelchal's tone was infinitely grave. "I am one of those who really *lived* in the shadow of Calhuacan aforetime."

Duke stared. The man was mad. *Must* be mad—or the rest of the world was! But Quelchal was speaking.

"I have waited long," he said, "for one in whom I could confide. A man who might understand. My friends, if you will be seated, I would like to tell you a story..."

IT was a new colony (Quelchal began) and one which our mariners had but lately discovered. It lay far to the westward of the homeland. It was a land of warm, blazing sunshine; of minerals, oils and vast forest resources. Its name, in the tongue of the brown-skinned natives, was Yuuktaan. But we called it "Mayapan,"* honoring the goddess and god of fruit and fertility.

---

* "The Abbe Brasseur de Bourbourg calls attention to the fact that Pan was adored in all parts of Mexico and Central America; and at *Ponuco* the Spaniards found, upon their entrance into Mexico, superb temples and images of Pan. The names of both Pan and Maya enter extensively into the Maya vocabulary...(as in)...the name of the ancient capital, Mayapan."—Introduction to Landa's "Relacion."

I was but a young man then, yet not lacking in experience. I had twice
I served with our foreign troops; our legions that held the barbarian
outside world in fee. Once, indeed, I served under King Theseus himself
when he led his expedition against the Gorgons.* Weird creatures they
were with their ebony-hued skins, their brightly painted faces, and
their wild, curly locks piled high on their heads in a fashion calculated
to touch the bravest heart with stony dread.

In recognition of my services, King Theseus granted me the post of
Viceroy to this new colony. I had little desire to leave the homeland, but
the proffered honor was a tempting one. Ten summers as Viceroy to
Mayapan, and I knew I could return to Aztlan as an important figure
in the royal court. So I accepted.

There was much to be done, I found upon my arrival at Mayapan.

First, the natives must be convinced that our conquest was a benign
one. They were a backward race; sullen and suspicious. They had no
culture, and less learning. In contrast to us Atlanteans, whose knowledge
of the sciences was greater than that which the world enjoys today.

Here Duke Callion interrupted.

"Come now, Quelchal!" he expostulated. "That cannot be so. Our
chemists...our astronomers...to say nothing of our marvelous mechanical
civilization..."

Quelchal smiled sadly.

"Your chemists, Duke Callion? You have tasted the ambrosia. Could
your chemists duplicate it today? And as to mechanical ability—well,
we shall speak of that later."

My duties, however, (the Atlantean continued) were not solely of
a social or altruistic nature. One important task was the study and
development of the natural resources of Mayapan.

Having studied chemistry, geology, kindred subjects during my
own youth—yes, Duke Callion, Atlantis had its institutions of higher
learning—I did not delegate others to head all of these expeditions,
but selected those which seemed most promising for my own personal
study. It was this which was responsible for my being here today.

Word was brought to me by certain of my engineers that in a mountain
not far from the capital city of Mayapan a wealthy mother-lode of gold

---

* The "Gorgons," whose enemies were turned to stone by gazing upon them?

had been discovered. Hearing this, I made arrangements to supervise the mining personally. I temporarily transferred my headquarters to a mining camp at the base of this mountain.

I will not bore you with the details of our mining operations. Suffice it to say that they were highly successful. The gold was there, as my geologists had claimed. It was, apparently, retrievable in great quantities.

Only one factor made the operation hazardous. The fact that this mountain was volcanic. From its highest peak there constantly fluttered a plume of white haze; while ever and again our miners were terrified to find the earth shaking beneath their feet in undulating temblors.

It was following one such shock—more severe than most—that my chief engineer came to me suggesting that we abandon our position as untenable.

"It is but a matter of time, Excellency," he told me, "before a major 'quake occurs. A temblor which may not only destroy all of our work, but take the lives of many of our workers."

I was reluctant to adopt his suggestion. Gold was the standard of exchange in Aztlan of old, as throughout most of the world today. I had already received many very pleasing communications from King Theseus regarding the shipments we had been sending home from our colony. So I hesitated.

"Our stopes," I said. "Our shafts and stalls are sound, are they not?"

The engineer shrugged. His gesture indicated the puniness of any man-made path through the bowels of Mother Earth when she begins to tremble.

"Very well, then," I told him. "I will make a trip into our farthermost shaft myself. If, in my opinion, there is danger, we will abandon the mine."

"Yourself, Excellency?" The, man looked fearful.

"Of course."

"And—how soon?"

"Tomorrow. Or better yet—tonight. Darkness and light have little meaning in the heart of a mine."

He sought to dissuade me. Begged me not to go into the mine. But I should have been a poor leader of my colonists had I not been willing to undertake what he called the "perilous journey" to the working face of the mine. I was determined to go; perhaps even eager. I dismissed his wild predictions as fantasy.

Would to Bel I had been less proud; what happened next?

QUELCHAL paused. There was a moment's silence and then the sound of Joey Cox drawing a deep breath.

"W-w-well?" he prompted, "w-wwhat happened next?"

"The end of the world," Quelchal replied sombrely. "Or, at least, the end of *my* world..."

It was at the entrance to the fourth stope (the Atlantean continued) that we first began to feel the temblors. For more than two hours we had been in the mine, carefully studying each working face, trying to determine once and for all the workability of the mine. Suddenly, as we were approaching the last and most distant face there came a dull rumbling sound that rocked and echoed in our ears like the beating of massive drums. The ground beneath our feet began to shake; slowly at first and with a sort of insistent rhythm, then more and more violently.

A loose rubble of shale and small rocks began falling from the rough-hewn roof above us, pelting our exposed bodies sharply. There was a curiously sharp odor in the air; a stinging, acid taint that made us cough and sneeze.

For the first time, misgivings struck me. My head engineer *had* been right. The mountain *was* volcanic—and actively so. I gave the only order possible under the circumstances.

"Flee!" I told my companions. "Run for your very lives!"

How can I hope to describe to you those next wild moments? A scant handful of men scrambling through musty corridors that rocked and swayed like the walls of an opium eater's dream world. The bedlam of sound that cascaded on our eardrums from every side! The groaning, crushing sound of nature in travail.

Panic struck my attendants, but I am proud to say that even in those dreadful minutes I was still their overlord and chief. They recognized my authority, and at the risk of their own lives gave way that I might move before them into higher ground and safety.

That was—until the torches went out. But as the gas increased about us, those flickering torches of grease wood spluttered and died, plunging us into Stygian darkness. Then it was truly every man for himself...hot hands pressing forward eagerly toward the still-open corridors...torn feet stumbling over piles of detritus.

As the last torch expired, I saw one man go down—his head crushed beneath a huge rock that had fallen from the tunnel roof. Once, beneath my feet, I felt the ground slip into a gaping hole. I leaped frantically; managed to find firmer footing. But behind me I heard an agonizing scream as one of my less fortunate followers tumbled into a hole that had no bottom...

It was no longer possible to tell where our original tunnel had been. Our clutching hands found great rips in the walls; shearings as smooth as our own borings. For a while our little party attempted to keep together; locating each other by shouts and cries. But as the hellish cacophony about us deepened in tone, our cries were lost.

How long I fled through those twisting tunnels it is hard to guess. But at last there came that dread moment when my hand, reaching out to find a companion, found no human to touch. When my shouts touched upon no ear. I was alone. Completely alone beneath the crust of a tortured earth that was ripping and tearing itself into shreds. And—I was lost!

Yes, I knew now that I was lost. Somewhere along the way I had taken the wrong turning; run, somehow, into one of those blind passages that had either been hewn by our own workmen or had been carved out of solid rock by the violence of the temblors. Still I continued to run forward; hopelessly, unthinkingly, as a trapped rat will continue to run the corridors of a maze.

But at last there came the moment when my headlong flight plunged me painfully into a solid wall. There was no more open space before me. I tried to retrace my steps, then. I moved backward, carefully, feeling the ground beneath me quivering and trembling like a wounded heart. My hands, widestretched, sought an opening—any opening—to gain another furlong...another yard...another inch...

I found-nothing! Behind me a huge segment of solid rock had fallen, blocking completely the path through which I had entered this small corridor. Before me there was no opening. The walls that surrounded me were smooth; sheer. I was trapped!

And with that realization, my resources came to an end. I suddenly discovered that I was worn and weary; exhausted with my futile scrambling. My lungs and nostrils were thick with the stench of dust and gas. Despairing, I threw myself on the ground. My chest labored. My heart's pumping was like the vast pulsation of a savage drum. But even as I lay there, panting, its tumultuous throbbing died down. I began to feel calmer despite the din about me. I understood, finally, why...

IT was the gas that was seeping into my chamber! Somewhere above me a slide had opened a vent, possibly from the very heart of the volcano. Through this aperture was filtering some strange admixture of noxious gases. These it was that were soothing my troubled mind; lulling me into a sense of false security.

I knew, then—or guessed—that this was to be my doom. To die alone and unattended at the bottom of this mine.

Yet—it was a better death than I had hoped for a few minutes before. It was, at least, a painless death. I made a brief prayer to the gods, feeling the soft fingers of drowsiness fog my mind as I mumbled the final words.

The ground beneath me felt somehow softer. Now my breathing was a slow and measured thing. Curiously, I felt the tiny pulse in my wrist. It was beating—but oh, it was slow! Infinitely slow. It was getting slower as my tired fingers fell away from my wrist.

No longer did the thick gases choke me. A feeling of utter abnegation suffused me! expunged all cares from my mind. My body seemed to float, suspended in thick, creamy softness. My eyelids were weighted. They closed of their own accord. I was tired...tired...and content. Death, I remember thinking, was not an unpleasant companion.

Sleep came upon me like a sable cloud. Beneath me the tortured earth groaned and twisted...rocked and swayed with the rhythm of a gigantic cradle...

CHAPTER IV
Escape

QUELCHAL paused, and smiled. So engrossed had Duke Callion been in the strange man's story that the smile seemed somehow eerie. As though it had been framed by the lips of a spirit.

Joey Cox must have felt it, too. He said, "B-b-but, Quelchal—y-y-you escaped?"

Quelchal nodded slowly. His voice was melodious.

"Yes, my friend. I escaped..."

My first thought upon awakening (he said) was that I had but dozed under the influence of the lethal gases in my imprisoning chamber. How long, I did not know. Perhaps a few minutes—or even a few hours.

This belief was strengthened by the fact that the ground beneath me still shook and trembled. I say "still." I should say "again"—but I did not know that then.

At any rate, I woke to discover that the air was free of the heavy gases which had caused my drowsiness. I first sensed the unusual when I scrambled to my feet. As I did so, I found my body to be strangely weak and stiff.

This I might have logically attributed to strain, had it not been for another even more terrifying and inexplicable thing. As I rose, dust, inches thick, fell from my body, causing me to sneeze and beat at the cloud which rose around me. And in doing so, I learned that I did not have a single stitch of clothing on my back!

Something tinkled on the rock beneath my feet. I bent over and fumbled for it in the darkness. It was the metal shoulder buckle with which my toga was secured. My feet were bare; my entire body the same.

There was but one logical conclusion to draw from this. Human agency. There must be someone beside myself in these depths; some thieving rascal whose base instincts had overcome even the fear of the eruption, causing him to strip me of my fine silk and linen raiment as I lay senseless.

I called. There was no answer. The cavern echoed the sound of my voice.

Enraged, I started to grope my way toward the near wall. One fact appeared certain to me. Where a thief found entrance, an honest man could find exit. And, in truth, I *did* find an opening which led into a tunnel which, in turn, led upward into a jumbled rock-covered path to the surface.

All this time, you comprehend, about me the tunnel walls and floor were trembling as before. The sound of tumbling rock, the grinding tumult of volcanic activity was in my ears constantly. But I scarcely noticed the din. I was fired with eagerness to escape from my underground prison; grateful to the gods who had seen fit to preserve me from the fate of my companions.

My heart was sore within me for those whom I had left in the dark vaults beneath. Yet I, myself, presented a sorry spectacle. My feet, shredded and bleeding from the sharp rubble through which I had picked my way, my bruised and dirty body, my face, grimy and coarse with stubble. In a short time, though, I promised myself as I neared the narrowed mouth of the tunnel and saw sunlight again, I would be laved and shorn, shod again, comforted with soothing pastes and unguents.

EXPECTANTLY, I staggered the final few rods; leaned at last against the shoulder of rock that concealed the tunnel mouth, and called weakly for help. By now, I knew, the entire population of the city would be out searching for us.

But—there was no answer. Save from the depths below me a dull rumbling as the mountain groaned in its labor, and from the sky above a high, thin screaming as some curious bird wheeled low to stare at this naked, bleating scarecrow.

Vainly I called again—and yet again. There was no reply. Now, for the first time, a feeling strangely akin to fear seized me. I looked at my surroundings sharply. They were the same...yet they were somehow different. I recognized the general outlines of the mountains that hemmed me in, the position of the sun in the sky (near high noon, I judged it) the undulant plateau land below me and to my right...

I had not, then, come out on the wrong side of the mountain. I had emerged from a passage that faced toward the capital city, Mayapan. As a matter of fact, all I had to do to view the city was walk a few yards forward. From that slight, cupped rise the staunch buildings and gleaming towers of my colonial seat would be visible.

Drawing a last ounce of strength from my incredibly weary body, I dragged myself forward those last few necessary steps. I mounted the rise; raised my eyes to look once more on Mayapan.

But—Mayapan was not there! I looked down upon a vast, parched, homeless plain, scorching beneath the rays of a torrid, merciless sun...

Quelchal paused. His great eyes rested somberly on Duke Callion.

He said, "You understand, Duke Callion, what it was I looked down upon?"

Duke nodded. He answered, "It was—today. Wasn't it?"

"You are right. It was today. The present. I who had gone into the bowels of the mount in the second year of Kan, had emerged twelve thousand years later—in that which you moderns call the Twentieth Century!"

JOE Cox said, surprisingly, "There was an eruption of Teolixican five years ago. In 1935. Was that—?"

Quelchal nodded.

"That was it, my friend. Do not ask me how these mysteries came to be. The gods have their own reasons for doing such things. I have pondered long on this which befell me, but have reached no decision. All I know is that through some strange chemistry I, Quelchal, Vice-Regent of the Atlantean colony on Mayapan, was put to sleep by gases in a subterranean chamber twelve thousand years ago, to awaken in *your* time.

"I will not bore you with the tale of my difficulties in this strange new world of yours. How I staggered into this shabby little village of Chunhubub, naked and weak, to find myself at once feared and hated by natives to whom I could not even speak.

"It was the Indians who, in the end, befriended me. To them I could at least make myself understood. Certain lingual similarities existed between their crude tongue and my native language.* They looked upon me as a sort of white god; nursed me back to health.

"From them I learned something of the history of the world through which I had slept for twelve thousand long years. From them I learned also a smattering of the Spanish tongue; enough that later I could establish relationship with the Mexican folk and live amongst them in peace and equity.

"For this came to pass after I had recovered a part of my strength and

---

*The language of the present day Quiches baffles science. Dr. LePlongeon who spent four years exploring Yucatan says, "One-third of this tongue is pure Greek! Who brought the dialect of Homer to America? Or who took to Greece that of the Mayas? Greek is the offspring of the Sanskrit. Is Maya? Or are they coeval? The Maya is not devoid of words from the Assyrian."

had revisited the mine. There I found a few handfuls of gold—enough to purchase the things with which to satisfy my needs and start working on that which I considered necessary."

"Necessary?" said Duke wonderingly.

Quelchal's eyes gleamed. There was a heightened color in his cheeks.

"But of a certainty, Duke Callion! Think! Of all the things I learned upon my escape from the depths, what one do you consider would grieve me most?"

Duke said uncertainly, "The—the vast changes that had taken place in our world since your long sleep? The sinking of Atlantis and the fate of your people?"

"That is it!" There was a hungry yearning in Quelchal's voice. "Duke Callion—it was more than a year after my escape that I even found one who knew what I meant when I spoke of my homeland, Aztlan. Then it was an old priest, a learned man, who thought I was crazed when I told him of my adventure.

"Yet it was from his lips that I learned that which is today considered a legend—the tale of the catastrophe which swallowed Aztlan beneath the waves. Of the utter destruction of our former fine civilization. Of the state of barbarianism to which the outer world descended, the loss of our mechanistic civilization, our learning, our science, our culture...

"I have already hinted to you, Duke Callion, of our science. You have doubted me. But—come! You shall judge for yourself!"

WITH a quick, herding gesture he from the tiny room to another even smaller one adjoining it. In one corner of this room rested a strange object of gleaming metal. It was spherical in shape, its welded smoothness marked on one side by the tight-fitting outline of a doorway large enough to admit a man.

Quelchal's fingers pressed a space beside this port. Noiselessly the door swung open, revealing an interior which glittered with strange gadgets and meters, the purpose of which Duke Callion could not even guess. Quelchal stepped in through the port; motioned his friend to follow him.

"There is room for all of us;" he said.

Wonderingly, Duke obeyed. Joey, close behind him, said dubiously,

"It l-l-looks like a machine of some kind. A v-v-vehicle?"

"That is it precisely," said Quelchal, "A vehicle such as no man has ever seen before. Or—that is, what it will be when I have completed it. Which will not be long, now. It lacks but a few minor adjustments to make it a finished product. A few minor changes to assure perfect accuracy..."

Duke said, "But what is it, Quelchal? What is its purpose?"

"Can you not guess, Duke Callion? Think again.

"Let your thoughts, your hopes, your dreams be as mine were four long years ago. My homeland gone—vanished beneath the waves of the ocean. The greatest civilization mankind has ever known lost; destroyed in its entirety. The world possessed by savages who lust for war, conquest; burn their resources with reckless abandon.

"Is it not only natural, Duke Callion, that I should dedicate myself to changing these things that be? I have said that our science was great. Here, before you, is proof of my claim. The machine you see is one on which Atlantean science was working at the time I was Vice-Regent of Mayapan. That they did not perfect it before the Deluge is now obvious. I cannot guess why. But I *did* perfect it! And with it—"

Duke cried excitedly, "It's mad, Quelchal, and I must be mad to even think of it. But everything is mad today. Do you mean to tell me that this machine—"

"I knew I had found one who could understand, Duke Callion. Yes, it is what you think. A machine in which we three can return to Aztlan the Eld, as it was aforetime, to warn my countrymen of their impending fate. And thereby alter the entire course of subsequent history. It is—a time machine!"

CHAPTER V
The Time Machine

DUKE said, "A time machine!" and his face mirrored his chaotic emotions. But it was practical little Joey Cox who pounced upon Quelchal's most significant statement.

"W-w-we *three?*"

Quelchal said, "But, naturally, we three!" There was a quiet simplicity in his voice; a tone which intimated he offered a privilege, an honor, which no sane man could refuse. He looked faintly puzzled. "Can it be that it is not your desire to accompany me?"

Joey said hastily, "N-n-not-me, thanks! You don't get me in any time-hoppin' buggy. Cincinnati is where I'm headed for!"

"Stow it, Joey!" ordered Duke curtly.

To Quelchal he said, slowly, "Quelchal, this *is* sheer madness. A time machine! Oh, I know what you mean all right. I've read a few strange stories about such contraptions. In science fiction magazines, and things like that. Wells wrote a book about a time machine, I think. But as for there actually *being* such a thing—" He shook his head. "I'm sorry, old boy. It's just too incredible."

The bronzed face of the great golden man turned a shade darker. For a brief instant, lines of hauteur tightened it, as in the *cantina*. His sea-faded eyes burned, and his voice was that of the Vice-Regent of ancient Mayapan.

"It is not yours to question, Duke Callion, when I, Quelchal, tell you—"

Then, suddenly; he seemed to remember himself and his sternness fell away from him like a faded cloak. He reached forward and touched Duke's arm.

"Forgive me. And do not judge too swiftly, Duke Callion. Listen to my explanation..."

For a moment he seemed to fall into a reverie, as though wondering how to put into words knowledge that the two young Twentieth Century soldiers-of-fortune would hear for the first time. Then he began speaking.

"Time, Duke Callion. Do you know what it is? Is there any man alive who knows what it is?

"We say it is the 'measurement of duration'—and our words are meaningless. We define Time by one of its own attributes.

"This we do know, however. That Time has strange contradictions. At the same moment in Time, a man in London and a man in New York look at their watches. The hands of one man's watch say it is five o'clock. The others declare it to be twelve. Yet, though the Time is different—Time is the same...

"This is a mere quibble, you will say. A bit of sophistry, based on our Time measurement system. And it is true, the argument is specious.

"But—" here Quelchal made a great, all-embracing gesture, "—who is to say that in this vast universe of ours, a similar situation does not exist on a macrocosmic scale so staggering as to defy our puny computations? Let us suppose that in this spacious arena of all-Time, the wee intervals which we call 'years'—" Quelchal's voice made the word sound insignificant, "—are but as fractions of seconds in Eternity. Less than that. Say that they are but one of the same piece—as a painted mural is one piece that the eye may scan and view in its entirety in an instant.

"Under these circumstances, would not all those events which mankind classes as 'historical' be occurring at one and the same instant?* A contemporary has pointed out that, viewed from afar, the entire history of mankind would have transpired in less than a year; the history of man's knowledge in less than a week. To this same watcher from afar, might not events which we consider separated by long periods of Time appear to be one and simultaneous; part of the same pattern?

"A pattern, Duke Callion! There is your answer! Even as I stand here talking to you, the Visigoths are raping Central Europe. Napoleon is marching confidently on Moscow, a Cro-Magnon man is hunkered over his tiny fire of dung and twigs, a 17th Century pirate is sacking a golden galleon of Spain. Yet these things are not happening *years* apart—they are happening inches apart on the gigantic tapestry we call, for lack of a better term—Time!"

---

*"To dramatize the recent increase in the rate of scientific progress, let us compress the time scale a millionfold. This means that a year ago the first men learned to use certain odd-shaped sticks and stones as tools and weapons. Speech appeared. Then, only last week, someone developed the art of skillfully shaping stones to meet his needs. Day before yesterday, man was sufficiently an artist to use simplified pictures as symbolic writing. Yesterday the alphabet was introduced. Bronze was the metal most used. Yesterday afternoon the Greeks were developing their brilliant art and science. Last midnight Rome fell, hiding for several hours the values of civilized life. Galileo observed his falling bodies at 8:15 this morning. By 10:00 the first practical steam engine was being built. At 11:00, Faraday's law of electromagnetism was developed, which by 11:30 had given us telegraph, electric power, the telephone and incandescent electric light. At 11:40 X-rays were discovered by Roentgen, followed quickly by radium and wireless telegraphy. Only 15 minutes ago the automobile came into general use. Air mail has been carried for hardly five minutes. And not until a minute ago have we had world-wide broadcasts by short wave radio." —Arthur H. Compton in *Science* Magazine

He paused, triumphantly. Joey Cox looked bewildered. Duke Callion fingered one of the shining metal knobs on the panel before him absent-mindedly; then said, "A clever concept, Quelchal. A damned clever concept, but I am afraid you are guilty of wishful thinking. You want to get back to Aztlan so badly that you have deluded yourself into believing it possible.

"Even your premises, were they right, would never permit the manufacture of a *machine* to pass through Time! Why, good God, man, it's impossible!"

"Impossible!" Quelchal seized on the word with a greater expression of joy than Duke and Joey had seen him manifest previously. "Then, Duke Callion—how do you explain *these!*"

HE jerked open a small drawer in the time machine; tossed before the astonished pair several small objects. A small silver medallion emblazoned with the head of one whom Duke recognized as the Emperor Caligula. A broken arrowhead of crudely chipped flint. Most astounding of all, a sabre-like fang of abnormal proportions.

Quelchal jabbed an excited finger at each in turn.

"From Rome, this first," he cried.

"Rome of about 40 A.D. The age of the second we can but guess. Probably around the ten thousandth year before He whom you know as Christ. The other is older yet. It is—but I see that you have guessed, Duke Callion?"

Duke nodded slowly.

"Yes," he said simply. "It is the tooth of the sabre-toothed tiger."

"Right! Well, my doubting friends, *these* objects came out of the past in my time machine on a grapple, when I sent it back, with set controls, to see how far it was progressing toward perfection.

"Thus, you see, my machine will penetrate the past. Or, as I prefer to think of it, it will rise above the Time tapestry and land again on another contemporary instant a short distance away."

"If you are right," demanded Duke, "why haven't you gone back to your time before now? What are you waiting for?"

A slight frown crossed Quelchal's face. He answered, "For a very good reason, Duke Callion. On these trial 'flights' I have also sent along small animals. Cats, rabbits, once a monkey. In each case they have returned to me—dead!

"I think I know why, now. During the past weeks I have been laboring to correct the mechanical fault which is responsible for the inability of animate objects to pass unharmed through the area above Time. Now I *think* I have it. But we must wait and make one more trial before we—"

Quelchal's words ended abruptly. A frown gathered on his face.

"Pardon, my friends!" he said—and stepped out of the machine.

Joey Cox grabbed his friend's coat-sleeve.

"H-h-hey!" he cried. "Let's g-g-get out of here! That guy's gonna send us off in his d-d-damn Time-buggy!"

But Duke's keen ears had caught the same undertone which had sent Quelchal hurrying into the other room of the adobe shack. Now he, too, was hastening after the man from Aztlan. Joey followed at his heels.

The noise was plainer in the other rooms. It was a dull sound, but an ominous one. The sound of many voices raised in growling anger. Duke had heard it once before in Alabama—at a lynching. He had heard it again in Tripoli when a horde of angry natives had stormed the white trading concession. It was an unforgettable sound, and an ugly one. The sound of a mob, bent on frenzied mob justice.

Swift strides took him to Quelchal's side near a small paneless slit in the baked wall.

"Quelchal!" he rapped. "Is it—us they're after?"

He did not need the Atlantean's answer. For as he watched, a horde of strangely assorted figures burst through the little *arceo* that screened Quelchal's dwelling from the street. Some men there were garbed in the tattered rags of peons. Others, like Fat Pedro, were better dressed. Yet their faces, too, were angry and drawn with mob fury. And in the vanguard of the approaching throng came a dozen men in khaki uniforms, with rifles unslung and ready for swift retributive action.

Joey Cox took one look at these latter, gasped and made a dive for his gunbelt. He tossed Duke's to him. He even forgot to stutter when he cried, "The Federals! They've found us! Duke, we're in for it now!"

CHAPTER VI
One Chance in a Million

TO Duke and Joey Cox, hardened and used to sudden emergencies in the crucible of war, their next actions were instinctive. They had not even time to feel surprised that Quelchal, too, was reacting so swiftly and with such quick knowledge of that which must be done.

The tall golden man rammed shut the only door, and placed across it a ponderous block of wood thick as three men's arms. While Duke and Joey, with unspoken accord, leaped to the two slit-like apertures, he jerked open a cupboard and—surprisingly—brought forth a rifle of ancient vintage.

There was regret but no alarm in Joey's voice as he called to his friend across the room.

"This l-l-looks like taps, Duke. We'll probably be too busy to talk in a minute, so—so long, guy!"

And the carefree young Irish-American, more soberly than was his wont, answered, "So long, Joey. I'll be seein' you somewhere."

"I wish," mourned Joey regretfully, "it was in Cincinnati!"

Then there was no more time for words. The throng had deployed now, as best it could, to scattered angles of the courtyard. From their vantage point, the three victims of the siege could see the hurried consultation amongst the army men. One, evidently *el capitan,* called in Spanish, "Americanos! Surrender—or be shot!"

Joey muttered, "Yeah! Surrender and we'll be shot anyway!"

Duke grinned across the room at him. He drew a deep breath. "I'll take mine," he said, "straight!" —and his finger tightened on the trigger on his automatic. Still he waited. If a guy was going to go down fighting, he could still be an American and a sportsman. Let the other fellow start the fight...

And then the storm broke. Broke as all tempests break, with a single, sharp, explosive crack! A gun spoke, and something hard *splatted* on the adobe above Duke's slit. Another shot...and another...and from every angle of the courtyard, leaden death began to hail upon the refuge.

Then Duke's automatic and Joey's spoke as a single voice. And where two riflemen had been crouching in the half-shadows, two khaki-clad figures slumped forward, guns and the battle forgotten forever.

The world became filled with the sound of gunfire, the thin, high screaming of bullets as they ricochetted off the adobe to waste their lethal selves, the stench of burnt powder. The detachment of Mexican Federals loaded and shot, pumped, reloaded and continued firing in a steady bombardment. Duke and Joey fired less often—but they made their shots tell.

Quelchal waited awkwardly, patiently, in the background. As Duke whirled to him, pointing at an automatic now empty, Quelchal nodded and stepped into the breach. There he raised his ancient firearm, sighted with careful aim and contributed his bit to the defense while Duke hastily jammed fresh cartridges into his still-smoking chambers.

"Nice work, Quelchal!" Duke tossed as he stepped back to the slit. Quelchal nodded; permitted himself a wan smile—then stepped over to hold Joey's portal as Joey's clip ran out.

How many times he loaded and fired, reloaded and fired again, Duke never knew. But at last there came that dreadful moment which, from the first, he knew must eventually come. The moment when, stepping back to let Quelchal take his place at the aperture, he rammed his hand into his ammunition pocket to find—nothing! Or, even more ironically than nothing, two final bullets.

Despairingly, he thrust these into the chambers. As he moved back to his slit he called, "Joey—any more—"

Then he stopped. For Joey, too, had now stopped firing. The expression on his face as he turned his pocket inside out was more eloquent than any words he might have used.

IT was a pointless question, and Duke knew it even as he asked, "Quelchal—there's no back way? No other way to get out of here?"

Quelchal shook his head. But from the wall he had taken down three *machetes*. Now, silently, he distributed these to the others. It was their last resort—and all of them knew it.

A bullet somehow found its way through the narrow aperture above Duke's head; sang past him and buried itself in the far wall with a *ping!* Duke's eyes narrowed, and he raised his automatic, trained it on the man whose marksmanship had been so accurate. Then—he lowered the gun.

Two shots left! It would be better to save those two for Quelchal and

Joey. They'd rather find quick death at the hands of a friend than—that mob outside!

There was a stirring movement from the besiegers now. For several minutes there had been no answering shots from their quarry. They guessed why. Duke could see the Federal captain gesturing his men to him. They were coming toward the house now...hesitantly at first, then more and more surely as the empty silence persisted. From scattered parts of the court were rising the enraged peons. Knives, bills, *machetes* in grimy paws, they too joined the macabre finale to the manhunt.

This, Duke Callion knew, would be the end. For a moment he felt a qualm pass through him. To die this way—in a strange land, far from home and those whom you called your own. To die *thus*—not in the heat of battle, but at the hands of a blood-lusting mob...

He shrugged off his misgivings. After all, he had bargained for this. He had been a soldier of fortune; ready to gamble at dice with Fate for his life or another's. Now he had lost the toss. A fragment of an old adage danced through his mind. "Those that live by the sword—"

The attackers were at the door now. Pounding with gun butts and eager hands upon its straining portals. With the cessation of gunfire, the tumult of voices was again audible. The besiegers kept up a steady stream of vituperative howling, screaming, shouting. The door groaned complainingly—and a shaft of yellow sunlight split through a hinge-joint to spill on the rough flooring like golden blood.

A *machete* blade split the upper panel; stuck there in the wood, quivering. Quelchal stepped forward calmly; smashed the fragment of steel with his own blade. It fell to the floor. But the door groaned again—and this time there was room for a man's arm to come through. An arm *did* come through—an arm bearing a revolver which leveled at Duke Callion's breast.

But even as a swarthy finger tightened on the trigger, Quelchal stepped forward again. His *machete* made one soft, *snicking* sound. The revolver exploded aimlessly. An insensate hand and forearm tumbled incredibly to the floor; grisly object that broke limply from the revolver. A gout of blood spurted across the sun-stained flooring. Outside a voice raised again...and yet again...in a terrible scream of agony and pain.

Quelchal's machete slashed downward with a swift motion, lopping the hand clean off at the wrist.

LIKE a flash, Duke scooped up the fallen revolver. It was half empty, but he poured its remaining shots recklessly, ruthlessly, into the close-packed sea of humanity that battered at the door; had the satisfaction of hearing hoarse screams as his leaden messengers of death went home. Then he tossed the useless instrument into the face of a soldier who suddenly loomed before the window-slit. The man's face fell away from the aperture, an angry red hole gaping where once an eye had been...

But not forever could the flimsy fort be held.

Already the door was falling from its hinges, and already the wooden bar that held it together was creaking and straining under the pressure from those outside. And now Duke shouted what might be his last order.

"The other room!" he cried. "We can hold 'em for a little while in that narrow doorway. With our *machetes!*"

And it was then, as they raced from the first room to that which was Quelchal's workshop, that Joey Cox cried, "The t-t-time machine!

Quelchal can't we escape in *that?*"

Quelchal's eyes lighted.

"By Bel!" he roared. "Maybe!" Then his face fell and he shook his head. "No! No, it is not completed. It might mean—death!"

"Death?" roared Duke. "It's sure death for us to stay here, anyway. Do you think there's an outside chance say one in a million—the damned thing *might* work?"

Quelchal groaned in an agony of indecision.

"It might. It might not. I don't know. The last time I sent it out, it killed the creatures I sent with it. But I have made changes since then. Changes which I hoped would—"

A hoarse shout of triumph drowned his words. From the other room came the sound of wood ripping at last like rotten paper. The trample of feet. The babel of the mob. Duke seized his two companions by the shoulders; whirled, and thrust them toward the metallic sphere.

"Then we'll take that chance in a million!" he decided. "To hell—or to Atlantis! What does it matter? Get going!"

Blindly, the three scrambled into the glistening machine. Quelchal began to press cryptic buttons with a frantic haste. A figure appeared in the doorway. Duke let loose a gleeful roar.

Quelchal's fingers found the final button. Something oddly silver glowed on the instrument panel. A deep hum rose from the entrails of the machine; shrilled into a high, piercing crescendo, and died in the tonic labyrinth of ultrasound.

Joey shouted, "The door, Duke! Shut it—*quick!*"

Duke slammed the portal. The machine seemed alive with a quivering sentience of its own. Duke barely beheld the way the outlines of the room faded and merged; became first shadowy, then a running blur of color as Quelchal's machine throbbed into motion. For stifling pressure bore down upon him...pressing...pressing...

He was conscious of Joey's agonized face staring into his own. Of Quelchal's lips writhing to form a half-sentence. "It's a fail—" Then darkness, sullen, brutal and complete, swooped down upon him.

Behind the three venturers, a vengeance-bent host of Mexicans poured through the doorway of the little room to halt in awed horror. Before their eyes, a huge, silver sphere was shimmering weirdly through the colors, beyond the colors, of the spectrum. An instant it shimmered...

then faded into a pale ghost...then evaporated into—nothingness! Nothing at all!

A howl, half of disappointed rage, half of superstitious awe, rose in the little hovel in Chunhubub. But Quelchal, Duke and Joey did not hear it. They lay senseless on the floor of a vibrant metal sphere that, untended and unguided, plunged down the dark passageway of Time toward a goal that Mankind no longer even remembered...

CHAPTER VII
Mayapan the Eld

A MILLSTONE was on his chest; grinding, crushing, until his shrinking flesh screamed and his very bones were turned to thin gruel. Duke strained, and tried to lift an arm that seemed weighted with lead. It would not move.

But—no! The pressure was less now! He felt an answering response from his fingertips. Now the millstone was lifting from his crushed body. The filmy shadows that had engulfed him were wisping away like scudding storm clouds.

He returned to consciousness with a start. Still breathing heavily, but—Duke struggled to his feet—but still *alive!*

He was in the silvery sphere that Quelchal called his "time ship." Before him, still unconscious on the palpitating floor, were Joey and the man from Aztlan. Duke dropped to one knee. He called, anxiously, "Joey! Quelchal!"

Joey Cox stirred. He said pettishly, "Aw, b-b-beat it! It's too early to—"

Then he was completely awake again; aware of the strangeness of his surroundings. Swift recollection swept the drowsiness from his eyes. "J-j-jumpin' jeepers, Duke! It worked!"

Duke said, "You mean—it wiggles. We don't know whether it works or not yet. For all we know, we're still in the room. Maybe those greasers are having trouble getting into this crate. It's metal, you know." He rose and moved toward the port. "By golly, I'll soon find out—"

"Wait!" That was Quelchal's deep, melodious voice raised in warning. The Atlantean, too, had now shaken off the gyves of unconsciousness. With eyes feverishly glowing, he was studying the instrument panel.

"Wait, Duke Callion! If you value your life, do not open the door! We're still travelling!"

Joey laughed raucously.

"That guy values his life? Hell's bells, if he *did,* do you think we'd be here now?"

And Duke said, curiously, "Travelling, Quelchal?"

The great golden man stumbled to his feet. For a long minute be bent over the instrument panel; then turned to the others.

"Yes. See?"

He pointed to a needle set in a dial. It moved so slowly that at first the eye could not detect its creeping. But as the slow seconds ticked by, the wondering Duke and Joey saw it cross one black dot...another...and glide inexorably toward the next.

"W-w-what are those dots?" Joey demanded fearfully. "W-w-weeks? Months?"

There was the faintest touch of scorn in the tall man's reply. Scorn—yet at the same time, pride.

"Not weeks," he said. "Not months. *Decades!*"

Joey repeated, "D-d-decades!" in a stunned voice. Then he drew his sleeve across his forehead and said, awfully, "Jeepers! If we started at that spot back *there,* I haven't been born yet! Won't be born—for a couple thousand years!"

DUKE frowned. He said abruptly, "Yes, Quelchal, how do you explain that? Haven't you created a biological paradox? If you are right—if we are actually travelling backward in Time as you say—how is it possible for Joey and me to exist in a Time that was before our ancestors even lived?"

Quelchal sighed and shook his head. "You must abandon your former concept of Time, my friend. Cease looking upon it as a measure of duration and see it as a broad tapestry in which all things happen simultaneously. Conceive of this machine as an airship in which we are traveling not from one *time* to another, but from one *place* to another."

Duke pondered a minute. Then, "I see. But if Time is but another dimension of space, Quelchal, there is only one medium through which we can travel. Through that which takes us above the tapestry. Through—the fourth dimension!"

"Precisely right!" Quelchal smiled. "And that is exactly where we are now, Duke Callion."

Joey Cox snorted. "You guys," he declared emphatically, "are nuts! I've got ten bucks says we're still back in Chunhubub, and right outside this here time-travellin' tin can there's a bunch of howlin' greasers waitin' to lift our scalps!"

"Save your money, Joey," smiled Quelchal. "Even though it will be valueless where we are going—" And he moved to one side of the sphere; touched a slide. A portion of the metallic wall slid back in an oiled groove, exposing a clear quartz-glass plate. "See for yourselves!"

The two men pressed their noses to the pane. Duke whistled. Even the dubious Joey paused and scratched his head. It was assuredly not a terrestrial scene that greeted them. It was no scene at all. It was nothing but wan, flickering *grayness*. Grayness through which, intermittently, flickered fantastic streamers of light and dark. Grayness that writhed and twisted.

Joey stammered, "W-w-what's that?"

"That", answered Quelchal, "is the passageway of Time. Days upon endless days. Years upon years. The way to the eternal. And we are the first to see it."

Duke turned away from the pane as Quelchal moved back the metal slide. He said, in a strangely humble tone, "And where is it taking us, Quelchal?"

"To Atlantis—I hope. Or to the Atlantis that was when I was Vice-Regent of Mayapan. To Atlantis, before the Deluge, Duke Callion."

IT was strange, at first, to be in that odd time craft of Quelchal's which, despite its apparent practicability, continued to waver and throb as though it might at any instant fall apart. But after a while the three time vagabonds became accustomed to their unusual surroundings, and with typical human adaptability began to look upon this as a quite commonplace journey.

The Atlantean had overlooked nothing in his construction of the machine. True, the sphere was not sufficiently large to provide sleeping quarters, but there was a tiny sanitary toilet, a tank of drinking water, and a supply of food, mainly of the tinned variety.

"Not any too *much* food," Quelchal admitted. "But enough to take us where we are going. After all, we aren't explorers in Time. Our trip has a definite purpose."

Duke Callion glanced at the dial. In the few hours since they had entered the time machine, the needle had traversed hundreds of small dots. He said, "And how long do you judge it should take us to reach our destination, Quelchal?"

Quelchal smiled gravely. "There is a slight element of chance involved there, Duke. It is not my fault, but that of your inept historians who believed Atlantis to have been a myth.

"The only Earthly record I could find of the date of Aztlan's catastrophe was that left by Plato who said in his *Critias* that the Deluge had occurred 9,000 years before the time of his famed ancestor, Solon. Solon's era was approximately 596 B.C. We left Chunhubub in 1936 A.D. So, on this somewhat arbitrary basis, it would seem that the Deluge must have occurred *about* 11,535 years before our departure...

"I have set the dials to take us back to my own era, which was approximately 11,600 years ago according to my computations. There we will find a ready ear to our warning. There will be sufficient time for my brethren to abandon the treacherous island; seek safety at the mainland. And the vast culture of Aztlan will not then be lost to the world."

Duke said, "I hope so, Quelchal. But still I am afraid."

"Afraid? Afraid of what?"

"I can't bring myself to believe that any man, any group of men, can change the history of mankind, once that history has been written on the books of Time. Or, to use your own simile, after it has been painted on the tapestry which is Time.

"Aren't these things done, now and forevermore, Quelchal? Is it not futile to hope we can go back and warn your people of the impending Deluge? Won't the Deluge come in spite of us?"

"Mayhap, Duke Callion. But to carry my concept a bit farther, I conceive of this Time tapestry as being one the twists and turns of which may be varied. At any rate, that is my hope.

"We will arrive in plenty of time to warn Aztlan. Despite the fact that for centuries the earth has been relentlessly pursuing its way about the sun; despite the fact that each 360 days have seen another revolution added to the interminable winding of Time—"

Joey burst in curiously, "T-t-three hundred and sixty, Quelchal?"

Quelchal said patiently, "Why, yes. The number of days in which the earth makes a revolution about the sun."

A SUDDEN, inexplicable pang of fear sank deeply into Duke Callion's heart. His voice was grave as he said, "An error, Quelchal. And perhaps a costly one."

The Atlantean's face darkened. "An error, Duke Callion?" he repeated stiffly.

"There is one thing at least," pursued Duke sombrely, "in which our moderns were in advance of those of your time. Astronomy. The earth does not, as you believed, revolve about the Sun in 360 days,* Quelchal—but in three hundred and sixty-five days and a fraction!"

Quelchal stared at him for a minute—then shrugged. "What difference does it make? A few years less; a few years more. "When we make our first landing we will ascertain the era in which we have landed. Correct our calculations and make a second voyage. It should not take us long. Look!"

He pointed at the time dial. Already it had gone far from its starting point. Now it was hovering close to a metallic marker Quelchal had set at the start of the time flight.

"Already our first journey is near an end. In a few minutes we will land. Brace yourselves!"

Joey said, "B-b-brace ourselves? Why?"

"Because in the haste of our departure we had to start from ground level. Ground level varies by many feet over a period of centuries. If we are fortunate, we will land easily. If not, there may be a slight crash."

Quelchal gestured toward a series of hand-grips set into the walls of the time-sphere. Duke and Joey took a firm grasp on a brace of these; planted their feet solidly. Silence fell over the little chamber as the needle groped closer and closer to its mark...poised fractionally above it.

Duke said, "All set?" and Joey answered, "L-l-let 'er rip!"

Quelchal's face was wreathed in glory. It shone with a joy

---

* There is evidence that the later Mayan civilization corrected their first calendars, allowing a space of five intercalary days to round out each year. However, this was not true in Quelchal's era. Early Mayan calendars show an artificial eighteen month year with but twenty days to the month. —Author

transcendent. His mobile lips framed a word. It was scarcely audible above the heightened throbbing from the heart of the machine, but Duke could read the movement. He was saying, "Aztlan!"

The dial needle hesitated, wavered, stopped. For a moment there was a breathless silence—then the machine gave a sudden, violent lurch. Duke's knuckles stood out whitely as he clutched his hand-grip. His feet slipped beneath him precariously.

"Look out!" he shouted. "We're falling!"

The nebulous, shimmering outlines that had bathed the ship throughout the weird backward journey into Time ended suddenly. The silvery sheen faded from the instrument panel. A new sound reached Duke Callion's ears. An eerie, whistling sound. Wind whipping past the dropping sphere. The machine wobbled and swayed beneath them. The muscles of Duke's arms corded with strain.

Then—they struck! With a grinding crash that jolted their feeble grips from the hand-holds; sent each of them crashing floorward. Duke was conscious of a startled shout that ripped from the throat of Joey Cox. The weight of Quelchal's body suddenly jammed against him, loosening his grip on the stanchion, crushing him back. Glass broke and fell, tinkling, about him. Metal groaned in protest. Then something rose beneath him to slash at his head with a fiery bludgeon.

There was a sudden, terrific shock. Pain burst upon him; over him, like a great, toppling wave. The inside of the sphere reeled, spun, collapsed. And from a vast distance, a brazen gong rose and roared, drowning out all else in the tumult of its clamoring...

CHAPTER VIII
The Sun-God's Greed

SOMETHING hard prodded Duke Callion. He mumbled in protest; stirred weakly. Every bone and muscle in his body ached with bruise. His head was alive with crimson devils who jabbed at his temples, his eyes, with flaming pitchforks.

He groaned, rolled over, and opened his eyes. A shaft of white-hot sunlight blinded him. He scrubbed at his eyes with the back of one hand and started to stumble to his feet.

Then suddenly, realization flooded back upon him.

He was no longer in the sphere. He was on a flat sandy shelf overlooking a city. And *what* a city! It was not the dingy Chunhubub from which their time-journey had begun. This was a great, sprawling metropolis gleaming in the sunlight with white, pyramidal temples, broad avenues, and green courts.

Behind him lay the ruins of the time-ship. It no longer was a shining sphere of seamless metal. The crash had split it from top to bottom. From a gaping hole there leaked shards of intricate coils and tubes; oily guts of the ill-fated machine.

But strangest of all were those who stood before him. A dozen brown-skinned natives, eyes wide with wonderment. Two or three feather-bonneted men-at-arms, lances dubiously leveled before them. And, at the head of all, a crimson-robed white man whose sun-bronzed skin, aquiline nose, and haughty, sea-faded eyes reminded Duke curiously of Quelchal.

"Quelchal!" With the thought, Duke's eyes sought his companions. Then he breathed a deep sigh of relief. They were all right—or seemed to be. Like himself, they had been borne from the damaged ship by the native slaves. As he looked, Quelchal stirred and moaned. Joey Cox was also beginning to regain consciousness.

Now, as Duke turned back to face the leader of the strange band, the crimson-robed one spoke. He rapped a series of unintelligible syllables, only from the intonation of which could Duke guess that a question had been asked. Duke shook his head.

"Sorry, buddy," he said, "but I don't get your lingo. Wait till my pal here comes out of it, and—"

The man spoke again; this time an imperious note in his voice. He raised the object with which he had prodded Duke into awareness, brandishing it. It was a short, thick-handled, braided whip bound with metal. There was a tinge of impatience in his tone.

Duke said, "Hey!" in a startled tone. Then, as the man lifted the whip ominously, repeating his question, Duke's quick, Irish temper rose.

"Cut it!" he snapped—and stepped forward.

Affronted, the man made as though to bring down the whip upon Duke's shoulders. But Duke never felt the sting of its lash. In one swift, sure move he whipped out his gun and shot the whip from the crimson-robed one's grasp.

The man snarled; his face mottling with anger. He turned to the armed men behind him; spat a hasty command. They pressed forward, leveling their spears threateningly at Duke.

Duke moved impetuously. He reached out and grasped the crimson-robed leader about the throat; twisted him, and jerked him forward until the man's body covered him as a shield. He gritted, "Now, call off your feather-headed buddies, mister, before something happens."

The man writhed in his grasp, but Duke's arms held him like iron bands. Finally he caught the sense, if not the actual meaning, of the young adventurer's words. Half-stifled, choking, gasping for breath, he coughed a single word. The spearmen fell back. Duke loosened his hold.

"That's better!" he said approvingly.

Joey's voice came from behind him. "Hey, Duke—w-w-what's gain' on here?"

Duke answered calmly, "Oh, nothing much. This guy in the red nightgown just tried to work out on me. I had to—"

Then Quelchal, recovered at last, came forward to join them. There was a look of joy, mingled with one of apprehension, on his face. He said, "You have been unwise, Duke Callion. This man is a priest. But all is well. These are my people." And he began to address the crimson-robed one in a swift, mellow tongue unfamiliar to the two Americans.

AT his first words, a look of swift astonishment swept over the face of the stranger. A look of surprise and puzzlement, which rapidly gave place to one of excitement. He rapped queries at Quelchal which the Atlantean answered. Duke and Joey waited expectantly.

Finally Quelchal flung them a few words of explanation.

"Our trip has been successful—or partially so. As you anticipated, we landed in a later time than was our intention. I am not yet sure how much later. But we are in Mayapan the Eld."

Joey said blankly, "M-m-mayapan? That's Yucatan, ain't it? I thought we were going to Atlantis?"

Quelchal smiled. "The time ship cannot alter our geographical position," he said. "It can only carry us back through the years. It is enough that we are here."

He turned back to the leader again. Now he said something, pointing to the city on the plain below them, and the man shook his head. He pointed at Duke and Joey. Quelchal raised his voice a degree—and there was in it a note of command.

The man nodded, but as he did so he shot from his lowered eyes a baleful glance at Duke. Then he barked some words at his followers. Quelchal gestured to his companions as the ill-assorted group started moving away from the time-ship and down toward the city below.

"Come," he said. "I have not quite succeeded in convincing him. But I have aroused his curiosity. We are going to seek an interview with the Vice-Regent."

Joey's eyes were wide with wonder as he stared at the high, vaulted colonnades of the auditorium in which they stood. It was a wide, roofed court; baked limestone walls frescoed with intricate lacework carvings, walls and roof inlaid with arabesques of gold and precious stones, tapestried with sweeping drapes and arrases. He whistled softly.

"Gosh, Duke, get a load of this joint! It looks like the inside of the Fort Knox reserve depot!"

Duke Callion's eyebrows had lifted, too, but for a different reason. Standing between Joey and the silent Atlantean, he had been watching the gathering crowd of spectators. Now he had seen something that made the whole screwy trip seem worthwhile. He said, "Never mind *that,* Joey! Take a look at the girl in the white robe. Over there in the archway."

Joey looked, grunted approvingly, then continued to stare at the rich adornments of the palace. Duke was less easily satisfied. He stared at the girl with unconcealed admiration in his gaze. Stared until at last she seemed to sense his gaze upon her, looked up and met his unfaltering stare—then flushed and lowered her head.

Duke smiled to himself. Girls were very much the same, he thought, whether in Mayapan the Eld or in America of the Twentieth Century. For even now the girl's head was raising for another stolen glance at this brash, handsome young captive who was so boldly staring at her. The blush, Duke thought, was both becoming and—quite modern!

Then, from some invisible source, came the golden note of trumpets. An expectant hush fell over the throng. An elaborately costumed man-at-arms approached the little trio; gestured to them. A gigantic tapestry fell back from one segment of the corridored court—opening a way into a still larger room adjacent.

The three stepped over the threshold of a court which for sheer luxury surpassed anything Duke or Joey had ever dreamed of. A council chamber; surmounted at one end by a raised dais on which there stood a throne of solid gold. On this throne, swaddled in ceremonial robes of indescribable splendor, sat a lean, hawk-faced man who leaned forward curiously to study them as they marched in.

Quelchal whispered swiftly to his companions, "The throne room! The Vice-Regent of Aztlan!"

NOW the crowd was pressing into the throne-room; its constituent members taking such positions as were allotted to their rank. Duke noticed that the crimson-robed sect stood to the right of the throne. These, he knew now, were the priests. The military leaders, garbed in tunics and a short kirtle like that of the ancient Greeks, took their places on the Vice-Regent's left.

Behind these two groups, indiscriminately, stood the common people. The women, tradesmen, workers. All but the brown-skinned natives. As slaves, these had no place in the commune of the colony.

The three men marched to a spot just before the throne itself. There a man-at-arms halted them; gestured them to drop to their knees as he himself did. Duke looked at Quelchal dubiously. The tall Atlantean stood erect and firm, smiling slightly. Duke grinned sideways at Joey and did the same.

The man-at-arms glanced back at them, a look of horror passing over his face. He muttered a few fearful words to Quelchal. There was a murmur from the crowd, and two or three of the militia took a step forward as though to press these oddly dressed barbarian strangers to their knees.

But the Vice-Regent, staring curiously at Quelchal, halted them with a word. They fell back. Then the man on throne spoke directly to Quelchal—and his words framed a question.

Duke felt curiously "left out" of all this. From time to time he seemed to recognize a single word of those that were being spoken between Quelchal and the Mayapan ruler. His knowledge of Mexican dialects enabled him to identify the Quiche words for "ruler," "mountain," and he once thought he caught the expression that meant, "time before tomorrow." But it was too much trouble to try to grasp the meaning behind that swift interchange of syllables. His attention wandered, and he found himself once again searching for the slim, dark-haired beauty whom he had seen in the corridor beyond.

He found her at last—and to his great glee, she had her eyes fastened on him when his gaze met hers. Once again he was treated to that soft, embarrassed blush. The girl turned her head away.

Quelchal and the ruler had done speaking at last. Now, as the Vice-Regent called several of his advisers to him, and they conferred in low undertones, Quelchal turned to his companions for a swift summary. The tall bronzed man was perspiring, and there was a worried look in his eyes.

"Everything fixed up?" Duke asked nonchalantly.

"It is harder than I had expected, Duke Callion," said Quelchal. "I am having some trouble understanding the things the Vice-Regent says. He is equally puzzled by my words."

Joey said, "What's the big idea? You speak the same language, don't you?"

"Yes, but with a difference. This period, I have learned, is one more than five hundreds of years *after* my time. The language has changed; become more involved. It is as though I were a Chaucer, attempting to converse with a man of the seventeenth century. Or an Elizabethan trying to talk with a New Yorker of your day."

Duke nodded understandingly. "But your name? Isn't that familiar to them?"

Quelchal permitted himself a grim smile. "They have a legend of a Quelchal, a Vice-Regent, who many years ago was devoured by the volcano Teolixican. But to identify that man with *myself*—" He shrugged.

Joey said nervously, "I can't exactly blame them. It does sound kind of goofy. I wouldn't believe it either, except that—well, here we are!"

"Still," said Quelchal , "there is no cause for apprehension. After all, these are a civilized people. We have no reason to expect anything other than sympathetic treatment at their hands. When I have spoken to their intellectuals...their scientists..."

He stopped short. For now, suddenly, had come a change in the atmosphere of the judgment court. Where all had been previously calm and studied, there was now an odd tenseness. A page had stepped forward and called, "Hurkan!" and from the ranks of the crimson-robed priests had stepped forward the one who had first met the adventurers. Now, at a sign from the Vice-Regent, he was telling his story. Prefacing it with an angry gesture in Duke's direction, he burst into a fiery flood of words; meanwhile graphically pantomiming the incidents attending the meeting.

Duke followed his gestures with amazement that a narrative could be so excellently delineated without words. First the priest, Hurkan, swept his arms widely to indicate open space. Then suddenly his arms came together in a great circle. "The time-ship!" Duke thought. Then Hurkan let his arms drop swiftly to the ground; separated them to show the rupturing of the sphere.

Next he pointed directly at Duke...half-crouched on his hands and knees to portray the young American rising from the ground. And he showed himself walking forward in a calm, friendly fashion...

("Yeah!" thought Duke. "But where's that whip he was prodding me with?")

But Hurkan did not show that. Instead he showed Duke springing to his feet; then leaping at the throat of the priest. Dramatically, the narrator clenched his own hands about his throat; staggered backward, choking, face contorted. A low rumble rose from the assembled throng. Faces turned wrathfully toward Duke. The Vice-Regent's face hardened and he stared at the three adventurers thoughtfully.

Duke could stand no more. Forgetful that these people could not understand a word he said, he sprang forward.

"This man's a damned liar!" he roared. "Look—I'll show you what *really* happened!"

He pointed at the outraged Hurkan; then at his own breast. "I'm him!" he shouted ungrammatically. *"This* is how he actually did it—"

He raised an imaginary whip; prodded it at something presumably lying before him. Then he stepped back a pace. As well as he could remember that scene, he acted it out for the watching assembly. Finally he reached the high spot of his pantomime...the spot where Hurkan took a whip and deliberately began to lash at the man before him.

Then Duke stopped, at a loss as to how to express justification for what he had done. He said simply, "So then—I defended myself. Tell them, Quelchal. Tell them I grabbed this Hurkan guy in self-defense."

But before Quelchal had a chance to say anything, there was a slight stir in the midst of the crimson-robed priesthood. The girl whom he had been staring at so ardently had pushed into that group; was whispering now, swiftly, to a gray-haired man of kindly mien. The elderly priest nodded and moved forward. He inclined his head graciously toward Duke, made a bow to the Vice-Regent, then addressed Quelchal.

Quelchal's answer evidently satisfied him. He turned to the Vice-Regent and spoke swiftly. The ruler of Mayapan turned questioningly to Hurkan. Quelchal explained swiftly, "We've found a friend. This priest, Lucan, is begging clemency for us. He understood your claim that Hurkan attacked you first. He—"

But now Hurkan was speaking again, with impassioned eloquence. And that the man had eloquence, no one could deny. He held the crowd breathless on the flowing cadences of his voice; swayed them with his words, and roused their rapidly mounting ire against the strangers to fever-pitch with the incontrovertible accusations he flung at them.

Even the ruler's impartial judgment was influenced by the man's words. As Hurkan's voice grew louder and more assured, his glances at the three captives became sterner. He, too, was feeling the effect of the mob-anger Hurkan was so perfectly arousing.

THE muttering heightened; became a low, rumbling undercurrent of menace. Lucan attempted to speak, and the crowd jeered him into helpless silence. Hurkan raved on; gesticulating wildly, threatening, demanding. Finally he pointed a quivering finger at the three; stamped his foot, and turned to the ruler. He almost screamed his challenge at that uncertain personage...

Quelchal said, "It's bad, Duke! He's got them under his spell! They believe—"

And then the Vice-Regent signaled for silence. Instantly a deathly stillness fell over the court-room—a hush in which Duke could feel the throbbing undertone of hatred beating against him and his companions in mighty waves.

The Vice-Regent slowly rose from his throne. He raised a hand importantly; glanced skyward. Through a high slitted window near the roof of the throne room, a lance of golden sunlight struck down upon his face, etching its hard lines into sharp relief.

It was like an omen. All present felt it. For an instant the Vice-

Regent held that pose; hand weighted like the hand of doom. Then his arm made a wide, sweeping gesture—and fell! A tumult of approval drowned out the word that left his lips...

A host of jostling, blood-hungry figures moved in on the three adventurers. Quelchal's face was a pale mask of fury. In a thunderous voice he cried, "The fool! He has listened to Hurkan! Sentenced us to die on the altar of the sun-god, Ray-moe!"

Then rude hands fell upon Duke, tearing him from his friends. As he lashed out about him in blind, futile wrath, he glimpsed, for just a moment, a white-clad figure in the background. A girl with horror-stricken eyes.

Then sheer numbers hemmed him in; overpowered him. He was grasped by a horde of eager hands, lifted and borne away...

CHAPTER IX
The White God Speaks

BY straining a little against the gnawing rawhide thongs that bound him, Duke could turn his head from side to side. He did so now.

It was an imposing spectacle. Were he on his feet to see it, rather than lashed to this pock-marked, circular stone, he might have appreciated it. But he could take no archeological interest in a temple when, within the space of minutes, he might become a human sacrifice to the god of that temple!

The mob had carried him and his two companions to the crest of a great pyramid which rose in several terraces, and was surmounted by twin temples, each three stories high. What divinity was served by the other temple, Duke did not know. This one was dedicated to the sun-god, Ray-moe.

"The life-giving god," Duke remembered out of a scattered knowledge of early mythologies. He smiled wryly. There was visible evidence that Raymoe was *life-taking* as well as giving. The coarse slab to which he was secured was brown with blotchy stains. The walls of the temple were spattered with a dirty encrustation certainly not native to the quarried stone. So, too, were the steps up which the captives had been borne.

Duke remembered, suddenly, the early Aztec custom of tearing the heart, still beating, out of the breasts of human sacrifices—then

Joey twisted and writhed as the priest raised the knife.

rolling the quivering body down the temple steps as a symbol of degradation. He shuddered.

Beside him, similarly bound to the altar, were his two companions. Quelchal, his, fury spent, lay in dignified silence; too proud to display an emotion before the watching crowd. Not so Joey, however. He was tugging at his bonds, muttering angrily as the rawhide merely bit deeper into his wrists, and groaning, "Out of the f-f-frying-pan, Duke. I w-w-wish we were back home in Cincinnati!"

Duke said quietly, "The Fates were against us from the beginning, Joey. There's no use struggling. You can't break loose from that rawhide."

Joey panted, "I know. But if I c-c-could just get into my p-p-pocket for a minute—"

The sun was almost overhead now. From the bottom of the pyramid steps rose the sound of a thin, high chanting. The voices of the priests, intoning the prelude to the sacrificial ceremony. High noon approached. The hour sacred to Ray-moe. The hour when he would claim his due.

The chanting drew nearer. There was the odor of fragrant incense on the air. A group of altar neophytes, barefooted, cassocked, appeared at the crest of the pyramid; shuffled forward slowly to pace three times around the slab. Solemn as carven figures, they looked neither to left nor right.

A cymbal crashed; its echo dying away with infinite slowness. As the last throbbing note died into muted silence, the priests themselves appeared in their crimson robes. As they passed by, Duke saw two faces not masked with frozen piety. That of the friendly priest, Lucan, was sad. Hurkan's eyes were hard; gloating.

They, too, made a slow circle about the captives; then halted in a great wheel, which took as its hub the altar. One man, whose crimson gown was crusted with golden ornament, stepped forward. The High Priest.

A hush had fallen over the assemblage. The High Priest of Ray-moe stepped forward to the altar; looked at the three captives for a long moment. Then, with a great cry, he lifted his arms high above his head, threw back his head, and looked directly at the sun.

It was high noon in Mayapan, and the sun was like a great, brazen ball of fire hanging low in the cloudless sky. It was a marvel that the sun-priest's eyes could stand the strain. But he held that pose without blinking, without flinching, while he recited a long, ceremonial prayer.

The dedication ended. The High Priest turned to those behind him. A close-tonsured neophyte handed him a silken cushion, in which nestled a jet blade of razor-edged obsidian. Again came the clash of the cymbal. The priest raised the knife; made a swift, cryptic gesture of blessing over it. The last act of the drama was about to unfold.

JOEY was twisting and writhing on the slab beside Duke. His face was dripping with perspiration, as still he struggled to get his hand into his pocket for a reason Duke did not try to guess. Quelchal maintained his haughty silence. Duke's own lips remained sealed as the sun-god's priest stepped forward and ripped the khaki shirt asunder at his breast.

Quelchal's was the next breast to be bared to the knife. Then Joey's. And now, with the sacrifices ready, the High Priest stopped before Joey and addressed a question to him.

Quelchal twisted his head to face Duke.

"I am sorry, Duke Callion," he said drearily. "I did not guess that this was to be our fate."

Duke tried to grin. "Skip it!" he said. "It's not your fault. It's just like Joey said—the cards were against us from the beginning. Anyhow, it was fun while it lasted."

Joey, still struggling, panted indignantly, "Aw, go sit on a tack, you jabbering monkey! Quelchal, what's this guy want? What's he trying to say?"

"He's asking you your name," replied Quelchal. "It is a part of the ceremony. He's dedicating your life to the sungod."

Joey snorted, "My name, hey? I'll tell him what my name is!" He had finally succeeded in reaching his pocket. Now, with a ripping of tortured seams, he jerked it forth again. In it was a small, glistening object. His thumb moved. He shouted, "All right, you in the red nightgown, I'll tell you my name. It's Joey Cox. Get that? C-cox! And I'm a bigger shot than your phoney sun-god ever was!"

He turned to Quelchal wildly. "Tell him that, Quelchal! Tell him what I just said!"

Duke said, "What's the idea, Joey? Have you—"

Quelchal was repeating Joey's words to the priest. Now Joey was shouting again; words spilling from his lips in an eager flood.

"Tell him," he roared, "that I'm the sun-god's son-in-law. Or his grandson. Tell him I'm going to show him a miracle. Make him look at me!"

Wonderingly, Quelchal repeated the words. Again the High Priest stared at Joey; this time hesitantly. He spoke briefly; began to raise his knife. He poised it over Joey's breast.

Duke's heart sank. For a moment he had hopes that Joey's bluff would work. Against these superstitious people, a claim to godhood *might* have succeeded. But now it was too late. He closed his eyes...

Then they jerked open again, suddenly, as a great roar of amazement rose from the crowd that thronged the temple of Ray-moe! Even the stolid priests were murmuring amongst themselves, and the High Priest, his eyes round in amazement, was moving backward. His black knife clattered to the stone pavement.

And Duke loosed a great roar of glee! Joey *had* performed his miracle! In his right hand, a tiny flame was glowing. A flame that already was licking at the rawhide thongs that bound him. Joey's miracle was—a cigarette lighter!

The thong spluttered, scorched, fell away. Joey fought loose of its coils; rose to his feet on the slab, towering above the stunned crowd. In his moment of greatness, he even *looked* godlike as he drowned out their cries of fear with his roaring.

"S-s-so you wanted to know my n-n-name, eh? Well, it's C-c-cox! Joey C-c-cox! And you'd better r-r-remember it, too!"

He leaped down from the slab; retrieved the stone knife that had fallen from the priest's nerveless fingers. Swiftly he slashed the bonds that held Duke and Quelchal. Then wildly, gloriously, he advanced toward the backward-pressing throng, still shouting his noisy challenge.

"T-t-truss *us* up like a Christmas turkey, would you? Well, w-w-we'll see! Quelchal, t-t-tell 'em what I'm saying. Tell 'em I'm the sun-god's favorite nephew. That the old boy died and left me some of his fire in this box. And that they'd better a damn' sight do what I t-t-tell 'em or I'll—"

Quelchal spoke swiftly. But he did not need to speak. The crowd had already accepted Joey Cox at his own self-evaluation. A miracle had been performed. A god had created fire out of a metal box. It was enough for them.

From the civilian crowd, first, came the response to Joey's raging demands. A faint, stifled cry, "C-cox! Aieee! Cacox!" Then the priests, too, acknowledged this new white god. Scarlet robes crumpled as they fell to their knees. The weak chant grew louder; gathered volume as more voices picked it up. "Coxcox! Aiee! Coxcox!"

Duke shouted gleefully, "You've done it, Joey! You've got 'em eating out of the palm of your hand!" And a dark cloud chased over his forehead. He gritted, "Hurkan! Where did he go? That's one guy I want to—"

Quelchal pointed to the plain far below them; to the base of the pyramid. A solitary, crimson-robed figure was racing across the sand. A priest who had perjured a god was fleeing for his life.

"We need trouble ourselves with Hurkan no longer," said Quelchal. "His life is forfeit—and he knows it!"

The mob, gathering courage now that the new white gods had not seen fit to bring thunderbolts crashing down upon them, was pressing forward. But this time there was no blood hunger in their forward

SONS OF THE DELUGE

surge. They grovelled at Joey's feet; eyes abject. A few of the more daring reached forth eager hands to touch his shoes, his trouser legs. The High Priest, his fine raiment forgotten, was foremost of the worshippers. In an ecstasy of abasement, he pressed his lips to the ground where Joey had trod. And ever the cry rose in volume, "C-cox! Cacox! Coxcox!"

Duke grinned. "Well, Joey," he said, "how does it feel to be a god?"

But Joey's sweating face was crimson with embarrassment. His anger gone, a new grief had risen to meet him. "L-l-listen!" he raged. "Do you h-h-hear them? The damn fools are *s-s-stuttering* my name!"

CHAPTER X
The Dangerous Quest

"TOPTLIPETLOCALI!"

Duke Callion repeated, "Toplipt—Toptlip—" and faltered into silence. "Come again, Pyrrha. I can't even get *near* the darned word!"

Joey Cox riffled the greasy deck of playing cards with which he had been dealing solitaire.

"I'm g-g-glad it's you that's trying to l-l-learn this language," he said amusedly. "Imagine *m-m-me* working out on a tongue-twister like that!"

Quelchal glanced up from his conversation with the friendly priest, Lucan, and smiled.

"Perhaps," he suggested, "you might ask Pyrrha the *meaning* of the word, Duke. I believe you're getting a bit 'nearer' to it than you think."

Duke said, "Hey? What's that?" and turned to the girl. In halting Atlantean he put the question to her. A heightened color came into her cheeks. Her laughter tinkled through the room; then suddenly she leaped up and ran away. Duke stared after her bewilderedly. Of Quelchal he demanded, "Now, what the blazes did you do that for? How do you expect me to learn this language if you're going to bust up my lessons with your wisecracks?" Then, suspiciously, "Well—' what *does* the word mean, anyway?"

"It means," answered Quelchal, smiling, "'Altar'! But, come. We have much to discuss. Lucan, here, has a map for us—"

Joey rose hastily. "If you'll p-p-pardon me," he said, "I've got to see a fellow about a p-p-pyramid. See you later!" Pocketing his well-thumbed deck of cards, he ambled out of the room. Duke grinned after him affectionately.

"Good old Joey. No use trying to make him discuss plans. He's a doer; not a thinker. I learned that years ago."

Quelchal shrugged and returned to the perusal of his parchments. "Well, it's all right. Joey is playing an important enough role as it is. The people here absolutely worship him, and he's making himself more and more popular every day with his card tricks and sleight-of-hand."

"Not to mention the fact," added Duke, "that he's responsible for our being here! Well, you've broken up *my* pleasant afternoon. Now let's get going."

ALMOST three weeks had passed since Joey's burst of genius had saved the time-travelers from sacrifice on the altar of Ray-moe.

By now, Joey Cox—or "Coxcox," as the Mayapans persisted in calling him—was the colonists' supreme deity. His every whim was their law. And why not? He was a "god," living amongst them as a mortal. A pleasant, friendly god on whom they could bestow their tangible admiration. And Joey, moreover, reciprocated their affection.

One of his first acts had been the elevation of Lucan to the High Priesthood. In the new and larger headquarters which became Lucan's abode, the three made their temporary residence.

Temporary, because by now Quelchal was burning to set sail for distant Aztlan, that his long-cherished mission of warning might be fulfilled.

Not so Duke Callion. Like Joey, he was perfectly content to remain right here in Mayapan—but for a somewhat different reason. A dark-haired and dark-eyed reason blessed with lissome grace. A reason answering to the name of Pyrrha; niece of Lucan the Priest. Duke Callion's interest in learning the Atlantean tongue was a passion less orthological than biological!

But there was upon him an obligation. In spite of misgivings which he had never succeeded in shaking off—an inner conviction that it lay within no man's power to alter the Past—he was still Quelchal's friend. He would accompany him to the end of their adventure. After that he would be free to return to Mayapan—and Pyrrha.

Lucan was troubled. He lay the parchment on which he had been working before Quelchal and Duke.

"It is unfortunate," he said, "that you will not be patient; wait for the next ship to arrive from Aztlan. As you know, we of the colony have never been great builders of sailing vessels. All that we can provide you is one of the smaller sloops left here by the King's fleet."

Quelchal said gravely, "It will suffice. Already we have wasted more time than is good. We must leave just as soon as possible."

Duke said, "But, Quelchal, I thought it was your intention to repair the timeship? Go back in that?"

"It was, Duke Callion. But now I find that is impossible. It was too severely damaged. And—" Quelchal smiled. "—surely you understand by now that in any Time it would return us to Mayapan. These are the maps, Lucan?"

"Yes. I think you will find them accurate."

"I am sure of it." Quelchal bent over the parchments; nodding from time to time. "Ah, yes, I recognize these small islands. 'Turnanogg,*' I believe, is the name given them."

Duke stared at the map curiously. It resembled a map of the Atlantic Ocean such as he had seen when a lad in school—but with several startling differences. There was, for one thing, a long neck of land standing far out into the ocean from that which Duke remembered as Guiana. Spain was an elongated peninsula stretching westward until it formed a long, narrow sea between Europe and northern Africa. This portion of the mainland included what Duke's memory told him must, in the twentieth century, be the island of Madeira.

A curious knob of land jutted from the Gold Coast section of Africa out to the sea. Duke, puzzled, thought of the islands of St. Paul, and the tiny Ascension group. These must have been, in his time—already he could only think of the Twentieth Century as some remote era—high, mountain peaks on the African extension.

B UT most amazing of all was the existence, right off the mouth of the Mediterranean Sea, of a huge island. And, Duke thought, it was really huge! As large as Iceland. No—larger still. Almost as large as Greenland, for the island which lay above it and to the westward was

---

*The Irish "heaven," St. Brendan's Isle of fable, song and story was known as "Tir-na-n'oge." It was an isle of golden wealth and beauty.—Author

almost as great as Iceland.

He placed a finger on the large island. "This is our destination?" he asked. "This is Aztlan?"

"Yes, Duke Callion!" Quelchal's eyes were glowing warmly. "That is my homeland. The source of all the world's culture. The land which, were it not for us, is to sink beneath the waves in—"

He paused abruptly and peered at Lucan from beneath his blond, shaggy brows.

"Have your calculations told you anything about that, Lucan? Have you been able to correlate the facts I gave you?"

Lucan sighed. "Very little, Quelchal. The legends of the Future whence you came are so faulty. Greek and Babylonian deluge legends mean nothing to me. I know of no persons called 'Greeks'. There *is* a country to the eastward which we call 'Biblon', but—"

"In Mexico," interposed Duke, "I once heard an old Quiche Indian tell a racial legend about a great flood. He said that in the fourth age, which he called Atonatiuh, there was—"

Lucan and Quelchal had both come to their feet of a sudden. Quelchal gripped the young American's arm.

"Atonatiuh!"* he cried. "The Sun of Water! Duke Callion, that is *this* age! Every man knows that the time of mankind is divided into four ages. The age of Giants, the age of Fire, the age of Monkeys, the age of Water!

"Remember! Remember swiftly! What did the legend say? When was this age supposed to have ended?"

Duke's brow furrowed in the intensity of his effort to remember.

"I was hardly listening at the time. I remember that a man and a woman were supposed to have escaped the Deluge on the trunk of a cypress tree. All other men were supposed to have been changed to fish..."

"Yes, Duke Callion! But the date? You *must* remember the date!"

"I do! I remember now. The old Quiche said: 'In the fourth age,

---

*Then comes the fourth age, *Atonatiuh;* 'Sun of Water,' whose number is 10 times 400 plus 8, or 4008. It ends by a great inundation, a veritable deluge. All mankind are changed into fish with the exception of one man and his wife who save themselves in a park made of the trunk of a cypress tree..."—from the *Popul Vuh*

Atonatiuh, whose number is ten times four hundred plus eight, came down the rains upon earth—"

"Four thousand and eight!" cried the two men simultaneously. And they looked at each other in sudden horror. Lucan's face paled. The life seemed to seep out of Quelchal's body. For the first time since Duke had known him, his proud erectness vanished. He let his head fall forward into his hands.

Duke faltered, "But—but I don't understand. Is there something wrong?"

Lucan echoed, "Wrong!" hollowly, and the Atlantean raised his head to answer Duke with a great bitterness.

"More than that, Duke Callion! It means our trip is a failure. For the Atlantean year 4008 is—this year!"

TO BE CONTINUED...

Brawny arms lifted Hurkan as though he were a child, and hurled him over the rail.

Sons of the Deluge

BY NELSON S. BOND

Intrigue and treachery sweep the Atlantean city as the day of the Deluge draws near, and Duke Callion battles to avert an ancient tragedy.

PART TWO OF A TWO-PART SERIAL

IT was Duke who rallied his friends out of the despair which had engulfed them. He stood up determinedly and faced the others.

"Well, so what?" he demanded. "It's not going to take us a whole year to get to Aztlan, is it? We've still got a few months to get there and warn your people, Quelchal. All this means is that we must move—and move at once."

His words put new hope into the Atlantean's heart. Quelchal forced a smile to his bloodless lips.

"You put me to shame, Duke Callion," he said in a quiet voice. "You—a modern American—have taught me to be a man. Yes, we must move—and swiftly. Lucan, everything can be prepared for our immediate departure?"

"Within the hour!" promised the priest, and left the room hurriedly. Quelchal turned to Duke again.

"And you, my friend? You are prepared to go."

"I suppose so," said Duke gloomily. "But—"

Quelchal asked softly, "Pyrrha?"

Duke's flush answered him. But before he had time to speak, a slim, white-clad figure raced into the room to toss herself, sobbing, into Duke's astonished arms. It was Pyrrha herself.

"Duke!" she cried, "Duke Callion! My uncle has told me. You are leaving! Take me with you! Ah, do not go and leave me behind. Take me!"

Duke tried to pry her loose tenderly, but there was a strange lump in his throat. He said, chokingly, "Pyrrha—I can't—we can't—"

And then, astonishingly, Quelchal said, "Why not, Duke Callion? There is room for the girl aboard. And these things can be arranged easily and swiftly."

Duke said hoarsely, "Don't fool me, Quelchal! I don't feel like joking!"

"Joking? I do not joke in times of stress, Duke Callion." Quelchal lifted the girl's head with infinite gravity. "You want to go with us, Pyrrha? You want never to be separated from this man?"

There was a sudden glory in the girl's eyes that humbled Duke oddly. "Never!" she said in a ringing voice. "And you, Duke Callion? You, too, want this?"

"More than anything on earth," Duke said simply.

"Then," said Quelchal, "you twain are mated in the eyes of the Gods, and I, Quelchal, Viceroy of the Atlantean colony of Mayapan, do bless this union! When Lucan returns he will sanctify it! And—" with one of his rare smiles he added, "—may peace and happiness attend you!"

"Y-y-you said it!" came a voice from the doorway, and Joey Cox entered. He stared at the sober trio thoughtfully. "Hey, what's g-g-going on here? It sounds like a wedding ceremony!"

"It is," grinned Duke. "Joey, in the words of the world we left behind us meet the wife!"

Joey stammered, "W-w-well, I'll be damned! Lucan told me outside that we were preparing to go on a dangerous quest. But he didn't tell me *how* d-d-dangerous!"

CHAPTER XI
Atlantis

THE slim ship rolled gently in the trough of the sea. Before them, as far as the eye could see, was water. Behind them was a receding patch of green, now nebulous with distance. The sun was like a great bronze disc hanging over them. Not a cloud marred the brilliant turquoise of the sky.

Joey Cox turned. He had been looking backward to the mainland. Now, as the ship dipped into a valley of white-capped emerald, he sighed. "W-w-well, that's that! You know, Duke, I kind of h-h-hated to leave that place. I liked it!"

Duke didn't take his hands off the wheel. There was no need to. Pyrrha fitted snugly into the circle of his arms as he guided the white-sailed vessel eastward. He smiled, "Cheer up, Joey. We'll return one of these fine days. After we've finished our mission."

Joey snorted, "Yeah, that's all right for *Y-Y-YOU* to say! You brought one of the n-n-nicest things in Mayapan along with you! But *me—*" He sighed wistfully. "You know, Duke, I *enjoyed* being a big-shot there. Mayapan was the swellest place you and I ever visited. Excepting for H-h-hurkan."

From the prow of the boat, Quelchal heard him and turned to glower darkly.

"You need concern yourself no longer with Hurkan, Joey. His life is forfeit when Lucan finds him."

"Funny he hasn't found him already," mused Duke. "Where might he be hiding, Quelchal?"

"Many places. In the jungles. The mountains of the peninsula. Anywhere. But wherever he is, he will return no more to Mayapan."

"And good riddance!" breathed Duke. Then, as he felt his bride of but a few hours shiver in his arms, he said solicitously, "Cold, Pyrrha? It *is* chilly out here on the water. Wait. I'll bring you a wrap."

He ducked down the companionway. An instant his footsteps clattered on the stairs—then his companions on deck heard a loud, amazed shout. "Hey, speak of the devil! Look what's stowed away on our boat!"

There was the sound of a scuffle, short and swift, then Duke appeared at the head of the companionway dragging behind him a disheveled figure in crimson robes. All the adventurers surged forward. Pyrrha gasped, and one white hand flew to her lips. Joey gasped, "The p-p-priest! Hurkan!"

Quelchal moved slowly, but his every movement was pregnant with menace. He strode forward; collared the ash-visaged culprit. In a level voice he said, "It is good! I will take care of him, Duke Callion."

Lean, bronzed cords tensed in his forearms as he marched the quaking ex-priest to the side of the boat. He muttered a few swift words in Atlantean. Hurkan struggled wildly; strove to break that iron grip. But Quelchal, like a great, golden terrier, lifted the quivering rat in his strong arms and—

"Quelchal!" cried Duke Callion.

Quelchal paused; turned his head impatiently.

"Yes, my friend?"

"You—you mustn't! We can't kill him like that!"

HURKAN sensed an intercessor. As Quelchal's grip relaxed somewhat, he tore loose from the one-time Viceroy; slithered across the deck-boards to Duke's feet and groveled there, mouthing frantic pleas. Duke drew back from him, sickened. But he said, "We just can't kill the man in cold blood, Quelchal. It's not civilized."

Quelchal folded his arms sternly. He said, "Was there mercy in his heart for us, Duke Callion? It is not wisdom to spare an enemy like *this!*"

Joey said, "D-d-duke's right, though, Quelchal. We just can't knock him off in c-c-cold blood." And hopefully— "Of course, if h-h-he'd like to scrap it out—?"

Once again Quelchal grasped the priest by the nape of the neck.

"He is our enemy. More than that, he aspires to the favor of your woman, Duke Callion. Did you not know that was why he was so bitterly turned against us during the trial?"

Duke said, "Is that right, Pyrrha?" and the girl nodded mutely. For an instant Puke's jawline hardened and he was tempted to let Quelchal have his way with the groveling Hurkan. Then his inborn American spirit of fair play won over his emotions. He said, "Nevertheless, he's defenseless now. Let him live. There are four of us to watch him."

Hurkan understood. In a paroxysm of surrender, he writhed at Duke's feet, slobbering over his boots. He raised his voice again and again in pledges of allegiance. Quelchal shrugged and folded his arms.

"So be it, Duke Callion!" he said. "But I fear we will regret this."

And Joey added his warning, "J-j-just one teeny-weeny regret, and he goes to f-f-feed the sharks!" He added, humorously, "Just as sure as I'm C-c-coxcox, the biggest god in Mayapan!"

Duke said nothing. Already he regretted his own soft-heartedness. But he knew he would do the same thing again, under the same circumstances.

DAYS passed. Fair days and foul days; days when the westerly wind was like the gentle breathing of a maiden's voice; days when howling tempests screamed across the waters to rip at the fabric of their reefed sails with hungry fingers. The mother sea was alternately the mistress of calm and the mistress of passion. Days upon endless days that stretched into weeks...

But inexorably, proudly, gallantly, the slim ship nosed its way through the swelling troughs; ever eastward. Once the adventurers paused at a small island for an overnight rest on solid land, and to refill their water tanks. Once, on the dim horizon, they saw the image of a feather-sailed vessel; tall and proud; towering high above the surface of the water.

Haze, and the indirect sunlight caused that form of mirage known to mariners as "looming." For a brief period it appeared to those in the tiny boat that the larger vessel was within scant furlongs of them. They could see its straining canvas; see, too, the hawk-like features of the captain on the poop, and the swarthy mates who paced the runways between the ranks of sweating oarsmen. Three high banks of oars raised, lowered, pulled in unison, and beads of spray followed the shimmering blades. Almost they could hear the groaning of the oars in their locks, and the sound of the horsehide drum beating the tempo for the crew in the galley. But as swiftly as it had appeared, the mirage faded. Once again the boat was a dot on the horizon.

Quelchal said, "A trireme out of Tyrrhenia. Sailing for Helluland, I suppose."

Joey said, "T-t-tyrrhenia? Would that be Tyre of our t-t-time?"

"Possibly. But not the Tyre of which your Christian Bible speaks. There were seven cities of Tyre. This was the earliest; peopled by colonists from Aztlan."

"And Helluland?" hazarded Duke.

"America?"

"The part which you knew as Nova Scotia," replied Quelchal. "A cold land, but a fruitful one."

For the thousandth time since their adventure had begun, Duke was reminded of its weirdness; its almost incredibility save for the fact that—as Joey had once commented—here they were!

He could not help but marvel at the smugness of Twentieth Century savants who, in his school days, had been content to allow that civilization sprang into being ("By spontaneous generation, I suppose," Duke thought wryly) at a spot in history scarce five thousands of years prior to the birth of Christ.

All the evidence was to the contrary. The fact that the Egyptian civilization showed no indications of a slow, tedious, groping development —but had sprung into being overnight, full-fledged and knowledgeable. Now Duke knew that Egypt was one of the Atlantean colonies.

Then there was that remarkable fact—the strange similarities between early Greek and early Mexican, Peruvian and American Indian languages! From his smattering of Atlantean, Duke now recognized that *this* was the mother of all tongues.

So many things! Every civilization under the sun had a legend of a "Deluge"—yet the scientists dismissed these as mere legends of a "small, isolated flood." True! It had been an "isolated" flood, mayhap—but a flood that had erased from the face of the globe the mother-country. Aztlan!

How, in the face of all this evidence, had science so long contrived to decry the existence of Atlantis? Duke did not know. But he *did* know that he was grateful for the combination of circumstances which had enabled him to live through this adventure. And—meet Pyrrha.

DAYS upon endless days. Days that lengthened into weeks. Once a windless spell stilled their sails, letting them drift aimlessly on the face of the swelling tide for three solid days, while Quelchal impatiently gnawed on his fingernails. Once Hurkan, grown more confident now that he had been allotted a special watch, and a time at the wheel, was found drinking surreptitiously out of the too-swiftly emptying water barrels. For that misdeed, Duke had given the ex-priest a good taste of American free-for-all roughhouse. After that, Hurkan attempted no more such tricks, but as he nursed a swollen nose and "moused" eye back to normal, many were the vengeful glances he tossed in Duke Callion's direction. Always in secret, however.

But by and large, harmony reigned on the vessel. To compensate for the sun's brazen outpouring in the daytime, there was the cooling silver of the moon at night. Joey played endless games of solitaire with a deck of cards rapidly losing their colors beneath a smear of grime. Hurkan nursed his grudge, but obeyed his superiors cautiously. Quelchal spent hours of hopeful-brooding on the forward deck. And in the comfort of the lee, Duke Callion and his bride loved and found reason to wish this trip might never end...

Until, one morning standing the dogwatch, Duke Callion's eyes saw a strange phantasm in the interminable blue-green of the dawn-streaked waters. A curious hooked smudge of brown that, rub his eyes as he might, did not disappear. Uncertainly at first, then with growing confidence, he roused the others with his cry: "Land ho! Land away!"

Sleepy-eyed but hopeful, the others gathered about him. There was long silence as they watched. Brighter grew the sky. Clearer grew the spot of brown.

Clearer...until it took form. A form that Duke Callion recognized. He had seen it before...in the book of Cosmos, the Mad Monk...and in Quelchal's ·collection of souvenirs from his lost homeland. A great cry ripped from his throat.

"Quelchal! The Crooked Mountain! Colhuacan!"

But Quelchal had fallen to his knees. There were tears of joy and thanksgiving in his eyes, and one word on his lips. "Aztlan!" Hurkan, too, was moved by the sight. He made a swift, cryptic gesture over his right breast and dropped to his knees.

Pyrrha pressed closer to Duke. Joey stood beside him, as ever. And thus they watched, in the first, golden glow of the rising sun, as before them, mysterious, lovely and beckoning, rose from the bosom of the sea the Golden Island of the Hesperides. The Fabulous Isle of Colhuacan. Atlantis!

CHAPTER XII
The Titans

DUKE called, "Hey, Joey—take over for a spell, will you?" and moved forward to where Quelchal stood staring at the green land before them.

Several hours had passed since the sighting of the island empire.

Blessed with favorable winds, their tiny craft had made good speed. Not that it was possible to see with fair clarity larger details of the mainland.

Quelchal stirred as Duke came beside him. There was *puzzlement* in his voice as he said: "I cannot understand, Duke Callion. It is incredible, but—there appears to be a battle raging!"

Hurkan overheard them and moved forward. Silence fell as the three strove to pierce the thin watery haze.

Then: "Damned if I don't think you're right, Quelchal," said Duke. "It looks to me as if those black ships are bombarding the city."

Hurkan said, "Black ships! Those would be the Titans."*

Quelchal rapped sharply, "Ridiculous! The Titans were quelled into subjection in my time! Four hundreds of years ago!"

Hurkan sneered belittlingly.

"That was in *your* time. They are a mighty, independent nation now. A state of warfare has existed between Aztlan and Titania for more than three decades." He added indiscreetly, "Perhaps it would be well for the Titans to win, too. They are—"

"Silence!" Quelchal's great, silverdowned hands twisted with the desire to spring themselves at Hurkan's throat.

"You see, Duke Callion? Not only a liar, but a traitor as well. We should get rid of him now. Here!"

"Wait," Duke soothed him. "Soon we will be able to turn him over to those who will try him. We don't want his blood on our hands."

Quelchal subsided, grumbling. Hurkan's face had paled before the golden man's anger. Now slow color crept back into it, mottling it unhealthily. He turned and left the two friends.

They scarcely noticed his departure. Both were engrossed in the spectacle being enacted before them.

A half score of hulking, black ships, deep-bellied with massive ebon sails, were knotted outside the crescent-shaped harbor of the island empire. Tiny crimson glows in the guts of these craft betold the presence of fires there—fires in which huge balls of pitched tar were being ignited.

---

*The legend of the Titans persists through every recognized mythology. Even the Christian Bible makes mention of the fact (in the chapter devoted to the Deluge) that "there were Giants in those days." —Author.

THESE burning spheres were deftly maneuvered into gigantic catapults, mounted on the ships. When the torque was released, the conflagratory mass arced high over the smaller, defending ships in the harbor to fall into the heart of the city of Aztlan. Here and there smoky pillars designated that a firebrand had found a mark.

The onshore defenders were utilizing a similar weapon, but for the main part their defense was futile. The mobile ships offered too tiny a target for the inaccurate catapults. Once, indeed, a spark caught one of the ship's mainsails, and a great sheet of flame rose over the craft: But a swarm of sailors roached high into the rigging to prevent the fire from spreading.

Duke thought, "Oh, boy! What one twenty-incher would do to that crowd! Or even a broken-down howitzer!" But aloud he said, "Quelchal—I don't understand? For a while you had me convinced that your nation was one well-versed in science and mechanics. How is it they use such primitive weapons?"

Quelchal, too, was puzzled. He answered slowly, "That is something I cannot understand. I did not lie to you, Duke Callion. I think my time-ship proved my contention. All I can assume is that—"

Joey Cox, who had turned the wheel over to Hurkan and come forward to join them, interrupted him suddenly.

"Well, that seems to be that. The battle's over. But w-w-who won?"

Duke and Quelchal looked swiftly. The battle *was* over, and now the massive black fleet was swinging about; preparing to leave the harbor. Duke said, "Hey—they're moving this way!" and leaped toward the wheel. He rapped sharp orders to his shipmates. "Reef the sails! Get down every inch of canvas. We don't want those black babies to see us!"

But his warning came too late. Already the black fleet had put about, and one ship was edging away from the others; scudding across the intervening water in the direction of the lonely little craft.

Duke countermanded his order.

"Never mind—we're in for it now! Get 'em all up again! Maybe we can beat out the big unwieldy bug!"

A big "bug" the approaching black bireme might be—looking, as it did, like a huge, many-legged spider as it crawled over the water towards them, its double row of oars dipping in magnificent unison. But unwieldy it most certainly was not. With the cadenced rhythm of the oarsmen aided by the wind that filled the sails, it literally flew toward their laboring little Sloop.

The harbor was still knots distant.

There was no hope of succor coming from the shore. It was catch-as-catch-can; the agility of the little boat against the superior lines and speed of the Titanian man-o'-war. Black as a thundercloud; ominous as impending doom, the vessel plunged down on the small sloop. The Titanian raiders, their bombardment of Aztlan having ended in a bootless draw, seemed determined to at least wreak their vengeance on this tiny Atlantean craft.

Nearer and nearer they drew. Now Duke and his companions could see the horde of faces glaring down upon them from the soldiers' deck; could glimpse, through tiny port holes, the straining visages of the slaves in the galley rack. The long oars seemed to yawn toward them... recede...yawn toward them again.

EVEN at that, they might have made it—had not Hurkan's treachery betrayed them. So intent was Duke at the wheel, curveting, twisting, writhing his tiny craft through the green like a live thing, that he did not have time to watch the venomous ex-priest. Nor did the others; their first intimation of anything wrong coming when, "The scoundrel!" roared Quelchal. "He has destroyed us all!"

And suddenly, beneath Duke's tensed hands, the boat seemed to go dull and lifeless. He looked up, an oath springing to his lips.

Hurkan had seized the moment. Scrambling to the fore deck, he had slashed expertly at the ropes which held the straining sails; had taken time to slash once...twice...thrice...at the sails themselves before leaping over the gunwale.

Now the boat, like a bird with two broken wings, shredded sails flapping aimlessly in the wind, came slowly to heel, stopped, and began to wallow in the forewash of the approaching Titanian vessel.

"At l-l-least," screamed Joey Cox madly, "I'll get h-h-him for this!" In a swift movement he was at the side of the boat. Then he, too, was in the water. His splashing body bore down upon that of the frantically struggling Hurkan.

Duke Callion took Pyrrha in his arms. For all too short an instant he pressed her close; then released her. To Quelchal he said, "We'll let 'em know they were in a fight, anyway—" From the water rose a frightened scream. Little Joey Cox had overhauled the traitorous priest. His hands were seeking, finding, Hurkan's throat...

There came a sudden, grinding shock. Wood struck wood; splintering. A shard of broken oar shattered the flopping jib of the tinier craft. Duke saw the butt of a crushed blade throb suddenly backward against one of the galley slaves' faces; saw wood and flesh and blood grind horribly together once while a piercing shriek broke from the oarsman's gushing throat.

He was conscious of Pyrrha at his shoulder, her scented hair fragrant in his nostrils. Of a wild-eyed Quelchal charging to meet a horde of gigantic invaders who dropped from the towering decks above to swarm their own small boat. He glimpsed, for an instant, a heavy figure hurtling down toward him; black bulk blotting the sun...

Then something silver gleamed, and lightning was crashing madly at the base of his skull. He felt strength sloughing away from him; his knees buckling forward. He saw a host of bestial faces writhe in taunting laughter; heard the voice of Pyrrha crying hopelessly, "Duke—"

Then all was silence.

CHAPTER XIII
The Dungeons of Titania

THERE was dampness about him; a moist and fetid chill that seemed to ooze into the marrow of his bones. The air his parched lungs gulped was rank and sour; smelling of old sores long festering. Duke gagged, raised up on one elbow, and peered about him.

Instantly someone was at his side. Pyrrha. Her face, against his, was wet with tears.

"Duke! You're all right?"

"It t-t-takes more than a crack on the c-c-conk," said the voice of Joey Cox, "to kill Duke Callion. Hey, fella! How's the head feel?"

"Lousy, thanks!" groaned Duke. He rose to his feet gingerly; peered into the semi-darkness about him. "Where are we, anyway?"

"In the dungeons below the castle-fort of Titania," answered Quelchal. "You have been unconscious for a longer time than you imagine, Duke Callion."

"It looks like it," agreed Duke. "How long?"

"Several hours. It is not far from Titania to my country. But—" Quelchal appended ruefully, "far enough!"

Duke saw, now, that he and his companions were in but one corner of a spacious, vaulted dungeon. The place was like a gigantic, filthy honeycomb. And it was peopled with others, captive like themselves.

Seemingly no concerted effort had been made by the Titans to keep their captives under bonds. Here and there Duke saw a prisoner chained to the wall, but for the most part the dungeon's inhabitants roamed freely within the limitations of the   moldy cavern. Ruddy spots in the darkness glowed where   they had built small fires to ward off the miasmic chill.   About each of these fires was gathered an evil-looking group of humans.

Duke said shortly, "Come on— let's see what kind of dump this is!" and led

Duke moved fast but Dwyfan was faster. In one swift stride he was on the murder-bent leader.

the way to the nearest fire. As he and his friends pushed into the squalid little circle, unfriendly faces turned toward them. One pock-marked captive snarled an oath at Duke; grabbed him by the arm and spun him around.

"Fair warning, brother," he spat, "before I slit your throat like a herring. This is *my* fire and *my* band! Go build your own blaze if ye'd be warm!"

Duke said thoughtfully, "So that's the way it is, eh?" and stared at the hostile circle of faces. "Every band has its own captain? And its own fire?" He faced the pock-marked one coolly. "And suppose I declare myself in on this band? Then what?"

"Then—*this!*" retorted the band captain. A grimy hand flew to his belt. Metal shimmered evilly. He rushed at Duke, the naked blade heart-high.

Pyrrha screamed. The scream turned heads from all parts of the room. A tall, black-haired youngster stepped forward swiftly; stayed his captain's hand.

"Let be!" he begged. "The captive is new here—"

With a foul curse the band leader jerked free and flung himself once more upon Duke. Joey chuckled. He said, under his breath, "What did I tell you? Wherever he goes there's trouble!" He didn't even stir. He knew Duke too well to waste movements.

Duke's left hand, darted out as the captain sprung in. He grasped the pock-marked one's wrist in an iron clutch; wrenched sharply. Bone grated dully. The knife clattered to the stones. The man fell back, screaming vituperative threats, nursing his shattered wrist in his good hand.

Duke said speculatively, "Now, if any of the rest of you—"

The dark-haired youngster who had attempted to befriend him stepped forward smiling. "There are no others," he said. "I will vouch for the rest. I am Dwyfan of Cym."

"And I—" began Duke. A sharp, warning cry turned him in time. The injured captain, maddened with anger and pain, had raised himself to one knee; crawled behind Duke. Even now he was lifting the blade to plunge it into the small of Duke's back.

Duke moved fast, but Dwyfan was even faster. In one swift stride he was over the murder-bent leader; had turned the blade in his band. He made a jabbing motion. The pock-marked one's scream died in a gurgle. Just once he twitched—then lay still.

Casually, Dwyfan lifted the body. "Thus we dispose of them," he said, "in this hell-hole!" He carried the dead body to a stream of evil-smelling water that entered the prison through a tube, splashed into a wide, deep trough running the length of the room, and disappeared into another circular aqueduct.

H E heaved mightily. The body arched into the torrent. Then, as the rushing waters plucked at it, it moved sluggishly downstream to disappear into the unknown beyond.

"We must provide our own sanitation," smiled the dark Dwyfan. "Our" captors forget us, once we are here. Oh, they throw us scraps of food from time to time, like wild beasts. But were we not needed as galley slaves, no doubt they would begrudge us even their slops."

They had rejoined the group at the fire now, and Duke noted a new respect on the faces of those who had before questioned his presence. Other prisoners, attracted by the commotion, had drifted from their own fires. Duke turned to Dwyfan wonderingly.

"There must be more than three score held captive in these dungeons," he marvelled.

"We were taking census just before you came," the Cymrian replied. "Three score and four, including yourselves. And—minus one, now—that makes sixty-three."

Duke's eyes narrowed.

"Sixty three", he mused "and two-thirds of them are sturdy fighting men. Tell me, have you never contemplated escape from your prison?"

A listener laughed hoarsely. Another said, "Escape? Traghol has just shown you the only escape!" Duke regarded the man thoughtfully.

"Traghol?"

Dwyfan the Cym shrugged and nodded toward the stream. "Folddhe means that the only escape is—death! We are on an island. An island of giants. Come, see for yourself!"

There was a small, barred window set high in the wall of the dungeon. Yellow rays of late afternoon sun filtered dustily through the narrow slit. Dwyfan gestured Duke to follow; began to clamber up the damp, uneven rock wall, clinging with fingertips and toes.

Dwyfan panted, "You are a man, stranger. Few can manage this climb," and motioned Duke to the window.

Duke saw, then, why there was no escape from the dungeon. Titania was an island, and to escape the prison was useless. The Titan soldiers guarding their rock-walled little empire would hunt down like a dog any stranger who succeeded in escaping the cells. But yet—

Duke gazed wistfully at the scene before him. The calm, green, unchanging sea; smooth and serene as ever. The horizon paling into the azure sky. And he sighed.

Dwyfan laughed mirthlessly, and began to clamber down again.

"You see? Escape is both impossible. And—futile!"

Duke nodded. "Impossible and futile. Yes." And for an instant a great dread swept over him. Time sped by, while they, the only ones who could save Atlantis from its impending fate, languished in this dungeon. His jaw tightened. "Yes—but it must be accomplished!"

THERE came the sound of a key grating in a rusty lock. The two men who had just reached the floor spun to see an armed group of their captors entering the dungeon doorway.

For the first time, Duke was able to see the men who warred upon Atlantis—and his eyes grew wide at the sight of them. Titans! They were Titans, indeed. Not a man of them was less than seven feet in height; and each was built in perfect proportion. Huge, broad men; raven-haired and dark of visage. Strong-hewed and mighty. And with them—

Joey gasped, and lunged forward.

"H-h-hurkan!" he cried.

The crimson-robed ex-priest of Mayapan edged cagily behind one of his stalwart companions. His smile was nervous but determined. He sneered, "So we meet again, my friends?"

Joey raged, "You grinning s-s-scoundrel! I thought I'd drowned you like the rat you are!"

"Hurkan lives to avenge his wrongs!" spat the man. He nodded to the tall captain beside him. "That one. The girl."

Duke gritted, "Oh, no you don't!" and raced to the side of Pyrrha. Joey and Quelchal, and their new friend, Dwyfan, also closed in to form a protective circle about her. But the unarmed guard was impotent before the strength and size of the Titan 'soldiery. With vast unconcern, the Titans broke them apart with cold steel; seized the girl and bore her to Hurkan.

"Pyrrha!" Duke quivered with rage, feeling steel press threateningly against his breast. She was fighting like a wildcat; clawing and scratching at her captors. But now she saw his own plight and subsided. Harkan smiled.

"Ah, that is better! Will you come quietly—or shall I have my friends quarter your groom for the crows?" Pyrrha's frenzy melted. She cried in an agonized voice, "Duke! Resist them no longer. I—I will be all right!"

Quelchal boomed devastatingly, "This will not be forgotten, Hurkan! Traitor and thief! With my own hands, I will rip your heart from your breast and feed it to the dogs that begat you!"

"Your bones will rot in this dungeon, braggart!" jeered Hurkan. To Duke he added, "Farewell, man out of the future! Despair not for your bride. When the conquest of Aztlan is concluded, and you rot here with your fellows, she will be safe and secure—lying in my arms!"

Then a word to the Titan captain—and they were gone. Once more the key grated in the massive lock. Dull silence fell over the dungeon. Dull silence which at last was broken by the voice of the Cym, Dwyfan, springing to his feet to address the brooding prisoners.

"Now," he cried 'in a voice of thunder, "we are become no longer men! It was evil enough that we allowed ourselves to be meekly herded into this stinking pest-hole, to rot here like caged rodents. But we have stood by and seen them take a *woman*—a young and beautiful woman! And a bride! Shall we stand for this any longer?"

A MUTTERING rose from the forward-pressing horde. It rose and grew to an ominous rumble of sound; an ominous growl of manhood long taunted, but finally spurred to rage. The sound of steel mingled with the rumble of voices. Angry shouts roused unholy echoes in the murky cavern. One man burst forward to confront Duke.

"The time is past for tiny bands and petty band-captains!" he cried. "I, Angha of Boeotia, do hereby bow to a mightier leader than myself. Duke Callion, my sword and heart are yours. And those of my followers!"

It was the trap that released the tempest. Fire swept through the other prisoners. One by one, from the most virile captain to the humblest serf, they surged forward to dedicate themselves to the single purpose. A motley crew they were; many of them gaunt and ragged. Their names were a roll call of the nations of earth. Like Babel their voices sounded.

"I, Ogyges of Attica...Yima of Iran...Valthgar of the Sunless Land..."

Something of their fire ignited the dulling flame in Duke Callion's own heart. He stared at his new rag-tag army with sudden hope. His warrior's eyes appraised, and found good, these men. Valthgar, the huge, blond man from the North. Ogyges, the broadchested Attican. Chiba, the great blackskinned barbarian from Afric. His eyes blazed.

"It is good! I accept your vows. Pick up your blades and weapons, and you leaders gather about me while we plan a council of war."

CHAPTER XIV
The Ancient Legion

HIS words were interrupted by the sound of a commotion outside the walls of the dungeon. Something metallic shattered against the stone abutments. A weird streak of glowing orange flared briefly in the tiny, slitted window: hiss and spluttered, and disappeared.

Dwyfan the Cym left the group; once more clambered up the wall to the window. From that height he looked down at the allies; cried excitedly, "It's a counter-attack! The Atlanteans' fleet is in the harbor, bombarding the city!"

Quelchal smiled grimly, "I knew retaliation would be swift!" he grunted.

Joey Cox said, "To h-h-hell with that! This is just what the d-d-doctor ordered for us! Duke—those Atlantean ships offer us a way of getting off the island!"

Only one of the assembled captains remained stubborn. It was Folddhe, the grim, dour-visaged Celt, who repeated the morbid warning he had made before. "There is only one escape from these dungeons! Death—and the tube!"

Dwyfan said scornfully, "You cowardly cur—"

But Duke Callion halted them suddenly as their eyes blazing, the two men wheeled to face one another.

"Stay! Folddhe speaks more truth than he knows! There *is* a way from the dungeons!"

Valthgar, the Viking, said, "A way?"

"The tube! The water tunnel! Has anyone ever attempted escape through there?"

The swarthy Iranian, Yima, shook his head morbidly. "It was told me once that a madman tried it. He was never heard of again."

And Joey pleaded, "No, Duke! You can't try that! We'll storm the door...break through the walls somewhere!"

Duke said, "Before this battle is ended? No, we must move now— and swiftly! Before the Atlantean fleet leaves the harbor. They are our one hope of salvation!"

Swiftly he stripped himself of all heavy impedimenta. His high field boots. His now useless gun belt and holster. The machete he had worn since the fight—oh, so long ago—in Chunhubub. Into his belt he tucked only a slim dirk. Then he strode to the side of the trough which fed the dungeon with water.

The exit tube was barely wide enough to contain a man's body. Duke looked at it—and for an instant fear and indecision weakened him. Then he remembered Pyrrha in Hurkan's lustful arms.

He took a deep breath; turned once to grasp Joey's hand.

"Gather at the door. If I succeed, I'll find some way to open it. If not—"

Joey understood. He said, "Okay, D-d-duke! Good luck!"

Then he turned away, reluctant to watch, as Duke drew a deep, lung-filling breath and plunged himself into the racing current, straight through the mouth of the tunnel tube.

HIS lungs were shriveled with fire, and the desire to breathe was a force that sapped strength from his failing arms and legs. The water pressed about him coldly; sweeping him out of darkness into darkness he knew not where. The sound of his beating heart throbbed in his ears like a threnody of death.

Duke Callion knew that it was a matter of seconds before his tortured lungs would have their will over his weakening body. Soon that insistent inner urge would open his clenched mouth and nostrils; let in a flood of slimy, stinking water.

His eyes, open despite the filthy scum that surrounded him, saw nothing but darkness. He fought his way to the surface, the top of the tube, hoping for an inch of fetid air above the water. There was none. The tube was completely choked with the offal drainage of the dungeons.

This, then, Duke knew, was the end. And even as he struggled to hold that stifling bit of air in him, he found himself thinking of Pyrrha...

Then, suddenly, the darkness about him was turned to a dull misty gray. Sunlight! There was sunlight on the water somewhere! And where there was sunlight, there was air!

His body met, locked against, something monstrously, distorted. Something fleshy, flabby, that gave before him like soft, unbaked dough. In the murky light Duke saw what blocked his passage. The body of the slain captain Traghol, somehow caught at the lip of the tube where it opened to the Outside—and freedom!

The irony of it almost forced a groan from Duke's lips. That he should be this near release, only to be defeated in death by one who had failed to master him alive. With a last, convulsive movement of despair, he lashed out with both fists against the swollen carcass.

And—it gave! Sluggishly at first, then as the cumulative force of the water behind gave it impetus, with explosive speed! Water pressure thrust inexorably against Duke's back. He felt himself popped like a cork out of a bottle...sprawling helplessly through air...falling...

But even while falling, he found time to draw into his lungs fresh, lifegiving air before he plunged once more into water. But, miraculously, this was *clean* water! Its grateful sting laved his eyes, cleansing them of their offal-burned smarting. Its bosom lifted him. He was atop the water, and—

It was sea-water! Clean, salt seawater!

The tube which fed the dungeons opened onto a sheer thirty foot drop into the ocean.

Again and again, Duke ducked himself, scrubbed at his hair and face and eyes with the emerald salt water to rid himself of the last vestiges of the filth through which he had swum. Finally, clean again, he circled back toward the shore, selecting the most likely vantage point from which to re-enter the fortress.

He found it. A narrow foothold staircase circling up the rampart walls; entering the fort through an arched doorway. On catlike feet, he stole up this walk, apprehensive that at any moment he might be seen from below.

But he was not. The Titans were too busy staving off the retaliatory attack of the ships from Aztlan.

Duke's sense of direction, earned through years of vagabondage, served him well. In the musty corridors of the castle, he chose unerringly the proper turns. And at last he gained a low-ceilinged avenue which he knew *had* to open on the dungeon's only doorway.

HE rounded a final corner—and knew at once that he had guessed right. For there were two soldiers standing beside a barred door. There was disturbed anxiety on their faces as they listened to the tumult of sound echoing through the grillwork.

As Duke waited, one guard said nervously, "I don't like it, Bursal! I don't like it at all. There's something strange afoot amongst the prisoners."

Bursal laughed carelessly, "Let be! Who cares if the rabble howls? Stone and iron will hold them!"

"I think we should call the captain of the guard. Perhaps a few lashes would quiet them?"

Bursal stroked his chin meditatively. "Well—a few lashes wouldn't hurt. I like to see them writhe, anyway. Wait you here, Herg. I'll call the captain."

Duke shrank into the shadows as the guard's footsteps approached. Now they were almost upon him. Harness clanking, he turned the corner—

He never had a chance. Duke's dirk was lunging at his throat even as the man's eyes widened in surprise and horror. His cry was stifled in a choking gurgle. His blood gushed a hot torrent over Duke's bared arm as the man sank lifeless to the ground.

From the far end of the corridor, the other man, Herg, cried nervously, "Bursal! Bursal! Did you call?" Then his footsteps came racing up the avenue. He almost stumbled over the body of the prostrate Bursal; recovered his footing just in time to see death, grim-faced and terrible, bearing down upon him. He reached for his sword...his hand never found it. Duke's dirk found his heart first.

Eagerly, Duke snatched the key-ring from the harness of the second warrior. In a trice he was at the door of the dungeon; twisting the rusted clef in the lock. A hoarse shout greeted him as the door swung open. Joey Cox was pounding his back; screaming delightedly.

"You did it! I knew y-y-you could, Duke!" Then the captains, the first taste of victory sweet on their lips, were gathering about him, asking instructions. Duke said swiftly, "The girl. Pyrrha. We must find her first, then steal a longboat. Row to the Atlantean fleet and safety!"

It was Duke who led the vengeance-hungry horde of prisoners forward and upward into the heart of the castle. Some sort of prescience seemed to guide him. It was as if the thoughts of Pyrrha were blazing a trail for him. But whatever the explanation, the ragged army found its way to the proper sector without once meeting opposition.

At the entrance to an ornate hall, Duke motioned his men to halt. Swiftly he ordered, "We split here! Joey, half of the men go with you in that direction. If you do not find Pyrrha; continue on to the shore and find there a boat or boats. "We others will go forward. May we all meet at the shore!"

"Or in Valhalla!"* added Valthgar. "So be it!"

The two groups split. Duke appraised those behind him swiftly. Joey's detachment had taken Quelchal, Ogyges, Yima and Angha and their followers. He had drawn the giant Nubian, Chiba, Valthgar the Viking, Dwyfan, and the morose Celt, Folddhe.

WITH whatever weapons they possessed—knives and clubs for the most part; an occasional rusted sword—the strange crew pressed forward over stone flaggings, past an ornate court, into the heart of the fortress. Finally, at the portal of a great bronze-studded door, dim voices came to them. Again Duke hushed them into wary silence.

Then his heart gave a great leap as he heard, on the other side of the door, a well-remembered voice. The voice of the rascally priest, Hurkan.

"The rulership of Aztlan," Hurkan was saying, "is all I ask for my services. That and one other thing. The girl, Pyrrha."

A rumbling, disdainful voice asked, "You seek to bargain with me, renegade?"

---

*Heaven where heroes dwell.

"There are many things I can tell you about the island of Aztlan," Hurkan persisted insinuatingly. "You did not know for instance that the fires beneath"

Chiba, the strong-hewed black, snicked his dirk in its scabbard and rumbled deep in his throat. But Duke laid a restraining hand on his arm.

"Wait!" he whispered. "The girl first! I have a plan to take care of the Titans. But we must get to Aztlan first."

Grumbling, the Nubian subsided. Duke's intuition was working with sweet perfection now. It was with a feel of utter certainty that he led his men to an adjacent doorway. With complete assurance that he flung open the door.

"Here!" he cried.

And he was right. As his detachment crowded into the room behind him, two women started and cried out with fright. One was an auburn haired girl with flesh the hue of alabaster. The other was—Pyrrha. Just for a moment did surprise shock Pyrrha into motionlessness. Then, with a glad cry, she was racing forward.

But there was another in the room, one of the giant Titans, an armed guard, standing beside a huge brass gong. One startled look at the raiders and he swung into action. He reached for the hammer; raised it to bring it across the gong's gleaming face...

Cro-o-o-onggh! The crashing sound filled the room with an ear-splitting din. Dwyfan roared, "He'll bring the whole fortress down on us!" and leaped at the guard, sword gleaming. With both hands he swung the heavy blade. The man's head wobbled loosely on a riven neck; fell forward on his chest. He fell slowly, ponderously, as a tall building might fall. In sections.

Duke shouted, "Get the other girl, Dwyfan. Let's get out of here!"

Pyrrha was at his side; sobbing with joy and relief. He saw the dark-haired, laughing Dwyfan sweep the auburn-tressed beauty off her feet, tuck her under his arm like a sack of meal, and charge toward the doorway. Then all of them were racing down the corridor toward an entranceway suddenly filling with Titans.

Afterward, Duke Callion had no clear recollection of that fight. It was like some wild, fantastic dream in which a warrior goes down, bleeding from a thousand wounds, only to rise again and struggle on a few feet farther.

He, himself, was like a madman as he carved a way through the mountain of flesh that stood before him. He caught fitful glimpses of his fellows about him. He heard Chiba's barbaric war-chant rising above the din of battle; saw the swart Ogyges rip a dripping sword from a Titanic opponent with his bare hands, and plunge the weapon down the man's gaping throat.

Dark Yima was a maddened dervish. Like a cat, he fought to disembowel his antagonists. A sadistic smile on his slender features, he fought his way through the holocaust with a lunge, twist, rip—and on to the next man!

But, from their superior height, the Titans wreaked havoc amongst the raiders, too. Twice Duke Callion felt a companion at his side gasp, choke, and slip to the floor. Once one of the prisoners stepped squarely into the blade of a sword lunging at Duke's heart. There was a smile on the man's lips as he died...and salt stung Duke Callion's eyes as, vengefully, he cleft the skull of the Titan who had slain him from pate to chin.

AND then, somehow, they were no longer inside the fortress. They were in the open, racing down across a sandy beach to where a wildly gesticulating Joey beckoned them on.

Pyrrha stumbled, and Duke lifted her bodily from the ground; swung her over his shoulder. No time to waste now in gentleness. Already a fresh horde of Titans were racing through the portals of the fort, charging down the beach after them.

And there were so few of them left! Even in this moment of haste, it sickened Duke's heart to see that of the score of men who had been in his *cortege,* a scant half dozen remained alive...

Then they were at the boats, and Joey's voice was screaming in his ear, "G-g-get in, Duke! We're c-c-casting off! He felt friendly hands relieving him of his precious burden; water splashing about his ankles, his calves, his thighs. A hard deck was under him. Over him a black sail was blossoming like an ebon flower before the wind.

And the angry roar of Quelchal, roaring above the din, "The harbor chain! By Bel, we're lost!"

Duke's heart sank. He had forgotten that this, as all ancient harbors, was secured against invasion by a great, metal chain stretched across the mouth of the harbor inlet. A massive series of links deep-set into oak stanchions on either crescent of land. Through this the ships could not pass!

It was then that something occurred that Duke Callion was never afterward to forget. For as the rebels stood dumb-struck on the decks of their bobbing craft, feeling hope die coldly within them, numbed by this culminating blow to their plans, one figure stirred into action. It was the dour Celt, Folddhe.

With a snarled oath, he wrenched the heavy blade from Duke's hand. Then, before anyone could guess his intention, he was overside, sword in his teeth, swinging toward the nearer arm of land.

Too late the stupefied Titans divined his aim. By the time their bewildered captain had given orders to intercept him, he was already dragging himself out on the far beach; racing to the sturdy stanchion into which was imbedded the harbor chain.

The blade in his hand hacked at the stubborn wood like the avenging wrath of a god. Slivers, of wood broke off; the gigantic stapling pin loosened. Duke watched him breathlessly. A few more strokes, now. Another. Another!

Then the Titans were upon him. A cast spear tore a gaping wound in his side; blood gushed forth to paint a gory cicatrix down one deep-planted limb. Another stroke. And another. Wood groaned. Metal grated. And—

A great shout rose from the boats. The massive harbor chain broke from its mooring; sank beneath the choppy rip. The straining boats broke free. Sails caught the wind and they spurted forward like racers.

Folddhe threw his broken sword into the faces of the raging Titans. Then once more he was splashing, stumbling, swimming through the sea. Duke heeled his vessel to. A host of eager hands reached out as the heroic Celt threw a dripping arm over the gunwale. Dwyfan the Cym cried, "Folddhe, you have saved us all! Come aboard. We are free now!"

But Folddhe shook his head. His lips were white with pain. Now Duke saw, with sudden horror, that where one limb dragged in the water, the emerald sea was stained a dull and dirty crimson. And Folddhe gasped, "Think you still...I am a...cowardly cur...Dwyfan...?"

He smiled that tight, dour smile they all knew so well. Then his pale arm slipped from the gunwale-and he was gone.

Duke's eyes were moist as he turned away. Dwyfan the Cym was weeping openly in great, wracking sobs, like a little child. Duke pressed his shoulders consolingly.

"We will avenge him, Dwyfan," he promised simply. "But later. For, see? Already the ships of Aztlan are putting about to receive us!"

CHAPTER XV
"Atlantis Is—'Doomed! '"

NATA, youthful captain of the Atlantean man-o-war *Kyklopes,* which had picked up the fugitives, nodded gently as Quelchal finished speaking.

"I do not pretend to understand all you say," he confessed. "But, then, I am merely a humble, god-fearing sailor. It is not for me to question your wisdom. Within the space of hours we will be in Aztlan, where you can communicate your warning to the Emperor, Zeus."

Quelchal said somberly, "Much time has been lost. Much precious time. Already the hour of the Deluge draws near."

Duke said cheerfully, "Well, it looks as if our troubles are all over now, Quelchal." And he pressed his wife's hand affectionately.

Joey Cox rose, disgust plain on his features. "S-s-soft stuff!" he snorted disdainfully. "I'm g-g-going out and talk to Dwyfan. You people in love—"

He stopped suddenly as the door burst inward to admit the dark-haired Cym. Behind him, blushing furiously, and trying to draw back, was the auburn beauty who had been Pyrrha's maid-servant in the castle of Titania.

"How long, Nata," demanded Dwyfan, "before this barge reaches Aztlan?"

"Very soon now," answered the captain. "Why?"

Dwyfan laughed uproariously, displaying gleaming white teeth. "Then very soon," he echoed, "this luscious morsel will become Dwyfach—wife of Dwyfan!"

Joey's face was a picture of dismay. He gasped for breath. Then, "Well, I'll be d-d-damned!" he complained mournfully. "They're all g-g-going crazy! I wish I was back in Cin—" He stopped and reconsidered. "No-I don't! But I w-w-wish I was back in Mayapan!"

DUKE Callion had travelled over much of the face of the twentieth century world, and had considered its culture to be a very high and worthy one. But now, after a journey about the capital city of the island of Aztlan, with Nata as guide, he was forced to concede that this ancient civilization compared favorably with the best he had known before.

Quelchal had gone to a private audience with the Emperor and his advisors. Joey, fatigued by their recent adventures, had remained in the apartment allotted to them vowing that he was going to, "H-h-hit the hay for a week or t-t-ten days!"

Nata had proven a sterling host. He had shown to them the palace with its gorgeous triple wall; the outer of brass, the second of tin, the third of the lost element—oralchium. He had shown them the temple to King Poseidon, one of Aztlan's early rulers; its interior a treasure-house of gold, silver and ivory; the gigantic statue of the King himself standing in a chariot-charioteer of six winged horses—of such a size that Poseidon's carven head touched the roof of the temple.*

He had shown them the fountains and the hot baths for which Aztlan was noted. ("Volcanic substratum," Duke Callion guessed.) Then the gardens, the canals, and the thousands upon thousands of homes, shops and amusement centers which made up the capital city.

Duke looked and marveled.

"But, Nata," he said at last, "This city is tremendous! What is its population?"

"More than an *alau*,"** replied the mariner proudly. "Twenty and one *kinchil* at the last census. In the city of Aztlan alone there are thirty *cabal*."

Duke whistled, translating the Atlantean figures into the more familiar Arabic numbers. "Larger than Chicago in my day. And from the looks of things, more active as well!" Then recollection of a former puzzling question came to him. "There's one thing Quelchal was not able to explain to me, Nata.

---

* For a complete description of Aztlan, see Plato's *Critias*.

"It was my understanding that in Quelchal's day the scientific progress of your countrymen was high. Yet today we have seen no evidence of great mechanical skill. No telephones, automobiles, electricity...nothing, to be brief, which would explain why Quelchal, your predecessor by some four hundreds of years, should have been able to construct the space-time craft in which we came here."

"As I have told you, Duke Callion, I am a humble sailing man. It is not mine to question the wisdom of my rulers. But—there is a legend amongst us that Aztlan once possessed these things of which you speak. And discarded them."

"Discarded them?"

"Yes. Quelchal lived in an era—" Nata grinned sheepishly, and Duke knew that the sea captain was, like himself, conscious of the constant incongruity of speaking of Quelchal as having lived *before*, when the man was alive *now*. "Quelchal lived in an era which boasted a mighty scientific knowledge. But as must be the case in a land densely populated, there came a time when civilization had reached the state where all mankind's normal work was being performed mechanically.

"Shortly after the death of King Theseus, it was decided that our race was retrogressing rather than progressing. The wise King Heracles decreed that the artificial age of machinery must end. That land culture and manufacture must return to the men themselves.

"So it was ordained. And lest some future civilization be tempted by the fruits of earlier knowledge, it was ordered that a great pyre be built. The savants conducted a ruthless destruction of all mechanical apparatus, all books treating of such subjects, all notes and facts and figures.

"Only vital discoveries were retained and utilized. The mariner's

---

** Mayan numbers...Arabic Equivalents:
hun...1
20 hun-1 kal...20
20 kal-1 bak...400
20 bak-1 pic...8,000
20 pic-1 cabal...160,000
20 cabal-1 kincbil...3,200,000
20 kinchil-1 alau...64,000,000
20 alau-1 hablat...1,280,000,000

compass, the knowledge of crop rotation, navigation principles, astronomical calculations."

NATA smiled wistfully. "Yes, there is even told that at one time Aztlan knew the secret of flight. Not of terrestrial flight alone, but of flight amongst the stars. To the sister planets revolving about the mother Sun..."

"It sounds incredible," murmured Duke, "but somehow I believe it. It explains so many things. The tales of ancient gods who descended from the skies in chariots of living flame—" Then, suddenly, "But there is one bit of knowledge which it was stupid of your people to destroy, Nata. That which would enable Aztlan to conquer its enemy, Titania."

"We did not need such knowledge aforetime," said Nata. "In those days, Aztlan held all the outside world in fee. Now our colonies rebel to loose themselves—" He stared at Duke with sudden hope. "*You* possess this lost knowledge?"

Duke said grimly, "Not all that which your people destroyed. But at least one thing—" Knowing no Atlantean word for it, he had to use the English term. "You have never heard of—gunpowder?"

"Gun...powder?" Nata's lips stumbled over the unfamiliar word. "I know its meaning not, Duke Callion."

"Then," Duke smacked a heavy fist into his other palm, "By Bel, you're going to! And so are the Titans! We are going to give those big, overgrown bums something to remember us by!"

IT was in a pitch of high excitement that the trio returned to their apartment. The idea of avenging himself upon the Titans by means of some snappy twentieth century ordnance was one much to Duke's liking. Already his hands itched for the feel of a .75 lanyard; his nostrils strained for the sharp, familiar stench of gunpowder. He felt sure that he and Joey, working together, could contrive to give such armament to Aztlan.

"And if we hurry," he promised himself, "there'll be time to blow Titania off the face of the map before the Deluge pops along and does it for us!"

Joey was so enthusiastic about the plan that he forgot to grumble about being wakened.

"S-s-sure we can do it!" he exulted. "I worked for a couple of y-y-years in the Frankford Arsenal, back in Philadelphia, Just g-g-gimme some paper. I'll figure it out. W-w-where's Quelchal? He ought to be here, too!"

As if in answer to his words, the door opened and Quelchal entered. Duke sprang toward him excitedly, "Listen, Quelchal, we're on the trail of some fun! We're going to—"

Then he stopped in amazement at the expression on the Atlantean's face. It was not anger that dulled Quelchal's eyes. It was despair. Sheer, stark despair—and discouragement.

"What is it? What's the matter?"

Quelchal turned lack-lustre eyes to him; to each of the others in turn. He said in a gray voice, "My friends—our mission has failed!"

"F-f-failed! What do you mean?"

"I mean—" Quelchal barked a short, sharp, mirthless laugh. "—that the Emperor did not believe my warning. He was friendly. He was sympathetic. But he heard my story as a child might hear a fable—then advised me in all gentleness to come home and rest. Much hardship and privation, he said, had given my brain to phantasms!"

Duke stared at him, stunned.

"Then that means—"

Quelchal's voice was high and shrill.

"Our efforts have been wasted, Duke Callion. The period of *Chuen* is upon us. The year of Atonatiuh draws rapidly to a dose. History is about to repeat itself. A few weeks...perhaps but days...and the Deluge will come!

"Atlantis is—*doomed!*"

CHAPTER XVI
The Builders

DUKE said disconsolately, "We might have expected something like this, Quelchal. I told you long ago that I did not believe it lay within the power of mortals to make changes in the recorded Past. The Deluge *was;* hence must it always be."

Quelchal shook himself out of his lethargy. His eyes blazed. "You are wrong, Duke Callion! It is that we are pawns of chance...and every step of the gambit has played against us. Had we returned to *my* time, instead of to this less enlightened age—"

Joey interrupted. "If t-t-that's the big drawback," he said reasonably, "W-w-why don't we try again? Go b-b-back to your time?"

"What do you mean?"

"Another time-ship. You know how to make one now. And you're in a civilized nation, with skilled workmen and plenty of materials at your disposal. Make a second ship, and this time we'll go back to an era where we'll find an understanding p-p-people!"

Quelchal said, "It might be done. By Dis, it *can* be done! I'll get right to work on it!"

"And in the meantime," said Duke, "I've a little project of my own that I want to carry out." Swiftly he told Quelchal of his plan. The Atlantean's lips approved.

"It is good, Duke Callion. The world will be the better with Titania destroyed. And Hurkan along with them; traitor that he is."

Joey nodded. "That guy's done us a lot of dirt. And I've g-g-got a feeling that he'll do us even more, if w-w-we don't watch out! But how about you, Nata? How do you f-f-feel about all this?"

The young mariner said quietly, "I am a humble man. I should not doubt the wisdom of my Emperor and his advisors—but somehow I do. I believe your tale of a Deluge to come. There is but one thing for me to do. Prepare my finest ship for it, that I and my wife and my children may ride out the storms in safety."

Duke grinned, remembering the old Christian tale of the Deluge. He said, "That's the smartest idea of all, Nata. Maybe we'll lick this thing; maybe not. Somebody has to give the world a new lease on life if we lose. So be sure to take plenty to eat. And maybe, like the old boy I used to hear about in Sunday School, you should take along animals and birds."

He grinned again, but the serious-minded Nata did not smile in return. To Duke's surprise he nodded soberly and said, "It is a good plan, Duke Callion. I shall start preparing now."

He turned and hurried from the room. Duke gazed at Joey and scratched his head.

"Looks like we've got one believer, anyway. And I know where we'll find some others. Joey, suppose you go out and round up the gang. Dwyfan and Angha and Chiba and the rest. We're going to need their help..."

A FORTNIGHT passed; two weeks of hectic occupation for Duke Callion and that loyal little band which followed him. Duke and Joey, pooling their knowledge of Twentieth Century armament, had "rediscovered" gunpowder for Aztlan; and vast was the amazement of the naive Atlanteans to find that there was potency in the measured combination of such simple commonplaces as saltpeter, charcoal of willow, and sulphur.

Joey found himself confronted with the problem of constructing a cannon that would not only shoot, but shoot without destroying itself and everyone about it. His initial attempts caused consternation amongst the Atlantean soldiery—and, on several occasions, almost decimation of the curious who gathered around his "proving grounds." At last there came the day, however, when trial and error resulted in the creation of a cannon. Ugly, it was, and but crudely rifled—but it worked.

"It's n-n-not much to look at," Joey confessed wryly, "b-b-but it ought to scare the living daylights out of the Titans. And that's s-s-something!"

Duke felt some misgivings about Nata. The quiet, simple sailing man had definitely proven himself a convert to the adventurers' warning of a Deluge to come. Asking leave of absence from his duties, he had bought himself a ship, and to this ship he had moved his wife and children.

Now, whilst crowds of highly amused and sometimes openly jeering Atlanteans gathered about this vessel, he was busily engaged in stocking it as for an ocean voyage. To all queries and gibes he made but one reply, "Duke Callion has said that the waters will come to cover the earth. And I believe him."

But it was not only Nata who believed the tale. Quelchal, Duke and Joey found their cause espoused openly—and with fists when the occasion arose—by those men who had been their companions in the escape from Titania. The blond Viking, Valthgar. Yirna. Ogyges.

As Dwyfan said, "Perhaps, as they say, you are mad, Duke Callicn. But if so, we owe our lives to your madness. Your cause is our cause."

And on a high ridge of the mountain Colhuacan a little colony came into being. A colony of those who believed the warning of the "future men." The selection of their site was at once determined by logic and chance.

"When the Deluge comes," Duke said, "if it *does* come, it will be prefaced by a great tidal wave. Craft in the harbor will be immediately destroyed. We should build our vessels of escape on a high peak, where there will be egress in any direction."

Unable to choose between several likely promontories, Joey tossed a coin. "Heads we stay here," he hazarded. "Tails we go to that other peak over there."

The piece of silver glinted momentarily; fell and rolled. Search as they might, none of them could find it.

"We stay here, anyway," laughed Duke. "We have a capital investment in this territory now."

And Joey said· ruefully, "Shucks! Good Atlantean money*—and I go tossing it away!"

B UT these were interludes. For the most part the little crew was kept constantly busy. While Dwyfan, Yima and the others carried on, atop the mount, the work which Nata was dedicating himself to below, Duke and Joey worked like Trojans on the rearmament of the Atlantean fleet.

Perhaps Quelchal was busiest of all. For he was laboring night and day over a second glistening sphere to carry him back to his own era—a *time* in which he would find ready ears to his warning of disaster to come. This time his sphere was being constructed on majestic scale. When completed, it would be large enough to hold the score of men who had pledged themselves to his cause.

And then—the day of vengeance dawned! At last the rearmament of the Atlantean fleet had been accomplished, and every ship had been supplied with a full complement of cannon. Stores of gunpowder had

---

* In 1867, archeologists discovered on the island, Corvo, in the Azores group, an unusual coin marked with the symbol of the Crooked Mountain; with the transverse depicting a great serpent twined about two stark trees. This coin was, in sheer desperation established as "probably Phoenician," though it did not correspond with the known coinage of that land; more resembling the "coiled serpent" of Central America. —Author

been prepared, and the ambitious Joey had even devised a crude sort of hand grenade for use against the Titans. And for the first time in more than three hundreds of years, Aztlan was in a position to prove itself queen of the seas; mistress of the world.

It was a gala scene when the huge silver fleet set out from the harbor of Aztlan, Titania bound. Banners flew proudly, bands played, crowds cheered themselves hoarse as one by one the Atlantean ships shook out canvas and swept gracefully out of the harbor.

Duke and Joey stood on the deck of the *Kyklopes,* beside Nata, feeling the enthusiastic mood of the crowd communicate itself to them. Of all their band, only Quelchal was remaining in Aztlan. His work was too pressing to allow even for such a foray as this. But all the others of their hard-bitten crew were aboard the commanding vessel. Last to leave the harbor, it would assume command as soon as they reached the open sea; would lead the attack against Titania.

Pyrrha and Dwyfach remained behind. Even' though this trip was a leave-taking, the two brides felt no fear. The result of the expedition, both knew, was foreordained. So they waved gladly, proudly, from the docks as the ship pulled away.

Dwyfan grinned and said, "Seems funny, doesn't it? Marriage, I mean—and settling down to a quiet life? Oh, well. We'll make this last scrap a good one."

Duke nodded; straining for a last glimpse of Pyrrha. And then suddenly Joey clutched his arm. He gasped, "D-d-duke-am I nuts? Did you s-s-see him?"

"Him? Who?"

"There! The guy in the white. Just disappearing around the corner of— Damn it! He's gone!"

Duke said, "What's the matter, Joey? Somebody in Atlantis who owes you money?"

Joey exploded, "Worse than that. It looked like Hurkan!!"

"You're seeing things," laughed Duke. "Hurkan's in Titania. And we're going to see him—*now!*" His jaw set tightly. Its cast did not bode well for Hurkan...

TITANIA did not wait for the Atlantean fleet to bring the battle to them. Its warriors sighted the silver vessels from afar, and broke out the huge black sails of their own ships. Ebon oars crawled from the Titan's harbor to meet the rapidly advancing biremes of Aztlan. And it was a mile from the island that the battle began.

"They'll be expecting," Duke said rapidly, "the same old kind of fight. Catapults of fire-balls. Lances thrown by *jaculins*. Ram's-head contacts and hand-to-hand fighting.

"Let them get near us—within accurate shooting range. And then let 'em have it!"

Joey Cox, crouched over the foremost and largest of the *Kyklopes* cannon, chuckled delightedly, and fingered the lanyard.

"Y-y-You bet! Boy, I haven't had so much f-f-fun since that scrap in Chunhubub. But—no hand-to-hand fighting, Duke?"

"Why should we? There's no use risking lives if we can mow them down this way."

Joey's face fell. "I was j-j-just thinking of Hurkan," he murmured dejectedly, "But if you f-f-feel that way about it—"

"I may change my mind," Duke's eyes glinted, "if we see Hurkan."

Then there was time for little more, for the slim black craft of Titania were upon them, diabolically sleek in the late rays of the afternoon sun; crowded to the aft rails with sable-armored warriors thirsting for battle.

Already a ram's-head grappling hook was being put out from the Titanian lead vessel. The rhythmic beat of the oarmaster's gong could be heard across the water. The starboard oars were being shipped so the black ship might be maneuvered closer.

Duke looked at Joey. "Ready?" he said.

"R-r-readyl" Joey's body tensed.

"Then fire!"

There was a burst of smoke, a belching of sudden flame, and thunder rent the air. Screams of wild fear and horror rose from the ill-fated Titanian vessel as one side of its wooden keel smashed inward as though struck by some massive fist. Planks ripped and tore. The cries of the living mingled with the groans of the dying. A violent shudder trembled the ship from prow to rudder. Terrified bodies, bruised and bleeding, fled the entrails of the ship to toss themselves, armor and all, into the water.

The doomed vessel made a gulping, sucking sound as sea water surged forward into the gaping hole. Men dropped like insects from the decks, the rigging. Chained galley slaves made the air hideous with

There was a tremendous explosion, and the galley lifted into the air.

screams of pain and fear.

Joey shouted, "A b-b-bull's-eye!" and swiveled about. "G-g-get me near another one!"

But his had been the shot that set off the guns of the other Atlantean vessels. All were firing now, and to the stunned Titans it must have seemed that the thunder and lightning of the gods were bursting forth. Flame and fire struck at their flimsy vessels in a tumult of raging sound; men died unknowing that death was at their sides.

It was not a battle; it was a slaughter. Within the space of minutes, the sea was clogged with the broken hulls of splintered fighting ships, scud of dragging black sails, shards of masts and spars to which clung clots of gory humanity until their grip loosened and their heavy armor dragged them into the cold, green depths.*

Here a captain-less vessel, rudder smashed away by an Atlantean ball, spun and struggled like a wounded duck on the surface of the water. There a desperate galley-slave, numb with fear, sought escape by slashing off his own feet to rid them of their shackles; then tottered on bleeding stumps to the railing to throw himself, dying, into the sea. And where scant moments before, a haughty black fleet had come proudly forth to do battle, now the sea was swept clean of all save the silver-bannered invaders who dipped from floating spar to spar, rescuing such bits of human flotsam and jetsam as had survived the holocaust.

Even Duke, hardened as he was to the grim reality of warfare, was sickened by the massacre. But he set his jaw grimly. "On!" he said. "On to Titania!"

B UT Titania had seen, from turrets and walls, the visitation of the gods upon their once mighty fleet. They had no wish to see their city tumbled into ruins; no stomach for the death and destruction they had witnessed from afar.

As the Atlantean fleet swung into the harbor with guns primed and trained, a sobered convoy of weaponless soldiery stepped forward to signal their surrender. Duke gave orders to withhold fire, selected a group of his own followers, and landed.

Through an avenue of weeping women and grave men his triumphal procession ascended the beach to the palace. There he confronted a thoroughly cowed Emperor of Titania.

The Emperor made obeisance; then, "It is futile to struggle against the gods," he said. "What is your will of us?"

Dwyfan, at his side, whispered, "Trust him' not, my captain!

---

* "The struggle lasted many years, all the might which the Olympians could bring to bear being useless, until on the advice of Gaea (Joey? NSB), Zeus set free the *Kyklopes* and the *Hekatonckeires* (i.e., "brought the ships into play"), of whom the former fashioned thunderbolts for him, while the latter advanced on his side with force equal to the shock of an earthquake. The world trembled down to lowest Tartarus as Zeus now appeared with his terrible weapon and new allies(!). Old Chaos thought his hour had come, as from continuous blaze of thunder-bolts the earth took fire, and the waters seethed in the sea." —"The War of the Titans" from the *Manual of Mythology,* by Murray.

Remember the dungeons!"

But a strange pity stirred Duke Callion for this once glorious, now crushed, nation. He said, "We seek only your allegiance to Aztlan. That and—"

Joey whispered something, swiftly.

Duke nodded. "That," he continued, "and the renegade priest of Mayapan who was your ally. Hurkan."

The Titanian Emperor said quietly, sincerely, "The allegiance I pledge, master of Thunder and Lightning. But Hurkan—he is not here."

"Not here!" exclaimed Duke, and Joey cried, in a suddenly fearful voice, "I k-k-knew it! That was him I saw on the docks of—"

"He is gone," the Emperor said, "on a mission of his own devising— to Aztlan!"

CHAPTER XVII
The Vengeance of Hurkan

DAWN was breaking over the amaranthine sea, and the first, slender shafts of orange stirred the ocean with pastels of beauty. But Duke Callion, restlessly pacing the deck of the *Kyklopes,* had no eye for loveliness just now. He paused to strike a moist hand on the pommel of his sword and plead, "Step up the beat of your oarsmen, Nata! Haste! There is no time to idle when that devil, Hurkan, devises God knows what hellish schemes against us!"

Nata said soothingly, "Peace, Duke Callion. Our oarsmen weary. But soon we will be in Aztlan again. See? Already the harbor lights glimmer."

Duke stopped grumbling, but his interminable pacing continued. Hours had passed since he learned from the Titanian Emperor the whereabouts of the scoundrelly priest, but each of those hours had seemed a century; each *moment* decades long.

Nor was the young adventurer the only one to experience this feeling of urgency. That foreboding which comes to active men at a crisis had descended over all of his companions like a sable cloud. Instead of returning home like the conquerors they were, their visages were as strained and drawn as those of defeated men.

But all journeys, howsoever tedious, must come to an end at last.

And finally, when the sun had come above the horizon to light the sky with crystal morning, Duke's ship put in to Aztlan harbor.

The crowd that had wished them Godspeed was but a fragment of the mob that turned out to welcome home its victorious heroes. Aztlan had once more come into its own—and its people were joyous. From humblest servant to most noble lord, all were there waiting on the docks. And a messenger brought tidings that the Emperor was waiting in his palace for a special audience with the conquerors.

But for once, Duke Callion was making no palliatory gestures toward a ruler. He said to Nata, "Give the old boy my apologies. Tell him whatever you want to. *I've* got to find Quelchal!" And he loped off toward the workshop wherein Quelchal was building his new time craft.

QUELCHAL was inclined to discount Duke's fears.

"There is no cause for alarm, Duke Callion," were his first words. "All Hurkan can possibly hope for is to prejudice the public in your disfavor. It must have been for some such purpose that he came here. But after today—" Quelchal shrugged. "There is no greater man in all Aztlan than you. Were Hurkan to speak a word against you, the mob would tear him limb from limb."

Duke said bluntly, "I don't like it, Quelchal. The man must have an ace up his sleeve. He would not risk his neck stealing into this country merely for the purpose you suggest. There must be something deeper—"

"What, Duke Callion?" Quelchal was smiling. "I fear you have listened to an old-wives' tale."

Duke grumbled, "Well—" and was silent, because he had no answer. "Anyway, I'm going to get my men together. Search for him. And *this* time he won't escape me!"

"It might have been better," agreed Quelchal, "if you had let me have my way with him weeks ago. Still, I approve of your aim. Now, the time-ship—"

"It's finished?"

"Not quite, but almost. This time there will be no mistakes. We will return to my era, and therein have a period of time sufficient to convince my people of the impending Deluge."

Quelchal sighed.

"You found it hard to understand, Duke Callion. Sometimes I find it hard myself. Look you! We have failed to convince these people of this era. Thus, when the waters come, disaster will strike them. And we know that on at least one other occasion in Time, those same waters drowned Aztlan.

"Yet there remains the paradoxical truth that as soon as I have completed this machine, we can return to Aztlan of four hundred years ago and *prevent* the Deluge! Is not that a strangely miraculous thing?"

"I've told you before," said Duke gloomily, "that I don't believe it's possible. This time your machine won't work, Quelchal. Or something will go wrong. Man cannot change the tapestry of Time."

"Nothing can go wrong now, Duke Callion," Quelchal contradicted him serenely. "One more day and it is done. The tapestry of Time will have to be rewoven. Are you ready for the next adventure?"

"Whenever you are," nodded Duke. "Or, that is, as soon as I've taken care of Hurkan in *this* era—"

He found his private "army," no longer a rag-tag collection of strangers, but now a well-clad, well-feted group of men, in the banquet hall provided by the Emperor for the heralding of the victors. Despite his anxiety, he could not help but grin at their discomfiture. They were frankly bewildered by all the fuss being made over them, and just as frankly bored. When he had gestured them to meet him outside, man by man they gave vent to an expression of relief.

"Another hour of that speech-making," confessed the swart Ogyges, "And I'd have gone back to Titania."

Valthgar the Viking scrubbed at his right cheek with an embarrassed, hairy paw. "Lip rouge!" he rumbled. "By the teeth of the Dragon—me with lip rouge on my cheek! These brazen modern women— Bah!"

Duke said, "Well, cheer up! I've got an assignment for you. Listen—" And he told them of Hurkan's being free somewhere on the island; warned them of what the priest's machinations might mean. "Find him!" he concluded, "And when you find him—bring him to me. I would prefer to meet him alive. But—bring him however you must!"

B UT it was Duke Callion himself who found Hurkan. And the way of their meeting was strange.

It was late afternoon. For some hours, Duke had been out searching for the ex-priest. Now, his own seeking fruitless, he returned to Quelchal's workshop in the hope that one of his companions might have returned with news.

Quelchal was inside the huge, shining oralchium sphere working when Duke entered the room. Duke had time to notice that the intricate wiring job was near completion before Quelchal poked his head out to see who his visitor might be. His lean, bronzed face mirrored astonishment at seeing Duke.

"Duke Callion? But I understood you were at the waterfront?"

"The waterfront?" Duke shook his head. "You're thinking of two other fellows, Quelchal. I've been up in the hills most of the day. Looking for that scoundrelly rascal, Hurkan."

"But I thought—" Quelchal stared at him oddly. "You're sure, Duke Callion? You didn't send a message for Pyrrha to meet you at the *Kyklopes?*"

"I haven't been near the *Kyk*—"

Duke stopped suddenly, and his face tensed. "Pyrrha! She was here? She received such a message?"

"Yes. She left...oh, some minutes ago."

Duke cried, "Hurkan!" in a rage-choked voice. "He has always wanted her! Now he has trapped her!" He started for the door. Behind him Quelchal cried, "Here! Wait for me!" but Duke Callion was waiting for no one. On feet winged by fear for his bride, he was racing for the waterfront; for the dock at which was moored the *Kyklopes*.

There was no one on the deck of the *Kyklopes;* no one in sight on the docks, either, until Duke loosed a shout. Then an aged watchman tottered from his little shed to peer at wild-eyed young man quizzically.

"A man and a woman?" he replied to Duke's frenzied query. "Nay, there was no— Stay! There *were* footsteps on the dock here but minutes ago. I called but got no answer. I thought it was children playing, as they do."

"Footsteps? Which way?"

"Down there!" pointed the old watchman. And Duke was already leaping in the direction he indicated; down by the lesser wharf where the small fishing craft and *feluccas* were moored.

He was just in time to see a small, slim sailing vessel pushing off from the dock. A tiny craft at the helm of which stood a figure Duke recognized all too well. Hurkan! And huddled in the stern, strangely limp and silent, was the girl, Pyrrha!

RAGE spurred Duke Callion to greater speed than he knew he possessed. Already the tiny ship was yards away from the dock, and now its slight canvas was beginning to belly to the breeze. But Duke's mind was racing along with his feet. There was a spot, three hundred yards distant, where the boat must edge past the end of the wharf to run through the channel-bar. He swerved; cut in that direction.

It was man's puny strength against the untiring wind. For a prize, for a wager, Duke Callion could never have made it. But now he was running for the greatest of all prizes—love. And it was love that gave him strength to streak down that three hundred yards of salt-crusted planking, devour the last few feet at a heart-wrenching stride, and lunge himself into the air over twelve feet of rapidly widening water to land, sprawling on his hands and knees, momentarily stunned and helpless, on the deck of the runaway sloop!

In that one moment, Duke Callion was at the mercy of Hurkan. But the ex-priest did not know it. He had not guessed that there was anyone within miles of him, and the element of surprise was Duke's salvation. Before Hurkan's stunned brain had time to react, Duke had regained his feet—and with his footing, his strength!

It was not love, now, but hate—complete, unadulterated and vicious—that drew back the corners of Duke Callion's mouth in a snarl. Like a great cat, without cry or warning, he flung himself upon Hurkan.

Hurkan loosed a great scream of rage. His hand tugged at his girdle; was locked there by Duke's iron grip. For an instant they stood there swaying, molded together by the sheer force of their enmity; then Duke's fist rose once, twice!

The anger mirrored on Hurkan's face faded into a look of numbed surprise. His jaw fell slack, and his eyes rolled backward, inward. He slumped to the deck.

In a flash, Duke was at Pyrrha's side. But now her eyes were open, and a tremulous smile hovered on her lips as she breathed, "Duke! I knew you would—" Then those eyes became wide with sudden fright, and her voice broke into a scream. "Behind you! Duke!"

Duke wheeled; crouched, ducked. Something hissed over his head. Steel death sang a crisp song by his ear; then whizzed past to splash into the bobbing depths beyond.

Hurkan had staggered to his feet and was reeling there drunkenly. Now, seeing that his cast weapon had failed to reach its mark, he spat like a caged cougar and turned. His sandaled feet scraped drily on the deck as he made to dive overside.

But Duke was off his feet in a diving tackle. He felt flesh between his arms; tightened them convulsively. Hurkan, now squealing in plaintive little mews, kicked and struggled. One foot glanced off Duke's head; streaming a shower of stars before the young man's eyes. But Duke's grim clutch grew tighter. His hands moved upward.

One instant they were straining there on the hard deck; the next Duke had sprung to his feet. His arm drew Hurkan to him; spun him around. The priest's throat was soft and yielding in the crook of his elbow. Duke panted, "Look you well, Hurkan! It is the last you will see!"

THE man's eyes bulged. His face began to purple, and there were dry, choking rattles in his throat. Duke tightened. Hurkan's chest heaved aimlessly; vainly. He was throttling. His tongue writhed out between bloody lips; spurted as his teeth locked into it. Then he made one last, frantic, slipping movement to the side—

There was a sudden short, harsh sound! Duke let his arm fall away as Hurkan's body sank limply to the deck. Pyrrha screamed and covered her eyes with her hands. An involuntary shudder coursed through Duke. He said dazedly, "He did it himself! Broke his own neck. But it is just as well, for I would have killed him..."

Then he stared down at his feet, startled. For a faint, choking voice whispered huskily, "I'm not dead...yet...Duke Callion."

Duke gasped. By all rights the man should be in hell now. His head sprawled at a weird, unnatural angle to his body. Only his indomitable hatred kept him alive at all. That and— "I will live...long enough," rasped that grave-cheating voice, "to see the end...of you all! Yes! Even now...it is *here!*"

The ship gave a sudden violent lurch. The afternoon sky, which had begun to dull into twilight, became a sheet of quivering flame that scorched Duke's eyes. There came a startled cry from Pyrrha. Duke looked shoreward.

The very sky seemed afire, and earth was atremble. Colhuacan. The guardian mount of Aztlan! It was spouting flame, smoke, ash! Erupting! There was mockery in Hurkan's eyes as Duke crouched over him; demanded wildly, "What is this? Speak, dog! You know its meaning!"

"Do not...move my head...Duke Callion. I would...lie here and see... the end of the world. Yes...I know about this. I did it. My workmen bored a shaft...to the core...of Colhuacan. Turned...the icy sea waters... into its glowing heart. Aztlan...and all that it stands for...is about to perish!"

Comprehension swept suddenly over Duke Callion. He shouted, "The Deluge! *This* is how it is destined to come to pass! The Deluge!"

There was the palest ghost of a smile on Hurkan's lips now. He whispered, "Yes. You have bested me in...but one thing...Duke Callion. I could not have her...in life. But I will take...her vision...now...with me in death..."

And slowly, deliberately, Hurkan moved. Turned his head for the last time. Turned his face to look upon Pyrrha—and died.

Thus passed Hurkan the priest.

CHAPTER XVIII
The Deluge

DUKE cried, "Quelchal! Joey! Nata and the others! We· must find them and get out of this!"

Swiftly he turned the drifting sloop about; began to maneuver it in to harbor again. It took but minutes; still his body was clammy with exertion and apprehension when he finally rammed the skiff headlong into the lower wharf and leaped ashore with Pyrrha in his arms.

Aztlan had become a madhouse. With the first dull rumblings, curious heads had poked from doorways; seen the sheet of greasy fire that screened the sky. Now all sixty-four million inhabitants seemed to be in the streets of the capital city; jostling, pushing, asking questions to which there was no answer; racing aimlessly from one place to any other. Fruitlessly seeking security—for there was no security anywhere. Momentarily the rumblings from the bowels of Colhuacan grew deeper and more ominous. Each succeeding belch of living flame that leaped from the riven crest of the Crooked Mountain seemed to spiral higher into the tortured sky.

Now a light, dusty ash, scorching hot, began to fall from the livid heavens. Duke knew what that presaged. Volcanic ejaculation. Lava would be flowing, white-hot, on the slope of Colhuacan. He redoubled his speed; recklessly jamming a way through the crowds that hemmed his passage. Everywhere voices screamed mad queries. Some raised futile prayers to the gods. Others cursed the Titans, intuitive that this was their doing...

Somehow, above the din, Duke heard a voice calling his name. A hand tightened on his arm, and he turned to look into the face of Nata. The young captain's face was not frightened. There was a look of ecstacy in his eyes.

"You were right, Duke Callion! It is the end of the world for those who would not heed your warning! Come to my boat with me. All is prepared!"

Duke had to scream to make himself heard. "I must find Quelchal and Joey! Go back and get ready to cast off! Get clear of the island before the sea rushes in!"

Nata pointed at Pyrrha; shouted, "Pyrrha! Shall I take her with me?" The girl opened her eyes, hearing, and shook her head. "Where Duke Callion goes, there go I, too."

Nata fell back reluctantly. He cried, "I will wait for you until the last possible moment, Duke. Do not tarry too long!"

THEN he was gone; fighting through the milling mob back to the sequestered section of the harbor where he had moored his ship.

Above the incessant roaring of the crowd came the sound of earth screaming. A loud explosion. The ground beneath them shook, and immense columns of hot water and mud, mixed with brimstone, ashes, and *lapilli,* gushed from the crest of Colhuacan like a water-spout. The stifling stench of sulphur made breathing difficult, and Duke Callion, when he tried to wipe the sweat from his streaming brow, found his hand smeared with gray volcanic ash.

And then he was at the doorway of Quelchal's workshop; was breaking into the room where Quelchal rushed to greet him.

"You are all right, Duke Callion?"

"I am—yes! But Aztlan is doomed! Come, Quelchal—we must flee to the mountains! Save ourselves while there is still time!"

Quelchal shook his head. "It is too late! There is but one chance for me. That is to finish my ship before the sea rushes in. But, here—" He pressed an envelope into Duke's hand. Duke clutched it instinctively; rammed it into a pocket. "This will explain much, should we never meet again. And now—"

The door burst inward, and Duke cried out, "Joey!" as his companion raced into the shop. Behind him was the smiling Cym, Dwyfan, and his bride. But none of them were smiling now. Their clothing was in tatters; their bodies wet with plastered ash and mud. There was a deep bleeding scratch on Dwyfan's face. Dwyfach's alabaster beauty was concealed behind a mask of fear and anguish; her auburn tresses tumbled about her shoulders in a bedraggled cloud.

Joey cried in a grief-stricken voice, "It is the end, D-d-duke! The e-e-end of everything!"

"The others? Where are the others?"

Joey spread his arms in a helpless gesture.

"God knows. We were on the mountain when the explosion came. The top of the m-m-mountain blew off, and lava flooded down the mountain side. Valthgar was in his ship. He never heard our cries of warning before—" He shuddered, wiping a grimy hand across his eyes as though to erase the memory.

"And Ogyges? Yima? Angha?"

"Out there—s-s-somewhere—in that screaming mob. You can't tell f-f-friend from enemy. Did you find Hurkan?"

"Dead!" said Duke. "I killed him. But it was he who caused this."

Quelchal muttered, busy again with his tools, "It was fated to be so, Duke Callion. there was no way to escape it."

Dwyfari said impatiently, "There are still ships in the harbor. Nata is there. We must go, my friends!"

Again Quelchal shook his head.

"You go!" he answered. "I must stay. Duke—you will understand why. Later." The bronzed Atlantean bent once more over his uncompleted time-ship. His hands flew from wire to wire as he tightened, arranged, rearranged.

Indecision slashed at Duke Callion with torturing blades. He could not desert Quelchal. Yet—at his side was Pyrrha. She must live. And she would not desert him. Joey was tugging at him; screaming frantic pleas. Grudgingly he moved toward the doorway; glanced back for one final look.

"Goodbye, Quelchal—"

The Atlantean's hands never stopped moving. His eyes were warm with something deeper than friendship. He said in that sweet, mellow voice Duke was never afterward to forget, "Not goodbye, Duke Callion. Just till we meet again..."

Then once more they were out on the streets, but things had become graver since they had entered the little workshop. The sun had disappeared completely, now, behind a veil of stifling smoke and mud. But in its place, casting a weird, unearthly glow over the maddened city, was a ruddy pillar of flame emanating from the volcano; a livid glare that quivered wild, unnatural shadows over the faces about them.

The ground no longer pulsed under their feet; it shook like a live thing stricken with the ague. Duke had all he could do to stay on his feet. About him frenzied Atlanteans stumbled and fell, tore bleeding sores in their hands and knees, rose and tottered a few steps forward.

Now stones and bricks and masonry added to the hazard of the journey. Buildings collapsed about them; narrowly missing them as they toppled. Once as they quitted a narrow street, Duke looked behind to see that both walls of the street had caved suddenly inward, burying a thousand screaming, writhing souls beneath tons of detritus.

The earth rolled, quaked and trembled. They were five specks of humanity caught in a plunging sea of fear. Five who strained every muscle, every thought, to keep together. They raced past the temple of Poseidon; saw how the walls had split asunder. The gold and ivory charioteer still lashed his silver, winged steads toward Chaos. But as they watched, the mighty statue trembled. The effigy of King Poseidon lurched drunkenly and toppled sideways with a mighty crash. An agonized scream rose as men saw that crushing weight plunging toward them...

Then Joey screamed, "Duke—jump for your life!" and suddenly their grasp on each other's wrist was broken. A vast crevasse was splitting the street asunder; a hole dark and fearsome gaped like a hungry maw, gulped bodies of shrieking humans.

Duke saw Joey leap to safety; saw Dwyfan lift his fainting wife and carry her beyond the gigantic crack. He felt his own feet slide precariously beneath him; threw all his strength into a frantic backward leap.

He made it—but now Joey and Dwyfan were separated from him and Pyrrha by a crevice too wide for leaping. He saw Joey cup his hands to his mouth; sensed, rather than heard, Joey's cry, "The harbor! To the ships..."

It was hard to breathe now. Each gulping mouthful of air seared his lungs as he drew in stifling ash and the foul stench of brimstone. Pyrrha was a drag on his arm. But still he staggered on; fighting, struggling, elbowing a way through the terrified crowd about him.

And now the docks were in sight. And here, indeed, humanity had gone mad. Every ship, every tiny *felucca,* was jammed to the gunwales with frantic, struggling humans who, oarless, made vain paddling movements at the turgid waters of the sound. Sails were lifeless in the oppressive heat; weighted by inches of muddy effluvium from Colhuacan.

But it was only a short distance to Nata's ship. There, Duke knew, he would find haven. He scourged his aching body for one last ounce of strength to carry him on.

And then, *"The sea!"*

The roar rose from a million throats; drowning out all tumult that had been before. Duke, looking seaward, saw that of which man had oft heard legend before, but never seen. The crest of the first tidal wave sweeping in on the doomed island of Aztlan. The forerunner of—the Deluge!

Like a great green wall, rimmed with white, it roared down upon the hapless port; a hundred feet high and terrible. It struck the ships at the harbor bar first; lifted them momentarily as though weighing them on a huge, cosmic balance, then chose amongst them with the cold imperviousness of a judicial god. Duke saw one ship...two...surmount that majestic crest miraculously. But others spilled over before it, dripping their screaming cargoes like shaken pods. And the mighty wave swept inward...

Duke's voice cracked on a great, forlorn cry. "It is the end, Pyrrha! The end..."

And then, in that last, terrible moment, Pyrrha was in his arms, her arms locked about his neck, her lips welded to his, whispering, "Then we die together, Duke Callion. It is all I ask!"

And their bodies were crushed together in a long, frantic, hungry kiss...

Then the flood struck! Duke felt a mighty force descending upon him; battening, wrestling, plunging. His arms tightened about Pyrrha's form. There was cold about him; cold and wet and horror. His lungs were stifled for air. He kicked out vainly, fighting even in that last terrible moment for another second of life.

Something hard and unyielding struck him in the small of the back agonizingly. He felt himself toppling over backward...rising...rising. Then soft bells were in his ears; pealing their dainty chimes. A vast weakness surged over him, soothing the anguish of his weary body.

This, then, was death. It was not hard to drown, Duke thought languidly. To drift off into nothingness like this; all harshness forgotten, the world gone mad and torn apart. His love in his arms...

CHAPTER XIX
Deucalion and Pyrrha

HE was dead. He was dead—and the old tales of a hell beyond the portals of death were true. This ghoulish light above him was the roofing of the underworld, and his nostrils shriveled at the sulphurous breath of demons.

But—Pyrrha was at his side. Was bending over him, whispering in his ear, "Duke! Duke Callion! You are alive!"

Duke roused himself. Every bone and muscle in his body was strained and sore, as though he had gone through a thousand battles. To move was to suffer, but—he *lived!* He lay in the thwarts of a tiny, bobbing craft; a single-sailed felucca that somehow wallowed on the surface of the waters! It was warped, the single sail ripped and flapping, inches of water in the bottom, but it floated!

He cried, "Pyrrha!" and gathered her into his arms once again. There was no need to say more. Both of them knew that a miracle had happened; that somehow the impartial sea had seen fit to spew them forth out of its hungry gorge with the craft that had been borne down upon them at the last moment.

The sea was a charnel house. All about them, on the mottled surface of the water, sprawled the bodies of the dead. Even the water seemed sluggish. Duke guessed why. Miles upon square miles of muddy land lay beneath; all the area of the Aztlan that was. Only one part of the doomed island still rose above the surface. That was the crooked knob of the destroying mountain itself—Colhuacan.

It was this which was spouting the lurid flames that Duke had thought the fires of Hades. But the glare was lessening, now; the streamers of greasy smoke twisting off in sultry spirals to die in the gray sky above.

And even as they watched, "See! It is the end!" said Duke Callion. They stood silent as there came one final, convulsive burst of belching flame and lava from the mouth of the volcano. Then, like a foundering ship, the whole mountain seemed to rear up momentarily, stagger, and slide into the cold bosom of the sea.

Waters churned and bubbled where it had sunk, and a vast whirlpool eddied toward the explosive mount with a horrible sucking sound. Gruesome, bloated bodies swirled and bobbed toward the maelstrom with grotesque, swimming motions. Pyrrha moaned once, softly, and Duke turned her head into the protection of his shoulder.

"It is the end," he repeated dully. "Our warning was vain. These things had to be."

Then suddenly he remembered the envelope Quelchal had thrust into his hand during those last, hectic moments at the shop. He fished it out of his pocket. It was water-soaked, but legible. The sky was lightening with false dawn. Hunkered in the weaving craft, Duke read...

"When you read this, Duke Callion, Aztlan will be no more. The hungry sea will have devoured it. The tapestry of Time will be justified.

"I write this in my shop, awaiting your coming. A strange sense of prescience is with me this morning, and I fear that ere the day ends, that will come to pass which I knew from the beginning must occur.

"Yes, I knew, Duke Callion! Forgive me—for I have lied to you, not once, but many times. Almost from the beginning, I knew that our journey into the past would end thus—but there was hope in my heart that through a miracle we might succeed in changing these Things that

Be. I worked toward this miracle.

"Almost from the beginning. Not at first, Duke Callion. When we met in my hovel at Chunhubub, I did not know that Time's demands were inexorable; that in finding you, I had merely done that which the Fates had decided. I knew only that I had found a friend.

"Then we returned to Mayapan the Eld. And there it was that I first discovered that these adventures we have undergone together are not *new* adventures, but were written into the tapestry of Time long eons ago.

"It was when Mayapan deified Joey Cox, calling him Coxcox, that I first suspected the truth. For my reading had taught me, Duke Callion, that in ages past the Mayans worshipped a white god, Coxcox, god of flame and mystery, who came to them once, left them, and returned again. His name was Coxcox, and he was known as the double-tongued god...

"My suspicions were verified when we met Dwyfan and Angha and Ogyges and Yima in the dungeons of Titania. You had no way of knowing it, Duke Callion—by my studies had taught me that these names were the legendary names of men who escaped the Deluge; founded new dynasties after the sinking of Aztlan. The Sanscrit legends mention Angha, father of the human race. Ogyges is worshipped by Greece as the founder of humanity. The Welsh claim descent from Dwyfan and Dwyfach—two who escaped the Deluge.

"ABOUT yourself, Duke Callion, I pondered long. It is odd that it did not occur to me earlier...and that your marriage to the sweet Pyrrha did not give the clue I sought. But I tried, vainly, to reconcile your surname, Callion, with a hero of the past-and could not. It was but a short time ago that I recalled the diluvial legend of the Arameans, directly derived from that of Chaldea, as it was narrated in the celebrated Sanctuary of Hierapolis, or Babbyce...

"The myth runs thus: that when the earth drowned in a sea of water, two escaped. A man and a woman. Their names were—Deucalion and Pyrrha!

"You, Duke Callion, are the 'Deucalion' of legend. This is so...this is constant...this is as it was and ever shall be. Our lives; yours and mine and Joey's and those of the men who suffered, laughed and fought with us, are inextricably bound, woven together into that huge tapestry we know as Time. Ever and again must we live this legend through;

returning ever from the Twentieth Century to act our little roles, then rest, at last, until the time comes for us to return again...

"Unless—and this is our sole salvation, Duke Callion—I can somehow contrive to finish my second time-ship before the Deluge. That is my prayer and my hope. If I can do this, I can return to the Aztlan of *my* time; give warning, and end forever this endless circle.

"You have no way of knowing that I fail or succeed. In this lifetime which now lies before you, we will never meet again.

"For my deception; I beg your forgiveness. In this strange new world into which I have led you, I ask you to remember only that of all things, Quelchal loved only one thing more than you. And that was—Aztlan!"

Duke finished reading. There was much in the letter which he did not understand. But slowly he began to see its meaning. And there were some things that gave him joy.

If Quelchal's words were true—and true they must be—Joey Cox was not dead. Somehow the "double-tongued god" had survived the Deluge. In good time Joey would find his way back to the Mayapan he loved; there to reign again as "Coxcox."

Dwyfan and Dwyfach, too, were still alive. From their loins would spring a new race which ultimately would people that which, centuries hence, would be known as the British Isles. So, also, with Yima the Iranian, Angha of Boeotia, Chiba of Afric. And Nata.

Duke's eyes opened wide. Suddenly he was seeing the broad tapestry of Time from Quelchal's objective viewpoint. He was remembering the "humble, god fearing sailor" who, with his wife and children, "listened to the voice of God" and "built himself a huge ship." Filling the vessel with provisions, with animals and birds, "of every clean beast," preparing for a Deluge whilst crowds jeered...

Nata! If the name of Duke Callion could become, in the distorted memories of men yet unborn, Deucalion—could not Nata's name become...Noe...eventually...Noah?

HURKAN,* too. Quelchal had not mentioned him, but Duke knew that somewhere in history *must* persist a legend of his perfidy. With so many who had hated him alive.

It was all very puzzling. And Duke Callion, ever more the man of action than of conjecture, roused himself.

False Dawn had ended, and the little ship rolled lazily on the bosom of a slothful, brackish sea. Off to the East shone the rising sun, now gallantly struggling to burst through the veil of sultry ash that sifted down from the heavens. A faint breeze stirred from westward, flapping the sails of his tiny craft restlessly.

Duke studied the damage. Yes, he decided, a man could restore the ship to good condition. And a man and his wife could sail it to land. To a bright new land of promise, where awaited them more adventures.

Upon their shoulders—his and Pyrrha's—lay a great obligation. A new race was theirs to found. They, it was who must preserve what little knowledge, what culture, remained of Aztlan the Eld. Until such time as, in the far-distant future, a bright-eyed, younger Duke Callion should once more set forth from Chunhub upon a backward journey into Time to prevent that which *was*, and evermore was to be.

Pyrrha interrupted his reverie softly. She said, "Look, Duke Callion. The sun is finding a way through the vapors!"

"It greets a new world," he murmured. "A world that is yours—and mine!"

He crushed her to him for a long moment. Her soft, sweet fragrance more than repaid the world he had lost forever. He kissed her again... and yet again. Then he turned to ponder the problem of mending that torn sail. There was a frown on his forehead; an itching impatience in his fingers.

For the father of a new race, there is much work to be done...

---

* "Then the waters were agitated by the will of the Heart of Heaven, Hurkan, and a great inundation came upon the heads of these creatures... They were ingulfed, and a resinous thickness descended from heaven... the face of the earth was obscured, and a heavy, darkening rain commenced—rain by day and rain by night... There was heard above their heads a great noise, as if produced by fire.

"Then were men seen running, pushing each other, filled with dismay; they wished to climb upon their houses and the houses, tumbling down, fell to the ground; they wished to climb upon the trees and the trees shook them off... Water and fire contributed to the universal ruin at the time of the last great cataclysm which preceded the fourth creation."—The "Popul Vuh," sacred book of the Central American Indians.

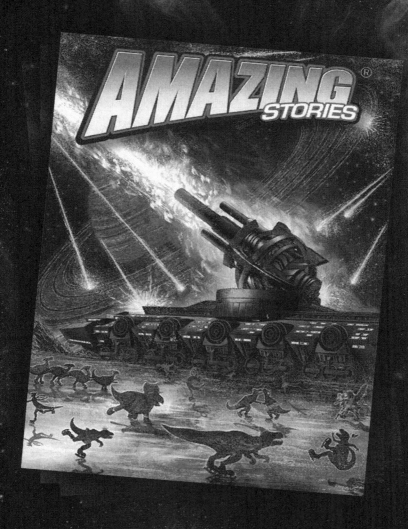

Made in the USA
Lexington, KY
03 December 2017